SCARLETT FINN

ISBN: 9781914517112

www.scarlettfinn.com

Also by Scarlett Finn

GO NOVELS
GO WITH IT
GO IT ALONE
GO ALL OUT
GO ALL IN
GO FULL CIRCLE

EXILE
HIDE & SEEK
KISS CHASE

WRECK & RUIN
RUIN ME
RUIN HIM

**THE BRANDED
SERIES**
BRANDED
SCARRED
MARKED

**FORBIDDEN
PREQUEL DUET**
ALL. ONLY.
ONLY YOURS

TO DIE FOR...
TO DIE FOR TRUTH
TO DIE FOR HONOR
TO DIE FOR VIRTUE
TO DIE FOR DUTY
TO DIE FOR LOVE

**LOVE AGAINST THE ODDS
STANDALONE COLLECTION**
SWEET SEAS
HEIR'S AFFAIR
RESCUED
MAESTRO'S MUSE
GETTING TRICKY
THIRTEEN
REMEMBER WHEN...
RELUCTANT SUSPICION
XY FACTOR

NOTHING TO...
NOTHING TO HIDE
NOTHING TO LOSE
NOTHING TO DECLARE
NOTHING TO US
NOTHING TO SAY
NOTHING TO GAIN
NOTHING TO YOU
NOTHING TO THIS
NOTHING TO DO

THE FORBIDDEN NOVELS
FORBIDDEN DESIRE
FORBIDDEN WANT
FORBIDDEN WISH
FORBIDDEN NEED
FORBIDDEN BOND

KINDRED SERIES
RAVEN
SWALLOW
CUCKOO
SWIFT
FALCON
FINCH

THE EXPLICIT SERIES
EXPLICIT INSTRUCTION
EXPLICIT DETAIL
EXPLICIT MEMORY

MISTAKE DUET
MISTAKE ME NOT
SLEIGHT MISTAKE

**RISQUÉ & HARROW
INTERTWINED**
TAKE A RISK
FIGHTING FATE
RISK IT ALL
FIGHTING BACK
GAME OF RISK

LOST & FOUND
LOST
FOUND

ONE

THEY WAITED IN that backyard until Harry and Styx were gone with their guys. Ares sent people to check. Funny that he could ever trust the skills of those currently under him. Maybe these mindless mercs had eyes, but they didn't have brains. Not super-agent brains. Just because they didn't see Styx and Harry didn't mean they weren't there.

A day of driving followed a night of driving. Their three vehicles stayed in convoy the whole time, only pausing long enough to switch drivers and gas up every few hours. The road seemed to go on forever.

She'd made the trip before. Under happier circumstances. Back then, she'd been ignorant of what waited at the coordinates deciphered by that guy at the RV park in Miami. It was just one big ball of string. She'd found the end, started to pull, and it hadn't stopped coming since.

One of the mercs spoke to their leader in the driver's seat, "Are we stopping tonight, Stratego?"

The label startled her. Stratego? That was what the men called Harry. Ares, if he was an asshole under Zeus's control, would probably relish taking his mentor's title. Daire? Her Heart? Yeah, he'd absolutely despise it.

While undercover as the dutiful Ares, he couldn't

reject the designation. In fact, his position demanded he command respect in that way. Snubbing Harry's dominion would be an added bonus. As it stood, the situation would be tearing her Heart up inside. Her body ached as her eyes dropped to her knees. She wanted to comfort him, to be there for him, to talk it out. His duplicity robbed them of that chance.

Between the three vehicles, there were enough operatives that they could keep driving in shifts all the way across the country. They didn't need to stop at all. Being sandwiched between two hulks in the back, she couldn't relax or close her eyes despite her desperate need for sleep.

"We'll drive another hour," Ares said.

"Thank Christ," the guy on her left said. "I need to get out of this truck."

The one on the right stretched, pushing his hot, hard, unwelcome thigh against her leg. "Me too. Maybe we can have some fun tonight."

Revulsion curled her lip. Like the situation wasn't bad enough already.

The left guy picked up the other's thread. "A lot of trouble she's caused," the guy said. "Don't get what's so special myself."

"Maybe it's hidden," the guy on her other side said. "Somewhere deep inside."

When the fingertips of the guy on her left touched her knee, her disdainful eyes fell to the point of contact.

"Guess we'd have to look inside real hard."

"Oh yeah, real hard."

The guy's digits ascended her leg, pressing harder. "Do you like it real hard inside, sweetheart?"

She'd be quite happy to pound him real hard… in the face. "Something you'll find out if you don't take your hand out of my skirt."

"You know you want it, baby."

The truck veered hard right, coming to a sudden, lurching stop. While those inside were still trying to figure out what was going on, Daire was already out. His door slammed, then the back opened. The handsy guy was ripped out of his seat, dragged around the trunk, and thrown down the grass verge.

But Daire wasn't done. Striding down the shallow descent, he grabbed the guy's shirt and pulled him up just enough to deliver two quick, hard punches. She flinched. Ouch. No less than the guy deserved. Maybe her Heart was a mind reader too. Nothing would surprise her at that point.

Bending lower, Daire grabbed the guy's jaw, yanking him high to growl something into his face.

The thug next to her unclicked his seatbelt.

She opened a hand to stop him going further. "I wouldn't," she said, still watching Daire as he hit the guy again. "Let him get it out of his system."

"What the hell is—"

"None of you know Ares very well, do you?" she asked, watching him drop the guy and deliver one last kick before turning his back to march up the verge again.

He slammed the back door and grabbed open his own to climb back in, pausing to put his seatbelt on before checking his mirrors and pulling onto the road like nothing happened.

"What the hell was—"

"That's what you get for not wearing a seatbelt," she said, answering for him. "Careless."

Their eyes met in the mirror just for a flicker of a second. Too short. The redness of his knuckles on the steering wheel drove a frisson of arousal through her. Her Heart.

"You're just gonna leave him there?" the passenger in the front seat asked.

"We no longer require his services," Daire said.

"But we—"

"You wanna join him?" Daire asked, his eyes cutting to his subordinate.

Didn't take long for him to shrink back in his seat. The guy next to her quickly fumbled with his seatbelt, connecting it fast.

Her eyes met Daire's again. If he wanted to keep looking at her like that… Was she supposed to get through the rest of the journey without revealing them? If he kept beating on guys who tried to get it on with her…

Inhaling, she closed her eyes. She couldn't think about it, or she'd do something real crazy… like undo her own seatbelt to slide up behind his seat and let her hands wander… or she might just climb between the seats and… No, mind blank, she couldn't think that way.

***

AS STATED AND EXPECTED, they drove for another hour. Probably exactly another hour. Precision was Ares's style. They stopped at a double-level motel and waited for one of the guys to go for the room keys. She didn't care. By the time all the checks were done and they let her out of the back, her body screamed. With a hand on her neck, she tried to stretch her stiff muscles and followed the pack into the room.

"Two on the front," Ares said, pointing at two guys next to each other. "Two on the back. Two and two west and east."

As he delegated roles all she could think about was a shower. The final stooge to enter carried the last thing she expected to see.

Her carpet bag.

She took a reflexive step toward it but doubted anyone noticed. The guy came over and held it out to her. They were giving it… She was…

Ares was instructing his people, paying no attention to her. Of course he wasn't, why would he? It didn't matter that the gesture meant the world to her or that it could only have come from his kindness. She was a prisoner. Angry. Upset. Annoyed. Rebellious prisoner… At least that was her cover.

Holding back her instinct, she went to the bathroom and turned on the shower. Hopefully, the steam would loosen some of her aches, physical and mental. Putting the carpet bag on the vanity, she opened it up, wondering what could be inside.

Her clothes. Toiletries. Damn, she'd actually be able to wear her own underwear instead of Kingsley's. Eager to get under the spray, she stripped to her bra and panties, only then realizing there were no towels in the bathroom.

Damn. Did that mean she had to go back out there?

Just at that thought, the doorhandle moved, and the door began to open. She gasped in a low breath, only releasing it when Daire revealed himself through the crack. He held a towel through the narrow space. Keeping his distance? Showing respect? Keeping to his cover?

She opened her hand for it without reaching out. He would have to come closer to give it to her. Were they alone? She didn't know and didn't want to take any chances.

Yet, he didn't hesitate, he came in to put the towel in her hand. As she laid it on the vanity, the door closed. Her attention pounced up. He wasn't gone, he was there. Behind her. The reflection of his eyes locked on hers. What was she supposed to do? Pretend to be offended? If his men were out there, the show had to be good. She needed direction; he was usually good at knowing that. At helping without her needing to ask.

The pulse of her heart soared while vulnerability trembled above it. Her Heart. Goddamnit, her Heart. Hadn't she lost him? Been torn from his side only to be betrayed by him?

He dropped to his knees, stealing his reflection from hers. His temple met her hip, his forehead, his nose and almost…

Her fingers sank into his hair as her eyes shut. The sensation was so familiar, need threatened to overwhelm her. She couldn't stay away, couldn't be distant, and descended to kneel with him, cupping her hands around his face.

"It's okay," she whispered against his lips. His eyes were closed, yet his pain bled into her. "Oh, baby, it's okay."

"I'm sorry," he exhaled.

"Me too. Baby…"

He caught her face in both hands, parting them just enough to find her eyes with his. "I had to."

As her lips quirked a fraction, tears tumbled from her lashes. "I know," she said.

After a stunned moment, his disbelief became relief.

"He told you."

"Whatever it takes." Both spoke in muted whispers. She didn't know the rules but cherished his honesty. "I told you to do whatever it takes."

"Losing you. Breaking this—"

"Nothing is too broken to fix," she said, smiling through her tears.

His startled blink preceded a frown. "Little Red…?"

"Yes?" she asked, moistening her lips. Whatever the question, whatever he wanted to know… the answer would always be yes. His lips moved as his attention flitted to hers, what was he thinking? Whatever it was… "Are they watching us?" His head shake was loose, almost absent. "Listening?" Another shake. She pulled his mouth closer to hers. "Forget everything and just be here."

So far, the line he'd drawn for himself stopped at her mouth. With her new permission, his eyes closed, and their lips met, sinking together like life only existed in their kiss.

It did.

All of her was him. That had never changed. Even when she'd wanted to hate him. When she'd believed his betrayal and doubted his heart…

His splayed hands skimmed down to her ass to pick her up and wind her legs around his hips. They were already so close to the floor that laying her down on the cool vinyl was an easy glide, much like their mouths, their tongues, their wandering hands. Easy was good. It was what she remembered and what had been withheld from them for so long. No Harry. No rules. No deception. Just them uniting in the way that always brought them completion.

Forcing her hands beneath his tee-shirt, she treated herself to the smooth muscles of his back for only a second. Her fingertips wandered to his abs and down to his belt. From their early days, their bodies had been playgrounds for each other, with only minor interruptions along the way.

He caught her arms and stretched them above her head, holding them straight in one sure fist. His kiss slowed as his other hand descended between their bodies. What was taking so long? Was he testing her honesty? Did he doubt she'd go through with it? Maybe he wanted to check if she was testing a theory. Was he sure Styx told her the truth?

Love was real. It was true. It existed so deep within her that there was no end. It slid into the abyss of infinity with every certainty she'd ever possessed.

Until he broke their kiss.

His nostrils flared when he inhaled deep. "No."

Letting her go, he rolled onto his back, covering his face with both hands.

"No?" He'd never said no. Never put up a fight. Was she supposed to seduce him? She'd never done that… well, never with forethought and effort. Everything between them had always been natural. He'd never said… "No?"

"If you let me back in, I'll never leave," he grumbled behind his hands. "Fuck, Temptress… Leaving the first time was…"

"You never left," she said, laying her head against the center of his torso, right over his heart.

Closing her eyes, she relaxed, listening to the beat she'd thought was gone from her life for good. Though there was a moment of hesitation, his fingertips found her hair to comb it from her temple over and over again.

"We can't stay like this," he muttered, his fingers still moving.

"Just another second," she said, skimming a hand down his tee-shirt to slide it back up underneath. Her palm on his skin, absorbing the texture of him was like a dream. "Your hearts beat differently."

"Has he been looking after you? Cover or not, I'll fucking kill him if—"

"You hit him in the face?"

"I did more than that."

"In D.C."

"In D.C.? He really did tell you everything… It was punch him or fuck you."

Smiling, she turned her head over to peek up at him. "For future reference, go with the latter."

He laid his hand on her hair. "Your father was right there."

"He's old. You can take him."

A whisper of a laugh teased his dimple. "I thought you'd never speak to me again."

"Why? The greater good is more important than us. I don't like it but can't argue against it." Sitting up, they didn't have the luxury of submerging themselves in each other. "What do I need to know? When we get there…?"

"We can't do this," he said, sitting up to take her hand.

"I figured. Are you going to hit me?"

"What?" he retorted, disgust narrowing his eyes. "No! No, I'm not going to…" He rubbed his forehead. "This is a fucking mistake. There's no way I'll be able to… In that lab, when you were…"

She took his hand to hold it on her face. "I didn't know the truth then. I know the truth now."

"You are… You don't understand how strong you are," he said, exuding nothing but truth. "The way you… You fought for them, not for you. You weren't even mad at me."

"I was sad," she said, nuzzling her cheek against his hand. "All I ever wanted was your happiness. You say I'm strong, but… You walked away, the things you did… You think I judge you for them?" She was overwhelmed. "Putting our relationship on the line… Hades and… your brother…"

"When we figured JARR was more than information gathering…"

She brought his palm around to her lips. "Every life is at stake. That's bigger than us."

"Nothing is bigger than us," he murmured, mesmerized by her. "If I was terrified for your life… in the lab when Styx said…"

Sitting straighter, worry tensed her. "It's not true. I'm not…"

"I know." He paused. "I drew your blood… When you were out."

"It's okay," she said, squeezing his hand in both of hers.

"I wasn't sure I'd even be able to do that, stick you with a needle," he said. "But when it was me or one of the other guys… I don't want anyone touching you. Not anyone at Beta."

Leaning in closer, she wanted him to understand her certainty. "I trust you."

"You trust me… How can you trust me?"

"In Vegas, when I first saw the Scepter…" Reliving it always sickened her. "I thought Zeus had hurt you. I was sure there was no other way that… Your brother is a good actor."

"He said what he did so I wouldn't hurt you," he said. "In the lab."

"I know."

His brow descended. "He had my back there… just like I had his in the shower… when you told him to…"

Emotion simmered so close to the surface that it was impossible not to show him her vulnerable determination. "You freed Harry… You helped us escape."

"I set it up so he could do it himself." Of course he had, knowing his mentor would seize the opportunity, even if he didn't realize it was presented on purpose. "In that shower, with Styx… Baby, how could you—"

"We had a deal. Him and me, we had a deal that…"

"What?" he asked, snatching his hand back, curling his fingers into a tight fist. "You had a deal that what?"

"We still have a deal, but he's not around, so I need you to make me the same promise."

Shaking his head, he pounced to his feet, then swooped down to scoop her onto hers. "I won't hear it."

"You won't have a choice," she said, reaching for him.

He yanked his arm away. "*'I can hurt the man I thought you were and the man you are now with the same act.'*" Those had been her words to him in D.C. "I know what that means."

"Yes," she said because she couldn't be anything except resolute. "If it comes to it—"

"I'm not capable," he said, somehow admitting weakness through his anger. "You can reason it out as much as you want. I might even agree with you in theory, in practice, I won't be able to do it."

She stepped closer, lowering her volume further. "I don't know how to do it by myself there. In that room—"

"You won't be in that room," he said. "You're a guest at Beta, not a prisoner."

"I'll be allowed to leave?"

"If you made it out before anyone got to you... yeah." She didn't need to ask to know how likely that would be. "But you won't be pacing in one room. I've made sure you'll be in the quarter block." Uh... what was that? "It's where we live, soldiers and officers..." His head dipped to the side. "Certain officers."

"If you're about to tell me I'm sleeping anywhere near Zeus—"

"You'll have your father's suite," he said, his fingers drifting across her cheekbone to her hair. "Next to mine."

"Next to..." she said, nuzzling his touch. "I prefer to be closer."

His hand dropped. "I will keep you close, baby, but we can't..."

"I know," she said on a sigh. "I'll be good, I promise."

Another flash of his dimple. "Didn't know you knew how."

"Around you? It will be a first."

He dipped lower, welcoming the rise of her chin. "Trouble is, I want you no matter what you're doing. I don't know how to be near you without..."

"Yes, you do," she said, licking her lips the moment they met his.

The sweet beginnings of their kiss were a silent promise. When he pushed harder, begging more, she eased away. "I'll do my best to have your back..."

"But?"

She tensed. "Evil or ally, I want you to be happy. Maybe I should've hated you, but I never did. If you want something, need me to do anything, I'll do it. I can resist the little stuff for show..."

"JARR," he said. "You mean if I ask you to bleed, you will." He scooped a hand around the back of her head. "You cannot tell Zeus that."

"I'd prefer not to talk to Zeus at all. We're hardly bosom buddies, but…" He might be incapable of hurting her, but she was incapable of refusing him. "I love you."

He sighed and pulled her forward to kiss her head. "I know, baby. I know… I love you too." The words in her hair offered salvation. Hope. They were the promise of their future. "I'll figure everything out. Don't worry. I've got you."

And she didn't doubt the truth of that. Navigating their new dynamic would be difficult with so many eyes watching, waiting to pick up on hints and clues of duplicity. They'd get through it… together. Somehow.

TWO

BETA.

The first time she'd arrived there, it was ominous in the night. The sensation of just looking at the building in its locale had settled an instinctual loathing deep inside her. The feeling provoked a desire to flee. Back then, she'd been ignorant to so much, what the beta site really was, Olympus, even the true identity of the man in the driving seat. The experience proved humans did still have their primitive ability to recognize evil.

In those early days of her quest, fleeing wasn't an option. Maybe she'd have tried, backed off for a few days or weeks, but she'd always have wondered. If she'd been alone at least. Danny's mission, Daire's mission, to put her in front of her father in Beta's control room would've prevented her retreating. He prevented her retreat.

All those months ago, she'd been ignorant to her father's identity too, and that he'd be at the end of the journey. Not that their first meeting in the control room was the end. It was just a step on the path she'd started in ignorance. Despite all she'd learned since then, clarity wasn't any richer.

Approaching the building again in the darkness, driving down the dirt road flanked by towering trees, she knew what was at the end this time. What awaited them.

Yes, there was still fear and, in some ways, ignorance. At least some facts were concrete. Zeus and Poseidon would be there. Also known as Ulysses Sherwood and James Garrick, they were two of the three Olympus leaders. The third being her father who they'd left behind in Miami.

Some of her fear was assuaged by her ally. The secret one. Her Heart. He'd never let anything grave happen to her even if it meant blowing his cover. It wasn't her own safety that played on her mind, it was the safety of others. Literally every other living being on earth. She didn't know what JARR would do if it was unleashed. Who would it threaten? Who might it kill? Would it start war or plague or nuclear winter?

In their precious time together in the motel bathroom, she could've asked her Heart for information, but wasn't sure he'd answer. In a selfish way, she wasn't sure she wanted to know. Either way, it was on her. Zeus might be the one pulling the strings, but it was her blood that would open the gates of hell, freeing the demons to swarm the earth.

Unlike her first approach, there was more life to the building this time as it came into view. She couldn't see lights, people, or movement, yet the aura around it was different. No longer stagnant and lifeless, it almost hummed with the intention of its purpose. Funny the structure should seem so optimistic while its replacement was being stocked hundreds of miles away. If only the compound could turn on those inside and deliver justice under the same secret shroud Olympus had cowered under since the loss of the alpha site.

They came to a stop at the gates. Daire, in the driving seat, lowered his window and punched in a code to open them. He'd once told her if the wrong numbers were input, explosives would take any wannabe intruders off the board for good. If they did that, humanity would be spared the horror of what may come. The responsibility would be taken from her door.

Except she didn't want those in her vicinity to perish. More specifically, her Heart who'd taken such a burden onto his shoulders. Always believing everything was his responsibility, this situation was particularly cruel. Truly, he was the only one with the ability to discover the truth. Zeus trusted him, not out of any innate love or loyalty, more likely out of sheer desperation.

Having been Olympus born and bred, the great Ares was the organization's best hope for the future. If the principals were wiped from the board, Daire was the only hope of the institution continuing. If they weren't, Zeus needed Daire to rally the men, to train, to fight, which was definitely a younger, more personable man's game.

They pulled onto the property and parked. Both rear doors were slammed in her face, so she assumed they wanted her to stay put. Not that she was eager to go inside the building. The men unloaded the kit and supplies, most of which hadn't seen the light of day throughout their journey.

Only after the directions were delegated did the back door open.

Daire peeked inside. "Come on."

He stepped back to open the door further. Given the choice, she'd stay in the truck, having no great desire to return to the place she'd been held at gunpoint, betrayed, imprisoned, assaulted, and so much more.

It was her role not to reveal Daire's true motivation for being there, working for Zeus, so she couldn't appear too compliant. She dawdled while exiting the vehicle, hooking her carpet bag higher on her forearm to smooth her hair and clothes as the others were piling inside. Some might consider leaving her alone with one man was reckless, that it lacked foresight and underestimated her. But this was the great Ares, she was hardly a match for his skill or awareness.

They went inside, her just in front of him. He guided her with a hand on her upper arm, being far more forceful than her Heart would be. They went toward the back of the space, through a door beneath the stairs that led them up a new flight she didn't remember from before.

Up those stairs, through another door, swing a right. Leaving wouldn't be easy in this warren of a vast building. That was probably exactly the point. With their failsafe measures waiting to take out anyone who tried to do Olympus harm, it was another kick that those intruders would be too lost to flee even if they did have time. The short corridor they reached was narrower than the others, the doors spaced further apart.

Kind of like the guy loitering in the middle. Was he waiting for them?

"Pandora," Ares said behind her, his voice deep and indifferent. "This is Havers, he'll be your shadow."

A new person. Had Daire picked him? Why couldn't she be her Heart's shadow? The answer to that was he was too important. Too busy being Zeus's right-hand guy to worry about ferrying her around. Still, her Heart might've given her a heads up about this Havers.

"Pandora," Havers said in greeting.

"Do you have to do that?" she asked, wincing. "Does he have to do that?"

Ares opened the central door. "Yes," he said, entering the room. "Your fingerprint is in the system."

"At the lowest security level no doubt," she said, following him in with Havers at her back.

She expected the same setup as her time imprisoned there. The room was around the same size, but had a desk, couch, and a much wider bed, though it was connected to the wall like last time.

"Closet, restroom," Ares said, pointing to the opening in the opposite wall. "Everything's been provided."

"Except freedom," she muttered.

"Havers," Ares said before starting toward the door again.

Hit with a sudden panic, she opened her mouth ready to appeal to him. What could she say? Nothing. He was supposed to be the bastard who'd betrayed her. How could she call out to him for reassurance? Watching him go without another word, she feared when she may, or may not, see him again.

"We work to a strict routine around here," Havers said.

He didn't seem as letchy as the guys in the back of the truck. Young, he did have an obvious air of military discipline around him. Was that from his history or had

Olympus drummed it into him already?

"How long have you stayed here?" she asked.

With a blink of surprise, his expression faltered. "Uh, we… uh… We start the day with a run, outside, sometimes it's grueling."

"Yeah, I won't be running," she said. "Just wake me up in time for coffee."

"You… have to come with us."

"No, I don't," she said, smiling as she took her carpet bag over to the bed. "Can I assume these are fresh sheets?"

"Yes."

"This is a nice room," she said. "Nicer than the last time I was here. I don't remember you. Were you around then?"

"I'm not really… supposed to answer questions."

She liked him. In the same kind of cute way she liked Zip and Milo. Her smile faltered. Were they in the building? "I want to see the others. The other prisoners."

"I can request—"

"Thank you.

"But I don't know if they'll allow—"

"Let's not say 'they.' Let's say what we mean. Zeus. You don't know if Zeus will allow me to see them. Probably not. He's sick like that." She looked at him. "Have you figured out the guy you're working for is a depraved individual so caught up in his own hubris that he can't see straight?"

"I…"

Man, her Heart had picked the right guard. Throwing him off-balance was easy, he was completely unthreatening. It wouldn't be difficult to broker an alliance with him. To worm her way in enough that he might think twice about pulling the trigger if the moment, or Zeus, called for it.

"What's your first name?"

"We go by our last names."

"I know," she said, sitting on the bed. "Doesn't mean we can't get to know each other. As you've probably figured out, I'm not Olympus." Shaking her hair from her face, she tipped her head back. "What do you know about me?"

"You're Pandora."

"And?"

"You're not to be trusted."

She laughed. "Oh, someone's a comedian. Who told you that? Zeus? Ares?"

"Everyone," he said, his expression hardening. "You have an ulterior motive."

"Yeah, uh huh." She played along while mocking the whole concept. "Yeah, I want to live. Ridiculous of me, right?" She exhaled. "You know, I feel sorry for you. Olympus it… I bet you were sold on the greater good too. Your country needs you. It's bullshit, Havers. And it always will be while Zeus sits at the top."

"You don't know—"

"What?" she asked, resting the heels of her hands on the bed behind her. "I don't know Zeus? He had me kidnapped and dragged across an ocean. I lived with him for weeks. I know Zeus. Or is it Ares? You think I don't know him?" Her snicker was ironic. "Believe me when I say, I know every intimate secret about the man you work under… 'cause I did the same thing for too long."

Deliberately leaving that ambiguous, she didn't mind if the operative thought she'd once been an agent herself. And if he took it the other way, well, it was the truth. She'd been under Daire plenty and would take the role again in a snap if offered.

Would she have to show her Heart resentment and hatred if they were in the same space? That wouldn't be easy. What would she gain by being bitter even if he was the lying betrayer for real? All that would achieve was showing everyone he could get to her, that he was still her weak point. Maybe just keeping things casual and indifferent would be the better way to go.

"I know Olympus way better than I ever wanted to," she said. "You probably have questions… that others haven't answered for you."

His shoulders went back. "My loyalty is to Olympus. To Zeus."

Curiosity tilted her head. "Have you ever had one on one time with him?" she asked and received no response.

"Have you ever even met him?" When Havers didn't reply again, she laughed. "Wow, he's the man behind the curtain… I suppose it's a reprieve for you and for him. Maybe he's finally figured out that he's just not a people person."

"At Olympus, we work as a team."

Yeah, right, Zeus didn't know the meaning of the word. Dictatorship. Yeah, he knew what that word meant. Repression. Persecution. These were much more familiar to him.

"Word to the wise…" Boosting herself off the bed, she snagged her bag. "I might despise him and everything he stands for, but if you want to pledge your allegiance to something, pledge it to Ares. He, at least, won't leave you in the dust for scraps. Zeus is an egomaniac who believes the world exists only to cater to his desires. Spread the word, he'll desert you all. You mean nothing to him."

Wandering in the direction of the bathroom, she was ready to wash off the day.

"Pandora—"

"I'll pass on the run," she said, pausing in the closet doorway. "Just wake me when the coffee's ready."

Havers was new. To Olympus and to her. If Harry was at the top, if Daire was, maybe the kid would have a chance of fighting for what he believed in. So long as he worked under Zeus, he'd be a puppet, and an expendable one at that.

THREE

DAY EIGHT

It's weird that I've never written a journal before. Okay, maybe not so weird. Mom would never have allowed it. Maybe I'd have been allowed to write only to watch her burn every entry as soon as it was done.

I miss her.

I know I should be conscious of leaving evidence, of admitting weakness, of confessing life is anything less than ideal. But I don't think it's any secret I didn't choose to be here. Secrets were important when we were running from the clutches of Olympus. Given that I now live here, yeah, secrets are less important.

Day eight and still going strong, which I completely put down to the fact I haven't seen Zeus. I hadn't given much thought to seeing him again, but knowing him, I would've expected he'd want to boast about his own magnificence. Guess the loss of his precious Six showed him that there were those willing to stand up to his tyranny.

With Six in his camp, Zeus would've always known if anyone was trying to creep up behind him. Now he's lost that safety net. Ha! Excuse me if I'm not weeping for him. Serves the bastard right.

Sure, okay, let's be honest, he has Ares at his back. His new number two would always see a threat coming. As to whether or not he'd alert the boss...? Who knows? His loyalty seems fluid.

So much has changed since the Exodus. It's actually been something of a blessing to have this time to stop and reflect. No, I'd never tell Zeus that... I probably wouldn't tell Hades either. For months, I've been pushed and pulled from here to there. Something's always been going on, there's always been a goal or a threat driving my purpose.

No one wants to kill me here. No, let me rephrase, no one will kill me here. I'd put money on Zeus's greatest fantasy being sticking a knife in my gut. But he needs me. Probably another reason I haven't seen him. He won't want to admit it. Won't want to see me smile as I taunt him... I have to stop, I know. Anyone could read these words any time. Again, it's no big secret that I'm not a fan of the asshole. If I was to suddenly begin pouring praise onto Zeus, no *one would believe it. I wouldn't believe it.*

Havers seems to be getting used to me. That's something. He's stopped trying to get me up to run outside in the great beyond with him and the other men every morning. The guy must be one helluvan optimist. Me? Run? My whole life has been dedicated to swerving the threats behind me. He hasn't figured out yet that I'm actually doing him a favor.

Anyone who knows me would never ask me to get up early and actually keep up with the pack. I'd slow them down. I'd ask questions. I'd rest. Styx couldn't handle it when we were running for our lives. My father thinks dawdle is my default, which, okay, yeah, maybe I should give him that.

Is it weird that I miss them? Staying put here might give me time to reflect, but it also leaves time for worry. They're out there. Capable, yes, I know, but if something was to happen... Would they tell me? Would Ares show enough respect to—

"Pandora!"

Looking up from the notebook propped on her raised knees, she saw the men were dispersing from the gym mats in the middle of the large space.

They spent a lot of time working out. When they weren't working out, they were training, learning, always doing something.

"What?" she asked the scowling guy in the middle of the pack. "Don't bark at me like that if you don't expect me to bark back."

The guys around paused, bracing to see how the barker would respond. The growling expression he wore suggested he wasn't the most patient guy. Let him come over and give her grief, she'd love to see how that played out.

The moment was broken by the doors opening.

Ares came striding inside, but almost immediately paused, assessing the mood of the room. "What's going on?"

"She's being difficult," the barker snapped.

Her mouth fell open. "I'm sitting here minding my own damn business. Who the hell do you think—"

"Enough," Ares said, impatient. Was that meant for her or the idiot with a chip on his shoulder? "All of you hit the shower then get out back."

The men muttered at each other as they filtered toward the door. When Havers got the nod to leave too, it took her a second to figure out Ares was the only one staying behind.

"These guys are amateurs," she said as the last of them departed. "Can I see the real power behind Olympus yet? H's people?"

"What do you hope to achieve?" he asked, coming over. "You can't do anything for them."

"I can tell them they're not alone," she said. "Not knowing is worse than knowing."

He offered her a hand. While suspicion narrowed her eyes, she closed the notepad and slid the pen into the spine to put her hand in his.

With little effort on her part, he pulled her to her feet, jerking her so close that her body bumped his.

"Classic Tess logic."

Hearing her name was odd. "No one around here uses my name."

"That's because they don't know it."

"Good. Especially that last guy. What the hell is wrong with him?"

"Daniels?"

"I don't learn their names," she said.

"Because?"

Licking her lips, she wasn't shy about telling the truth. "Because I met a group of people once. Good people. I learned their names. Got to know them. And wouldn't you know they went and got themselves kidnapped. So now they're being held against their will, kind of like I am, and there's a huge chance none of us make it out of this alive. That, my former friend, is what they call learning from experience."

"Former friend," he muttered, his gaze dropping to her mouth.

They hadn't been alone. Not completely. Not since the motel. Being there in Beta, she couldn't take the chance of anyone overhearing or spying. They may not be alone. In Beta, she never assumed privacy was guaranteed.

Stepping back, she smacked his arm with her notebook, startling him from whatever was going on in his head.

"You make me watch your people fight each other every day. Doesn't look that hard, you know."

"No?" he asked, a semi-smile quirking his lips for a brief second. "Show me."

He bent down to unlace his boots. Now it was her turn to be taken aback.

"Show you?"

"Yeah," he said, removing his boots and socks to back up onto the mat. "Come on."

"Oh, you think I'm lying?"

"I think you're weak," he said, with enough of a glint in his eye that she could read his playful taunting. "Bring it, Pandora."

Tossing her notebook to the floor, she toed off her shoes. She'd started it and wasn't known for backing down, so she marched across to join him in the middle of the mat. Keeping her balance on the soft surface wasn't easy.

"Widen your stance," he said, gesturing at her legs. "Open up."

"Okay, well, you can't say stuff like that."

Another glimpse of his smile. "Don't lock your knees. Eye contact is always first."

"Usually, if someone's trying to kick my ass, I don't stop to gaze at them."

"Okay, then come at me."

She raised an arm but paused. "You're not packing

tranquilizers, are you? That seems to be Olympus's assault of choice."

He opened his hands in surrender. "No drugs. No weapons."

"And you do remember that I'm important…" He frowned. "To Olympus. I mean you can't actually kill me because my blood is—"

"Shit."

He grabbed her arm, yanked her forward and swept his leg in an arc to take hers out from under her. With a whoop, she landed on her back with him coming down on top of her.

"I wasn't ready," she panted, her heart rate climbing.

"Your weapon would be talking your attacker to death," he said without hiding his smile this time.

Was she…? Oh, damn, it felt good. To be under him again. He was thinking it too. The yearning in his gaze stole his smile as it drifted down to the mouth he'd tasted so often.

"Daire," she whispered, snaring his eyes again. The line between his brows deepened. He wanted to respond. Wanted to be them just as much as she did. If one of them didn't break, they'd lay there all day… or worse. "Up!" Smacking his shoulders, she played the affronted victim as best she could. "Goddamnit, get off me!"

Holding onto her, he pounced to a crouch, putting her on her feet as he stood, the rough act more Ares than Daire. Maybe he needed to remind himself.

"You want to speak to your father?"

She'd been working up a lather. Ready to make a show of berating him for taking advantage. The moment his words sank in, that steam depressurized.

"Yes," she said, actually stepping closer. "Yes. Please."

His side-nod indicated the exit, but he went first, leading her through various corridors until they reached a small room with a fixed desk. Small was accurate, it couldn't be more than six feet square. Painted light blue with a single light on the ceiling and no windows.

She squeezed around him to sit on the static stool and

picked up the corded handset that was affixed to the wall in front of her. Apparently, she wasn't a prisoner, but it sure felt like prison.

The door closed. Ares was gone.

FOUR

THIS WOULD BE THE FIRST TIME they'd spoken since Miami. Over and over, she'd asked to speak to her father and Styx. Every time she'd been ignored or denied.

She took a breath before raising the phone to her ear. "Dad?"

"Light-Sprite?"

Harry.

Relieved tears pricked her eyes. "Are you okay? Where are you?"

"Don't worry about us. How are they treating you? If anyone's laid a finger on you—"

"No! No, Dad, I'm fine. It's more boring than traumatic. They've given me your quarters; I'm trying to keep them neat for you."

"That I'd need to see to believe," her father said, a warm almost laugh in his voice. "You won't have to be there much longer."

Was that a comfort? If they were setting up Gamma, as she believed was the plan, they could take as long as they wanted doing the job. But what was at the end of that journey? What would happen next? A consolidation of everyone would lead them back to exactly where they'd been before. With

Zeus eager to extract JARR, there had to be something else, a plan she wasn't aware of. It wouldn't be the first time she'd been kept in the dark.

"Is he harassing you?" Harry asked. "There are forms of torture other than physical."

"I know." Which *he* was her father referring to, Zeus or Ares? "I have a shadow who keeps his eyes on me, but I am allowed to move around the building. I mainly stick with the men."

"Our men?"

"No, the new ones," she said. "I haven't learned their names. Where's Styx? Is he okay? Are you driving each other crazy?"

"No more than usual. We haven't forgotten about you."

"I haven't forgotten you either. Your life probably got much easier when I was taken out of the equation."

"We'll get through this, Light-Sprite."

Being father to a daughter hadn't come natural to him. Their relationship had endured its bumps... so far. Maybe they'd hit them again in the future, but her father had proved he'd be there for her if and when she needed him. He could've abandoned her rather than save her. Could've left her behind instead of taking her along.

Maybe it was for JARR. Although she wanted to discount that completely, experience taught her to be aware of any possible outcome. Sometimes the people she thought cared about her were actually prioritizing other things.

Of course, Daire came to mind. The last double-cross had been part of a larger plan, but it still stung. Some mornings she woke up grieving him and had to remind herself that he hadn't actually used her to further Zeus's nefarious agenda. Not for real.

"I need—"

"Lady?"

Oh, God, it was Styx.

Clinging to the mouthpiece, she clutched the phone closer. "Hi, Prince."

"You better be keeping your head down."

"Does that sound like me?"

"No," he said. "You'd get in trouble there even if you were completely by yourself. How are the teamsters doing?"

She guessed that meant their cohorts. "They won't let me see them. I've asked. I keep asking, but they won't let me... Do you think that's bad? That they've been hurt?"

"Take no news as good news. We can't fix a problem we don't know exists. Most of them are smart enough to keep themselves in line... only one or two who might not."

"And what about them? It's not easy to be locked up and powerless, you know that."

"They're not powerless, they've got us. They're holding onto that, and you need to as well. This part, the waiting, it's tough. Remember what I told you about waiting?"

That most of their game was waiting for something to change. "Yes."

"Hold onto it. Stay alert. Stand ready."

"For anything?"

"Hey, you never know," he said. "Luck is always on your side, Lady."

"I'm not the one out there..."

Anything could go wrong at any second. And Zeus wasn't to be trusted. He could circumvent Daire completely and send someone out to take down Harry and Styx.

"Worrying achieves nothing. Keep that chin up."

She opened her mouth to respond, but a click on the line silenced her for a second. "Hello?" she asked. "Styx, are you—"

Behind her, the door opened, so she swung around.

Ares was gesturing her out. "That's it."

"Was that you?" she demanded, throwing the phone to the desk, surging to her feet. "Did you disconnect me?"

"Everyone got what they needed."

"No, they didn't. I didn't! What was the rush? Not like I've got a full day. You can't just—" He grabbed her arm to pull her into the corridor. "Let me go! Stop!" Pulling back, she at least got his attention. "I wasn't finished!"

"If you act like this, we won't let you talk to them again."

"Who the hell do you think you are?" she asked, angry tears blurring her eyes. "What gives you the goddamn right to—I thought I wasn't a prisoner. I thought I was to be treated as a guest." Her chest tightened. "You can't just cut me off from the people I care about! You can't just decide to…" The pain in her chest grew as her lungs shrank. Gasping in one breath and then another, she couldn't seem to fill them. "This isn't right." Another gasp. "You can't just— you can't—"

"Breathe," he said, grabbing her again, only this time he planted her back on the wall.

"What's…" Her throat screamed in stinging agony. "I… I…"

"Look at me," he said, guiding her to the floor when her legs buckled. "Breathe out, all the way out, slow… Tess! Look at me!" He grabbed her chin, forcing her eyes to his. Tears dropped from her lashes when she blinked, clearing her vision enough to read his gaze. "That's it…" He blew out a breath. "Slow it down. In…"

He breathed in and out.

Mimicking him wasn't easy. "I… I can't…"

The pain in her throat eased a little.

"Yes, you can," he said, smoothing the hair from her face as he continued his measured breaths. "You can do it. You can do anything, baby."

Pulling in another breath, it was easier to calm herself while looking into him. They were in Beta, probably being watched, anyone could walk by any second. This wasn't right. She wanted to see her Heart, to lean into him and gather strength from his courage.

Her eyes closed. "I can't do this."

Breathing was one thing, but what did it matter. Whether she lived or died, everything was out of her control. No one was who they said they were. Loyalties were confused and inverted. The whole world was topsy-turvy.

"Come here," he said, pulling her onto her feet.

He kept one of her hands as he walked down the corridor, leading her wherever he was going. "I don't want to go to that lab again," she said, pulling back.

"We're not going there," he said, tightening his grip.

"I'm taking you somewhere else."

"Where?" she asked, following as he went into a stairwell, though it wasn't easy to maintain the pace with her head still spinning.

"Wait and see."

That hadn't always worked out in her favor. She trusted Daire. Had to. But he wasn't himself there. If this was the time he chose to put her in front of Zeus, she'd seriously question his—

He burst through a door at the bottom of the stairs. Before she registered light, air hit her. Fresh air. Outside. Freedom.

Letting him go, she rushed past him, eyes closed, just breathing it in. The concrete beneath her feet and the obstructing perimeter wall detracted from the illusion. From the hope that there really could be a world beyond this confinement.

Weight lifted from her chest. "Oh, God," she exhaled.

"Better?"

Spinning around, she rushed to him until their bodies met, taking both his hands in hers. "Let's get out of here."

Concern touched his brow. "What?"

"Let's just go," she said, tipping her face to the sky. "Let's get the hell out of here for an hour."

His fingers did stay in hers, but she had to open her eyes to judge his reaction. He looked to the side, his jaw moving like he might be considering it.

"Fuck," he said, but strode off, pulling her with him.

The smile she wore was the brightest it had been in weeks. They rounded one corner to a fleet of vehicles just lined up waiting. Daire took her to the third in the line, lifted her into the passenger seat, and got in the driver's side.

Somehow, he started the engine and then they were driving. Right up to the gate. Out without any hitches. No one stopped them. No one asked questions. They were just... free.

Exhaling a single laugh, she couldn't believe liberty was so simple.

"Breathe easier?" he asked once they were shrouded

by the trees.

"Yes," she said, her smile becoming a grin. "Much."

"Good," he said and stopped the truck right there in the middle of the road.

"What? What's wrong?"

"Nothing. One second," he said and jumped out.

She tracked him going around to the back of the truck, then he disappeared. Looking this way and that, she wasn't sure where to expect he'd reappear. Whatever he was doing didn't take long. Within seconds, he was coming back, jumping into the driving seat again.

They were moving before he looked her way.

Her brows rose in question. "What was that?"

"Disabled the tracker."

The corner of her lips responded. "Will you get in trouble for that?"

"The only one above me in the hierarchy these days is Zeus," he said. "You think he checks the tracker logs?"

That sounded more like an Ares job than a Zeus one.

"If he doesn't check, what does it matter if the tracker works? What are you protecting?"

"You'll see."

What did that mean? She wasn't sure but could see the smile that flirted with his lips. It was too much to hope they were making a break for it. Though, they could, and pick up Harry and Styx on the way south of the border.

Shame that was the same as signing the death warrants of those held captive by Zeus.

Still, they were free, even if it was only for a short while. Slipping off her shoes, she put the seat back and just breathed.

"You feel safe?"

He'd asked her that question when they left Vegas together after London.

"Maybe," she responded in a semi-tease.

"Just relax. I've got you now."

She didn't really sleep, but her muscles were definitely looser, even in spite of the uneven dirt road beneath their tires. Near the end of the road, rather than head for the highway, he took them into the forest. They bumped and swerved, avoiding this tree and that for quite a while, like miles and miles.

A vigilant passenger wouldn't question the driver while they were concentrating. Though anyone who knew the man next to her would never assume he was incapable of doing more than one thing at once. If only she could be sure they weren't being watched or listened to. Okay, so no one could track them, but just asking if they were being recorded would raise the suspicion of anyone who might later hear their voices.

She intended to put her theory on his ability to multitask to the test. Except they stopped. In a weird, middle of nowhere place. Surrounded by trees and little else.

"Where are we?" she asked.

He got out and came around the hood, smirking just enough to make her suspicious. Without a word, he opened her door and retrieved her shoes, turning her in the seat to slip them onto her feet with full entitlement.

What was going on? Did she want to ask?

He lifted her out of the truck, setting her on her feet right up against him. That smirk grew until his dimples made an appearance. Goddamn, she loved this man.

Linking their fingers, he led her away from the truck. They rounded a fallen tree, passed a boulder or two and… Something in the distance began to take shape. Not that far in the distance. As they got closer, she stopped, mouth open, submerged in shock.

"Don't stop there," he said with a slight laugh and came back to sweep her legs out from under her.

It was. She couldn't believe it. She couldn't… Her cheeks prickled and warmth rushed to her eyes. Getting so emotional was ridiculous. It might be, but…

FIVE

ANCHORED BY HER ARMS looped around his neck, she stayed against him while he took the keys from his pocket and unlocked the door. As he stepped inside, she held her breath. It was… They were…

"Home," she whispered when he put her down. "God, baby, how did…?" She turned to see him locking the door behind them. "Are we being monitored? Followed?"

"No."

That was all she needed to know and rushed to him, throwing her arms around his neck, trying to pull his mouth to hers.

He resisted. "Wait a minute," he said, unhooking her arms. "We need to—"

"What's wrong?" she asked, losing her happiness in an instant. "What happened?"

"Nothing happened, just…" He exhaled and set his contrite eyes on hers. "He told me to seduce you."

"Who?"

"Zeus."

"When?"

"A couple of days after we got to Beta."

Relief relaxed her muscles. "Geez, and you waited all this time? I thought you were going to… Who cares?"

He frowned. "Who cares?"

"I don't," she said, coiling her arms around his waist. "He gives you orders every day. You have to follow them. You have to… For now anyway. Here's one you get for free."

"Yeah, but I didn't want to—"

"You didn't want me to find out later and wonder if everything was a lie." He shrugged in confirmation. "It's a gift, my Heart," she said, slipping her feet from her shoes, then bobbing her brows as she took her top off. "I appreciate you telling me. Thank you. You should always tell me. But he's given us a gift… even if he doesn't know it."

"A gift?"

"You have permission to be with me," she said, tossing her top to the couch before wriggling out of her jeans. "Even if we get caught, you have a cover story."

"He wants me to seduce you because he thinks it'll make you more pliable when it comes to releasing JARR."

"And because he probably wants to mock me about it some time." And Zeus was proud of being that kinda guy. "Think about it logically," she said, going to unbutton his pants. "If we get to a point where I'm in the JARR control room and my blood is needed, I won't be able to resist by force. I'll try, but it won't make a difference." As her experience in the Beta lab last time proved. "They don't need my consent. In fact, I can be unconscious, and they can still use it. I don't know what releasing JARR will do." She slid her hands under his tee-shirt to stroke his body. "But I do know that if it brings plague and death and horror…" She smiled. "I'd regret not being with you, I'd never regret the opposite."

"I didn't think…" His hands rose slowly, creeping under her hair to her jaw. Rising further, they hooked around her head beneath her ears. "I've never endured a torture like this." Pain touched her expression before it found his. "All I want is you, Little Red."

"You have me," she said, still stroking him. "You'll always have me. Didn't I promise we'd always find a way back to each other?"

"I stand in the room while he talks about you…" The way he gritted his teeth in a snarl suggested his leader wasn't always complimentary. "I want to put a bullet in him."

"But you haven't. Because we need intel. The sacrifice you're making is… I would never be able to do it."

"You are doing it," he said, his thumbs moving in a gentle caress. "Every time you ignore my cruelty. My betrayal."

"This is not a betrayal," she said, curling her fingers into his tee-shirt. "You are my heart. My soul. My breath. My being."

"Goddamnit, baby," he said, lunging down to capture her mouth with his.

In their home, the first place they'd ever been together, it wasn't possible to resist their pull. In his arms, off the floor, she knew he'd take her to their bed. Even so, a zing of thrilling anticipation zipped through her when he lowered her onto her back.

"I love you," she whispered when he kissed her chin, her throat. Unhooking her bra, he continued his feast as she tossed it aside. "Oh, God, baby…"

Had she thought it was possible to exist without this? Without the tender touch of his famished mouth. He needed her. She knew it, her body was in withdrawal from his. A spasm clenched her gut as his palm drifted down it. The feather-light touch heralded his finger's entry to her body. Her panties were just an inconvenience, they didn't slow him down.

"Daire," she said, moving with the probing of his digit, gasping as a second joined in. "Please, baby."

"I can't…" He rose to meet her eye. "I don't know if I'll be able to walk away again."

In the motel, he'd resisted, thinking it would be too difficult to turn his back on her again.

Scooping her hands around his face, she smiled as a warm trickle of moisture left the corner of her eye. "You live in me, baby. You never went anywhere."

Guiding his mouth to hers, she pushed up, forcing her tongue deep into his mouth, reminding him of the power of their connection. It didn't matter if they were apart. Yes, she'd choose to be next to him every minute of the day if she could. Life wasn't that simple.

In London, with an ocean between them, the potency of their love hadn't faded. Distance, physical or mental, didn't change the truth of what they were. Soulmates was a corny word that didn't go far enough. He was her. Her reason and her meaning... Maybe her father was right.

Easing back, she licked his lower lip. "Your cock," she said, alight with a need just as potent as it had been on their first night together. "I need your cock..." Frayed, his conflict was heartbreaking. Pulling away, refusing, would be the easier, more sensible course. But he'd brought her there. He'd brought them to their bed. He had to know how this would end. "Please don't deny me."

"I can't," he said, his mouth touching hers again. "Temptress..."

His words didn't match his actions; his hand descended between them and...

Completion came when he slid into her. It was exactly the medicine she needed. The truth that enlightened her. The meaning of existence.

With her eyes closed, her body arched into his every thrust. "Daire," she whispered.

They needed this. Both of them. There in the forest, surrounded by trees and wildlife, they could do what they hadn't before. Yelping in response to the deep push of him consuming her, she wanted every second to stretch, to linger, to envelope her the way her body did his.

"Little Red," he said, his speed growing. "Look at me, baby."

Opening her eyes to his, their obvious adoration curved her lips. "I love you." Slamming her fists on the bed, a surge of endorphins pushed her higher. Lighter. Hotter. Desperate. Everything was clarity. Nothing made sense. "Oh, goddamnit, Daire. I love you!"

When she screamed it out, he exhaled a laugh and ducked to kiss her head. "I love you too, baby. I love you too."

She only kind of heard him as the rush of blood in her ears rang.

Gasping in one breath, her muscles clenched around

him. "Yes! Oh, fuck!"

No matter how much she wanted it to last, this was the first time she'd climaxed since the last time he was inside her. There hadn't been much to celebrate or many opportunities. The only time she thought about sex was when she was with him.

Her orgasm kept on going so long that his almost passed her by. Her whole quivering form wasn't ready to surrender his, but when he pulled out, she was stolen from the bliss she'd missed.

"Every time we think we have nothing left to give, no fight left, our strength is tested."

"What does that mean?" he asked, leaving the bed. "Thinking of your mom?"

"I think…"

Him taking off his tee-shirt distracted her for a second. She hadn't even moved, couldn't really, but that act suggested they were in no hurry to rush back to Beta. Thank God for that.

He opened the fridge. "Think what?"

"That I was a really stupid kid," she said, digging her heels into the mattress to push up the bed until she was sitting against the pillows.

Beer in hand, he closed the fridge with a flat hand that remained against it. "Didn't take us long to get back to it."

No, and until it was dealt with, they'd always keep circling back to Olympus.

"When can I talk to my dad and Styx again?"

"Next week maybe," he said, pushing himself away from the fridge.

"Why does it have to be so long?"

"It's better to talk when there's information to exchange," he said, handing her the beer as he got back on the bed. "Too much and it's more difficult to pick out what's relevant."

"Styx said I would have to be the conduit… I didn't know if there was anything I should—"

"This one went the other way," he said with a smile, lying on his side next to her, holding his head on a hand.

"The other way?" she asked, tipping some beer into her mouth. "What does that mean?"

"Styx gave me intel."

She frowned, her beer hand dropping to the bed. "How did he do that? Did you talk to him while I was talking to Harry?"

"No," he said, his smile almost pitying. "The teamsters are—"

"The prisoners."

"No."

"That's… what?" She was confused. "I thought he was asking me how your people were doing."

"He was talking about the team he's building."

"Him and Harry?"

"Yes," he said. "No news is good news means all is going well. His comment about one or two not being smart enough to stay in line means a potential recruit or two are reluctant. But he said 'stand ready' which means we're in the final stages. He feels ready to proceed, so it could happen any time."

"Even if the recruits are reluctant?"

"Remember, H will think this is all his plan. As far as I know, Styx hasn't told him about my mission."

"H is prepping with the team."

"They're probably still trying to encourage whoever's reluctant, but we can't wait forever. It will come down to a do or die moment."

"What a nice way to put it." She offered him the beer. He shook his head while sliding a hand behind it. "You won't drink with me…? Because you're on Omega?"

Skimming a hand up her thigh, he gave her a squeeze. "Because I'll have to see him when I go back. The sex I can explain. Alcohol?" He shook his head again, still stroking her leg. "Ares doesn't drink unless it's required for a mission."

"Always clear headed."

"Right." He tipped his head back to find her eyes. "I know this isn't easy for you."

"It isn't easy for anyone," she said, drinking more beer. "Sometimes I want…"

Saying the words aloud wouldn't be fair.

Sitting up, he took the beer from her to set it on the windowsill behind the pillows. "If you say the word…"

"I know," she said, pulling him closer. He hadn't said it since his mission started, at least since she learned about it, but that didn't matter. "If I asked you to walk away right now…"

"I would," he said without a second of hesitation. "But it would mean…"

"The murder of every person left behind. The pursuit of Harry and Styx… We'd be running forever."

"Because no matter what, he needs your blood."

She licked her lips. "How does this play out? What don't I know? Styx is putting a team together?"

"Yes," he said. "Assets. People we know. We can trust."

"Like Wreck and Tulsi."

"I don't know them, but Styx trusts them. That's enough for me… I don't know that Tulsi would—"

"I met them," she said, smiling. "He's a scary guy. Big and mean looking… Tulsi… she was the oasis I needed… And she witnessed me screaming at Harry, so, you know, she knows what she's getting into."

"Don't know that Styx or Wreck will let her in on this, but I'm happy you had some comfort."

SIX

WRIGGLING DOWN THE BED, she lay facing him. "You know I never stopped loving you," she said as he tucked her hair back from her face. "I was mad. I really was. I was… angry at everyone."

"At me?"

"At me," she said. "Harry was right. He said I was so mad at myself that I was taking it out on everyone else. I was. All I wanted was you and I… I'd have come with you if you'd asked. But you didn't ask, so…"

"You thought I never loved you."

"It seemed logical…" Growling out her frustration, she dropped onto her back, pressing the heels of her hands into her eyes. "I thought about every moment like this. When we were alone… The things you said… It was all so unnecessary if all you wanted was the Scepter. But you're the best, right?"

"I wanted to tell you," he said. "When Styx and I were putting the mission together, I thought it was a given I would. When I told him I wanted Harry on the outside…"

"Why didn't you want to loop him in?"

"He'd have taken over… If he let it happen at all. He'd know the stakes here." He paused. "You have to understand, Little Red. This could be a suicide mission."

Searching his expression, she sought any sign of doubt, any reluctance. There wasn't a trace. He believed this mission could cost his life and it was a price he was willing to pay.

Breathing out a laugh of disbelief, she shoved down the bed to climb off the end. "Guess it was nice knowing you," she said, marching down the trailer to swipe up her jeans.

"Baby—"

"No, you don't get to 'baby' me," she said, whirling around, ignoring the frustrated tears threatening her eyes. "Do you love me?"

"Yes."

"No," she said, taking a step back his way. "I don't want a kneejerk answer. I want you to think about it, really think about whether you do. The least you could do is look me in the eye and tell me the truth just once."

"Wait a fucking second…" he said, leaping off the bed to stride down to her. "I did this to protect you."

"Without consulting me?" she asked. "Your brother said no, and you just went with it? How could you do that to me? How could you go off on a mission you might never have come back from and let me doubt our love forever? What if you'd died? What if—"

"Styx would've told you."

"You don't know that," she said, shaking her head. "You don't know that for sure. I could've gone the rest of my life thinking you were just a bastard who used me!"

"If that was the price for—"

"What?" she asked. "Protecting me? You know why it was so easy to make that deal with Styx? Why I was so willing to die in that shower?"

He turned his back to walk away. "I don't want to hear this."

"Because you can't face the truth that this is more likely to cost my life than yours. How would you have lived with yourself if Zeus dragged me in there for JARR before you got the chance to tell me the truth?"

"That would never have happened. We've

orchestrated this so it's impossible for him to access JARR before we've mobilized."

"So all this is treading water? Wasting time? Whose time? Mine? Yours?"

"Yes, we're treading water," he said, spinning around to look down the passageway. "We need time to get people in place. All this back and forth is for a reason, it's maneuvering. We were at a disadvantage; we've bought ourselves time to get the advantage back."

Between her return from camp—when the brothers figured out releasing JARR meant more than accessing data—and the detachments leaving, way back when, the brothers had forty-eight hours to come up with a plan. Some of what had happened between then and now was made up on the fly, that much Daire had confessed. They'd swerved this way and that, adjusting and adapting, which had given Daire enough time to bed in deep with the new Olympus men, and prove his loyalty to Zeus.

In that same window, excluding the time he'd spent locked up in Beta, Styx had gathered information and created his own team in hopes of liberating the old one. Some members of that team she had faith in, like Tulsi and Wreck. Others, she wasn't so sure would work well with a group.

"I met Exile too," she said, her fist, still holding her jeans, landed on her hip. "You trust that guy?"

"He's the best… and with Swift there too, we'll keep a leash on him."

She laughed. "A leash? This is the guy you're trusting to take JARR apart. To save all our lives. How is he supposed to do that without being inside? Are you going to kidnap him too?"

"He's not an easy guy to capture, we need his compliance."

"But you don't trust him."

"You want to know what I trust?" he asked, leaping closer. "The guy's in love." She blinked, a little deflated. "He is in crazy, obsessive, ridiculous love with a woman who drives him insane. That's what I trust! I trust that love because I know it. I'm in it! Even when it makes no sense, when it might be the last thing I need, I can't help it! I can't help loving you so much I'd tear myself apart for you! So, yes! We trust him! Because he would never, ever, let anything happen to the woman he loves! How can I trust that? Because it's the same reason I am here sucking up to that motherfucker's ass every day! I want to hurt him! I want to take my time and do it slow! He's the fucker who took you an ocean away from me!"

"Baby…" she tried to soothe.

"You stand there and scream at me about wasting time? I wish this was over! I wish this was done! If it was, either we're both dead or he is! Least that way we know. The fucker doesn't deserve to live, and he doesn't deserve to chain you! When the time is right, he'll know he lost! I'll make damn sure! And then I'll put a bullet right between his eyes! Same as I did for Six!"

He turned away again. She faltered. Six. Styx took the heat for the assassination of Six, also known as Lowell Parr, one of the Olympus benefactors. Shit. She should've known. Her Heart wanted Six dead. Had from the start. If Styx had taken the shot, her love wouldn't have had his vengeance.

"Did he know?" she asked, dropping the jeans. "Styx? Did he know you were going to—"

"No," he said. "I didn't know it until Six was out there with you and… He grabbed you and I reacted. I didn't think; it was instinct. Shitty timing, but we take what we can get."

All this burden. This responsibility. Every minute there was something else. No reprieve. Not a second to himself. Living at Zeus's beck and call, she couldn't imagine it. Any second Daire could be summoned, and he had to be ready and eager to please.

Approaching him, she rested her hands on his back and leaned in to kiss his spine. "I love you," she whispered against him. "I can't lose you. I won't survive it."

Turning around, he cupped her face to tip it back. "I will never leave you," he said, his eyes burning with certainty. "I live in you. Whether I'm breathing and walking on this earth or not, I will always be in you. Always, Little Red."

A tear slipped down her cheek to his hand. "If you

leave, I'll follow. You go, I go."

"No," he said, pulling her close to kiss her head once before meeting her eye again. "You will live happy and free. My mission is to free you, nothing else. I don't care about the world, just you. If I go, I'm taking Zeus with me. I'm clearing the board. There won't be another person or reason endangering you. That's all I want. That's what will make me happy."

"You're the only one who can make me happy."

He smiled. "If I've done my job right, you'll know you gave me the greatest happiness just by being out there, living your life."

She couldn't imagine it, being in a world without him. They'd talked about stakes in the past, but with both of them living at Beta surrounded by people who could turn on them at any moment, it was all becoming far too oppressive.

"I don't want this," she said. "I don't want it to be like this." She swallowed, but another tear escaped. "This isn't fair."

"No." Though he agreed with her, his calm acceptance was resigned. "It isn't fair. You don't deserve this."

He'd said that to her before they entered Beta for the first time. Back then, with Danny, for a brief glimmer of time, they'd been free. No, not free, because Danny had protected her, even if she hadn't known it.

"Neither do you," she said, her hands sliding up his chest. "You shouldn't have to sacrifice yourself for anything."

"Sacrificing myself was always in the cards. Never blinked. Never once." His warm smile squeezed at her heart. "I found my limit in you. I will never sacrifice you, Tess. Whatever it takes. Whoever else I have to lose, I don't care, so long as you get through this."

Her throat narrowed. "It's not much is it?" she whispered. "All we want is to be left alone. To be us. Why does karma want to screw with us? Why can't it just leave us alone?"

"Because twenty-eight years ago, your parents produced my reason for being. That blessing was so huge, it has to come with a price."

"I don't want to pay it."

Dipping down, he brushed his lips across hers, his eyes remained closed. "I'll pay it and be free of their chains."

Absorbing the reality they were in wasn't easy. He said he'd pay the price. Except if he did, she'd be the one left behind alone. It was so sad, so heartbreaking, that in addition to saving her, he saw losing his life as the only way to escape the tyranny of Olympus.

"Don't go looking for it," she said, linking her fingers at the back of his neck. "I want you to get us both out. One step at a time. We deal with this and then we'll face whatever's next. Together."

"I'll try," he said, his eyes opening to show his doubt. He didn't mean to be condescending, but she could see he believed the request was naïve. "Whatever happens, baby, I love you."

"I know," she said, tightening her hold to pull his forehead to hers.

For a moment, they just breathed together, existing in these stolen seconds with one another while the danger loomed out there on the horizon. Her need for him grew again. Every time she thought their love was maxed out, it would surprise her and overflow. Having an excuse to at least get close at Beta was one thing. But it wouldn't be like this, it wouldn't be exposed and vulnerable. True to be free.

"You want me to keep my distance at Beta?" he asked.

As much as she wanted to be with him, it wasn't easy to imagine being close to her Heart at Beta with all those eyes on them. Especially while they were supposed to be on opposing sides. But they had to be smart, to show Zeus what he wanted to see.

Even if it meant her humiliation, her falling under Ares's sexual spell would lull Zeus into a sense of security that could ingratiate Daire further. Zeus had mocked her need to belong, to be close to someone, anyone. He'd relish being right. He always did.

If she had to play the naïve, horny idiot who fell into bed with her enemy, she'd do it if it meant strengthening

Daire's position.

Exhaling, reality once again squeezed its way into their intimacy. "Zeus will know you left the compound today. I suppose you can tell him it was an opportunity."

"I won't tell him the Beast is here."

"No," she agreed as he wrapped her in his arms. "You can tell him we did it in the forest, we've done that before."

"The truck," he said, a smile raising one corner of his lips. "You forget how scraped up you got the last time we did it in the dirt?"

Only a month had passed since then. Why did it feel like so much longer?

"Okay, in the truck… If you were my enemy and determined to ruin my father, I'd hate myself for giving in to you."

"Yes," he said, tucking her hair behind her ear before letting her go to retrieve the beer from the windowsill. "I'll make some moves and you can't respond." He handed over the beer then sat on the bed. "You have to resist."

She huffed, dropping back to lean on the bathroom door. "I won't be good at the secret-agent stuff."

"You don't have to be," he said. "Tell yourself you're mad at me."

Just looking at him, it was obvious he was thinking the same as her. "Even when I'm mad at you, I don't stop having sex with you."

"Which works for me," he said, bending down to swipe his tee-shirt from the floor.

Panic hit her. "No," she said, rushing over to push him back enough to straddle his lap. "I'm not ready to leave."

"We have to talk business," he said, giving up the tee-shirt when she grabbed it to throw it away. "There are things you'll need to tell Styx."

"On the call?"

"No, in person. The next stage will happen soon. When it does, it'll happen fast, and I won't have time to say goodbye."

She didn't like the sound of that. "Why are you saying goodbye? You mean you'll… I don't understand."

"Styx is gonna come get you," he said, his gaze growing more intense. "And the Scepter."

SEVEN

STYX WAS GOING TO… All she'd learned came into sharp focus. If the Scepter was taken from the control room, Minotaur, the main computer would shut down. When that happened, it was programmed to trigger its protection systems… those involved killing everyone left in the compound.

"It'll be like the Exodus. Everything will shut down," she said. "What about the failsafes?"

All he'd said when he told her about them was "*certain timeframe*." She couldn't remember if he'd been more specific about how long they'd have to clear out before the building murdered the stragglers.

"You don't have to worry about that," he said.

"Why?"

"Because Styx knows what he's doing. They can't build a reliable force without our guys. Two teams will come into Beta… under the radar… at first anyway. I'll do what I can to cover their tracks, but I can't be blatant about it. Someone you know will come get you."

"You?"

"No," he said, his fingers combing through her hair. "I'm playing for the other side, baby. I have to go with Z."

Her stomach dropped. "You have to act surprised by the break-in. Angry."

"Yes."

"Why can't you just kill him?"

"Because I don't know his contingencies. This is our only shot. If I blow my cover, Z will never let me back in. Convincing him the first time wasn't… easy," he said, the specter of his past deeds flitted across his face. After abducting his own people, imprisoning them, injuring them, it may not be easy for her Heart to gain the trust of his old allies. "And right now, the new merc guys work for me. Most of them have never set eyes on Z."

Which meant they'd be more likely to trust and follow Ares. It wasn't guaranteed, but it was always useful to know Daire could call off the squads if necessary. The longer he had control of Zeus's army, the less chance they'd kill anyone on their side.

"Styx will come in with two teams," she said. "One to get me and one to get Harry's people?" He nodded. "Who gets the Scepter?"

"The team with Harry's men. They can provide back up and know the building."

"Whoever gets me will know—"

"No, you're the primary objective," he said. "I told Styx if you're not secured first, I'll pull the lever and we'll disappear."

"We?"

"Yes. We," he said. "I can't take the risk of you being trapped in there. If I have to pull you out of Beta myself, we'll be left with only two options. Either I take you on the run with Zeus or I betray him and the whole thing is blown."

"Why not take me with Zeus?"

"Because he'll be mad, baby. He'll be mad and, if you're with us, only one person will suffer for it. How long do you think I'll stand by if he raises his hands to you? You don't want to know how close I came to breaking his neck in the lab."

Zeus had hit her then. He'd done it before that too, but her Heart never witnessed those other times.

"So you'd end up blowing your cover anyway."

"Yes."

Single word answer. Direct. To the point. Clear. Concise. Certain.

"What about Garrick?" she asked.

"You need Garrick," he said. "If he cooperates, you'll get him in the raid. If not, I'll send Styx word where we are and it'll be a smash and grab somewhere down the line."

"Why do we need him?"

"For you," he said. "After you guys are out, you'll need to get the keys. All three of them."

"You know where the other two are?"

"I did," Daire said. "He moved them."

"When? Why?"

"About a week ago and because it's smart."

"A week ago," she exhaled in disbelief. "You mean Styx was here, close by, and I didn't know?"

He lingered. "How did you know he was close?" She didn't answer. "Only way you know that is if he told you where the keys were."

What was she supposed to say? Should she lie? Why would she lie to Daire? She trusted him. "Not completely exactly."

His head went back on a groan. "Goddamnit."

"What?" she asked, stroking his face, his hair, trying to bring his attention back to her. "Why are you pissed I knew?"

The glare he landed on her was almost reminiscent of Ares. "Because it puts you in danger. Every fucking thing he—"

"I wasn't in danger. I didn't acknowledge to him I knew until a couple of days before the handover… Same day I found out about this… about you… being my guy on the inside."

Okay, so he wasn't exactly *her* guy on the inside. Though he was on the inside, and he did belong to her. Her eyes flirted with his as she laid her arms around his neck, the beer still loose in her fingers.

When she tried to kiss him, he resisted. "When did he

tell you where they were?"

"I've known since… a while."

"If he'd let it slip you knew," he said. "In Beta while we were questioning him…"

"He would never have done that," she said, appreciating Daire's fear. If Styx told anyone she knew, Zeus may have demanded Ares raise his hands to her in the same way he had to Harry and his brother. "You knew where they were too."

"Do you know where he moved them to?"

She shook her head. "No. And you don't either?"

"It's a good bet they're somewhere somebody can find them."

"Anyone but Zeus," she said, cupping his chin to raise it up. "A week ago means Styx wasn't far behind us… arriving at Beta."

"No."

"He's worried about you," she said, stroking his jaw. "Feels like he's letting you down."

"He told you that? We came up with the plan together, how is he letting me down?"

"Because he's used to being at your six. He doesn't trust anyone here and hates that you're working alone."

"I've worked on my own before. Plenty of times."

She shook her head. "This is different. It's the lion's den. It's your home. Olympus is like this tyrant you're up against, and he just let you… He wants to be with you."

"And he would never have pulled it off," he said. "Him and Zeus didn't always get along. Their relationship is a lot like Z's relationship with H."

"My Heart," she said on a sigh. "Always the peacemaker caught in the middle."

That wasn't necessarily a good thing. Him being forced into the role of mediator meant his own feelings and opinions were sidelined, they went unvoiced in lieu of others stomping their feet louder.

"Think you're the one stuck in the middle of this right now, Little Red."

"As long as I'm stuck with you, that's fine," she said.

"Thank God Styx didn't come get me while he was moving the keys."

"He can't get you out of Beta alone. Carrying you and the keys simultaneously would be massively irresponsible anyway." Which she could believe of Styx. "And the only reason Zeus isn't tearing up the earth looking for those keys is because right now, he believes he has the upper hand. He has you and the Scepter, that's two pieces of the puzzle. The keys are the other two."

"So we're tied."

He took the beer from her and leaned back to put it on her nightstand. Picking up her arms, he coiled them around his neck, then slid back on the bed to lie with his head in the pillows, her on top.

"H and Styx are setting up Gamma."

"Which Zeus believes is for him," she said. "How can he be secure in that? Isn't the Titan chip already there? When we were talking about it on the road, it seemed a big deal that you set up security at Gamma. Why does it matter?"

"Because if I wanted to code the building to be a bomb, I could."

"Okay, why don't we do that to Zeus?"

"Zeus is not going to wander into Gamma without someone else securing it first."

"You," she said, and he nodded. "So they're down there, apparently getting the building ready for Zeus to move in, which he plans to do when he liberates Minotaur and JARR. Can Styx and Harry use a key to turn Minotaur on at Gamma while it's on at Beta?"

"No, to move Minotaur there, you'd need the core. Doing it remotely… It's never been split between two locations, and we only have one Titan chip. Exile might be able to steal Minotaur's data, but that would bring everything crashing down. Zeus is ready for H to try something, that might be the trigger he needs."

"To what? Stop playing nice?"

If their current situation could be called nice.

"Fighting over Minotaur would be dicey while the core is in place here… it's too messy to take that chance. Zeus could shut it down fast, then we lose the status quo. It's not worth the gamble when JARR is the real problem." That she knew. "And it's more complicated than we thought."

Her attention pricked. "Why?"

"Because the key in Minotaur, the one responsible for running the system, has to be removed and used in the JARR operator station within ninety seconds."

"Ninety seconds?" Her eyes bugged. "Is that even possible? How far apart are the rooms?"

"The width of the building and two floors," he said. "It's tight, but it's possible."

"And then there's the code. And the blood…" Breathing out, she sank down on top of him. "This is so… Even without Zeus, we have a tough job on our hands. Do you know which key goes first?"

"No. Only Asclepius did."

"Garrick said that?" she asked.

Both men seemed determined to put the onus on the other. Unfortunately for Garrick, Asclepius was dead. That made it much more difficult to put pressure on him to reveal anything. Garrick was the only one left in the firing line.

"Yeah."

"We got all Asclepius's stuff," she said, rising to meet his eye. "Harry stashed it somewhere."

"Yeah, and they've been searching through it. Harry was pretty sure the doc would've written about it recently, given that's what he was asking about. And after the Exodus, he must have known Zeus would want to move it. He was a compulsive recorder of his thoughts."

Though the doctor had told her the opposite. She forgave him the lie given how well it worked out for them that his intel was left behind.

"Okay, that's good. We just need—"

"His notebook is missing," he said, guiding her back down to lie on his chest. "They went to go get it and it wasn't with everything else. It's strange…" She sat up. "If someone was going to steal the doctor's work, why wouldn't they take everything? Unless they knew there was something relevant in that—" She touched his lips. Almost incredulous in the way she shook her head. "What?"

"What do you think I write in every day?" The blink of his surprise was unmistakable. "God forbid anyone ask the woman who sat beside that pile of papers for days."

His fingers curled around her wrist to lower her hand from his mouth. "You stole it?"

"I didn't steal it," she said, climbing off him and the bed. "I'm on your team, remember?"

"Why did you take it?"

"I was reading it," she said. "And maybe, it's possible, I might have a tiny smidge of trust issues with my father."

He rose to his elbows. "You haven't told me anything about how he took this… me going to Zeus's side… betraying you." His mentor and brother too. "Except to say you were screaming at each other."

"That was about the non-existent baby," she said, her hand rising to her stomach. "You know I told Styx I wanted the test to be negative right up until the moment it was."

His expression softened. "A baby complicates things."

"I know," she said, throwing up her hands and wandering to the fridge. "It was an irrational disappointment. We can never have a kid. I know. I just think…"

"For a second there was the chance of normalcy."

"It would never have lasted," she said, opening the fridge to check for food. "And how would I have told you? I couldn't have told you."

"This sounds rich," he said, sliding down the bed to plant his feet and pick up his tee-shirt from the floor. "But I don't want you keeping secrets from me."

Closing the fridge, she landed a smile on him. "Yes, that is rich."

"You'd be an incredible mother," he said, putting his tee-shirt back on. "And it would've been my honor to share something so precious with you… I'm sorry Olympus stole that possibility from you."

She strolled back his way. "I don't know that it did." His brows rose. "I have faith in you, my Heart. In us." She rested a palm on his shoulder. "Maybe it's something we can talk about again when this is over."

"Little Red—"

"I know," she said, pushing him down to climb on top of him again. "You think all is lost. But I…" She bowed to kiss him. "Don't think this is over yet."

"Yeah?" he asked, his half smile revealing his dimple as his hands ran up her sides. "You think there's a chance for us?"

"Oh, I do," she murmured, working on unfastening his pants again. "We're home, baby… let's not lose another second."

They'd have to go back. Too soon they'd be within Beta's walls playing it like they were enemies… while possibly sleeping together. It was complicated, but at least he wasn't alone anymore. And if the plan played out like he said it would, they'd be torn apart from each other again. Soon. Too soon. She needed to relish every second with him while he was still within reach.

EIGHT

Some days I want to tear my hair out. This is one of those days. Every second since I woke up, I've wanted to go back to bed. Not because I'm tired, I just want to bury my head under a pillow and forget about the shitshow that is Olympus.

It's like there's an axe swinging above me, like I'm lying under the guillotine blade. Maybe it's just a crash because I've been so high for the past couple of days. I still put that down to getting out, breathing fresh air, and just being free. I try not to think about what happened when I was out there. Is this it hitting me now?

Talking to H and S, it gave me hope. No, not hope, it just... talking to an ally, a friend, it's comforting. Makes me feel like

I'm not alone. My vulnerabilities should've learned their lessons by now. I can't live like this, so focused on the fact that I'm alone and at the mercy of others. I want... something. I don't even know what.

I've never lived a normal life. Even if someone was to set me free and tell me I could do anything I wanted, I wouldn't know where to start.

The routine is driving me nutty too. Up at the same time, eat at the same time, I'm surprised they don't schedule bathroom breaks too. I'm writing in here so late because I wanted to give myself a goal for the day. If I had something to look forward to, an aim, I thought it would be better than writing early and being aimless for the rest of the day.

It's not working. Yes, so I have something to do, but that doesn't suddenly make me forget about the rest of the crap that—

Her door opened and Havers came inside.

"It's time for dinner."

"I'm not hungry," she said, remaining on her bed, back against the wall, knees pulled up to act as a table for her journal. Repositioning her pen, she intended to continue, except he just... stood there. "What?"

"I don't think it's optional."

"You can't order me to eat," she said. "I'm not hungry."

And she didn't want to go into that mess hall full of rowdy mercenaries who liked to whisper or jeer, depending on their mood and how close they got. There were no women in the ranks these days. She hadn't known Kingsley well but got a stark view of how her life had been living with men all day every day.

"I can't go back without you either," he said. "You should come with me. Even if you don't eat—"

"I should come and watch the rest of you eat? No, thank you."

"But they'll—"

"They won't do anything," she said, aware that "*they*" actually meant Ares, his superior. "How many times do I have to tell you that they need me? They can't hurt me or they'll hurt themselves. Why do you think they have me here? It's not because I'm such an excellent soldier or a hoot to be around. I'm a thing to them. An object. A vessel." Containing valuable blood. "And they don't care if the vessel skips a meal." Her eyes stayed on him. Yes, he seemed uncertain, but she didn't need an audience. "Go on. Get out of here."

He waited a second before taking a step back, obviously dithering on what to do. Another moment passed before he turned to depart, closing the door behind him.

You know, I feel sorry for Havers. Poor guy is stuck with this assignment. S would sympathize, he always said I was a pain in the ass. I don't mean to be. I really don't. It's not easy to live a life dictated to you by others. To constantly feel as though you're out of control. My existence has been driven by what Olympus wants, what Olympus needs, is it any surprise I resent the shit out of them for it.

It's not the guys' fault, I know. They're just people doing their jobs, given objectives to carry out. No one seems to appreciate how it is to be on the other side, to be driven by something, but still have no aim. No direction.

I've written about my mom plenty

before. I miss her. Yes, I do. And I didn't appreciate our relationship as I should've when she was alive. Until she was gone, I didn't face how much I depended on her, how much I needed her to validate my life.

Without her, it seems like I've stumbled from screw up to screw up. I try to make her proud. Try to think she'd be proud or would do things the same way. But when I pause to look back, I have to admit she wouldn't. My mom wouldn't have walked into half the messes I have. Did I learn anything from her? Anything at all?

I know why I'm beating myself up. It's that my weakness took over. How could I...? Being with him again, it was insanity. How can I even look at myself in the mirror? I shouldn't. I'm surprised I've eaten anything since it happened.

Everyone loves to tell me how he's the best. How can I be aware of that and still fall for his—

The door opened again.

"Havers, I said—"

Ares walked in. Alone. And the door closed behind him.

Writing in her journal about her guilt was one thing. Good cover if anyone took it from her. Being faced with him, it wasn't the same thing. The game was obvious. Hate him. Blame him. Resent him. But doing that while she was looking at him... He was her Heart. Her Daire. The man she wanted to scoop her up and hold her closer.

Inhaling, she steeled herself to playing the game. He needed this from her. The mission needed it. Zeus would love to see her tied up in knots, hating herself. Giving the asshole a show might be enough to distract him from other things just long enough for her people to do whatever they needed to on the outside.

"Are you going to just stand there?" she asked when he didn't speak. "Don't you get enough time to ogle on your cameras?"

"Cameras are off."

That was a lie. His eyes remained on hers and he showed no outward signal that he'd just been dishonest. But she knew it. Zeus wouldn't give up a chance to see this. More than that, her Heart wouldn't stand there rigid, shoulders back, hands clasped behind him, carrying that indifferent air, if they really were alone.

"No," she said, shaking her head. She closed the notebook and put it on the pillow as her knees descended to the bed. "Turn them back on.'

"Don't trust yourself?" he asked, smug in his smile as he sauntered closer.

"I don't know why you think you're here—"

"I'm here because you refused an order. No one's allowed to do that around here."

"Call me the exception," she said. "I don't take orders from anyone. I'm not one of your soldiers." Something she'd reminded her father of many times in the past. "And Havers isn't exactly the most intimidating guy."

"I don't know if it's possible to intimidate you, Tess. You don't seem to know when it's time to admit defeat. You should be intimidated, but you still don't get it."

Looming over her, the shutters over him were unnerving. That was her love. If she told him right now that she wanted to leave all of this behind, he'd switch in an instant. He really was the best, in more ways than most knew.

"Is that why you came here? To intimidate me?"

"The men are eating," he said, lowering to sit on the bed beside her. "Occupied."

"You should join them," she said, shoving closer to the pillow to avoid his attempt at touching her knee. "There's nothing here for you to do."

He snickered. "I could find something."

"How do you think your boss would feel about that?" she hissed. "You know how much trouble I could cause for you? If I told him—"

"If you told him what? That you're weak? That he was right about you? Tess, you need this…" When his fingertips met her knee, she stilled. "You need a human connection. Need to be touched."

"Not by you," she said, getting off the bed to put some space between them.

God, it was like pantomime. Running her fingers into her hair, she probably appeared harried and stressed. She was both. Not because she hated herself for giving into him, but because she was so desperate to do it again.

"You know what we were," he said, softening his voice. Ares voice, not Daire's. Some might consider the difference subtle, for her it was stark. Her Daire would never talk to her with such a false inflection. "You don't have to feel guilty about your needs." He came up behind her, close enough that she could feel his heat. "You're here. This is your home. You can relax here."

When his hand landed on her shoulder, she shrugged it off and walked away. Avoiding him, darting here and there, it was part of the game. She got that. She understood that they were putting on a show for anyone who might be watching. Resisting was important. She had to show the guilt, the disgust. Zeus wanted her to hate herself. Giving him what he wanted would ultimately give them what they needed.

Except turning around, back to a perpendicular wall, it was difficult not to reach for her Heart. At the other side of the room where she'd left him, he hadn't even turned around. Was it hurting him? Was she hurting him? It had to be difficult, not only to force himself on her in this way, but to have her shun his touch, to rebut his affection, to recoil.

They loved each other. It shouldn't be this way. As if she hadn't hated Zeus enough already, she now had another reason to add to the list.

He turned so fast that she swayed back. "We give you everything and this is how you repay us?"

"Everything?" she asked. "You locked me in a room

with your brother. Beat him and my father. You—"

"They're soldiers. They know the cost of insubordination."

"Hades isn't subordinate to you… and Styx shouldn't be either."

He stormed over. "Always his big defender."

"I'm amazed you turned out this way," she said. "That you can live with yourself."

His teeth clenched as he bowed lower. "I'm not the one sleeping with the enemy."

"And that's what this is about, huh?" she asked and raised a hand meaning to shove him back.

Instead, he slammed it back against the wall, forcing it high above them.

Damnit. Bad move. On her part or his? It didn't hurt. His grip was strong, sure, but oh so fucking arousing. Their words didn't mean anything, not really, but their actions… She could tell her mind not to respond to her Heart. Her body? That operated on a different wavelength, one his knew just how to infiltrate.

"You've got a secret," he grumbled, bringing his body nearer hers. "You're no good at hiding it."

She tried to remain defiant. "I don't have a secret. You don't know what you're talking about."

"Oh, I know," he said, his finger grazing her cheek. "Because it's me. You want to hate me. You should hate me. But you just don't know how."

"I know exactly how," she said, trying to wrench her wrist free, but he held it in place. "Let go of me."

"See, you say that," he said, one corner of his mouth tilting higher in an arrogant slanted smile. "But it's not what you want."

"Screw you," she said, pulling harder.

Rather than release her, he got hold of the other wrist and trapped it with the first. "Maybe you do hate me," he said, bending his knees to align their mouths. "But it doesn't change what you want… How do you think Daddy would feel about that? About his little girl being caught up and desperate for the cock of the man who ruined his world."

"You're sick," she spat the words. "You don't know what you're talking about. You know nothing about me."

"I know everything," he said, his hand sliding from her throat to her breast and down to her waist. "I know just what you like and exactly how to give it to you."

His hand kept on going, descending her hip to curve around her ass.

"Don't you—"

He yanked her hard, forcing her against him, showing her just what he was ready to give. His eyelids grew heavier. Their bodies were crushed together, and he was… Was she supposed to be disgusted by that too? By arousing him? Damnit. Her heart was racing, her breathing shallow, he'd see it, he knew. Her Heart knew when he had her. He always had her.

She could push him away, fight him, but she couldn't. If she put up too much of a fight, the man she loved would taste guilt.

"Pandora," he said, his chin tipping to bring their mouths closer.

Her codename. He never used that word when they were alone. But she had to… she needed to…

"Why do you do this to me?" she whispered, swallowing hard. "Is it a power kick? You do it because you can? Is it sport? A way to pass the time?"

"You're looking at it the wrong way," he muttered, those drowsy eyes descending to her lips. "This isn't being done to you, sweetheart." Something else he never called her. "You're doing it to me. With me."

And she wanted to do it with the man she loved. Daire. Licking her lips, she closed her eyes for a brief moment, just enough to breathe in his proximity. She needed to savor him, just for a second.

Then sucking in a bolstering breath, she redirected all of her desire into portraying disgust. "Take your fucking hands off me this second or I'll go to that mess hall and tell every guy there how you really treat the female prisoner."

"I didn't lay a hand on Kingsley… that she didn't deserve."

"I didn't mean her," she sneered. "You think they'd like knowing their superior gets his ya-yas out with the woman they're holding captive? Maybe I'm not much of a threat, but I am your enemy. You don't want my father to hate you anymore than he already does."

"I don't give a shit about your father."

"Maybe not, but if the guys know, the truth will get back to Zeus… You think he wants to know what you did to me out in the forest?"

His expression reacted a second before he pushed away. "Do you know who you're threatening?" he asked as she rubbed her liberated wrists. They weren't really sore, but it wouldn't hurt Zeus to believe Ares had been more threatening than he had to be. "You want to think carefully before threatening a man like me."

"You say you know me? I know you too," she said, shoving away from the wall. Now she needed to put some space between them for a different reason. "I know what you want and it's got nothing to do with sex."

"Nothing wrong with doing both."

"Okay," she said, folding her arms. "How about a trade?"

That intrigued him enough to look closer. From the crook of his brow, she could almost see both men. Her Heart was as interested as Ares.

"What is it you think you want, Pandora?" he asked. "'Cause if you think I couldn't get pussy any time I wanted it—"

"Information," she said. "It's only right that I should know how this will play out. What's going to happen to my father and Styx?" Man, was he… impressed? And who was that? Ares or Daire? "What will happen to the people you're holding prisoner?"

"What about you?" he asked. "You don't want to know our plans for you?"

"I know what you plan for me. Regardless of how this plays out, you have no long term need for me. Any asset that comes to the end of its usefulness is disposed of."

"You have been paying attention."

"So tell me, what's going to happen to my father?"

"The more you show us you care, the more we'll hurt him," he said, his attention wandering. "Free lesson for you."

"Why thank you," she said, put on alert when he started toward her bed. She sidestepped away from it. "What are you doing?"

Rather than approach her, he swiped the notebook from the pillow to flick through the pages. "You write about me in here?"

"Why would I do that?" she asked, leaping around the bed, trying to snatch for it.

He held it higher, out of her reach. "Mean something to you?"

"Privacy means something to me," she said, shoving him. "Give me it."

"Tried that," he said. "You threatened me instead. Gotta work on your bedroom skills, Pandora." Walking away, notebook still in his hand, he took the base unit from his hip, read something and hooked it back on. "You're in luck."

"I'm in luck? Somehow it doesn't feel that way."

He stopped, looking her straight in the eye despite the fifteen yards between them. "He wants to see you."

"He who?" she asked, except the moment she did, clarity struck her. "Zeus? He wants to see me?"

After being there for twelve days, she'd given up on the idea he might want to see her. Although she had no desire to hang out with him and shoot the breeze, one lesson stuck: intel was the key to survival. The only way to maximize her opportunities for info gathering was to get time with the man at the top.

"Yes," he said. "And that's one invite you don't get to refuse."

"What are you going to do? Force me?"

Except he folded her notebook and stuffed it into the pocket on his thigh before marching her way.

"Yeah," he said. "That's exactly what I'll do." He grabbed her arm. Instinct forced her to resist, except when he gave her a hard shake, she froze. "Haven't you learned fighting never works. You're not strong enough to stand up to us.

When we want something, it's your obligation to give it to us."

"No," she said, shaking her head. "Fighting is the only thing that works. And strength comes from within us. Keep your muscles and your martial arts. The only muscle that matters is in your head." That and her heart, but Daire owned that. "Our strength is tested when we think we have nothing left. You might be bigger and stronger, but there's one thing your boss will never have."

"What's that?"

"My surrender," she said. "Drug me and strap me down if that's what it takes. He will not break me."

Ares leaned closer. "We might just take you up on that."

NINE

BEING LED AROUND THE BUILDING was par for the course. Though she couldn't say her knowledge about it increased much. She could get from her room to the mess hall and to the training room. Other than that…

They were going somewhere new. The corridors became an ominous rich red color she hadn't seen at beta before. In situations like that, blood red didn't signal anything good. Slowing down, it was difficult not to trust Daire, yet he wasn't exactly acting in her best interests these days. Still, nothing would harm her if he knew what was coming. That was a big if. Anything could be landed on either of them at any second. If he blew his cover, that would be it, the chance for the raid would be over. They'd have to flee alone. What would that mean for the prisoners? For the Scepter?

Daire stopped at a door with a gold handle unlike any in her block. Man, the guy just couldn't get over himself. When they paused, she waited, then looked up at him. He wouldn't want to walk into the unknown any more than she would. Did he know what Zeus wanted?

After exploring her eyes for a second, he winked. In the shroud of the door, he might know how to avoid the cameras. She didn't, so didn't react. Any smile or clue picked up by cameras could be enough to raise suspicions.

As for what it meant? Either he knew what awaited and was reassuring her or he didn't but was letting her know he was with her. If only that were true.

With little choice other than to proceed, Daire turned the handle to open the door. He went inside first, something he'd do if he was securing the scene for her. Ares wasn't supposed to care if she walked into a gunfight but—

Just two steps into the room, she paused. "What the hell?"

Zeus wasn't even there. James Garrick was the only one in the out-of-place reception room. Luxe, it was mismatched to the rest of the industrialized building. Around the long couch and armchairs, the walls were painted red and beige, a massive desk stood at the head of the room. With carpet on the floor and a hanging light, it could almost be in a real home somewhere far from the clinical detachment of Olympus.

Garrick got up from his chair by the fireplace. That couldn't be real... could it?

"I thought Zeus wanted to see me," she said to Ares. Instead of answering her, he left the room, and the door was closed. "What's going on?"

"Zeus will be ready soon," Garrick said. "It's good to see you, Tess."

"Yeah, I can't say the same."

"I understand your anger. How is your father?"

"How would I know?" she asked. "I've been here for almost two weeks. And I've got to say, it's stupid of you to ask. Do you think I believe you care?"

"I didn't know any of this was going to happen. Ares's decision to..."

Of course he trailed off. No interaction at Beta was certain to be private.

"They'll kill him, you know," she said, rounding the couch. "My father. If you don't stand up to Zeus."

"This is not about sides."

"Oh, come on," she said, throwing up her arms. "Don't be naïve. Your decision to side with Zeus, to help him, it signs my father's death warrant."

His head shook. "Why do you care? Your relationship with H is… You hardly see eye to eye."

"Do you see eye to eye with him all the time? What about Zeus? Do you agree with every order he gives?" She went closer. "You have to stand up to him."

"He's our leader."

What was Garrick supposed to do? She got it. She understood his need to live. Even if he didn't agree with Zeus's plays, there wasn't much Garrick could do about it. The men worked under Ares who Garrick believed was on Zeus's side. And the so-called leader needed Garrick to liberate JARR, he wasn't going to let the tech genius just walk away.

The door opened and she turned, expecting to see Zeus enter. Instead, it was Havers… carrying her carpet bag.

"What is going on?" she asked.

"Come with me," Havers said.

"Come with…" Ares appeared behind him. Stoic, stony-faced, extreme even for Ares. Something had spooked him. Something he was trying to conceal. Something unexpected had happened. She wasn't looking at Ares's conflict, it was Daire's. "What's going on?"

"We're going on a trip," Garrick said, walking around her to head for the men at the door. "We don't want to be late."

"Late for what?"

Havers moved aside to let Garrick pass and her eyes met Daire's. This was bad. Really bad. Styx and Harry could show up any time. If they came to get her and she wasn't there… They could liberate their people and get the Scepter. But if Zeus lost those advantages, she'd be his only play. And he'd be mad, just like Daire told her.

"Come on," Havers said, gesturing at her when he leaped back into the room. "He's waiting."

He could wait all damn day for all she cared. Except if she was difficult, Zeus would order her sedated and she'd miss the trip. Anything could hold a clue, she couldn't be out of it again.

She went to Havers and snatched her bag. On the plus side, it was still packed. She didn't put things in drawers or closets, she traveled light and was ready to move fast. That didn't mean Havers hadn't rummaged through it, but there was nothing incriminating in there… she didn't think.

After negotiating their way through corridors and stairwells, a door burst open ahead of them. The noise from the darkness beyond stopped her dead. That was… it sounded like…

The others went outside, but she stayed put. "I can't."

"Move," Havers said, grabbing her arm to pull her outside.

In the inky night, floodlights were aimed at the helicopter with its rotor going. This was a different side to the building, not the one they'd used to go in and out before. It stood to reason there would be a helipad. Olympus was well funded. They needed tech to do their job.

"What is the matter?" Havers hollered over the sound of the helicopter as Zeus, Garrick, and others boarded the craft.

Guys came over to force her forward and bundle her into the chopper, eliminating her freewill. Still numb, it took Daire leaning over to fasten her safety belt to even notice he was there. Where were they going? The men outside rushed back, and they rose, wobbling as they escaped the shadow of the building.

They were in the air. She couldn't see outside, nothing but night. In the center of the craft, men sat either side of her. Daire. He was there. That meant something, didn't it? Curling her fingers into her palms, she took solace in the pain of her nails digging in deep. What she wanted to do was grab his hand, to turn and bury her face against his arm.

Beta was gone. Her father wouldn't know she'd been moved. Styx wouldn't know it. If her interpretation of Daire's expression was accurate, he hadn't known this was happening. He couldn't get a message to Styx, not that night. The plan they'd put in place needed small adjustments along the way, but the raid was important. Key to their success. Also key was her being present. This unexpected development could throw everything off. They couldn't tell their people not to go in. Couldn't tell them the plan had changed.

Goddamnit. Would they recover from a failure? Was there a contingency? Yes, but it meant people losing their lives. That was one burden she didn't want on any of their consciences.

***

HOURS WENT BY, that was what it felt like inside. Every mile that passed took them further from Beta and from the hope of returning, at least that night.

As they landed, she saw lights. City lights. Streets. Buildings. They were in a built-up area. She didn't get much chance to look for landmarks because they stopped on the roof of a building. They didn't even wait for the rotors to stop before the men were disembarking, taking her with them.

They went inside, down a stairwell and out into a hallway. Carpet. Wallpaper. They were in a hotel. Which hotel? Where?

There weren't many options for where to go next, the elevator seemed the most tempting, but of course, that wasn't their aim. Zeus walked straight past her just as the door ahead opened and a guy in a three-piece suit appeared.

"Good evening," he said, his smile broad. At least until he glanced at her, surrounded by big guys in black security gear. Was she being protected or a threat to those in the building? Neither, but the guy didn't know that. "Uh, we would like to welcome you to—"

"We want this floor sealed," Zeus said to him. "None of your staff are to come onto this floor. Do you understand?" The guy took another look around, then nodded. "Good. Go."

The suited guy didn't even wait for the elevator, he went into the stairwell they'd just used and the door closed.

"Ares," Zeus said.

Saying his name was redundant, Ares was already on his way inside. Alone. Just like Miami. Always sent into potential danger first and he never blinked. Everyone waited on pause for him to return.

She didn't find the silence so easy to bear. "What's the play?" Zeus ignored her. "Do your men know everything about you? About the organization you've tied them up in? Maybe if you won't give me answers, I'll start giving them some. Secrets fester, right?" His lips narrowed. He wanted to ignore her. Wanted her to shut the hell up. Threatening the leader, in front of his people, was risky. But what the hell did she have left to lose? "How about we start with your real name and what you did to your former—"

"You don't want to threaten me here, Pandora."

"Why don't you use my real name?" she asked, almost offering the gesture. "Seems right the men should know it before you order them to kill me."

The sinister smile on his face grew as his focus came around to hers. "I would never dream of giving them the pleasure... I've been waiting for it myself."

Yeah, and the feeling was mutual.

The elevator interrupted them. Hoping for a clue, she didn't anticipate former President Byron exiting with his own posse of security agents.

"How was your flight?" he asked Zeus, ignoring everyone else.

"Uneventful."

"My favorite kind," Byron said and only then turned to her. "It's good to see you again."

"The feeling isn't mutual, believe me," she said. "You want to tell me what's going on here?"

"He doesn't get involved in our internal business," Zeus said.

Fair point. That wasn't meant to clue her in on anything, but it did.

"Are the others here?" she asked. "Gosh, ranks at the top are thinning. Four still missing? Six is gone..." If these men were together... "Is my father here?"

If Garrick was needed and Zeus was present... It could be a meeting of the principals. Would she have to watch her father walk away? Again? Would she be allowed to see him? Speak to him?

Ares appeared to give Zeus the nod, so everyone poured inside. Another hotel suite. Another bland, boring, vanilla space. Sweetness in the air, modern convenience within the plush décor. How was it possible to be surrounded by so many normal things but be in such an abnormal situation?

"That's your room," Zeus said, nodding to a door in the corner.

Her own bedroom or did he mean cell?

"I'm happy to stay with the group."

Partly because she didn't want to give him the satisfaction of trotting along in response to his orders. Also, staying with the group increased her chances of hearing something that could be useful.

"You'll do what you're told," he said. "We have a meeting in an hour and you're the garnish. Shower, get changed. Everything you need is in that room."

Shit, a meeting could mean her father. Would it mean Styx? Her attention rose to the window. Was he out there somewhere like he had been in D.C.? Looking at her through the scope of a rifle. If only he could take the shot. If he could clear the room… maybe this was the chance. If they could—

"Ares," Zeus said.

She heard it but didn't think much of the command until her arm was snatched from her side and she was being forced to move. On impulse, she objected, but the grip wasn't sore, just sure. Daire. He pulled her into the room and closed the door behind them. He went straight past the four-poster bed to seal them both in the shiny marble bathroom.

"Upgrade from the crappy motels," she murmured, but doubted he was listening. Daire went over to open the glass shower doors and turned on all the jets. She put her carpet bag on the floor. "Why do I have to shower? Who are we impressing? H won't care if I'm clean."

"He's not here," Daire said, marching back to her. He didn't stop and picked her up to seat her on the vanity. Scooping a hand around the back of her skull, he angled her ear up to his lips. "There are no devices in here, but we can't take any chances."

"What's going on?"

"I don't know." Her hands slid onto his chest, but he pushed them down. "Don't be familiar, you don't like me, remember?"

"I don't understand."

"Heat signatures can be picked up. Do what you're told, okay? Just play along. I'll do what I have to."

"Will we go back to Beta?"

What she wanted to know was if he could get a message to Styx. What would happen if they went in while she and Garrick weren't on site?

"Eventually."

That wasn't an encouraging answer. "He said I was the garnish. If he's prettying me up to trot me out to some guy—"

He swayed back, his eyes meeting hers. That was her answer. It didn't matter if that was Zeus's plan, her Heart would never let it happen.

"Get ready, okay?" She nodded, bereft when his hands slid away. "If I can't trust you to do it, I have to watch."

That was a tease and it was difficult not to respond in kind. She always felt better when he was close by, but him out there, with the others, increased their chances of finding out the purpose for the trip.

"I'll get ready."

"Good girl," he said and departed.

Ready? She could shower and put on clothes, but without knowing what was going on, how was it possible to prepare herself?

TEN

THE BEDROOM DOOR WAS LOCKED. Of course it was.

Daire had said there were no devices in the bathroom, so she probably wasn't being watched. Though it was possible something had been set up in the bedroom while she was showering. That was why she took the things laid out on the bed into the bathroom to finish getting ready.

Doing her hair, putting on makeup, it felt ridiculous. At the same time, some part of her craved the tedium. All over the world people were putting on clothes and fluffing their hair…

She sighed and fixated on her reflection. "Are we going to get out of this?"

The unknown usually spelled some kind of drama or disaster. That's how it played out walking into Beta for the first time. What happened when she got on that plane with Three. When Boze didn't come back in Vegas. When she was taken from her Beta cell. The list went on and on.

Figuring they would come get her when it was time to go to their meeting, she waited. It didn't take long. The door opened and Havers came inside.

"They want you out there."

Except he didn't seem to be heading out too. "What's going on?"

"I don't know," Havers said. "They told me to wait in here."

Which sort of suggested Zeus didn't want the goons listening. At the principals meeting in Vegas, the goons had been excluded too. Curiosity took her to the door. That and she didn't want to give Zeus the satisfaction of seeing her being forced to do something else against her will.

She opened the door to enter the living room. Zeus, Garrick, Byron, and Ares were by the entrance, greeting someone it looked like.

"Come in, please, relax," Zeus was saying in that completely fake jovial way that piqued her disgust.

"Thank you. I have to say it's good to finally meet you."

The group opened out as they came into the room and that was when she saw him. When she registered their guest's identity.

Everything screeched to a halt. Instant panic became sheer terror. "No," she murmured. "No. No. No."

Spinning around, she went back into the bedroom. But, damnit, now she was penned in. What the hell should she…? How was she going to…?

"Get back out there," Havers said as someone else joined them.

Ares stood just inside the door. "Pandora?"

He got her focus. Pain and guilt collided in her, sorrow welled in her eyes. "I can't."

"You can't, what?"

They couldn't talk with Havers there. Couldn't be themselves. Yet, she couldn't let the truth just slip away, not again.

"It's an ambush," she whispered.

"An ambush?" Ares asked, wearing a frown. "What are you talking about?"

If only she could tell him. "Why is he here?" she asked.

"You know him?"

"I know who he is."

"Who?"

"Richard Merrill," she said, her mouth drying.

"Yeah. A presidential wannabe."

Her head shook as her clasped hands rose to her chest. "That's not why he's here."

His scowl deepened. "You've got to get out there."

Her jaw loosened. What could she say with Havers present? While others may be listening? She'd put it off and put it off and now…

"This isn't about me," she said, frustrated by the invisible gag that kept her from uttering the truth to her Heart.

"Did you forget we can't hurt you?" Ares asked like he was impatient, but she could hear his concern beneath. "Whatever you're afraid of—"

"I'm afraid that this is an ambush."

"What is this Merrill guy to you?" Ares asked. "How do you know him?"

"I don't."

"Then why are you—"

"I'm not the one being ambushed." His eyes moved, searching hers. "I know things…" she said, grateful for the flicker of recognition that crossed his face. Those were her words in the woods, after they'd had sex. "It was never the right time." Time had been against them. Things happened so fast, so much was up in the air and then they were apart. "I'm sorry."

His concern hardened to something like anger and he glanced at Havers. What was he supposed to do? Kill the guy? He couldn't send him out into the living room if Zeus had specifically sent him away.

"You think it's me," Ares said. "That they want to ambush me?"

"I know it."

And if they were enemies, she might enjoy seeing that. Showing this weakness, this contrition, it wouldn't help their mission, but it could hurt their relationship. More than hurt it, the truth could obliterate all of Daire's trust in her and Harry. His trust with Zeus wasn't secure, he didn't care about him, but if the Olympus leader was the one to tell him the truth… Either he'd kill him, or his mission would cease to be about the security of the world and possibly become about annihilating it.

"Ares!" that call came from the living room. From Zeus.

Her jaw tightened. If only Styx was out there. If only she could save her Heart from the pain and embarrassment that may lie ahead.

"We don't have time for this," Ares hissed and marched over to get hold of her.

He dragged her out into the living room. The minute they were there, she yanked her arm free. The men standing around the couches, sharing a toast with their scotch, all looked at her.

"She's beautiful," Merrill said.

"Thank you," Zeus said.

Why were they talking about her like she was chattel? And why was Zeus grateful, she was nothing to him. Any redeeming quality she may have, physical or otherwise, was a product of her parents and experience.

"What do you want from me?" she asked, her focus on Zeus. "Why do I have to be here for this?" Whatever it was. "I have no reason to keep secrets for you."

No, and if Ares had betrayed her as Zeus thought, she'd probably relish seeing him ambushed and embarrassed.

"I thought you would enjoy being part of this," Zeus said. "Given you brought us all together."

"I didn't bring anyone together."

She'd never even met Merrill.

"This is a celebration," Zeus said, raising his glass. "Ares, get the woman a drink."

A drink? A celebration? Could her Heart know the truth? No. If he did, this trip wouldn't have surprised him. Not knowing Zeus's plan was unnerving. This was no innocent play. Something deeper was going on. Something that would drive a wedge between her Heart and her father.

"I don't want a drink," she said. "I want to know what's going on."

"Richard is here to discuss joining us," Byron said.

"Us?"

"As you stated yourself, ranks are thinning at the top," Zeus said. "Richard is a great patriot. He believes in this country. After Lowell's tragic death—"

"Oh my God, you're replacing him," she said. With Six dead, their money pool got drier. They needed cash. Money. Green. Olympus couldn't do what it did without free flowing funds. "You're asking Merrill to be the new Six."

"As we said, he's a great patriot."

Shaking her head, she retreated until her back hit the door. This wasn't about choice. It wasn't about whether or not the man wanted to get involved with Olympus or if he cared about their objectives. Merrill might be rich, she'd never investigated him to find out. And he might even believe this was an offer, like he actually had a choice.

He didn't.

Because if he refused…

"I don't want to be a part of this."

"You are a part of it, Pandora," Zeus said. "Come and sit with us."

"Go to hell."

"Don't make me regret bringing you."

"It was that or leave me with the men you don't trust at Beta," she said. "You don't want me to be a part of this. You're flaunting your power, or you think you are. Tell him the truth." Zeus frowned. "Quit the fakery and lay it out for him. This isn't about choice. This isn't an invitation. You don't invite anyone to do anything, you force people into things. You leverage their secrets against them."

"Do I?"

"Yes," she said. "So feed him the bullshit about your mission being about the greater good." She switched her focus. "Spoiler alert, Mr. Merrill, it's not. It's about this man's ego… actually about Byron's too. You don't know it yet, but you're already in the tar pit. Hand him your checkbook now because there's no way you're getting out of this. No one does."

With that, she tried to go back into the bedroom. The

door was locked. Damnit, Havers might be placid, but he was smart, and knew how to give Zeus what he wanted.

"Looks like you're stuck with us," Zeus said. Closing her eyes, she wanted to be free more than ever. The last thing she wanted to do was watch Zeus play with Merrill and Daire like they were mice being toyed with by the cat. "Philip, would you excuse us?"

She turned, leaning back on the door. The former president was confused. Why wouldn't he be? Few people excused former leaders of the country. Fewer probably kept secrets from him.

"I… yes."

Byron put down his glass to disappear from the room.

"This is a family matter," Zeus said, opening a hand to one of the armchairs. "Would you like to sit down?"

Daire wasn't looking at her. As always, he was absorbing the room, his mind working, his intrigue alight. It didn't matter. This was one secret he'd never be able to guess.

"You don't have to do this," she murmured.

Zeus ignored her. "Our organization is extremely important. You must understand how important it is to the running of the country, to global peace."

The sales pitch made her nauseous. Somewhere in the depths of somewhere, Olympus was once righteous. Maybe the men at the top still convinced themselves it was true. She couldn't believe it.

"After all he's done for you," she said. Zeus straightened, but she couldn't see his face. It wasn't necessary, the man hated that she couldn't keep her mouth shut. "This is repayment for a lifetime of service."

Zeus spun around. "You had your chance. Didn't you? Whatever you didn't say isn't my responsibility. And why do you care? Why do you care what I—"

"Because it's sick," she said, shoving away from the door. "Telling me was cruelty, but you played it like you were doing me a favor. This is exactly what you're doing right now! You're feeding Merrill a bunch of bull! Say it! Tell the truth! He has no choice because you have dirt. On him. This is not an appeal for aid, it's a shakedown. You're using your greatest ally, your primary instrument for success, against a man guilty of making a mistake three decades ago!"

She couldn't take it. Couldn't stand there and watch the drama unfold. Striding across the room, she didn't hide her intention to leave.

"How far do you think you'll get?" Zeus barked.

With a hand on the doorhandle, she twisted to look back at him. "I could ask you the same thing, Ulysses."

Someone, somewhere, would stop him, eventually. He couldn't win forever.

Opening the door, she wasn't surprised there were men between her and the elevator. Some were Olympus, some were not. It was clear none of them knew what to do about her. She got as far as pressing the elevator button before anyone got hold of her. And it wasn't some random security agent, it was Ares. He dragged her through the men, but rather than take her into the suite, he pulled her into the stairwell.

"What the hell is wrong with you?" he snapped when the door closed.

Unsure if they were alone or being observed, it was impossible to be explicit. Or at least as explicit as she wanted to be.

She swiped a rogue tear from her face and raised her chin. If she was going out, she'd at least give her Heart the chance to save himself from humiliation.

"Hera." His scowl loosened to surprise. "That's what this is about."

ELEVEN

"WHAT DO YOU MEAN?" Marching closer, he crowded her up against the wall. "Tess?"

Her real name? Either he was shook or happy to blow their cover.

"I learned the truth in London. The truth that compromised you."

Did he remember? Please say he did. In Miami, it was the mention of Chester Buford that got Harry worried. That name inspired Harry to tell Daire he'd been compromised.

"I don't understand."

"I didn't know he would do this. That we would find ourselves here. I didn't want it to happen like this."

She wanted to take his hand. To hold and reassure him, but the door opened and one of the minions poked his head out.

"You're wanted," the minion said.

"In a minute," Ares said.

Not Ares. He wouldn't refuse a request from Zeus. This man wanted time with her. She could've prepared him for this. Why hadn't she? Because it had the power to explode his relationship with Harry. Why did it have to happen now? When they were light years apart? She couldn't go to his bed or comfort him. Couldn't apologize like she wanted to.

"We'd need more than a minute," she said and took a step toward the door.

The minion came closer, producing something from behind his back. "Turn around."

"Most men say please," she muttered, but did as he asked. What was the point of fighting? As her wrists were zip-tied together, she searched her Heart, his concern, his turmoil. "Don't believe everything he tells you. Only we know the truth."

And those were the last words to leave her lips before the minion tied a long black gag over her mouth.

His eyes came to hers. There was doubt in them. Doubt and determination. For what? She didn't know.

"Take your hands off her," he said.

The minion's hand dropped from her shoulder. "We got orders from—"

"I know," her Heart said. "But she's not an easy woman to handle."

He came over, his eyes on hers until he was near to her. Until the moment he spun her around to clasp the back of her neck.

Being directed through the security men felt like being led to the gallows. She had no choice but to return to the suite with Ares.

"She's your prisoner?" Merrill asked, trying to stand as the door closed behind her and Ares.

Zeus gave his shoulder a pat strong enough to put him back in the seat. "She's an asset. Useful. Or she will be. Once she's fulfilled her purpose, she'll be executed."

No flies on him. Not so much as a blink from the Olympus principal. Merrill visibly paled and sort of stuttered in breaths. If she could comfort him, she might offer a smile. A pathetic comfort maybe, and she couldn't even offer that with the gag across her mouth.

"I don't—you can't—"

"I can," Zeus said, smug as he strolled to the couch to sit in the center. "I will and do. Something to bear in mind when we request your assistance." Which would look a lot like cash on demand. Maybe more if the man did get into the big chair. "Here's what happens next. You go back to your life, live it completely as normal, as if this never happened. Former President Byron will coach you on how to get funds to us. When we need more, we'll be in touch."

"You don't scare me," Merrill said, trying to laugh him off. Yeah, it was a bluff, the man was clearly uncomfortable. Rather than have compassion, Zeus laughed. "I'll expose this. Expose you for—"

"For what?" Zeus asked, his laugh dying immediately. "Dedicating ourselves to the cause? You have no idea who you're dealing with."

But she did. Her, Ares, and Garrick, the three of them watched Zeus work. Not just do it but enjoy it.

"I have connections," Merrill said, shifting to the edge of his seat.

"Oh, we know you do, Mr. Merrill," Zeus said, relaxing. "And we're happy about that because it's those connections that will guarantee your allegiance."

"What are you talking about?"

Seeing his disbelief was painful. The man was confident in his own importance. Did he believe he was untouchable? No one was untouchable. Unfortunately for Merrill, his weakness wasn't locked in JARR, it was in the minds and memories of those involved.

Garrick at least appeared somewhat contrite. Merrill wasn't looking at the man standing in the background. His focus was on the threat in front of him. The real threat.

Zeus retrieved his glass from the coffee table and sat back, straightening a crease in his pants as he did. "You worked closely with former Vice-President Buford at the start of your career…" He made eye contact with the ashen Merrill. "Didn't you?"

The man had gotten away with his crime for decades. She didn't blame him for believing it was forgotten, lost to the mists of time.

"How do you know that?"

"I know everything about you," Zeus said. "I know he wasn't guilty of his crimes… Poor man fought the case against him, proclaimed his innocence to the world, but it was undeniable… without the right documentation."

Harry said the evidence had been destroyed in Alpha. Hadn't it? If something like that existed, wouldn't Daire have seen it? Was there really a part of Olympus he didn't know? If he found out the truth, it would be like the institution itself lied to him. What would he do then? Isolated. Betrayed. He'd be desperate. Vengeful. Could her Heart grow so bitter that he'd become the threat they all feared?

"She's right," Merrill said, resigned as the truth deflated him. "You're blackmailing me. Threatening me."

"It's something I do very well," Zeus said, sipping his liquor.

Not so well. It had never worked with her. At least, even in the times she was afraid, she didn't back down.

Zeus wasn't the one she worried about. Neither was Merrill. He was guilty, whatever he got, he deserved. Her shoulder went back, just a little, just enough to push into her Heart's touch. He was still there, just behind her. She wanted more than that simple contact. But it wasn't her right to ask for it. She couldn't control or manipulate him, couldn't console or empathize with him.

Whether Zeus revealed the full truth in this meeting or not, Daire's father was back in his life. That bomb would always be waiting to drop. It would hang there above him like the axe that swung over her.

"You won't get away with this," Merrill said.

Sad. Pathetic. Pointless. Though what was the man supposed to do? Of course he'd object, he had no clue what he was up against.

"Providing you comply, none of the evidence we have will see the light of day."

"I don't believe you," Merrill said, though she wasn't sure that was true. "I'll deny it. I'll deny everything."

"You can do that," Zeus said. "If it comes to it and we have to release the truth to the world, you can deny it… until the feds come to arrest you."

"You don't have that kind of pull. I don't know who you are. Why should I believe—"

"Men like me endeavor to conceal our acts and our existence. We work in the background, pulling the strings. True power has nothing to do with democracy and jockeying for position in a city built to put on a show."

"I won't listen to any more of this," Merrill said and rose.

Zeus didn't stop him this time, not until he got half a dozen steps toward the door. "How is June?" Merrill stopped. "She's stood by you through a lot. Your wife is a strong woman. A man open to affairs early in the marriage is always going to be open to them later."

Merrill whipped around fast. "That's an insult."

"Yes, it is," Zeus said, taking another sip from his glass. "I'm sure your wife would feel the same way. And your mother, Ruth, does she know about your proclivities?"

"Why would you—"

"You have children with June," Zeus said. "Won't they be delighted to learn they're not your only offspring?"

"Hera," the man behind her murmured, so quiet that she didn't think anyone else heard him.

She wanted to apologize for keeping the truth hidden. Guilt was all-consuming when she recalled his assertions to Harry about them being partners who shared everything. Would she forgive him for keeping such a huge secret? Even without knowing they'd end up in this position, she still should've told him the truth. Yes, she'd worried about damaging his and Harry's relationship when they needed each other, but this wasn't better. With the men apart and no one able to explain their reasons for concealing the facts, more damage could be done.

Harry said Daire knew better than to ask a question he didn't want the answer to, but choice was gone. Zeus was taking that choice away from her Heart right before their eyes.

Trust was Daire's religion.

When Harry hadn't shown it with Zulu, it did enough damage to set Daire on a path for revenge. What would this betrayal cause?

"Are you saying—"

"Consider it a shot across the bow," Zeus said. "To

ensure you're truly with us, I'll give you twenty-four hours to deliver a hundred thousand dollars to this room. If you don't, your wife will learn about your secret love child."

What a sick way to put it.

"How dare you! I would never—"

"You knew she was pregnant," Zeus said. "You accepted the news of her death and the child's with relief, didn't you? You accepted it and went on with your life. You didn't bother to verify their deaths. You didn't ask to see their bodies. You did nothing… And now you pay the price for your carelessness."

"I can't—"

"You can," Zeus said, rising to his feet. "You'll thank me in the long term. The work we do makes the world a better place. We're patriots of humanity. You should consider this an honor."

"I don't believe you."

"What? That your child lived or that I'll release the news?" Zeus smiled, exuding a wry pleasure. "A simple DNA test will prove I'm telling the truth. And releasing the news? Of course I will, it's sport, and the world loves a sex scandal. Your marriage would crumble and your shot at the White House? I wouldn't hold my breath for that if you make an enemy of me." Opening a hand toward the door, he was not-so-politely telling the guy to leave. "Byron will assist you."

Merrill turned for the door, pausing just long enough to meet her eyes before continuing.

No one said a word after the door closed. The room, suspended in silence, seemed to be getting a measure of those in it.

"That was drastic," Garrick said eventually. "Was it wise to threaten him so quickly?"

"We don't have time for hand-holding," Zeus snapped, landing a glare on her. "You can't help yourself. You have to make a scene, take advantage of my kindness." Her urge to scream, to spit and fight and kick was hampered by her bonds and the gag, still he scowled. "Take her to her room."

When Daire's hand strengthened on her shoulder,

she fought to push back, not caring when her body came to an abrupt halt when it met his. Did Zeus plan to carry on as normal? Like he hadn't just slammed Daire with a truth he didn't want.

Moaning and shouting behind the gag, she wanted to be free of it. Despite her objections, Zeus went to the bar to pour more alcohol into his glass as though she didn't exist. Daire didn't help either. With a strong arm around her stomach, he picked her off the floor and carried her to the bedroom, bucking and screaming. She kicked the door, which must've signaled Havers inside because he opened it fast.

Daire carried her inside. "Get out of here," he said to Havers who quickly scurried away. His chest rose and fell, much like hers, a sign the adrenaline was rising, that tensions were growing. "You knew about this? About Merrill?" She nodded. She hadn't known that Zeus was going to trot him out and use son against father. "They told him I was dead…" His eyes cut to hers. "H knew about this." She nodded. "Styx?" She shrugged. His brother had never brought the subject up with her and she'd never asked. "Okay." He turned as if to leave and she screamed behind the gag again. He paused, looking over his shoulder. "You want to speak?" She nodded as a frustrated tear fell. "I don't know if I want to talk to you right now."

Maybe it wasn't a tear of frustration. Her soul was filled with pain for him, for her Heart and the lies he'd lived surrounded by.

Her whimper was the only way to ask, to beg, for a chance to speak. On an exhale, he came over to turn her around. A second later the binds were cut from her wrists.

She pulled the gag down and spun around. "Baby," she whispered.

"No," he said, taking a step back. "This goes in a box right now. Don't open the lid, just let it be."

"You can't ignore this. You can't pretend it doesn't matter."

"It doesn't matter. It's not the mission."

"I don't care about that," she said, trying to get closer, but he backed off again. "Don't shut me out."

"You're a prisoner. Our prisoner."

The cool shutter that went down over him tightened all of her muscles. "He made sure I was here to see it. It's sick. He's playing with you."

He shook his head. "It's a means to an end. A step closer to our purpose."

She frowned. "Why are you talking like this? You always marginalize your feelings. You're allowed to be mad. You should be mad. He didn't even warn you. He gave you no notice of what was about to happen or who his mark was. You didn't have to be there. I didn't have to be. Garrick either. He made sure he had an audience because he's sick. He enjoys seeing others in pain."

"You don't understand what's at stake here," he hissed. "He's doing what has to be done."

Was she talking to her Daire or Ares? She didn't get it. They were alone… or were they? Glancing around, was anything out of place? Could Havers have left a device lying around? When Daire told her they weren't being listened to earlier, they'd been in the bathroom, not the bedroom.

"You should hate him," she said, creeping in, sliding her hands onto his body.

If they were being listened to or watched, it wouldn't be a stretch to consider she might use this revelation as a way to get close to Ares, to poison the well for Zeus. But that wasn't why she touched him, wasn't why her hand rose to his cheek. Whether he compartmentalized or not, she needed to give him some kind of physical comfort, even if it had to be under the guise of something else.

"The mission is what matters," he said like he meant it though his eyes said something else. There was a conflict in them, a sorrow, a pain, and anger. "If anyone's at fault for me being in the dark about this, it's H."

She couldn't tell whether he meant that but kept stroking his face and chest. "He was trying to protect you. He didn't want you to be hurt by what went down." And more that she couldn't say in case Zeus was listening in. "You have to understand that."

"I don't have to understand anything," he said, taking

her hands from his body to retreat. "Stay in here until someone comes for you."

She wanted to go after him, to call out to him, but what would she say? They were both prisoners of the lies swirling around them. The only one winning was Zeus and that made her sick. Someday, he'd have to pay for all the pain he'd caused.

But, as she sat on the bed and breathed out, she had to admit the blame didn't stop with him. Harry hadn't told Daire the truth, about so many things. One more lie could be enough to topple the stack. And while in this double-agent predicament, Daire couldn't show his real feelings. Maybe he did understand, maybe he was plotting H's demise. Could go either way. While they were under Zeus's shadow, honesty would be impossible.

TWELVE

"TELL ME!" The masculine shout startled her awake. In the darkness, it took a second to orient herself. "I want the fucking truth."

That snarl wasn't in the room, it wasn't there with her. Where was she? The hotel. Zeus. Merrill.

"Daire," she said, leaping out of bed.

Instinct took her to the door, but she paused before opening it. If Daire was shouting, there was an argument, anger. Was it directed at Zeus? She couldn't imagine him losing his cool with an underling like that.

"We did what we thought was best." Garrick. That was Garrick's voice, she tipped her ear toward the door. "H said if you wanted to know, you'd ask. We simply didn't volunteer the information."

"You think you get out of this on a technicality? You sent my mother to prostitute herself with that scumbag, framed an innocent man, and she died for your sins?"

Oh, this was bad. Had she ever heard her Heart so riled? Would going out there calm him down or enflame the situation. Where was Zeus? Why was Garrick the one facing this wrath?

"No one knew Buford would find us. It was a

different time. Olympus wasn't as strong then as it is now. Your mother accepted the missions. She knew what she was getting into."

"I don't think she knew she'd find herself pregnant," Daire snapped. "What happened when she did? When she told you?"

"Your father took it to Zeus."

"H. You mean Hades took it to Zeus."

"Yes."

The tremble in Garrick's voice was completely understandable. Who was out there? The newbie mercs might be around offering security, but she doubted it. A secret like this, Daire wouldn't want it advertised.

She opened the door to enter the living room. Garrick was at the other side of the room, apparently using the dining table as a barrier between him and Daire. The latter stood beyond the opposite couch.

He whipped around to glare at her. "Get the fuck out of here."

"If I can hear you…" she murmured, raising a calming hand, "whoever's on the other side of that door can hear you." She nodded to the suite door. "I don't care if you yell at him, I do care if you're giving out intel." She shouldn't, but she did. "Where's Z?"

"Downstairs with Byron," Garrick said, eyes pinned to Daire. "I thought I could make him understand."

"You don't get out of this either," Daire said, rounding the couch to stalk her way. "You knew about this. For months, you knew."

"Yes. And I have no excuse. I was as disgusted as you when I heard what they sent Hera into. Zeus said it was a choice too, her choice. But I doubt in a platoon full of men, she could've gotten squeamish about a mission." Daire stopped. "You have every right to be angry."

"I don't need your permission."

"No, I don't suppose you do."

"You have to calm down before Zeus gets back," Garrick whispered, perhaps more aware of eavesdroppers. "He won't tolerate a confrontation."

"You think I give a shit what he'll tolerate?" Daire growled. "It's lies on top of lies in this place. I can't trust any of you."

"We only wanted what was best for you. I know this is a shock. Learning about your mother… how she met your father—"

"What did Zeus tell her to do?" Daire asked, his focus returning to Garrick. "When he heard she was pregnant?"

"I don't… I wasn't…"

"Tell me!" Daire demanded.

"He told her to abort," she said because it was true. "H was the only one in her corner. She said she didn't want to, that she wouldn't, and Hades stuck by her."

"You think that earns him points?" Daire asked. "That all's forgiven?"

"No. You asked the question and I answered it. H didn't know how you'd react. I'd guess this is a good bet of what he assumed… he would've told you, if you'd asked. Garrick's right, H said the same thing to me, that you knew better than to ask a question you didn't want the answer to. You didn't know they met on a mission? That it happened that way?"

The door opened; Daire turned fast.

Zeus came in, slowing to a stop as he assessed the scene. "What is going on?"

"You'd have left her to die," Daire said. "Wouldn't you?"

Zeus looked at her. "I won't leave her to die, I'll put a bullet in her. Once it's over."

"Not her," Daire said, striding closer to the principal. "Hera."

Awareness flickered across Zeus's face. Fear flitted within it. He tried to hide it, but it was definitely there, subdued by his bravado. With Daire, the great Ares, this amped, she didn't blame Zeus for being worried. Though a not-so-small part of her wanted Ares to snap, to put the haughty principal in his place. Zeus was nothing without Ares behind him. If that relationship fractured, he'd struggle to hold onto command.

"That was a long time ago," Zeus said, attempting to cross the room.

Ares got in his path. "You knew it was Buford who destroyed Alpha."

"Of course I did."

"So you know he was looking for my mother."

"He didn't know who Merrill shared the secrets with. Though I imagine if he saw her, he'd have put the pieces together."

"Who killed her?" Daire asked, zeroing in. "Who killed Hera?"

Zeus's silence was conspicuous. It lingered as he tried to hold eye contact, tried to stand up to the threat that could flatten him like a bug. Maybe he was regretting all that training he'd been so proud of when Daire was fighting in the ring.

"Why are you dredging up ancient history? This is not part of your mission. I—" He stopped and grabbed for the base unit hooked to his belt, Garrick did the same. "Goddamnit."

"Oh my God," Garrick said, his gaze flitting around the room. "How did they know?"

"How did who know?" she asked.

Zeus moved aside. "Get the men together. We're leaving. Now."

"Leaving?" she asked. "What's going on?"

"Beta's shutting down," Garrick said. That didn't much enlighten her, and she shook her head. "The Scepter's been taken from Minotaur. It's dormant."

"What does that mean?" she asked, fearing she knew the answer. "What about our people?"

"This is you," Zeus barked at her. "You did this!"

Her jaw swung loose. It defied comprehension. "I've been here with you! I was asleep, I wasn't making calls—I don't even know what the hell's going on!"

"It's over," Daire said. "He lost it."

"This is not over!"

"With everyone else here, only one person would know how to run an op like that," Daire said. "This was H."

"Yes!" Zeus agreed, thrusting a pointed finger her

way. "Her father! Her fault!"

"I can't trust any of you," Daire said, taking a few loose steps backward. "You're gonna fuck this up."

"We're going to win!" Zeus said, surprisingly optimistic. "We'll take them down and—"

"This is the Exodus all over again," she said.

"H will have freed his people," Garrick said.

"And the new mercs there wouldn't know to get out," she said.

"Yes, so they're likely already dead."

"H has all three keys now," she said, trying to disguise her gloating… just a little. "And his people back. You don't stand a chance, Ulysses."

"We have one thing he wants," he sneered, his eyes narrowing on her. "He'd give it all back for you. So long as I have you—"

"Go get your bag." Daire. His attention rounded to her. "Now."

Her? She was to…?

Hurrying back to the bedroom, she ran to the bathroom and scooped all the hotel toiletries into her carpet bag. In the bedroom, she emptied the minibar into it. She didn't know Daire's plan, but if they were going on the run, it paid to be prepared.

"Stand down," Zeus said. "This is a minor setback. We'll regroup—"

"Beta was our advantage," Daire said, gun in hand. "Without it, you'll just slow me down. Move, Pandora."

Was she supposed to be reluctant? Even if Ares was Olympus Ares, she'd still choose him over Zeus any day.

"You can't take her!"

"She's the only advantage now," Daire said. "Like you said, H will do anything to get her back in one piece."

"What is your plan?"

"I plan to get the keys, get Minotaur back online. And kill whoever gets in my way."

"You can't do it without me. Without leadership."

"Your leadership got us here," Daire said. "How many lives have been lost under your leadership?"

"You don't care about body count."

"I care about Olympus," Daire snapped. "I care about the mission, about getting things done. All this bullshit, this pissing match between you and H, it's ruined us."

"If you succeed, how will you run Olympus alone? How will you—"

"When the job is done, I'll let you make your case. Maybe I'll let you back in. Maybe I'll kill you. That's up to you."

"We can support you," Zeus said, an odd thread of glee in his words. "You were always meant to take your place at the head of Olympus." Like Zeus would ever actually work under someone. The man was power mad. "It is your birthright. You have grown so much. This is what we nurtured you for. With me at your side—"

"The mission has to be achieved before I let you suck my cock," Daire said, startling everyone, though her impulse was to smile. "I'll move faster alone. I don't need you for this. Not yet. Pandora, get over here, now."

Rushing to him, she clung to her bag as he guided her toward the door.

"She'd be safer with us," Zeus said. "You could take down H and come back for her. Once you have the keys—"

"You lost the keys. I gave you the Scepter and it still ended up in H's hands," Daire said. "I am not taking the risk you'll lose her too."

Zeus leaped in front of him. "But we—"

"Get out of my way," Daire snarled. "Or I'll move you… and that won't end well for you."

She shouldn't have smiled. From what she could tell, Daire wasn't declaring himself loyal to H or shunning Z, he was playing it his own way, like he'd just figured out he was actually stronger alone. Still, it was nice to see Zeus put in his place. It was about damn time.

Though the principal's lips thinned, and his nostrils flared in anger, he really had no choice except to step aside. He'd never win in a fight and that was an embarrassment he'd do without.

Daire pushed her to the door and paused to address

the principals. "Stay here," he said. "I'll find you if I need you."

And if they needed him?

They did. That much was obvious to any onlooker, but it wasn't in Zeus to beg.

Daire reached over her to open the door and grabbed her shoulder, holding her back against his chest as he took them out of the suite. The men in the hallway moved for him. Whether they'd heard what went on or not, no one would get in Ares's way, especially not while he was armed.

They got into the stairwell.

"We don't have a vehicle," she started. "How will we…?" Except instead of going down, they went up. Back to the roof. "Can you fly a helicopter?"

Maybe the question was stupid because he was opening the door and boosting her inside. Obviously, he must have some idea what he was doing.

"Fasten the safety harness," he said and slammed the door.

It took her trembling fingers a minute to figure out what the hell they were supposed to do. By then, the rotors were going and Daire was putting on a headset. He leaned over to put hers on too and then they were rising. Leaving the hotel, they went out across the city heading for… she didn't know where.

Whatever was at the end of this flight, she hoped Daire had a plan because they were on their own again. Just like the old days.

THIRTEEN

THE DARKNESS BENEATH THEM was foreboding. It was almost ironic that when they landed and Daire killed the rotors, they were back where they started.

"Beta," she said, taking off her headset and working her jaw.

Helicopters weren't comfortable. With the noise and the vibration, it was impossible to hold a conversation. She didn't want to distract the man in charge either. With all the buttons, lights, and switches, helicopters seemed complicated.

Silence lingered for a second before Daire took off his headset and got out. She took hers off too and had unfastened her safety belt when her door opened.

"Did they wait for us?" she asked, putting a hand on his shoulder, accepting his help to get onto solid ground again.

"No," he said. "They'll consider tonight a failure. As I do."

"Why?" she asked. As far as she was concerned, their position was a hundred percent better than it had been that morning. "If they'd waited—"

"They didn't know you wouldn't be here," he said, striding toward the building.

She hurried after him. "Maybe they waited. How do

you know they didn't wait?"

Stopping, he moved out of her way to show fewer vehicles in the lot than had been there before.

"Oh," she said, moving again when he did. "So they got the prisoners, the Scepter and then left?"

"That was always the plan. They need to give their people a chance to recuperate, get back in shape, and to give Zeus a chance to put distance between them."

She stopped. He walked down the center aisle of the parking lot and stopped at an Olympus vehicle. When he was in front of it, he noticed she wasn't in his wake and looked back at her. Waiting.

"You said 'their' people." In the night, it wasn't easy to pick out his features, but he was definitely tense. Snappy. On edge. His tone was less Ares the soldier and more angry Daire. "Aren't they your people too?"

"We don't know where they are," he said. "It wasn't necessary to have a rendezvous point when you were supposed to be with them and me with Zeus."

"Can you communicate with them?" she asked, taking a few more steps. "Put the code in like we did the first time?"

"H doesn't have his base unit," he said. "And we'd as likely summon Zeus and Garrick. Without a key, we wouldn't be able to regroup here. If we're going to be on the move, they'll slow me down."

"I'll slow you down."

"I need you," he said, turning to her as she reached him.

"You need me?"

At least that was an indication he wasn't irreparably mad at her. Except when she reached for his face, he caught her hand in his.

"We need a key," he said. "It's the only way this gets back on the tracks."

"A key? I don't have a key."

"No, you don't. But Styx talked to you. Told you more than I knew. He wouldn't put all three keys out of reach. Not when the stakes are so high. Someone knows where he stashed the keys."

"Someone," she said. "Me? You think I know?"

"You might not know it, but you do." He left it at that and went around the truck. Ducking and rising, he would be checking it out and probably disabling the tracker like he had before. He opened the driver's side door. "Get in."

"Why did you bring me?" she asked. "Because I might know the location of a key?"

"We don't have time for this now. Get in the truck." What was her alternative? Wait out there in the freezing cold? No one was coming back to Beta, not for a long time. "Tess."

Okay, she didn't need that tone of warning. She didn't need her Heart to be threatening her either. Yeah, he had a right to be mad, but that didn't change anything. They were together, on the same side, even if he wasn't happy about it.

Styx and Harry had made their attempt to take back the upper hand. They'd succeeded, to a degree. Her Heart obviously wasn't happy the plan had gone awry, but that was hardly her fault.

"Where are we going?" she asked. If Styx had given her some secret clue, she'd missed it. When he hid the keys before, she'd always had her suspicions. It wasn't like that this time. "Why did we come back to Beta if we're not going inside?" And just to drive away from it. Something was close by. "Are we going to the—"

"Don't talk."

Because he hadn't fully checked out the vehicle for monitoring equipment or because he didn't want to hear her voice?

"I just want to know where we're going."

"And you'll see when we get there."

Hoping that meant it wasn't far, she pulled her carpet bag closer to her chest and waited. When they turned off the road to head into the forest, the answer was clear. They were going to the Beast.

Thank God. With all that was going on, life didn't offer many comforts. Home would go a long way toward reassuring her. And Daire, he couldn't remain distant and angry when he was reminded of all they'd been there… could he?

They bumped and swerved their way to the Beast. Stopping closer this time, Daire left the engine running and reached down to take something from his boot. The Beast's key. He held it toward her.

"Go inside and wait."

"For what?" she asked, taking the key. "Where are you going?"

"To salvage what I can," he said. "I have to get rid of this vehicle and check something out."

"How long will you be? Can't I come with you?"

"I'll be quicker alone," he said. "Shouldn't be more than an hour."

So she was to sit alone in the Beast in the middle of a forest for an hour… alone?

"I don't like us being separated. We should stay together. What if something goes wrong? What if they followed us here?"

Lifting his hips, he withdrew something from the back of his pants and put it in her palm. The gun. "You said you know how to use these."

"You always said I wouldn't need to."

Not while he was around anyway, but he wasn't going to be around.

His eyes met hers. "Will you trust me on this?"

"You're mad," she said, more worried for him than scared of being in the Beast alone. "At me. At Harry. At Zeus. Everyone."

"Tess," he said, reaching over to scoop a hand around the side of her head. "You're safe. Do you believe I'd let anyone hurt you no matter how mad I am?" She shook her head. "Go wait in the Beast, I'll be back as soon as I can."

She got out of the vehicle with her bag and went to open the Beast. He waited until she was inside before turning to disappear into the night. Things had gone wrong. The plan wasn't playing out like it should. With no one next to Zeus, they'd have no way to know if he planned something dangerous or if he got intel on their locations or objectives.

She locked the door and put her carpet bag in the

closet. It was late. She was tired and they hadn't eaten. Still, she sat on the end of the bed and looked down the length of the trailer. They'd had their first kiss there. First made love in the bed beneath her. Though she wouldn't have thought of it as "making love" at the time.

They'd said goodbye to each other in these walls and greeted each other after time apart. She'd cried in his arms. Laughed at his jokes. Craved him and hated him there. Okay, so maybe not hated him, but she got close.

Their home was their sanctuary. Yet it was cold and isolating. She didn't know where she was, not exactly. What if he didn't come back? What would she do then? He'd never abandon her, but she didn't like doing nothing.

FOURTEEN

JUST UNDER TWO HOURS LATER, at the first rumble of an engine, she vaulted onto her feet. Was it him? How could she tell? Even peeking through the closed blinds didn't help. The light obviously came from headlights, but she couldn't see anything beyond their glare.

When the vehicle pulled around in front of the Beast, she scrambled to the living room, eager to check who was out there.

Daire got out of the driving seat. Relief took on new meaning. With the gun still in her hand, she leaped out of the Beast and ran around to where he was crouched between truck and trailer.

"Get in the truck," he said before she could utter a word, taking the gun from her hand to put it back in his waistband.

"Want me to help? Everything is secure inside." Because she hadn't really touched or moved anything. "I can get the stabilizers or—"

"Baby," he said, standing up. "Please."

She nodded. At least he was using endearments again. "Can I do just one thing first?"

"What?"

Narrowing the space between them, she ran her hands up his chest to grasp his neck and pull him down. At first, it felt like he resisted, but she persisted. He eventually came down to meet her mouth with his.

Maybe it wasn't the time. There were other things to worry about. But there were always other things to worry about. No matter how mad he was or how much he wanted to focus on work, his experience with Merrill must have been a shock.

When her arms coiled around his neck and their tongues began a more passionate battle, he quickly withdrew and laid a hand on her arm.

"Okay," he said on an exhale. "I get it."

"I love you," she murmured. "No matter what. I love you."

His eyes closed and he rested his forehead against her for a second before taking her arms from around him. "Get in the truck. It's late. I want to get on the road."

He left her to go down the other side of the Beast.

This tension, his need for control, to do tasks he could center his focus on… it only confirmed what she knew about the night's events. Her Heart was uneasy. Maybe it was all Merrill and his mother being brought to the fore. Maybe it was the abrupt change in the plan.

She got into the truck and waited, as he'd requested. He did his checks, backed up the truck to connect the Beast, and then he was back inside.

"Are you hungry?" he asked as they started moving.

"No," she said, curling her feet up beside her.

He glanced her way. "Put your feet down," he said. "And you are hungry."

"We're going at two miles an hour," she said, but put her feet down. "I had a cereal bar."

"Nutritious."

"I don't care about food," she said. "Not while I'm worried about you."

They broke through the trees into a clearing. When the truck turned and she saw the water, she realized where they were. He'd picked a spot not far from the location she'd last been intimate with Danny. Their spot. Where they'd made love in the grass, gone skinny-dipping, grilled steaks and just been them. Before everything got complicated.

"There's nothing to worry about," he said, snagging her attention. "I have everything under control."

"I know, you always do."

He turned on the heater and redirected the vents. "Are you cold?"

"My Heart," she said, putting a hand over his. "Talk to me."

He shook his head. "We can't get into it. I can't get into it. We need to focus on the plan."

"The plan to find a key?"

"Yes," he said. "H and Styx will be taking care of our people. Until we know how to remove JARR, there's no point returning to Beta. Where did you go with them?"

"Tulsi's. D.C. The doctor's place."

"Okay, Tulsi won't be at her home base if Wreck is with Styx. They'll set up somewhere secure. Somewhere inaccessible." Which wasn't great for anyone who wanted to find them… like her and Daire. "D.C. is out, it's too public. They'll avoid cities, anywhere too built up. The doctor's might be—"

"Styx torched it."

"Okay," he said. "No Asclepius."

She gasped. "Do we have his notebook? His bible with the—"

"We have it."

Of course they did, he knew its importance. "I don't know how we'll find them." She searched her memory. "We stopped at an abandoned factory place in the middle of nowhere. Styx and I did. Harry went to stash the doctor's stuff. I don't know where he went. The building was pretty run down, but there was running water."

"I know where that is. They won't be there either. It's too exposed and remember they have numbers now. They need somewhere to spread out," he said. "It doesn't matter. We don't need to hook up with them."

"Won't they just go to Gamma? They have the keys."

"But no Minotaur," he said. "There's no point extracting Minotaur when we'd only have to put it back to remove JARR. Gamma's a target and the first place Zeus would look. Without Minotaur and with our people not at full strength, H would never go there. He can't defend it and we know Z doesn't care about blasting buildings to shit."

No and they'd lost a comrade the last time Zeus seriously lost his temper. Maybe they'd lost more people. Maybe H and Styx. They had no way to know if everyone got out of Beta or if there were casualties during the raid.

And suddenly, it made sense.

"You're mad," she murmured.

"Yeah, you said that already."

"No," she said, shaking her head and pulling her seatbelt out enough to pounce onto her knees facing him. "You're mad that you're not at their six. You're mad just like he was mad. You're mad you're stuck babysitting me."

"This is not about you."

"Maybe not. But you are mad you weren't there when it all went to shit."

"I was supposed to be there. You were supposed to be there." His fists tightened on the steering wheel until his knuckles whitened. "After busting in and realizing we weren't there… it would've been a shitshow."

"At least they got your people out," she said. "They have numbers now."

"Do they? We don't know who got out. All we know is Minotaur is offline… which means the failsafes kicked in."

And if they'd wasted time looking for her…

"They'd know better, wouldn't they?" she asked. "Than to waste time—"

"H would've got an answer out of one of Z's mercs. Fast. Styx…"

She waited, but he didn't finish. "Styx what?"

"Let's just say I don't know how many of those mercs were dead before the oxygen was cut off."

And the gas released. Beta did know how to say goodbye with a bang.

"People say I hate when things are missed? Styx hates

it when things go wrong."

Which was probably another reason he'd been so mad after they escaped Beta with Harry. Adapting might be part of his remit, but when it meant leaving a man behind, his brother behind, she could understand why he'd felt the strain.

"The mercs didn't treat him or Harry well," she said. "I'm not sure they didn't deserve whatever he gave them."

"What do I deserve?" he asked, negotiating their way onto a narrow road. "I did most of that damage."

"So they didn't do worse," she said. "You know how to pull your punches without making it look like you are. You wouldn't do any long-term damage. They might."

"You're so damn sure—"

"Don't," she said. "Do not try to push me away." He glanced at her. "You've had to do some horrible things recently, to people you love. You think it would be easier on your conscience if we all hated you. If we treated you like the Ares you had to be. My Heart..." Leaning closer, she slid a hand to the back of his neck and the other across his chest. "If you want to be mad, you can yell at me. If you want to pretend we're strangers, you can do that too. But we're not. I'm your something. I'm as much your something now as I was when you decided to go through with this mission. You did it to give us an advantage. To buy some time and gather some intel. That worked. All of that worked. The mission was not a failure. In fact..."

When she suppressed her words, he laid a hand on hers on his chest. "In fact, what, baby?" She could feel the beat of his heart, almost like it slowed beneath their stacked hands. "Don't shut me out, Little Red," he said, a serious warning weighing his words. "No matter what, we have to be honest."

And she was Little Red again.

Boosting herself over the center console, she kissed his cheek, nuzzling her mouth against him. "I've missed you, baby. I thought I lost you and... I'm not sorry things went wrong if it means being together with you again. I'm never safer..."

"Than when you're in my eyeline."

"I'd die for you, baby," she breathed against him. "I asked you to do whatever it took to get back to me and you did. I love you, but please, please… don't ever leave me behind again."

"That look in your eye when you turned around in Vegas… I wanted to rip my heart out and hand it to you right there. I thought I was sacrificing this. That you'd never touch me again."

"I can't help myself," she said, curving her arm around his neck to pull herself closer. "I love you so much, I don't want to breathe without you."

"Sit down," he said as they pulled onto the blacktop.

"I want to be near you."

"We need to put some miles between us and Beta."

"Because…?" she asked. "Whether it's Styx or Zeus that catch up with us, you will get us through it."

The way he'd left it with Zeus was pretty genius. Yes, he'd stood up to his superior, but he hadn't blatantly betrayed him. Knowing Zeus, he'd still be hoping Ares would ultimately choose the side of Olympus. His side.

"Because when I lay you down in our bed, Little Red, I don't want there to be interruptions or a time limit. I need more than stolen seconds with you." She sank back to her seat. Tension radiated through him. "I don't want to think about disobeying orders or getting caught. I don't want the threat looming over us. When was the last time we had peace to just be together?"

She had to think about it. "Miami." And even then, Styx had been on the other side of the door the whole time. And the imminent, potentially explosive, reveal of their relationship hung on the horizon then too. "If we don't count that, it was before Three's house was destroyed."

"Months ago. And you're surprised I'm ragged?"

He flashed her a dimple and she settled back in her seat. "You always tell me if I said the word, you'd walk away from it all."

"And I would."

"You know the same goes for me, right? If you're tired of this and just want to get out of here, we'll go. No hesitation. I'd do anything to make you happy. Follow you anywhere."

He gave her knee a squeeze and left his hand there. "Close your eyes. I want to see you sleep."

"There's so much to talk about."

"Yeah, and it's not going anywhere. You're so peaceful when you sleep. It calms me down."

How had he never told her that before? "Okay. But if you find somewhere to stop—"

"I'll wake you up."

Closing her eyes, she had an affinity for him drawing calm from her. She did it too, the other way. Knowing he was there with her, in the driving seat again, there was nowhere safer. Safety wasn't something to take for granted. It could be stolen from them at any second. While they had it, they needed to cherish it.

FIFTEEN

CLEAN, FRESH AIR refreshed her lungs. She stretched and blinked into the light. Daylight.

They were no longer moving. Daire wasn't in the driver's seat. Rising a little, she checked around. He wasn't in the truck at all. And they were… parked. Grass. Trees… People. Why were there people? Not looking at her, they were… It was an RV park. Where was Daire?

Putting her shoes back on, she opened the door and got out, still stiff from sleep. The Beast and truck were connected. Had they just arrived or were they leaving soon? Trees hugged the back of the trailer. They were on the edge of the park. No one was right next to them, no surprise Daire elected to put a considerable distance between them and listening ears.

She reached for the Beast's doorhandle.

"You think I'd let you out of my eyeline?" Startled, she looked left and right. That was Daire's voice, but where did it come from? "Look up."

"Up?" What did he…? It was only when he moved that she noticed him sitting in the tree next to the Beast. In it. Actually up there sitting on a branch. "What are you doing up there?"

"Height gives a good vantage point."

"You think these people are a threat?" No, he didn't because if he did, they wouldn't be there. "Why didn't you wake me?"

"You needed to sleep."

"And you?" she asked, going over to stand beneath him. "Are you going to come down?"

He did. Sort of. He slid off the branch to land on the bough beneath and descended to the one just above her head to extend an arm her way.

"Give me your hand."

"You want me to come up there? I never climbed trees as a kid."

Wasn't something her mom taught her.

"Then you can do it as an adult." She hesitated which relaxed his neck. "You think I'd drop you?"

"No," she said, reaching up.

He locked his hand around her forearm, so she did the same thing. He'd picked her up plenty of times, but never like this. Her feet left the ground and she grabbed for the branch, hauling herself up onto it with his help.

Straddling it, she swept her hair from her face. "Risky to have sex up here. So many people watching."

His smile was a good sign. "You were right. There's a lot to talk about."

So they were sitting in a tree, in public, to distract them from prioritizing getting naked. Probably smart. How many times had she berated herself for missing opportunities to talk because they prioritized sex instead?

"Okay. What do you want to start with?"

"I put a communique out for Styx."

"Telling him where we are?"

He shook his head. "No point. We won't be here by the time he gets it. I just need proof of life."

Because they still weren't sure who made it out of Beta.

Shimmying closer, she rested her hands on his torso as he leaned against the trunk of the tree. "They made it. I know they did."

"I can't help but think it would be easier if we just joined them."

"We can do that."

"I need to know the process for JARR… If we get a key, I can go into Garrick's vault and search his archive."

"He has his own vault?"

"For his many, many prototypes… Some of Asclepius's potions ended up in there too."

"His bible notebook didn't help?"

"It did," he said, nodding. "But it didn't tell me everything."

"And we need every detail?"

"Without knowing everything, we're going in blind. We have to know everything because once the process starts, there's no going back. We'll have to act swiftly. There's one important thing I don't know… We could trace where Harry stashed the doctor's papers… But I need to get a look at the panel itself. In the JARR control room. I need to…"

"What are we scared of?" she asked, relaxing more of her weight onto him. "We have the keys. We need the password and the order of the keys. Can't Exile take it from there?"

"You're missing one vital piece of the puzzle."

"What?"

"You."

She licked her lips. "Yeah, well, we have me."

He touched her face, exploring her like he'd never seen her before. "But how much of you will they take?"

Her blood? "A lot," she said. "I don't know the number, but Asclepius made a comment about the subject bleeding into the system being too weak to screw over anyone." Paraphrasing, but that was the gist. "I guess that means they'd lose a lot of blood."

His nod seemed tight. "You're A positive."

It took her a second. "My blood type?"

"Right. I'm O negative." Which might make sense to someone who knew what he was talking about. "We're going to do something, might seem weird, but… You trust me?"

Folding her forearms, she gave him all of herself.

"Always."

"Okay," he said, tucking her hair behind her ear. "If Styx reaches out, if he's alive, he'll need time with the guys. This will end at Beta. One way or another."

"And after?" she asked. "What happens after?"

"Let's just get through this first," he said. "One thing at a time."

"We get a key. Go back to Beta. I need to know the order of the keys. We get that wrong and it's over before it starts."

"What did you get from Asclepius? From his notebook."

He paused. "I know how to get into the security panel... and which key's first."

"The one we need to take from Minotaur and put into the JARR system within ninety seconds?"

He nodded. "I think the information's been split up on purpose." He exhaled an ironic snicker. "Makes you wonder why we're surprised things ended up this way. It's the Olympus way not to trust anyone. Someone always knew we'd end up destroying ourselves from the inside."

"Three keys. Three locations of information... If Asclepius has one and Garrick has another... who has the third?"

"No one."

"No one?"

"If we know the order of the other two, the third, by default, goes in the final place."

Right. Yeah. Duh. "Garrick knows. Do you think he's told Zeus?"

"Maybe," he said. "But he's smart, so probably not. I didn't know the order was split between them until I read Asclepius's notes." She sighed. "We need the head start." He cupped her face. "If we get a key, I can go into Beta."

"Zeus will be notified."

"It doesn't matter," he said. "If we're inside, I'll turn on Minotaur and put the building on lockdown. No one will get in without our say so."

"You can do that? Why didn't Zeus—"

"Because you need an authorization code from each of the three principals. Zeus had access to Garrick's." Because the guy was there. "He didn't have access to H's."

Except… "You know Harry's access codes," she said, astounded and impressed.

"Yes."

"But Zeus and Garrick's…"

"Garrick hasn't changed his master code in ten years, even Styx knows that damn code and he never pays attention," he said. "And being Zeus's right-hand man… I was closer than I've ever been… in every room, every meeting."

"Seductive," she said, grazing her lips on his jaw. "That's what he wanted to do. Seduce you."

"Yeah, I guess."

His dismissive attitude and casual discomfort spoke volumes.

"It's a shame," she said, resting her temple on his body, trying to peek up at him. "I feel sorry for him actually."

"You feel sorry for Zeus?" he asked, tipping his head back to the side. "Is the sky falling?" She laughed. "Why do you feel sorry for him?"

"Because he didn't know I'm the only one who can seduce you," she said and boosted up to kiss him quick. "It must've been difficult being back there. Without Harry and Styx."

"I've been at Beta without them plenty."

"Yeah, but… this was different. They weren't out on a mission and on their way home. Do you think Styx has told Harry the truth yet?"

"I don't know. I didn't know he was going to tell you."

"I wasn't in a good place," she said, laying her palms on him to push back, then watching her hands stroke up and down his tee-shirt. "I could've screwed everything up."

"I told him not to tell Harry," he said. "The trade-off—"

"I know," she said, hazarding a smile. "Looking back on it, what I went through… it's nothing to what you endured."

"No," he said, grasping her chin to meet her eye. "We're not getting into that. We can't get into it. I can't get into it."

"We need to focus on the plan."

"Right.

This distance, his need to bracket his time as Ares and set it aside, was understandable. Though she worried about what it was doing to his head... and their relationship.

"You have everyone's codes?" she said, reveling in how smart he was though it didn't appear he gave himself credit. When did her Heart ever give himself credit? "We get inside. Lock the doors..."

"Once we're inside, we're safe. Zeus won't target a strike on Beta. There's value inside... as well as JARR, Minotaur... and you. They'll be pissed, but no one will harm us."

"We'll have Beta to ourselves."

"We'll call the shots. I can take as long as I have to with Garrick's notes. With the vault... I can examine JARR. I'll send a message to Styx, tell him to get to Beta when it's time."

"We need a key," she said, coming around to his thinking. "Why not just send a message to Styx and ask where they are?"

"He's not that stupid," he said, his hands settling around her head again. "If he sends that message and Zeus or Garrick are monitoring our channels... For all he knows, they could be the source of the message."

Inhaling, she felt some of his burden. "I have to remember."

His thumbs moved in a delicate caress. "You have to remember."

She winced. "The big problem is—"

"You're not good with subtle," he said, his arms dropping to his sides as he sagged back against the tree trunk again. "I know."

"He should know better. Everyone should know better. I'm not good with hints. It took me a month to figure out the Beta coordinates and even then I only did it because you set me up."

Considering her, his brow strengthened. "You went to the factory to meet Exile. Then where did you go?"

"A motel. We walked forever, into the city, and got a room to talk… about the thing you don't want to talk about." His time as a double agent. "From there, Styx got us a ride, I don't know where from. We met Harry in Tallahassee."

"You've got a real thing for Florida, babe."

"Did you know Harry and my mom lived together in Florida? That I was taken from there." He shrugged. "I can't believe Harry owns the house." Their eyes met. "You don't think… Would Styx have?"

"Maybe," he muttered. "You went from there to Miami?" She nodded. "And to the house. Nowhere else?"

One place… that she hadn't told him about yet. She hooked her legs over his to get closer. "I got your letter." Such an indecipherable man, yet she couldn't keep her shit together. "I couldn't believe that… I don't even know why I… thank you for writing it."

"I didn't think you would get it so soon. We were only in Miami a day. I couldn't be there and not… I knew if this all went to shit, it would be the only place you'd look."

Kissing him slow, she enjoyed the texture of his lips, the heat of his body, the way his breath merged with hers. All those little things she took for granted now meant more to her than it was possible to express.

"I wanted to crawl inside you," she whispered, her eyes still closed. "I wish I could just be inside you. Always."

"I know the feeling," he said with enough innuendo to make her draw back. He laughed. "I'm sorry, Little Red."

"You made something sentimental sexy… I'm not even surprised." Wasn't like he didn't have previous. "Styx was with me. Not when I read the letter. He wouldn't let me go out alone, so he came with me."

"He knows about the locker?"

She shook her head. "He wasn't with me there. I sent him to the milkshake bar."

"Did you watch him go to the milkshake bar and sit down?" Did she? No. Which she told him with a headshake.

"He knows about the locker." He took her hand to his lips. "No doubt."

"So that's where it is? The key?"

His head angled left to right in a back and forth bob. "Maybe and it's a good place to start, but…"

"But?"

"H knows about the locker. I don't know that Styx would put it somewhere everyone could get at it."

"Harry doesn't know Styx knows about the locker," she said. "He was scouting the house when we went. Styx didn't even tell him after, he told Harry we went to check out the RV park for the Beast… which we didn't."

"It wasn't there."

"Harry knew that." Which meant they weren't the only ones going on secret excursions. Her father hadn't mentioned the RV park being on his itinerary until they told him it was on theirs. "H doesn't know we went to the Rotunda. At all. Did you tell Zeus about the locker?"

"No," he said, brushing her hair from her face. "I'm sorry for the things I did tell him."

"You have to stop apologizing," she said. "It was a means to an end. I know why you did it."

"I'm glad one of us does." He wasn't going to give himself a break any time soon. "Before the Exodus, I… Guilt was easy to process and set aside. It was naïve of me to assume it would be that easy with you."

"Okay," she said, slapping her hands to his shoulders. "We need to get out of this tree."

"Why?" he asked, though did shift away from the trunk.

"Because you need to remember us."

"I didn't forget."

"I think you did," she said. In a way, she had too. Those moments of doubt put space between them. While she was eager to erase it, he was reluctant. "Either way, it's like you said, we need more than stolen seconds together." His expression didn't change. Clasping his face, she brushed her thumb across where his dimple should be. "Come home to me, baby… I'm here. I'm yours."

"I don't know I deserve your devotion."

Searching his face, something occurred to her. "You thought you lost this," she said. "That we could never be together again. That's what Styx told me… That we would never be what we were."

"H was right in Miami. I told him you knew what we were capable of… Knowing it and facing it are two different things."

She'd been so eager to be with him, to show him that she didn't judge him for what had happened while he was Ares. Enthralled in that, she hadn't noticed his reluctance. She couldn't help but wonder if Zeus had got his way.

"You had sex with me in the Beast last week. I know, I was there."

"This is not about my attraction to you," he said. "I want you like… It's not even possible to describe how much I want to be inside you right now. Last week I thought…"

"That the raid would happen any second and we'd be apart again." That had been another goodbye. The things he'd said… Of course it was goodbye. "I want to get down now."

The ground seemed far away. Further than it had when she was looking up from it.

"Little Red—"

"You can help me, or I'll break my neck doing it myself."

"Baby, I…" Glaring at him, she showed her resolve and he exhaled. Turning around, he sat with his legs to one side. "Put your arms around my neck."

She did and he hooked her legs around his body. When he edged closer to the edge, she closed her eyes, letting him do the difficult part. As soon as his boots landed on the grass, she let go and stood herself before he'd even straightened all the way up.

"We should get back on the road," she said, starting for the truck again. "We have a lot of ground to cover."

"We need to do something first." Yeah, he had said that. What was it? Looking back at him, she got no clue. He went to the Beast and opened the door, releasing the stairs before gesturing inside. "Please."

SIXTEEN

NOTHING INSIDE WAS DIFFERENT.

Daire closed the door and squeezed past her. When she stepped back to give him more space, he fixed on her.

"I expected this reaction from you after the mission. Not after being honest about my feelings on it."

"You haven't told me your feelings on it," she said, folding her arms. "Every time I bring it up, you say we have to focus on the mission."

"Because it's easier to focus on what needs to be done than what I did to hurt you."

"Shouldn't I be the one to decide how hurt I am? I want to be with you. You're the one throwing up barriers every time I make that clear."

"Little Red," he said, erasing the space between them to wrap his arms around her to haul her close. "I want to be with you more than anything in this world."

Her muscles relaxed. "Then I don't understand, why are you pushing me away?"

"I need you to face what I did, what I was… I lied to you. Hurt you. Hurt people you care about… I shared information about us with an enemy."

"You did all of that to protect us. It's the greater

good, right?"

"And I need you to see that you are my greater good."

"Do you think I doubt that? Don't you think I have guilt of my own? I doubted this. I doubted us… Even then, during the escape I… I didn't want to leave you. I tried to stay behind. Styx forced me out and… When I found out about the mission, about you being the man on the inside… We left you behind."

"You were supposed to," he said, dipping lower while tightening his embrace. "I'm supposed to be behind enemy lines, that's my job."

"And it's my job to be with you. No matter where that is."

"If I'd taken you with me, he'd have used you against me. It was too dangerous. If he thought I didn't feel like I do, he couldn't turn this against us. Think about it, think of what I did to get us what we needed. Imagine what I'd have done if he held a knife to your throat. You think you've seen it all. That you've endured the worst. That's nothing, baby. Nothing to what I'd do if he meant to hurt you."

They'd been protected by JARR in that regard. Zeus couldn't threaten her life so long as he needed it.

"Is that what you're scared of?" she asked. "That I'll take away your goodness. That I'll make you do terrible things?"

"I have done terrible things."

"In the name of our love."

"I'd die for it, Little Red. Our love is my world."

"You'd die for our love," she murmured.

"Without hesitation."

"I want you to hesitate," she said, filled with her own anger. "Goddamnit, Daire, how many times have I told you we have a future? I am your something to live for, to survive for, remember that? If you go out there and get yourself killed, who protects me then? What do I live for? You're my something too. God, you're so stubborn—" Pushing at him, she fought to free herself of his arms. "I don't want you dead. I want us to live… together. Not—let me go."

"Not a chance," he said, yanking her to him hard,

crashing his mouth over hers.

She was sick of his need to be a martyr for her. How could he miss that her need for him eclipsed his for her? His tongue forced its way into her mouth, delving deep, dominating the moment. The asshole always with his control, always in charge. Throwing her arms around his neck, she returned his fervor with her own.

Damn him. Damn them.

He stood straight, picking her up to take them to their bed. Being home, this was another greeting after being parted. How long would it last? When would they say goodbye again?

As he stripped them both, his eyes stayed on hers. So much had to be said. In the tree, it seemed he wasn't going to be intimate with her. Was it possible he just needed her that much? She didn't utter a word, too afraid that he might stop, that she may not get to experience him again.

Once upon a time, being together was a given. An inevitability. Even in their Danny days, keeping their hands off each other was impossible.

He planted his hands on the bed above her and levered down to merge their mouths again. This was a language they spoke together, in a place they always agreed. Maybe words were the problem. As she lay there accepting his kiss, his arms closed around her head, holding her close as her legs coiled around his hips.

She'd berated herself for prioritizing sex believing words were more important. Now it seemed words were the problem. They couldn't talk without disagreeing, without arguing, without the institution insinuating itself between them. Would they ever get over it?

"Temptress," he murmured against her lips.

That sounded like a request… a desperate request. Was he asking permission? Her breath caught in her throat as his kiss descended her body. He could have her. All of her. Didn't he realize he already did? Her fury took a backseat in that moment to his guilt. Before, he'd never worried about living with himself. He'd done what was needed for the mission. No negative emotion plagued him then. Did that mean she was bad for him?

"My Heart," she said, clasping his head to draw him back up to meet her eye. "Your cock. Give me your cock."

In a way, they were starting over. It seemed fitting to use the words she'd used then. Something like relief overcame him and he kissed her again, aligning their bodies to push himself into her. The need was real. More than a hormone overload, her world became complete when he was inside her. Sometimes in their frantic moments, she forgot about all they'd been through, forgot how they'd fought for each other through it all.

Would it ever change? Would her love and need for him ever dwindle? "God, I hope not," she hissed through gritted teeth. "Baby…"

The determined resolution set on his expression revealed something much more profound was going on within him. The shiver that rocked her belly was both pleasure and fear. He could be claiming her again, reminding himself that she belonged to no one else or… The alternative fled her mind when he shoved in hard and slid out slow, his hand moving between them to torment her clit as desire darkened his gaze.

Those sinister eyes saw within her. They read her soul. If only she could bear her all to him every minute. Whatever he doubted, it would never be her. Whatever they had to endure, he needed to know his past misdeeds wouldn't influence her love for him.

"Baby," she gasped, her body tightening. "Oh, Daire…"

Her volume rose in a yelp that thrust her body into the pit of pleasure that arched her against him, pushing back against the love he poured into her. But she accepted him. All of him. And she always would.

When he dropped onto the bed beside her, she focused on the ceiling, listening to the pant of his breath.

"Is Olympus what you want?" she asked, her voice a little hoarse.

"What?"

"Olympus. Being back there with Zeus… I understand if that reminded you of… If Olympus is what you want—"

"No," he said, rolling onto his side to loom over her. "That's not what this is about, baby."

"You don't want to talk about the future," she said, her knuckles grazing his chest. "Maybe it's because you know your future is there. It's still possible for you to have it."

He frowned. "Yeah, and to get there, I'd only have to kill you, H, and Styx."

"I think he would join you. Styx. This mission was a ruse. He couldn't join Zeus when he was withholding the keys. But if you want—"

"Stop it," he said, swiping the hair from her brow. "I am not going to hurt you or let anyone hurt you. I can't think about the future because I need to have my head in the game. I can't be thinking about being with you or dreaming of a future that may never come."

"You have to be willing to die," she said, sitting up as clarity captured her. "You don't think about what comes next because it might hold you back. You might hesitate."

"Hesitation gets you killed."

"Please don't feed me Harry's lines," she said, her forehead sinking into her hand. "I can't do anything else to convince you. If you want to kill yourself…" She pushed to the end of the bed. Technically, she'd been willing to die to prevent Zeus getting his way. If Daire wanted to throw himself on his own pyre, she'd have to find a way to get over that. "Can I have a shower? Is there water? Do we have time?"

"Yeah," he said.

She turned on the water and went to grab a towel. With her hand on the shower door, she paused to tip her chin toward the bed without looking at him.

"It's hands off, Agent. If we think distance will make it easier to lose each other, we'll keep this professional."

"Baby—"

"No," she said, resenting the pressure behind her eyes when they met his. "I lost you once and barely survived it. The greater good wins. It always has. So we keep this professional."

"If that's what you want," he said, his voice deep. "I'll respect your boundaries."

Hadn't he been the reluctant one in the tree? When was she going to learn that he knew best? She got into the shower. Distance wouldn't be easy to maintain, they'd tried it in the past. Though back then, they'd never been so precariously close to the finish line.

Losing each other would be difficult either way. It wasn't like they'd fall out of love just because they kept their hands to themselves. Maybe it would last, maybe it wouldn't. But she couldn't live through losing him again. Despite their proximity, in some ways, it felt like she'd never got him back.

***

WHEN SHE GOT OUT THE SHOWER, the accordion door was closed across the bedroom. Good, that gave her privacy to dry her hair and change. Once done, she opened it up, intending to put her towel in the laundry bag.

Daire stood by the dinette, dressed though his hair was wet. Where had he washed? That wondering fled when she saw the setup further down the trailer. A low metal table with an empty bag hooked to the side, tubing, and in Daire's hand? A needle.

"What is going on?" she asked, opening the closet to put her towel in the laundry bag.

"Will you come lie down on the couch, please?"

"Why?"

"That weird thing I said we had to do," he said and produced another bag, that one filled with blood. "This is it."

"Blood? You want me to give blood?"

He nodded. "I have a refrigeration unit behind the kick-plate here." He tapped his foot against the kick-plate under the sink. "I did one before joining Zeus. This is the second," he said, raising his blood bag again. "If you do one now, that gives us three."

"I don't understand. My blood has to be living."

"For JARR, yes," he said. "These are for you."

"So you can replace my blood after," she said on a rush of breath.

"We have medical facilities at Beta, but our blood

stores were lost. We also don't know for sure that we'll be able to hang around at Beta after JARR has been accessed. If we're on the move and have stores at hand, I can treat you."

"Daire—"

"I need this," he said. "I need to plan for every eventuality. It's not much, but… H is A positive, and you can have as much of mine as you need. Styx knows how to set up a transfusion."

They still didn't know if Harry and Styx were alive. But that was a worry for later. How could he keep doing this to her? Just after she told him to keep things professional, there he was declaring he'd bleed himself dry for her.

Rather than argue with him, she went to sit on the couch and offered her arm. "Thank you," she said when he crouched next to her.

He didn't look at her. "It's just a precaution," he said. "It'll sting for a second." She averted her eyes as he pushed the needle in. "I don't know how long H will need to get the guys back in shape. He wanted longer before we split with our detachments. The more time we can give them the better. If that's as much as two months, we'll donate again. Styx and I talked about the need to do this when we were planning the mission. He should get the guys who can to donate as much as possible."

He really did plan for everything. Blood. It wouldn't have occurred to her. JARR needed living blood, but if they stored it right, she could be replenished by any compatible blood.

She wanted to reach out, to run her fingers into his hair and show her gratitude. Keeping their distance might be difficult for her, but wasn't it exactly what he'd asked for? By refusing to talk in detail about his time with Zeus and his feelings on their separation, he was compartmentalizing. Right now, he needed to be mission oriented. The future he didn't want to talk about? That would have to be reserved for later. If there was a later.

SEVENTEEN

"ANYTHING?"

She already knew the answer. His brow had been pulled down when he opened the newspaper. In the three or four times he'd gone through it, his scowl only darkened in hue.

"No," he said, closing the newspaper to toss it into the backseat of the truck.

"It's been five days," she said, reluctant to say what had to be said. "They're dead, aren't they?"

"We don't know that," he said, nodding ahead. "You want me to go in here alone?"

The Rotunda loomed large before them. This was it, the moment they'd find out if she was right… or not. After five days on the road, the pressure was immense. She had to be right.

"I can do it."

"No need," he said, grabbing for the doorhandle. "I'll just be a minute."

For a brief moment, she considered jumping out after him and following him across the parking lot. What would be the point? He was a man on a mission, growing more and more distant every day. Sheer desire for his happiness wasn't enough. No matter how she tried to will it, bringing him peace was impossible.

He needed rest. Since their bloodletting, he hadn't set foot in the Beast. Not for a second. Not for anything. The only place he slept was in the front seat. Ready to drive again at any moment.

If they got the key, they'd have to turn around and go back the way they'd come, just like before. She'd mentioned flying, getting this over and done with as quickly as possible, but he'd reminded her Harry and Styx needed time with the men. To train. To plan.

And maybe some part of him didn't want to face the truth. A part of her felt the same. Every day they stopped for coffee and bought a newspaper. Every day Daire pored over each word. Nothing. She might think he was withholding something or trying to protect her by concealing a message, but his mood said it all. The dark cloud hovering over him grew denser and gloomier every day.

Without Harry, without Styx, it was on him to do it alone. She didn't know if that was possible. Even if they got the key and back to Beta to lock the building down, they'd still have to leave it at some point. Maybe Daire could destroy JARR and extract Minotaur… though without Exile, they may not complete the former. If they didn't, some as yet unknown hell would be unleashed. Fighting that alone would be impossible.

But for argument's sake, even if they completed both, they'd still have to leave Beta. Zeus would be lying in wait. Depending on how long it took, he may have rebuilt his ranks. Byron may provide personnel… How would Daire fight his way through all of them and protect her at the same time?

She'd never felt like such a weight around his neck. When he had Styx on side, working in the background, there was focus, possibility. With each day that went by, that prospect, the hope they'd triumph got dimmer and dimmer.

Just like he said, it only took a minute. Sort of seemed like a lifetime, but there he was, striding across the parking lot toward her again. It didn't appear there was anything in his hands. Maybe he'd put it in a pocket to conceal it from anyone who may be watching. Though who would be?

He opened the door and got back in. His still furrowed brow didn't bode well.

"Did you get it?" she asked, bracing for the answer.

"Wasn't there."

"Shit," she said, dropping back in her seat.

"It was too obvious. I should've trusted my instincts."

"Don't beat yourself up," she said, gravity growing stronger. "This was on me. Goddamnit."

What came next? Nothing. How could she be so wrong? Frustrated with herself, she got out of the stifling truck hoping to breathe easier. How could she? Why should she? Her father was dead. Their other ally as well. And they had no way to access what they needed.

South America came to mind. Making a run for it. But even that was shot to shit because she'd put limitations on them. Professional? Who was she kidding? Every part of her life was a hot mess.

His door closed too, jolting the truck she leaned on.

"You have to think."

"Don't," she said, walking away from the truck.

"We need a directive." And he was looking to her to provide it. "Tess."

Grabbing her arm, he hauled her back. Her Heart. He was looking to her. In need of guidance.

Something else crowded her emotions. "I need you to tell me the truth… Are they dead?"

"I don't know," he said. "I have no way to know that for sure."

"What does your gut say? You're good at this. You know how to—"

"I can't divine intel from nowhere," he snapped, his hand dropping from her arm. "Could they be dead? Yes! It's possible all of them are dead."

At Beta, they'd walked past the compound and possibly their allies' corpses without realizing it.

"Oh God," she said, nausea rising in her belly.

"Don't worry about H," he said, tempering his words.

"Unless Styx clued him in on the mission, he's still in the dark. H wouldn't send a message even if he read mine because he won't trust it."

Okay, that was something. "And Styx?" she asked, reading the answer in his flat affect. "It's my fault."

Turning her back on him, she tried to keep the tears from her eyes.

"Your fault? How is it your fault?"

"Because he would've been looking for me. The only reason he'd be stuck in there—"

"If that's true, I'm the one at fault. I made it clear you were the primary objective. But we don't know anything." When she turned to him again, the tension was back in his form. "If he is dead, it's possible there was a shoot-out. Possible someone took him by surprise. Possible he was outnumbered."

And Styx had already endured more than a beating at Beta. Had they expected too much too soon?

"He was alone." Her words grated the inside of her throat. "He died alone."

"You don't know that either," he said, but took a pause that wasn't encouraging. "If H went down too, he went down with him. They went down together."

"You just said we didn't have to worry about H."

"We don't. Not yet. He's a stubborn bastard. Both of them are. If anyone made it out of there, I'd put my money on them."

"Funny, Styx said something similar about you."

"All we can do now is work to complete our objectives. We need to know where that key is. I can do anything, Tess. Anything you tell me to. I just need direction."

The desperation of his strained plea spoke to his own torment. None of this was easy. He was supposed to be her guiding light. Yet he worked best when he was focused. Right now, she was the only one able to give him direction.

"I never wanted to be your master," she whispered.

He must have sensed her disappointment in herself because he softened. "You can do this. I know you can."

The super-agent stuff was always someone else's

responsibility. Giving her blood was easy. But if the cause rested on her ability to decipher a secret signal, they were monumentally screwed.

"I can't give you an answer," she said. "I don't know."

"Okay," he said, standing down, releasing some of his tension. "Let's go inside and have something to eat."

"Something to eat?"

"Sure," he said, stepping aside.

"How will that help?"

"Are you hungry?"

Her stomach growled. "Yes."

"Then come on."

They went inside, got a table, rather than sitting at the counter, and ordered.

"You can recite entire conversations," she said. "My memory isn't—"

"Don't worry about it," he said, watching the skaters. "Want to go on the rink after we've eaten?"

Like they didn't have a care in the world. Why was he so calm? Maybe it was a psychotic break, the guy was running on very little sleep.

"We could try the house. Harry's house... We weren't there for long and I don't know where he'd stash something, but we could look." His head went back. "We spent most of the time in vehicles and it wasn't always the same one... We wouldn't be able to track those vehicles down, would we?"

"I see why your mother called it the glitter."

"Daire," she said, moving from opposite him to the chair perpendicular. "What's wrong?"

"Nothing's wrong, baby," he said, then faltered. "Sorry."

"Is that what it is? Us? I'm not mad at you..." Though she was a little. "I didn't say what I said about being professional because I don't love you." Edging closer, she hooked her pinkie around his on his thigh. "You need to be objective. I get that. I am trying to give you what you need."

"Yelling at you won't help you remember. Forcing it

won't help either. Sometimes what you need to do is think about something else. Something completely different. Take the pressure off."

The yelling hadn't helped. Would clearing her mind do it?

Their food came and both began to eat.

"Would you look at me?" she asked. His eyes rose to hers. "You don't look at me when we're at odds."

He swallowed his food. "I don't like disappointing you."

"I know."

"And I get mad when I read hurt in your eyes... mostly at myself, which makes things difficult. I can't kill myself."

That altered the already tense mood. Because he could, just like she could, and they might end up there... sooner than they wanted to if she didn't figure out the location of the key.

She pushed her plate away and set her elbows on the table. "Remember when we were here together before?" He nodded. "That blonde wanted to sleep with you."

The corner of his mouth curled. "Yeah, but you took care of that quick."

"I was a woman on a mission."

"I remember."

They shared a smile. Everything seemed so much easier when they were happy with each other.

"And I found my mother's letter... You took on a lot for me that night, I never said thank you."

"You did."

"Not to Daire," she said.

Their eyes met again.

Distracting himself, he tried to push her plate closer. "You should eat."

"Why did you do that for me? In the Beast? Why let me cry all over you and calm me down? You didn't get sex and made me breakfast in the morning, why?"

"I'm a human being, Tess. It might not always seem like it when I'm doing my job, but... I cared about you. And

I meant what I said before we went into Beta. You don't deserve any of this."

"Do you?" she asked. "I don't think so."

When he took another bite of his burger and his attention returned to the skaters, she knew he wasn't going to answer.

"Harry said I can't reveal what I don't know… Maybe Styx didn't trust me with this. Maybe we're not thinking about it the right way. You're his brother. He knows what you're capable of. It would make more sense to tell you the secret, not me."

"How did you find out the previous location of the keys?"

"He told me a completely random story when we were in London… About you and Harry… I wanted to hear it, but he didn't know about us back then, so it was just… odd that he'd tell me something so personal." An idea straightened her. "Maybe he didn't move the keys at all. Maybe he just wanted you to think that he—"

"I checked," he said. "When I left you in the Beast, that was one of the things I did."

Okay, well, she'd got there just a little after him. "In D.C., he disappeared and came back with supplies. Guns, earpieces—"

"That was our cache for the Titan mission," Daire said. "We had a safe house."

"Should we check there?"

"If you want," he said. "Did he take you there or talk about it?" She shook her head. "It's unlikely he'd be that subtle."

And Daire had already ignored his instincts on that. Hence how they ended up in Miami at the Rotunda. Keyless.

"What about Fox Den?"

He nodded. "We can try there."

"Feels like you're humoring me."

"It won't be somewhere a lot of people know about," he said. "Fox Den is a flophouse for dozens of people. I didn't get the impression he trusted anyone there, not enough to give them this confidence."

"What about our apartment in Miami?"

"We're here, and in the absence of another target, I'll go round them all. Are you going to eat?"

"I'm not hungry."

"You were outside," he said. "You need your strength."

"I'll eat when you sleep," she said, crooking a brow at him.

"Don't think it's good form to dump someone then tell them what to do." He stood up, pushing his chair back with his legs as he scooped up a handful of fries. "If you won't relax, we should get back on the road."

Off he went while she just sat there. So she was supposed to pretend she didn't care? Wasn't supposed to have an opinion?

EIGHTEEN

"YOU DIDN'T TALK TO LUZ?" she asked when they were back in the truck, pulling out of the Rotunda's parking lot. "We could've stayed where we were like last time."

"It's the middle of the day, they'll want to keep their lot clear."

And it would be difficult to sleep if they were in a built-up area.

"Where do you want to park?"

"Somewhere familiar."

Twenty minutes later, she knew exactly where he was taking them. The RV park. Their RV park. Where they'd spent time together, doing nothing but enjoy each other. That time had been the closest to their dream, to living the life they'd choose. Or the life they would've chosen.

They were allotted a spot and Daire slotted them in without any trouble. He unhitched the truck and pulled it in beside the Beast. She didn't expect him to stay in the truck, but he killed the engine, took out the key, and reclined the seat.

"No," she said.

"No?"

"You've been doing this all week. You sleep in your seat for like an hour and then hit the road again. No more."

Opening her door, she was quick to jump out and go around to his side to open his. "You're going to get out and sleep in a bed."

"I don't need to sleep in a bed. Here is fine."

"For you maybe, not for me."

"Your panic button's in the nightstand just like every other night. You can sleep in the Beast."

"That's not what I meant. It's not right that you choose here when your home is beside us." She took his hand and tried to lead him out, but he stayed put, just looking at her. "What?"

"We've never slept in separate beds in the Beast."

So it would be traumatic for him, or did he think going into the Beast together meant they'd sleep together? Now that he'd pointed it out, the second possibility distracted her.

Stepping into the shadow of his door, she hooked his arm around her waist. "If you need me to lie with you, I will."

"I won't force you to do anything you're uncomfortable with."

The man was infuriating. "You're pouting."

Startled, his shoulders went back. "I'm what?"

"Pouting," she said. "And it just so happens, I have had enough sleep. I plan to stay up and write down as much as I can remember about the trip with Harry and Styx. We won't be sleeping in separate beds. You'll just be going to bed before me." Which they'd done before. Though usually it was the other way around. "This is important. You're better when you have sleep and I'm better when I don't have to worry about you."

Backing away, she coerced him out of the car using the arm she'd hooked around herself. He didn't let go, which was just fine by her. She took the keys from his hand before slipping her fingers between his and guiding him around the hood to the Beast's door.

The door slammed shut behind them and Daire locked it. Then it was… When they'd first brought Harry back to the Beast, when she'd learned Danny was Daire, the Beast felt claustrophobic. At least then they'd had her father around to keep things focused on business, on the problem.

Without moving a muscle, her eyes ascended to find his already on her. Damnit. In their home, their safe space, which had been restricted by her father and circumstance so often, it was difficult not to appreciate their freedom.

"Don't," he said.

She blinked in innocence. "Don't what?"

"Don't look at me like that," he said, tossing the keys on the counter and bending down to unlace his boots.

"I'm not looking at you like anything."

"You think I can't tell?" he asked, toeing off his boots, then grabbing them up to stash them in the closet.

"Can't tell what?"

He slammed the closet door. "What do you want from me, Tess?"

"Why are you yelling at me?"

"Because this is like its own kind of torture," he barked, running a hand through his hair. "I get it. I did shitty things. I didn't expect your forgiveness. I didn't—"

"Hey!" she said, marching up the center of the trailer. "You are the one who won't forgive yourself! I came back to you. I was yours! I am yours! Shit, baby, you think I like seeing you like this? What happened to my guy, huh? The guy who included me? The guy who trusted me?" Twisting around, she thrust a finger toward the couch where he liked to sit. "You are the one who sat right there and told me everything you knew about JARR! You said trust was your religion and—"

"I know! I lost your trust. You think I don't know that?"

She exhaled an ironic laugh. "Would you listen to me? Once upon a time, you were the only one who would. You were the only one who understood me! Who wanted to see things from my perspective! Now you've made up this narrative in your head and won't let it go. You won't forgive yourself, Daire! I wanted to talk about it! I wanted my guy back. The guy who never shied from sharing with me. Harry said I looked to you…" She took a breath. Crushing grief exploded inside her, instantly flooding her eyes. "You said you looked to me. You told him we were partners and I… I was so proud of us for making it. Everything wanted to tear us apart and we—" Her words lodged in her throat. She sniffed hard, resenting the shit out of her weakness. "We made it through everything... I thought we'd..."

"Don't cry," he said, rushing the last few feet to her, wiping the tears from her cheeks. "Please, baby, don't cry."

"I love you," she said, losing the fight. "Even when I tried not to, I... I've loved you through everything. Through every single second."

"I know," he murmured, his hand settling on her cheek. "I know, baby."

"But you want to be a stranger. You want to put up these walls and block me out. You've never done that! Never and I... I don't know how to reach you."

And that was what shattered her heart. They'd always worked. It always just... was. They understood each other's nuance. Making it work, forcing it, felt foreign. But she'd never felt like she was the only one pulling on the oar either. For the first time, he wasn't at her back, supporting her, holding them up with the same passion that burned in her.

"Everything I did before I met you, that was another life," he said, stroking her face. "I put it in a box and... It was the past. With you... everything was different. I was different. I knew I'd always do whatever it took to protect you, but I never thought I... I didn't think I'd have to deceive you in the way I did. And the truth is..."

"What's the truth?" she asked, fixated on his gaze while grabbing for the hand loose at his side.

"Even if I'd told you about the mission before, if Styx hadn't asked me not to... I don't think it would change anything. I would still feel this way."

"Because you never thought you'd be my jailer."

"No," he murmured.

"You didn't think you'd ever be the one locking my restraints..."

He swallowed. "With H and Styx, we've done the duplicity thing, we've all beaten the crap out of each other, for missions or training. I could forgive myself for that... I can't forgive myself for letting you witness it. For pushing you to such a desperate corner that you wanted to…"

"That I asked Styx to take my life." Something the brother wouldn't want her saying aloud. "My forgiveness isn't enough."

"You said you didn't want to leave me behind… I wanted you out of there so fast, it took every ounce of willpower not to come down to that room and bust you out myself. But then you were out in the world… all I could think about was your safety. If something happened to you and I wasn't there…"

"You're here now."

"No," he said, withdrawing his touch. "Because it was then I realized… I wasn't your protector. I was your pursuer. I was the threat you were afraid of."

"I was never afraid of you," she confessed. "After D.C., when I said it… Harry pitied me, told me I should be, but I couldn't do it… Locking a door is one thing, but I knew… I knew you could never put your hands on me in anger."

"Getting you out when we did saved me too," he said. "If he'd ordered me to…"

"We're not in that position and you have to stop reliving it. No one hurt me. Styx gave me comfort. He and my father kept me safe. And we're together again."

"You were right to stop this," he said, certainty tensing his muscles. "We should keep this professional. Staying in the truck, separating myself from you, it's the best thing I can do for you now."

"No," she said, shaking her head. "I know why you did what you did at Beta. I know why you gave Zeus the Scepter, why you had to hold us prisoner. I even understand why you had to hurt Harry and Styx. But this…" She gestured between them. "This I don't understand."

"You told me to stay away."

"Because I was scared! Because I am scared! I'm terrified!"

Concern lowered his brow. "Terrified of what?"

"Of losing you! What the hell am I supposed to do if something happens to you? I can't protect you! I can't keep you safe the way you keep me safe!"

"You're not safe," he snapped back. "You'll never be safe with me!"

"I'll never be safe without you! Damnit, the way you shut down, the way you… I know Ares is a different beast, that you compartmentalize and block off all distractions…" Her skin shivered. "These could be our last days together… You seem so damn determined to sacrifice your life… and for what? Is that your penance? Is that what you think you deserve for what you've done as Ares? What about me? What do I deserve?"

"You deserve to be free," he said. "You deserve to be happy."

She closed in to take his hand again. "The only way that happens is if we're together. And I don't mean physically, I don't mean like this. I mean like we were. I need you to come back to me. I need Daire back, my Daire. The man who loves me more than anything else."

"I love you," he said like it was an offense to question that.

"Really? Then where are you? After Fox Den, when I found out about H's message, when I was mad, accusing you of lying about being with me because of my father's orders, you wouldn't let me hide. Where's that guy? The guy who told me he was a resource at my disposal? That his primary mission was to keep me safe?"

"How was locking you up in Beta keeping you safe?" he asked. "Not much of a resource when I stood by and let them shoot you full of drugs."

"What did we learn?" she asked. "You got into Beta again. You got authorization codes from two principals, and you got up close intel on the men under Zeus now. You know what they're capable of, their weak spots and strengths. None of them can come at us now without you knowing exactly how to take them down. You also managed to get me out of there without cutting ties with Zeus. The only chance I have is you… Don't you see that? Don't you see why it's so hurtful that you talk about sacrificing yourself for the greater good? Even if I am that greater good, there is only one way I get out of this complete. That's with you at my side."

"I don't know how to fix this. It's never been… broken like this before."

"Nothing's too broken to fix, baby," she said, resting her hands on his chest. "You said you lived in me. If you're lost, broken, there's only one place you have to look for rescue, and that's in me."

The emotion in his eyes as he searched hers became almost desperation.

Adoration bled from behind his desolation. "Little Red…"

"Come back to me, baby… please."

She needed him more than even she'd realized. It wasn't about pride or triumph, they each had something the other needed. An intangible piece of them only became real within them when they were in sync.

He ducked a little closer and hesitated.

"Yes, you should," she whispered, showing a gentle smile. "You absolutely should."

Taking his head in her hands, she drew his mouth to hers. Professional wasn't going to save anyone. Losing each other would always devastate them. And he needed her, even if he didn't want to.

His arms came around her to lift her from the floor and take her to the bed. They couldn't do it. Couldn't be apart. Their home needed their hearts to belong. When they were at odds, neither of them truly existed.

His lips trailed down the side of her neck as his hands explored her body. Whatever he was looking for, she held it within her. Despite being unable to identify it, she'd hand it over without hesitation.

"I am yours," she murmured, her eyes closed as her head moved in time with his mouth traversing her throat.

He tucked his fingers under the hem of her top and drew it off as she helped him shed his. Their relationship had seen its share of roadblocks, but this… his own torment, she didn't know how to save him from himself.

As they wriggled from their pants, she gave him a push, rising enough to climb onto him as he lay down. This was her choice. Being with him. She'd neglected her duty. If he needed proof, certainty, that there was nothing in her world except him, she had to show him. She never wanted him to doubt it again.

NINETEEN

"YOU NEED TO FALL IN LOVE with me again," she said, watching their tangled fingers play.

Shifting his head on the pillow they shared, he looked at her. "I love you. I never fell out of love with you."

That wasn't exactly what she meant. "Was it difficult? Going back to Ares, working under Zeus?"

"Yes."

"And some of that was my fault," she said. "Because you could be you with me. The honest you." As she'd requested. "Reentry to Olympus was difficult because of me."

"Because I wanted to be with you. I always want to be with you."

Her head moved, so she could look him in the eye. "And that's what this is, reentry to us. It's a transition we've never really had to make before."

"I'm sorry."

Freeing her hand from his, she rolled over to tuck herself against him. "I don't want you to apologize anymore. No more sorry. There's nothing to apologize for. You did what you did for me. For us. I'm in awe of you, baby. I'm proud and grateful—"

"Okay," he said, tipping up her chin to kiss her lips.

"Don't lay it on too thick."

His smile was real. His whole being was more relaxed than it had been all week. Maybe it was the sex. Or the Beast. Or their location. She wanted to think their conversation had something to do with it.

"Did you think of me? When you went to Zeus?"

"I think of you every second, baby," he said, tracing his lips across hers. "I was more afraid of facing you than I was of cold-cocking H."

"He'd have loved that."

"Betraying our people was difficult, but they're soldiers. I at least had some hope they'd understand the need for my duplicity. Walking in on you…"

"Styx knew it," she said, unable to believe he'd played it so straight. "About three seconds before Zeus walked in, he told me to move. I thought we were going to run. Now I guess he was just putting on a good show."

"We knew Zeus would want you at Beta. The need for your blood kept you alive."

"And Styx concealing the location of the keys kept him alive," she said. "You knew where they were the whole time." He nodded and she breathed out. "The trust you two have… it's incredible. It didn't occur to you for a second to use them or to give Zeus the information. Styx knew you wouldn't. He trusted you so much that he took the beating. You knew where they were, you could've told Zeus Styx was useless any second, but you didn't. I knew it before, but seeing it in action… You trust him so much."

"If I didn't, you think I would've left him alone in bed with my girl?"

"I didn't—"

He kissed her again. "I trust both of you. You needed comfort. Your relationship with H is too messed up for you to rely on him."

"Actually, he was surprisingly comforting," she said.

Her father once said he knew Daire didn't love her because he'd never have been able to act in the same way with Carrie. She didn't need to tell her Heart that.

"When he wasn't yelling at you."

She laughed. "Right. And he still didn't want me to have the whole picture. He thinks he's protecting me, but it just… So many times I wished you were with us because I knew you'd include me. Where is Four by the way?"

"Four can disappear. It happens sometimes."

"How did you convince Zeus not to kill Harry's guys?"

"Wasn't that difficult," he said. "They're valuable and well-trained. Since the Exodus, there's been plenty of time for distance to grow between them and their Stratego. Some may have turned."

"You didn't give them the chance to join Zeus?"

"No!" he said. "Because the ultimate play is to back H. I couldn't set any of our guys up to be on the other side when I wasn't on the other side."

"Some of them might have followed you just because you're you."

He shrugged and used his chin to tuck her head under his. "Maybe."

"I would follow you," she said, rubbing her face against his throat.

"I made a choice," he said, his voice a little deeper. "You said you'd have come with me if I asked. I chose not to ask. I could've taken you with me, but it was too big a risk."

"Because Zeus knowing you cared about me would give him a weakness to exploit."

"It's one thing when he's spouting orders and only I suffer for it. But Z is… he's sick."

"He enjoys others pain," she said. "I've noticed that about him."

"I didn't ask you to come with me to protect you from that. The less direct exposure you have to Z, and Olympus, the better."

She kissed his throat. "Can we talk about what happened at the hotel? About Merrill?"

"If you want," he said. "But there isn't much to say."

"Of course there is," she said, wriggling back in his embrace to meet his gaze again. "He's your biological father. The way Zeus set you up, to have you in that room without warning…"

"He's sick, Little Red."

"I know, but… When I think about… I get so mad! He didn't even set it up so you could meet in safe, positive circumstances. He didn't even pretend he was doing either of you a favor, it was all about him."

"He wants to put a wedge between me and H."

"Like you haven't proven yourself to Z?" she asked. "There's a wedge there already."

"Yeah, but he needs me to pull the trigger… and soon. If I hesitate…"

"If you hesitate, what?" she asked, her fingertips meeting his jaw to encourage his attention back to hers.

"Z doesn't want to doubt. And, I'd say, after Zulu he's paranoid. He trusted me at Beta. It took time, but I'd say he did relax and believe I wanted Olympus back, and under his leadership. Me walking away—"

"He had no choice. He knows what the rest of us have known forever. If you wanted to take over and leave the principals in the dust, you could. They almost did their job too well. You're stronger and smarter than all of them. Olympus is more yours than anyone else's. If you want to build it up and keep it for yourself, you can. If you want to burn it to the ground, it's yours to do that too."

"There is nothing after this," he said, his eyes probing hers. "Do you understand that?"

"Are we going to talk about your readiness to sacrifice yourself again?" she asked, repelled. "Please don't bring that sadness back to our bed, my Heart."

"No," he said and smiled as he stroked her hair. "I meant there's no Olympus after this. If you and I make it through, we're doing South America. We're getting away from everything and everyone in our past life and building the life we want together." She wanted to clarify he didn't mean get away from Styx and H. Except that only reminded her of their probable demises. If they were dead, they couldn't have relationships with anyone. "Or not."

Her attention leaped to his frown. "No, I wasn't…" She showed him a broad smile. "That's perfect. Exactly what

I want."

"You got all serious for a second. If you'd rather we—"

"No," she said, guiding his mouth to hers. "I want that. I want you and us making our own future." Pushing up, she deepened the kiss until his arms came around her and he shifted her onto her back. They could get lost in each other. Right there, in that special place, they were themselves. She eased from their kiss. "What about Merrill?"

"What about him?" he asked, skimming his lips across hers.

"Do you want a relationship with him? He might know things about your mother—"

"I know about my mother," he said. "I know who she was. I read her service record and her mission reports."

"Were there reports about Merrill? About Buford?"

"No," he said. "Which was enough to confirm I was conceived on a mission." A shiver went through her. "It's okay." His nose brushed hers, tempting her mouth higher. "She was dedicated to Olympus. I knew the story of Hades and Helen; I knew love wasn't afforded to those in our position… I knew enough from her service record too that if she wanted to be with someone or free of Olympus, she'd have found a way."

"Do you think she was scared?"

"When she found out she was pregnant? Maybe. It wasn't part of the plan." He paused, his head tilting the opposite way. "I guess I don't know that for sure."

"I wish you could've known her… My relationship with my mother was so vital. So important to me."

Rolling away from her, he opened his nightstand drawer, something slid along wood, then he came back, holding his hand up between them. "It still is," he said. "I know that."

When her pendant dropped from his fingers, it was impossible to subdue her elation. "You kept it safe!"

"I kept it safe."

She smiled as he put the chain over her head. "Where's the rest of her?"

"In the truck," he said. "Has been all week."

"I don't understand." The point was to hide anything personal that could be connected to them. "Weren't you worried someone might find her?"

"I buried her," he said. "Picked her up before we left... When I was checking for the keys."

"You buried her," she said, he braced for her reaction. "Where?"

"In our spot," he said. "Behind the rock at the tree line where you left your clothes safe and dry when we went skinny-dipping."

She remembered using the words *"safe and dry"* and being teased for them. "You're incredible." She kissed him again. "You even keep a dead woman safe."

"I know what she means to you."

Present tense, not past. "That's why I wish you could've known your own mother. Was there anything in there about Merrill? What came at the end of her service record and mission reports? Did her file just stop? No explanation?"

"Yeah. And the dates didn't add up. The last two years of her life were unaccounted for."

"So you knew they were hiding something."

"I did."

"Why didn't you follow up? Look deeper into it? Find out the truth?"

"You know better than just about anyone that my relationship with H hasn't always been the best. I didn't want to invite trouble. She died a long time ago. And until the Exodus, until you, I always believed there was no life for me outside Olympus. Why make a sometimes fraught situation worse? I figured I was the product of a mission. And, again, before you, all of my encounters with women were Olympus related. No reason to believe my mother's life was any different. She still chose me, chose to have me. Until Zeus's play in the hotel, I was never leveraged against anyone. So whoever my father was, I hadn't been born to take him down... That's what I always believed anyway."

"Until now. Now Zeus is trying to use you against

him."

"He can try, but it won't work."

"It could. Isn't there DNA evidence that you're his son?"

"My DNA is stored in the Olympus vault," he said. "But I've never seen it matched to a father. For the extortion play to work, I have to be present. I have to be willing… That won't happen. Z can announce to the world that Merrill has a secret son, yes. He can even provide DNA proof… if we let him into Olympus. But I won't stand in front of the cameras and stir the pot, I couldn't care less about Merrill or him having a place with the Six."

"Because once this is done, we're done with Olympus."

"Right," he said, kissing her again.

Given the greatest threat to Olympus was exposure, it was unlikely Zeus wanted to put himself in front of a camera and open himself to scrutiny.

She laid her hands on his chest, pressuring back enough to talk. "You know, he's a criminal. And not just a petty criminal either."

"Buford took the fall for Merrill's crimes?" he asked. She nodded. "It's funny. Before, maybe I would've been intent on putting him where he belongs."

"And for what was done by Byron Senior. I'm pretty sure getting rid of Buford was a political play."

"It absolutely would've been, yes," he said and sighed. "It's all so long ago. Who benefits from the scandal?"

"Buford's family might like to know the truth, that their relative wasn't a traitor."

Though Buford was responsible for razing Alpha to the ground. The guy may not be a saint, but he had just had his career and reputation blown to pieces by Olympus. It wasn't any wonder the guy wanted his revenge.

"When we're in Beta, I'll see what I can dig up," Daire said. "We can send it anonymously to sources who'll get to the truth… if that's what you want."

"I want what will make you happy," she said, squeezing her arms from between them to coil them around his neck. "I don't want you pushing your feelings aside or hiding them from me. You have a right to be mad that no one ever told you the truth."

"I didn't ask," he said, magnanimous in his honesty. "I could've pushed. If I wanted to, I could've cornered H about it."

"But he taught you not to ask questions you didn't want the answer to," she said, trying to subdue her smile. "Sometimes you really are his son, you know."

"Was I curious? Of course."

"You do like to know things."

"I do. But who would've benefited? If the information wasn't offered to me, it was nothing good. Who benefited from me asking questions and learning truths that would disrupt my home? Remember, before the Exodus, Olympus was my life. I didn't want to lose it. Olympus was all I had."

"You could ask now," she said. "If we get through this, if H is alive... He'll tell you if you ask."

"I might," he said. "But if we both get through this, there will be other considerations."

"Such as?"

"Such as..." He kissed her. "Do you have enough bikinis and sunscreen to make it through our trip?"

Her lips curled and she pulled him closer. "Your something to live for," she murmured against his mouth. "I need you, baby."

"Whatever it takes."

"Whatever it takes," she agreed and surrendered to his kiss.

The world and all its troubles seemed so far away. This was what she wanted. He was what she wanted. Visiting the Rotunda again, returning to Miami, it was their time in a bubble. Freedom from their chains.

If he'd checked in the locker, he'd have got her letter. She hadn't seen it. Had he read it? Maybe he was saving it for another time. She wouldn't blame him for leaving it there either. With so much uncertainty ahead, concealing the truth of their love could be vital. It wouldn't pay to leave evidence lying around.

Though she was grateful his letter to her couldn't be found by interested parties, she would love to read it again. To relive his love in those words. Maybe one day she would…

She broke their kiss.

"Baby?" Daire asked, his voice gruff and definitely ready for something more intimate.

"Oh my God," she whispered, pushing him back so she could sit up.

"What?" He rose beside her. "What's wrong?"

She exhaled a laugh and turned to him. "I know where the key is."

It took a second, but his dimples gradually came into view. "Told you if you thought about something else it would come to you."

"You…" she said, raising a hand to his cheek. "You're the only one who can put me at peace like that." They enjoyed inspecting each other for a second before she winced. "It means driving across the country again."

"We have to do that to get to Beta anyway," he said, taking her hand. "We're going back that way."

"Should we go now?" she asked. "Do you want to move fast?"

"What I want…? Is to try that seafood place and spend the night with my girl."

"It can wait?"

"It can wait," he said, using his body to ease her onto her back again.

TWENTY

"I THOUGHT YOU and Earl had a fight," she said as Daire navigated the trailer around to the back of the office building she'd met Danny in.

"Earl loves me. All the guys here love me," he said, backing up a little more. "If I don't have to cut ties with an asset, I don't. It can pay to have allies in different areas."

"So you lied to me?"

He paused to check her teasing expression. "Only to get in your pants, baby."

His wink made her laugh. "You'd been in my pants by then. Plenty."

"Yeah, but I wanted to keep getting in there."

"What would you have done if I said no? If I was completely categoric about you not coming with me?"

"I wouldn't have taken no for an answer," he said. "If I had to follow you, I would've followed you... I'll always follow you." He killed the engine. "You want to come in and say hey or go take a breather?"

"I think I'll pass on hanging with your stoner friends," she said, leaning over the center console. "I'm going to scrounge up some food in the Beast. We'll eat and take a walk over... unless you don't want to come with me."

"Do you need ID?" he asked. "I'll put something together if you don't have anything on—"

"It's thumbprint accessible," she said. "Which is great for someone like me."

"Yeah, you can change your name, no problem. Your fingerprints are trickier."

"Try impossible."

His head shifted to the side. "No, not impossible."

"Okay, no more freaking me out." Curling her fingers into his shirt, she pulled him closer. "Kiss me goodbye."

"No goodbye," he said and gave her a quick peck. "That's as much as you're getting before we're back there alone. You know what happens when I give you more."

All week had been the same story. She'd lost count of how many times they'd pulled over to have sex in places they really shouldn't pull over at all, let alone to do… that.

"It's sort of sexy though," she said, taking off her seatbelt as he did the same. "Being back here, where we met."

"Baby, the way we're going, there's nothing we can't make sexy."

"Like when you were drinking that water?" she asked, reaching over to press both hands on his thigh. "Driving and drinking and your throat—"

"Okay, yeah, see, that," he said, snickering as he picked up her hand to kiss her palm. "Show me your panic button."

She retrieved it from the glovebox and hooked it around her thumb. "Safe."

He kissed her again and got out to come around and open her door. "I'll be ten minutes, tops, okay?"

"I know we want me to be right," she said, her hand in his as he closed the truck door and led her around to the Beast. "But there's a chance—"

"Don't second guess yourself. You were sure when you thought of it. Optimistic. Don't doubt yourself."

She'd gone back and forth between the two. Sometimes it felt like the most obvious and certain place in the world. Yet she was hyperaware of their useless trip to Miami. They'd driven across the continent on her completely inaccurate intel.

He unlocked the door and opened it to lift her inside without freeing the stairs. "Have something to eat. I'll be back."

He closed the door. She was almost tempted to go open the shades to watch him until the last second. Their love was more than combustible these days. Yes, it was amazing to be so hot for each other, but she did her best to ignore the reason.

They'd lost each other. Though it had only been for a short time, that was enough. If she was right about the key being where she thought, that would be a victory. Or would it? As she made sandwiches for them both, she considered returning to Beta. To sneaking in as they had before… What would it mean? Going inside would alert Zeus and Garrick that Beta was up and running again. Would they expect to saunter back in? What would happen if Daire didn't let them inside?

What would they find there? Bodies. Maybe the bodies of people they cared about. It almost didn't bear thinking about. Her father and Styx might be lying there, in wait. Unliving. An omen of what could be their future.

Beta could be the last building she ever entered. Crossing the threshold could be the same as signing her death warrant. At least with Daire it would be her choice. If Zeus had her, he'd force her, push her further than was required just for his own sick pleasure. The principal already said the truth aloud. His plan was to kill her. As soon as JARR was accessed, she was as good as dead.

With the sandwiches on the table, she crouched to retrieve the doctor's bible from behind the kitchen kick-plate. Daire had pored over every page, understanding every symbol like it was plain English.

Sitting in the dinette, she took a bite of her sandwich and opened the notebook. It didn't mean much. Her Heart had translated some symbols for her. When they lay in bed together, he'd read sections aloud. Most of it was scientific gobbledygook, but it felt good to be included. Usually, she fell asleep. God only knew how much longer her love remained awake after her.

Though he didn't say it, the pressure of what was to come was getting to him. Without word from Styx, he had to be feeling isolated. Survival could rest on his shoulders. Not just theirs, but the whole of humanity. She wanted to be a comfort, a support for him, but what could she do? When the moment came to hook her up to the JARR machine, he'd be alone. He couldn't keep their enemies at bay and care for her too.

The door opened just as she took the last bite of her sandwich.

"Time to go."

Sliding to the end of the seat, she had to boost up a little to see him leaning in from outside. "You're not coming in? I made food for you."

"Bring it," he said. "Sooner we get there, sooner we know."

"Okay, I have to put this away."

Down she went to return the bible to its hiding place.

"What were you looking for in the doc's notes?" he asked.

Although he couldn't have seen the notebook, he'd have heard where she put it and deduced what she'd been reading. "Nothing in particular."

The plates she put on the sink cover would bother him when they got back, but there wasn't time to wash them. She gathered his sandwich and went to put an arm around him so he could help her down.

"It'll be soon," he said, locking the door then taking half his sandwich from her. "Are you worried?"

"It's difficult to be scared of something when you have no idea what to expect."

He ate his sandwich as they walked from Buckhorn and headed deeper into town.

"I'll show you around Beta and the JARR system," he said. "Make sure you understand what every part does before we start. And I'll show you the route to the nearest exit. I will make you walk it over and over until I'm sure you've got it."

"If this machine needs so much of my blood, it's

possible I won't make it out even if I do know the route."

"It will make me feel better," he said between bites.

"I'm not saying I won't do it, but… We'll have to adjust the plan if we don't have Styx and my father backing us up. If they died in the raid, the team they're putting together probably didn't hang around to help us."

"Garrick didn't bring the Zone device to the Merrill meeting. That means it's still in Beta."

"You think you can track some of your guys? Your original guys? Harry's guys."

"Maybe. Except the problem is…"

"You duped them once before," she said on a sigh. "They trusted you when you walked them into Zeus's trap."

"Right."

"Now it might seem opportunistic to switch sides and feed them the, 'this was a secret plan between Styx and I,' line."

"Fool me once…"

"What about the others? Exile? Could you get in touch with him?"

"Yeah," he said. "Maybe. He doesn't like me."

"Why not?"

"I don't bend rules… typically."

"You're much more flexible now," she said. "I'm against the rules and you do me all the time."

He glanced her way, flashing a dimple as he took the other half of his sandwich and tossed an arm around her shoulders. "And do we plan to tell him that?"

"Why not? If you trust his love, why shouldn't he trust yours?"

"Maybe 'cause I imprisoned mine. Not a lot of guys in love would understand that."

"Kero will understand that level of trust… if she loves Exile too… He got her out of captivity, and you've done the same for me."

"Difference is, he didn't put her there." He stopped to turn toward her. "Did he bring her? Did you meet her?"

She shook her head. "No." Before he could start walking again, she caught his pinkie with hers to keep him in place. "Styx told him about you, that he had a man on the inside. If we tell Exile you're that guy, it might be enough to convince him to work with us. That way he knows it's a mission and you're not flipping sides."

"Maybe."

They started walking again. "He has a link to the Laird, but so do you…" He didn't say anything. "Who's the Laird?"

"Prison warden," he said. "Sort of."

"What's sort of?"

"His prison isn't official or on any record. It's hidden. In the mountains. Far from anywhere it could be found."

"What is it for? Who funds it?"

"He does," Daire said. "Him and the assets of his prisoners… or those who want them held."

"That's terrifying. That someone could be locked up without due process."

"You surprise me, baby. After all you've seen, it should encourage you that there's at least someone trying to keep order of what goes on outside the mainstream. The Laird doesn't act on maybes. He has a team of people who adhere to strict criteria. If someone doesn't meet the criteria, they're not taken there."

He had a point. Olympus was a secret. How many other organizations and groups existed where people operated with impunity, believing themselves above the law? And they may be. With connections like Zeus had, he could probably get himself out of any official jam in a jiffy.

"Is that the plan? To imprison Zeus?"

"Unlikely," he said, finishing the sandwich. "But we have to be prepared for any eventuality. The Six may have to be taken care of too."

"Two and Five are new. Wouldn't it be unjust to tar them with the crimes of their predecessors?"

"Maybe."

"Right. Maybe. We're not operating in black and white and don't know how this will play out."

"Exactly," he said, pulling her closer to kiss the top of her head.

"What about Swift? Who's that?"

"Swift is…" He inhaled through his nose and held the breath before releasing it from his mouth. "Exile's counterpoint… sort of. He's as skilled with tech, but less… mercenary about it."

"So Exile is more about himself?"

"And Kero. Yes… Swift works with a group… a private group."

"Like Olympus?"

"No, the Kindred are much smaller scale, but often just as effective. They're close knit and have the skills to take down a threat like Zeus… in theory."

"Theory?"

"We're operating without a net," he said. "And if Styx didn't make it, it's possible the Kindred are doing their own investigation. They wouldn't drop a lead on a global threat, regardless of who was alive or dead. But I don't know what they know, how much Styx told them, and getting in touch with them is—"

He stopped again. Both speaking and walking.

"What?" she asked, curling in close to stand against him. "Getting in touch with them is… what?"

He exhaled a laugh. "What a fucking idiot."

"Excuse me?"

"Not you," he said, cradling the back of her head to pull her in and kiss her hairline. "Me. I'm the fucking idiot."

"Why?"

"They're alive."

"Who's alive?"

"Styx," he said, a smile in his eyes when they met hers. "And H."

"They are?" she asked, filled with relief. "How do you know?"

"I don't," he said. "But I know how to find out… I know where to look."

"Where?"

"We need a helicopter."

Another helicopter?

He put his arm around her to get them moving again.

Each step led to the next, down the asphalt and on their journey. For now, they had to worry about the key. If she was right and they got that, the next step would take them on their travels again. Though she didn't know why they had to abandon the Beast and take to the air. He'd explain that… or he wouldn't. Wherever they went, they'd be safe. She'd be safe. With him at her side.

The post office was still there. Good. Progress. Sort of. No reason it wouldn't be. Only a few months had gone by since she had last been there. Somehow, it felt longer. She'd changed so much, some part of her maybe expected the world around her to change too. But, no, it carried on as normal. Unaffected. Hopefully, that would last.

She gave her details to the woman behind the counter and used her thumbprint to clear security. The woman disappeared into the back.

"I guess we'll know soon," she said, nerves dancing like ants in her belly. "If I'm completely wrong again—"

"Have faith in yourself, Little Red. I do."

In that moment, it was his duty to tell her he was nothing but confident. Optimism alone wasn't enough to get them what they wanted. Still, her anxiety eased when he pulled her closer. Love. For all the trouble it caused in her life, she wouldn't choose to be without it.

"I don't want to let you down," she murmured against him.

"You couldn't if you tried," he said, stroking her back. "Whatever happens, we'll get through it."

And that was about more than just the next ten minutes. Whatever happened… It didn't bear thinking about.

Seconds ticked by until it felt like an age had passed. Eventually the woman returned to the counter with a stack of mail.

So as not to hold up the line of people behind them, they took the pile to the table affixed to the wall. There, people could fill out forms or do whatever they needed behind semi-private screens positioned at regular intervals.

She tossed aside the skinny envelopes, pausing for a moment on the one bearing her handwriting. Daire's letter.

Beneath it was a small bubble mailer.

Daire squeezed her shoulders. "That's his handwriting."

Relief. The weight in the envelope further confirmed what was inside. "Thank God."

"Are you going to open it?"

Was she? That was the whole point of them being there. "No. Not here, out in the open."

The secret-agent stuff might not be her purview, but she felt exposed. Not vulnerable, Daire was with her, so she was definitely safe. That just wasn't the place to go flashing things around.

"Okay," he said. She gathered everything up and slipped it into her purse. "Let's get out of here."

Because they had to find a chopper, apparently. Daire knew where their family was. Or he thought he did. She wanted to see them, so much, to know they were okay. But if they weren't, wherever they went next, they'd have to face that reality too. Have heart, wasn't that what her father said to reassure her? They were okay... they had to be.

TWENTY-ONE

PAY ENOUGH and you can get just about anything. That was Daire's explanation while choosing a helicopter emblazoned with a specific company's name. He needed it and that meant bribing a guy. Unfortunately, there wasn't time to ask more about the why. Once they were in the air, casual chitchat seemed inappropriate.

Land gave way to sea. She couldn't see anything beyond and had to wonder where they were going. What was the range of a helicopter? Surely not as much as a plane. Being out over the vast water was unnerving. Just as her anxiety edged toward fever pitch, she saw it, an island. Out there, surrounded by the blue, gray waters. Was that it? Their destination?

Yes.

They landed in a clearing near the shore. Daire switched everything off and got out to come around and open her door.

"What is this place?" she asked, her hands staying on his body even after her feet were on solid ground. "I don't understand how they would know…" Obstacles penned them in from every side. Wherever there wasn't forest, there was wild, dark water. "How could they survive here? It's so…

harsh. How would they survive—"

"You trust me?" he asked, bending his knees to align their eyes. "You have to do everything I say if we're going to get over the threshold alive."

"Threshold? What threshold?"

"Stay close," he said, taking her hand to tuck it in at his lower back as he hustled into the trees.

Still confused, she did as he said. He had direction so had to know where he was going, but she didn't get it until they reached the tree line and he stopped. Up ahead, across a clearing, stood the most magnificent house she'd ever seen. Gray, gothic, it was beautiful and terrifying at the same time.

"Oh my God," she said on a rush of breath. "What is this place?"

"My tomb if Maverick is watching," he muttered, crouching to assess the area. "We should've brought a white flag."

Dread straightened her shoulders. "I don't like this. If it's dangerous, we shouldn't take the risk. Let's go back."

"Here's hoping, brother," Daire said to himself, rising to snag her hand again.

His speed increased as he rushed them across the exposed area, past a smaller stone structure and on to the grand double doors in the middle of the main building.

"Should we knock?" she asked when he touched one of the doorhandles. "Seems rude not to."

"Trust me, they already know we're here," he whispered. "I'm still alive, which is a good sign they're willing to hear me out."

"We were quick, if—"

"Speed doesn't matter," he said, fixing her in his sights. "Raven doesn't miss." Ducking, he kissed her quick. "Stay behind me and follow my lead." He smiled. "And if they put a bullet in me the minute I open the door, I love you, it's been swell."

There couldn't be a more inappropriate moment for a joke. She didn't have time to tell him that because he turned the handle and popped one of the doors from the other. Unlocked. A good sign? If they weren't allowed in, they wouldn't leave the door unlocked, would they? Though, being out there, far from land, they might think locking the door would be redundant.

Daire opened the door further, tucking her in at his back and creeping forward. Just as he stepped over the threshold, someone cocked a gun.

"You twitch, I pull."

The growl of menace stopped them both. Well, it stopped her. When she peeked up, she just saw the barrel of a handgun against her Heart's temple. Whoever held it hid against the unopened door. Terror infused her so fast she squeezed his hand hard.

"It's okay, LR," Daire said, returning her squeeze. "Just relax."

"Tell me why I shouldn't put a bullet in you right here," the growler asked.

"I'm looking for my brother."

"That's not an answer," the growl grew deeper.

"I have the necessary package."

"All the more reason I should take you out the picture."

"Your wife here?"

"Mention her again and I'll do it with my bare hands."

"She's always more reasonable," Daire said.

Snatching her hand out of his, she ran around to put herself between her Heart and the huge, gun-toting guy with his back to the static door.

"Please hear him out," she said, wishing she could do a better job of protecting Daire. As it was, the broad man with his sights fixed on her Heart didn't even have to adjust his angle, she was too short to get in front of the weapon. "Don't hurt him."

"I told you to stay behind me," Daire said, putting an arm around her to pull her back against him.

"If he shoots you, I'm fodder, where the hell would I go?" she asked. Unable to fly a helicopter, it wasn't like she could make a run for it. "Why didn't you bring a weapon?"

He took one everywhere else and they hadn't been threatened anywhere except there.

"If I was armed, I'd be dead already," Daire said. "Right, Raven?"

"You've got some nerve showing up here."

"No, not nerve," Daire said. "Faith, in my brother."

Another sound caught her attention. For the first time, she took in the spectacle of the grand cavernous foyer. It was incredible. Stone stairs with an ornate banister went up so far then turned in two separate staircases perpendicular to the first. Those flights led to a mezzanine that overlooked the... Someone was up there, another figure, loitering in the shadows.

Let's get out of here," she said, fumbling behind her for Daire's hand. "Let's just walk away."

"We're safe here," Daire said. "The Kindred want the intel they can only get from me. Doesn't matter that Styx didn't tell—"

"He told us," this Raven said. "After spending time in the enemy's camp, I need to know you didn't drink the Kool-Aid."

"I wouldn't be here if he had," she said, anger rising, despite her attempt to subdue it. "You know how valuable I am to this? He wouldn't risk bringing me here if he was loyal to the enemy."

"We need to know if they're alive," Daire said. "Things get dicey from here on out without back up. If I'm on my own, I need to know."

Easing away from the door, Raven put a meter or so of space between them before nodding backwards. "Move," he said. Daire came inside and immediately put himself in front of her. "No, I want to see her."

They kept crossing the foyer, Raven walking backward, gun trained to his target.

"I'll use her as a shield the same day you put Swallow in front of you," her Heart said, his voice gravelly. "If you try to hurt her—"

"You don't try anything, and no one gets hurt."

They went under the mezzanine and Raven opened a door into a corridor. Without looking, he navigated his way to another door and reached back to toss it open before reversing into the room.

"Beau, what are you—oh, God," the woman's voice was light.

A beacon of hope perhaps?

Daire stopped, just inside the door. This time he put both arms around her, forcing her to stay at his back. "Swallow."

"Look what the cat dragged in," a new male said.

Her mouth opened. That was her hope right there. Styx. That was his voice.

"Want me to put a bullet in him?"

"Put the gun down," the female said. "You never used to be so trigger-happy. No. Wait. I take that back. You've always been trigger-happy. I knew your trigger before I knew you."

"Wondered when you'd show up," Styx said. "Where's your lady?"

Her Heart's arms dropped, which she took as a sign to show herself. Rushing into the room, it was a relief that Raven's arms were at his sides, the gun no longer aimed at her Heart. But it was the man at the end of the room, standing in a seating area, who got her absolute attention.

Running across the space, past the couches, she threw her arms around him, welcoming his embrace in return. "We thought you were dead."

"Maybe I am," Styx said, easing back to look at her for just a second before fixing on his brother, probably still at the door. "Guess you blew your cover."

"Not exactly," Daire said, his voice coming closer. "But we do need a new plan."

"Where's H?" she asked, rubbing Styx's chest. "Is he here? Did you get your guys out?"

"So many questions," Styx said, moving her away when Daire appeared at her side. "You got your sanity?"

"Jury's still out… I'm sorry the—"

"Everyone's alive," Styx said. "Well, almost everyone."

"Almost?" she asked, clutching his arm in both hands. "Where's H?"

"Downstairs," Styx said, flopping an arm over her shoulders while Daire stayed in his focus. "He doesn't know."

"Guess it's time we brought him into the fold."

"Yeah, but he's downstairs with the guys," Styx said. "Think we better separate one from the other first." Or he might order his men to take down the Ares threat before they got a word in edgeways. "He took the raid failure hard."

"We all did. We didn't know we were moving out until it happened."

"Where were you?"

"LA," Daire said, growing more serious. "There's a lot to talk about."

"How imminent is the threat?"

"As imminent as I say it is."

"We have the keys and the necessary package," Styx said. "You know what happens after we use them. Can we eliminate the threat?"

"We'll talk about that," Daire said. "After we get through with the hard part."

"I'll get him," Raven said, drawing her attention. "Watch him."

She hadn't even noticed the other guys in the room. Two were at a table, behind the door, seated opposite each other.

"Might start a fight," the guy with the scar on his neck said. "Get some exercise."

"Yeah," Raven muttered. "Please do. He'll kill you."

When Raven, and his gun, left the room, a woman stood up behind Daire. "Can we all relax now he's gone?"

"You married him," Daire said, bowing to kiss the woman's cheek and accept her hug.

The ebony-haired beauty had perfect skin and the kind of figure only seen in action movies. "You look good."

"Better than I did last time you saw me," Daire said, finally slapping a hand into Styx's to greet his brother properly.

"Yeah, I'd say that amount of anger isn't healthy," the woman said. "But your trigger's nowhere near as sensitive as my husband's." When the woman looked at her, she froze.

"Pandora… Finally, temptation has a face." She offered a hand. "Swallow… or Zara, whichever you prefer."

"Tess," she said and shook the woman's hand.

"I'm tempted," came a shout from the table. "Send her over here."

"You shut up," Zara said without taking her eyes away. "Ignore him. He's bored and wants to get a rise out of someone."

"I'm the one rising over here," the guy shouted back. "Send the guys downstairs to sweat, I'll keep her entertained… and sweating."

"That's Griffin Caine," Zara said, wearing a tight smile.

When Daire turned to head in that direction, alarm spiked in her. If he started a fight—

"Don't worry," Styx said, resting a hand on her shoulder. "Everyone knows Caine's an asshole. Ares won't give him the satisfaction."

Zara moved aside to let Styx join his brother. "Yeah, he just saves it for when Rave's not in the room. Especially an armed Raven." When Daire reached the table both Caine and the unknown man stood up to do the handshake greeting thing. "The other guy's Swift. Our very own hope for the future."

The computer guy. Exile's opposite. Morality wise anyway.

"You've all been here? Since the raid?"

"Gave us time to lick our wounds," Styx said, dropping to sit on the couch.

"Who'd we lose?" Daire asked, returning to them with Swift not far behind.

"No one. We're good," Styx said. "Couple of gunshot wounds, some bruising, nothing serious. Can't say the same for the other side."

Curious how Daire would feel about the men he'd trained being injured, she tried to be subtle about checking his reaction.

As if he could read her mind, his focus locked to hers and he smiled. "We're at war, baby. Sometimes that means a body count."

"The more we take out now," Styx said, "the less we have to deal with later. Gotta say it felt good to be in the field again… until we realized it was a cock up anyway."

A failure. Just like Daire said.

"We're all together now," she said. "Isn't that what counts?"

The smirks and snickers that went around the room weren't appreciated. Yes, okay, so she sounded like an after school special and these were hardened super-agents, but pessimism wouldn't get them anywhere. Thinking that was sort of ironic. She'd been ready to give up herself recently. But all the people she loved were safe in one place. Life was about as good there as it had been for a long time.

"Bright and bubbly," Zara said. "Not what I'd expect for the great Ares."

That wasn't really accurate. Bubbly definitely wasn't a word that would describe her, not in her head anyway.

"Are we staying?" she asked Daire because there was really nothing to say to Zara's teasing.

"Depends on H."

"You got a chopper from our supply firm," Zara said. "That was smart."

"I've been accused of worse," Daire said, laying a hand on the woman's cheek. "Can't tell you how much I appreciate this."

Zara shrugged. "Ah, it's nothing," she said. "My guy doesn't do so well with the good life. He prefers a moving target."

"I know, I've seen you two fuck with each other."

"We've still got it."

"I'll say," Styx said. "After seeing how you two take failure, I'm not sure you don't go looking for it."

"He gets tense," she said. "Better he vents that on me than someone else. I won't end up dead."

Having been that pressure release for Daire, and using him as one herself, she understood Zara's position. If only they could be that relief for each other right then. With every second that passed, her awareness of her father drew nearer. He'd come in and… she had no idea how he'd react. Her response hadn't been so measured and she admitted her love still existed.

Did Harry's? Would he forgive his protégé? Both of them? And her… what would happen when he found out the truth?

TWENTY-TWO

WHEN THE DOOR OPENED and Harry walked in, the air changed. He hadn't expected to be faced by what awaited him. Or, more accurately, who awaited him.

"What the fuck is this?" her father demanded.

"We'll give you privacy," Zara said, drifting away from them to head for the doorway Raven loitered in.

"Just when there was something worth watching," Caine said, but got up in time with Swift to leave.

The door closed, sealing them, and their tension, inside.

"Think you can come crawling back?" Harry asked. "Your master stop cutting the crusts off your bread?"

"I never left, Harry," Daire said, ignoring the ridicule.

"Oh, is that it? Do you think we're dumb enough to fall for that? Zeus send you to gather intel? Guess that's why you brought my daughter, you thought she'd soften and distract us?"

"He's telling the truth," Styx said. "We've been running an op since we left camp with our detachments. He never intended to go to Beta with Zip and Milo. The plan was always to slip into Zeus's ranks. He's been gathering intel for us. Not the other way around."

"Yeah," Harry said like he didn't believe it. "Convenient how he ricochets back and forth as the mood takes him. I hope you don't think you can put your hands on my daughter this time around. We're smarter than that now."

He might be. Her? Uh… not so much.

"I know this is a shock," Daire said. "But we don't have time to argue about it. We're here now. We need a plan. Who have you got lined up?"

"And this isn't information gathering? You think we'll just hand you a list of our allies?" Harry asked and looked at her like he was just seeing her. "Are you hurt? Did they hurt you?"

"No, Dad, I'm fine," she said, squeezing between the brothers to go to her father at the back of the couch to take his hand. "I didn't know either. I didn't know that… They figured something out, JARR is not just hoarding intel. It's a trigger. Accessing it will set off a chain reaction."

"Leading to what?" he asked, but she didn't have that answer. He appealed to his boys. "Leading to what?"

"We didn't know," Styx said. "That's why someone had to get close to Zeus to find out. The more information we have, the more chance we'll have of shutting it down."

"You want to destroy it," Harry said, his eyes narrowing like he didn't believe it, telling her he wasn't looking at Styx anymore.

"Yes, I want to destroy it," Daire said. "But I'll do whatever it takes to keep Tess alive. If that means letting the world burn, I'll do it."

Swinging around, she glared, shaking her head. "He doesn't need to hear that right now."

"Just being honest."

"We don't have to be that honest right off the bat, do we?"

"Where is Zeus?" Harry asked. "How did you get away from him?"

"I walked out the door," Daire said. "You think he'd be dumb enough to get in my way?"

"I think he'd be smarter than to let you walk out with Tess given she's the only card he has left."

"Yeah, well, he screwed up and gave me an excuse, so I took it."

"What excuse?"

Daire didn't respond. Yeah, only family were present, but salting a wound while there was tension between father and son wasn't going to mend this rift.

"He knows," she said, filling in the blank so her Heart didn't need to. "Zeus brought us into a meeting with Merrill."

Shock hit her father hard. "What?"

"He's got some ingenious idea about Merrill being the new Six. And, of course, he didn't hesitate to apply a little pressure."

"Blackmail? Extortion?"

"Bingo," she said. "He didn't go as far as pointing at Daire as the illegitimate child, but he made sure we were in the room."

"It was Zeus who told you, Light-Sprite."

"Yes," she said.

"He knew you knew."

"And didn't mind letting Daire know we'd hidden the truth from him, all of us."

"'Cept the guy standing over here in the dark," Styx said.

She smiled as she glanced back to see him raise his arms in a wide shrug.

"VP Buford didn't betray king and country," Daire said. "Turns out my biological father did. Perfect leverage to bring the presidential-hopeful into the fold."

"Merrill," Styx said, his attention landing on her and Harry. "And you both knew this?"

"I was there," Harry said. "Hera's principal at the time."

Which was an indirect way of confessing he'd been the one issuing orders.

"How do you know about it?" he asked her.

"Zeus told me in London."

"And you didn't tell me?"

"It was the last night," she said. "The night of our op."

Though using that term seemed pathetic in light of everything else the agents had done.

"And every night since?"

"It wasn't my secret to tell you," she said. "If I didn't tell Daire the truth, why would I tell you?"

"Why didn't you tell him?"

"Time. Opportunity and..."

"You didn't want to rock the boat with everything being so tenuous," Styx said on a sigh. "You couldn't have known this would be Zeus's play. Damn... How are you taking it, brother?"

"Am I pissed? Yeah, I am," he said. "And H is damn lucky Tess was the one with me as I processed it. If it hadn't been her..."

"You'd have walked away," Styx said. "Or killed him."

"Maybe."

It was a wonder they hoped to achieve anything as a cohesive unit when there was so much mistrust between them. Suddenly the previous pessimism seemed much more realistic.

"This is never going to work, is it?" she asked no one in particular. "We'll never be able to stop this. To stop him."

"We're going to stop him," Daire said. "I didn't risk losing you on a maybe. The only reason I walked away, the only reason I planned this op with my brother was to guarantee your safety."

"I know," she said on a breath as she laid her hands on the back of the couch. "But there's no trust here. This doesn't work without trust. Zeus knows how to play you off each other and he's done it perfectly. And we might be together when we're next facing him. He'll push buttons, twist and contort all of us until we can't bear to look at each other. Manipulation is his specialty. How can we have any faith this will work? That we'll follow through on what we want, what we say we want?"

"What did I tell you about the raid?" Daire asked. "What was the primary objective?"

"Me."

"Right," he said. "And if you weren't pulled out?"

"You said if you had to pull me out of Beta yourself, you would."

"And I did, didn't I? Because…"

"Zeus was mad."

"No way I was going to let you suffer for that," he said. "We were just lucky that he gave us a third option and I didn't have to blow my cover. But if he hadn't given us that reason, I'd have slaughtered every man in the building to get you out of there. Do you doubt me?"

"Of course not!"

"Tess," her father warned.

"I know," she said, her head dropping. "You told me to be careful. That he'd use what I felt for him against me." She looked over her shoulder. "He didn't have to take me out of there, Dad. And he didn't have to bring me here. He could've taken me back to Beta. To Zeus. Any time. He didn't. And maybe it's naïve, but I believe him. Everything he's told me makes sense."

"He needs you. He needs you at Beta to access JARR."

"That he wants to destroy," she said.

"You don't know that. We can't be sure."

"No?" she asked, her brows rising. "Because the first thing he did when we were safely away from Beta was donate blood and collect mine too. He has a contingency for his objective, just like you taught him."

Surprise switched her father's attention. "You're planning for a transfusion."

"It's a last resort," Daire said. "We don't know how much of her blood JARR will take. Having something to replace it is just smart. And you're A positive too, so you're next in the chair."

"If you dilute her blood with ours, JARR won't accept it."

"Fuck JARR," Daire said. "Tess is my primary mission. If that machine needs more of her than I'm willing to give, I'm pulling her out. We'll be in Beta. There are bunkers—"

"You disconnect her prematurely, it could damage

her. Any doomsday event—"

"We'll get through it," Daire said, marching to the front of the couch. "Whatever it takes, she gets through this. If I have to sacrifice you, my brother, my goddamn unit, I will. You want honesty? That's it. Tess is my priority."

"How can you say that to us now and expect us to believe it? You let them drug her, kidnapped her, locked her up—"

"I have my own penance to pay for that."

"And he was willing to," she said. "He didn't expect forgiveness. Didn't ask for it. The truth is, it doesn't matter what we say, forgiving himself is going to be his biggest obstacle."

"He did it for her," Styx said. "Even agreed not to tell her about the op when I vetoed it."

"You wanted it to be real," Harry said. "She got hurt because you two—"

"I got hurt. We all got hurt," she said. "But when you strip away everything else, we're all doing what we think is best. We're doing it for the people we love. To keep our family safe. Like it or not, this is it. With Olympus facing extinction, all we have is each other."

"Not so long ago, you were saying Styx and I were all you had."

"You should be happy, Dad," she said. "Daire didn't betray you. He's fighting for the greater good. Everything he's sacrificed has been in deference to the big picture."

"No," Harry said, shaking his head. "You're his bigger picture. He isn't thinking Olympus. He's thinking with his heart, and I definitely didn't teach him that."

"If your daughter isn't your bigger picture, old man, we're walking out right now."

"We need to do this together," Styx said. "Tess is right about that. If we can't find a way to trust each other, Zeus wins."

"I trust everyone here," Tess said, taking the first step. "I believe in all of you."

"I second that," Styx said.

Silence lingered. Who was going to break first? Father

or son? Sometimes she wanted to scream at the two of them. One was as stubborn as the other.

Her pleading eyes blinked to Daire's. The strength of his resolve only took a second to falter. Not that he wasn't as determined, but that he'd read the look in her eyes and had no defense against it.

On an exhale, he surrendered. "For the most part, we agree on our objective. JARR has to be destroyed. Telling you where my priority is gives you more information. If it comes to the crunch, if a decision has to be made, I choose Tess… How can that surprise you?"

"How can that surprise me?" Harry asked, incredulous. "Because I saw you sit next to her watching her heart break as she begged you to care."

"That's between Daire and me," she said. "We've dealt with that. And can you honestly tell me you wouldn't have done the same thing if it meant saving mom's life? You sent her away with a new life and tore yourself from her side to return to Olympus. That wasn't out of desire, you didn't want to be there, you did it because Zeus gave you no other choice. Daire made the same choice."

Her father's shoulders rose before they fell. "History plays on repeat."

"Okay, can we get over the personal shit and get to work?" Styx asked. "Everyone take a seat, we have to thrash this out."

"Should we invite Raven and Zara back in?" she asked as the men went to sit. "This is their house and if we're expecting their help…"

"They should be in on it," Styx said, starting for the door. "Sure. They deserve to know everything we do." He smiled. "But this isn't their house."

If it wasn't their house, who did it belong to? Caine? Swift?

Details like that didn't matter, so she didn't ask and went to take a seat while Styx retrieved their allies.

TWENTY-THREE

EXILE'S VOICE CAME THROUGH the laptop Swift had set up on a low table in front of the fireplace. "This better be important."

With them and their Kindred allies settled in the seating area, they were ready to put their plan together.

"Where's Wreck?" was Daire's first question.

"Getting some people together," Styx said. "People we've worked with before. People we trust… and getting his girl supplied. Don't worry about him, clue us in on what you learned. Do you know what JARR will trigger?"

"I know of two components," Daire said. "There may be others. I can't guarantee he doesn't still have an ace up his sleeve."

"If I know Z," her father said, "there's always an ace."

"What are the two components?"

"Like we thought, there's a financial factor. The system will dump all stocks. All over the world as each market opens. And they won't be able to stop it. The markets will open and dump regardless of what they do."

"Shit."

"Yeah," Daire said. "The world's economies would never recover. And that's not the worst news."

"What's the worst news?" Zara asked, resting a hand on Raven's thigh.

"There's a biological element," her Heart said to be greeted by silence. He let that linger for a few seconds before continuing. "An infectious agent is awaiting pick up. It's likely the lab storing it doesn't know what it is, so when the order comes in to send it out, they'll have no reason to hesitate."

"I think I'd prefer nuclear winter," Styx said. "Where does it land?"

"Population center," he said. "Not another lab, a hotel."

"They'll open it without having a damn clue what it is."

"Yeah, and it's one of Asclepius's potions. It's slow acting, so someone can be exposed without realizing it. They'll go about their lives for a day, maybe two, without knowing they're spreading the virus. It's highly contagious."

"How is it stored?" Zara asked. "No lab would put something in an envelope and just mail it to wherever. Why hasn't it spread already?"

"They're storing it safely. It will be safe until… It's triggered by light. As soon as the package is opened and the virus is exposed to light, it will be activated and begin to spread."

"And if it's a hotel, they'll open it, figure there's been a mistake or someone's pranking them, and they'll just set it aside."

"Right."

"Hundreds of people could be exposed to it. How is it spread?"

"I don't know. We have to assume it could be any and every way."

"Okay," Zara said, patting her husband's leg. "We find out where it's being stored and buy the company. CI has the facilities to study and dispose of it."

"Buy the…" Tess wasn't sure that was a realistic option. "You want to buy the company?"

Zara's focus moved to Swift. "Can you trace it? Find out where it's being kept? JARR can't send something that no longer exists."

"I can try," Swift said. "Bear in mind this might have been done manually…"

"Manually?" she asked.

"If someone literally walked the package into a lab and handed it over for storage," Daire said, "that means no digital record of where and what it is… Though, like I said, it's likely they don't know what they have. Either it has no classification or it's been classified as something benign they wouldn't think twice about."

"JARR would need an identifier, a bar code or serial number, to request the item be shipped," Zara said. "Unfortunately, the labs out there run the gauntlet. It could be somewhere state of the art that takes cataloging seriously."

"Or it could be some back to the stone age dotty professor type place or in some country where they don't pay much attention to rules and procedures," Styx said to which Zara shrugged. "We could look into where the doc had access to back then. Was there somewhere he could just walk in and ask to store something without questions being asked?"

"Probably several places," Harry said. "But it's a place to start. What about the stocks? If he wipes out the stock market, financial institutions crash, people lose everything, companies dissolve. The things we take for granted would stop working."

"If JARR's been learning all these years, and locked down, that information may not be accessible until we start to open it up," Swift said.

"The stock market is easy to manipulate," Exile's voice came through the computer. "We can handle that… and make a little green on the side."

"Flame…" the sultry female voice that oozed from the laptop was both unexpected and intriguing.

"Thought you were alone," Swift said, smirking.

"I am. Kero doesn't count," Exile said. "She's honorable and decent."

"Unlike you," Kero said.

"We were on our way to somewhere when you called," Exile explained. "I'm happy to disconnect and get back on my ride."

"I'll still be naked no matter how long the call takes," Kero said, confirming they were an intimate couple. If anyone had doubted it. "Saving the world takes priority."

"So you keep saying, Cupcake," Exile said. "I've gotta say, giving a shit about anything outside my self-interest doesn't feel good."

"Flame, you're the only person in the world who feels guilty about doing good not evil."

"Word is," Zara said. "You can get us the government if we need it, Exile."

"I can get you anything you need, baby," Exile said. "But we don't need the government."

"Would be better to have a third in case this ace crops up," Swift said. "Anyone you trust?"

"I trust Kero, but she can't even use the internet to order pizza."

Not very hopeful when they needed a world class hacker covering their asses.

"Warren?"

"Distracted," Exile said.

"Rourke?"

"Self-involved."

"There's gotta be someone—"

"White don't fight, and this is war," Exile said. "We don't need any more of you vigilante, white knight heroes on this… Speaking of, where's Knight?"

"Working," Zara said. "So who do you think we need?"

"Swift handles the biological shit, I'll deal with the financial."

"In real time?"

"If I have to," Exile said. "You say this system is inaccessible because we need blood to open it up."

"Yeah."

"You're talking about going in the front door," Exile said. "The system can only learn, adapt, and gather, if it has a connection to the wider world."

"Minotaur is its connection," Daire said. "If you want

to sneak around the back, you'd have to go through Minotaur and that's no easy hack."

"That could set off a chain reaction," Swift said.

"Put me at the JARR terminal. I say there's an indirect way in."

"It doesn't work that way," Daire said. "The JARR operator station can only be accessed by using the gatekeeper's blood."

"Your girl?"

Although she laid a hand on his leg, Daire remained intent on the computer. "Yeah."

"Gimme the process."

"Minotaur has to be running on the first key. There's a coded panel in the JARR operator station. We use a sample of living blood to gain access. From there, we need to input the right code to open the JARR entry system. Then the real fun begins. We have to shut down Minotaur in the central control room and get the first key into JARR within ninety seconds."

"Possible?"

"Just," Daire said. "The next two keys have to be entered in the correct sequence. If they are, the blood inlet opens."

"It takes the blood into its system for analysis. If it accepts it, carnage begins."

"Does the blood have to keep running into the system while it's in use?" Zara asked.

"We don't know," Daire said. "Which is why I'm asking everyone who can to give blood."

"Unpopular opinion," Exile said. "But the only surefire way to guarantee JARR never sees the light of day is to slit her throat, you know that, right?"

Daire took her hand from his thigh. "Not an option."

"Figured. Where are the creators?"

"Dead."

"Sure, stupid question."

"Who do we know in biometrics?" Zara muttered.

"You asking me?" Raven asked.

"No," she said, patting his leg. "Shooting things is

your specialty, honey. The company is more my…" She twisted to look at her husband. "You know who knows a little about this field."

"No," Raven said without equivocation. "Try somebody else."

"Okay. We have contacts at ThornCorp, I'll work those," Zara said. "Regroup in twenty-four hours?"

"Works for me."

"Don't go too far," Zara said, though the laptop screen declared their connection to Exile had already been severed. "Tess, you mind giving us a blood sample?"

"Uh… no."

"Why do you want her blood?" Harry asked.

"Because we have a doctor, a hacker, and an inventor in the building," Zara said. "If all we're doing is killing time until the pieces are in place, what harm is there in them trying to replicate the system? If we can figure out how it works, maybe we figure out how to circumvent it."

"You try that and everyone in Beta dies… You could set a wider disaster in motion."

"Don't get defensive, Dad," Tess said, hearing the frustration in his voice.

"You're not hooking her up to any system."

"Don't worry," Swift said. "If we need to tie someone into any potentially deadly machine, we'll use Caine."

"Or Saint," Raven muttered.

Zara smacked his thigh but widened her grin on the guests. "Who's hungry?"

"Did you cook?" Daire asked.

Zara laughed as she stood. "I specialize in heating up whatever Bess left for us."

"She's not here?"

"Back east," Zara said, retreating toward a door in the far corner. "She goes where the kids go."

"Right," Daire said. "You know, I'm sorry about—"

"Don't worry about it," Zara said. "Beau, you want to set the table?"

She didn't see the look he landed on his wife, but by her laugh, she could guess.

"I can do it," Tess said.

"Thanks," Zara said and pointed to a unit in the corner. "Everything's in there."

Doing something was better than dwelling. So many people had mobilized to take down a threat that could end the world as they knew it. Would they succeed? They had to, didn't they?

TWENTY-FOUR

THANKFULLY, they were given a bedroom on the mezzanine that overlooked the foyer. If they'd been taken any deeper into the house, chances were she'd be lost forever.

Folding her things into her carpet bag, she was ready for bed, ready for sleep, it had been a long day.

"You're quiet."

Daire's words drew her from her daze. He stood in front of the closed bedroom door on the opposite side of the room.

"And you're playing soldier," she said, smiling at him. "I don't think you have to worry about standing alert here. Doesn't seem to be the easiest building to penetrate."

"It's not impossible," he said. "The getaway is the real test."

"Said the voice of experience."

"We ran some drills here. Just for fun."

"Of course you did," she said and sighed as she dropped into one of the wingback chairs that flanked the bistro table in the window. "Zara said we were killing time until the pieces are in place. How much do we need? How long will we be here?"

"I don't know. Harry will need time to get the guys

into shape. Our casualty list wasn't high, but there are some injuries. Ideally, we'll be on form in a month, maybe two."

"Two months?" she exclaimed.

"Don't worry about it," he said on an almost snicker. "The time doesn't matter. If we need it, we take it. We want this done, but we don't want to rush it." And, as usual, he took everything in stride. "Is that what's on your mind?"

"Your friends are incredible."

"We don't hang out on holidays," he said. "We only see each other when shit like this crops up. We've backed each other up a few times. I came here after the Exodus."

"Whose house is this? Styx said it wasn't Zara's."

"Xavier Knight," he said. "Falcon. It's his house. Raven has an identical one on the east coast."

"That's where Bess is?" she asked, and he nodded. "With the kids… Did Zara really mean children? Are we pulling babies into this?"

Dinner was great, but more reflective than chatty. The men preferred to brood and getting to know anyone any better could backfire in the long run.

"Falcon and Finch have a couple," Daire said, wandering over. "And she's pregnant again, it seems to be their thing." Except his joke fell flat. "Swift's wife is with them in the east coast house. Far from this."

"On purpose," she said. "Because it's dangerous." On an exhaled groan, her head fell into her hands. "This is wrong. It's so completely wrong."

When his palms slid onto her thighs, she dropped her hands onto his and opened her eyes.

He was crouched in front of her. "What's wrong, baby?"

"These are good people. People with lives and families. How can we ask for their help? What if someone gets hurt? What if someone's killed? Are we going to take a father from his children?"

"Falcon doesn't go into the field anymore. He and Zara keep the family companies going. He uses his brain for the Kindred, and that's why he stayed here. For the backstage work."

"He wasn't at dinner."

"Yeah, he's not wild about people," he said. "If Finch is around, he comes out of hiding. She's his sort of conduit to the world in a lot of ways."

"I don't want anyone to get hurt."

"They won't. We'll be at Beta when this goes down, one way or another. There are bunkers there—"

"Will Finch be at the bunker? What about the kids? Will they be in a bunker?" His hands slid out from under hers and descended to her calves. "Zeus will have an ace. Harry's sure of it."

"You want to walk away?" he asked. "Leave this behind?"

"That won't make them any safer," she said. "I know why we came here. I know why we need people, numbers, but even after everything, we still don't know what Zeus plans. What trick will he pull out of his hat at the last minute? I don't know Exile or Swift enough to know if they're capable of what they claim. Let's say they are, let's say we don't need a lot of my blood. We get in there, hook me up to the machine and they complete their missions… There's still an x factor. An unknown."

"And you want to know what that is."

Leaning forward, she stroked his face. "I don't want Z to win. If we lose each other, or any of these good people lose their lives or the people they love, he wins… I just have a bad feeling about this. Someone isn't making it out alive."

"Okay," he said, offering a tight smile. "Just remember you're my Pandora. Always."

She frowned. "What does that mean?" she asked, caressing him. The contact, the texture, it was so important to relish every second. "You never call me that."

"No, I don't, my Pandora. But you need to remember it. Maybe you can be good with subtle."

"I never was," she said, her guilt redirecting to something else. "If I was, I'd know what danger my mother felt before she died. She knew something was there, someone… I don't know, but something scared her."

"With all this family around, you've been thinking of

her?"

"Of how much easier this would be if I had her? Yes. I feel like I can't… It doesn't feel right to do it without her."

"She'd be here if she could be."

That wasn't much comfort. "We don't even know why she can't be here," she said, searching him. "Why did she die? Why did she have to…? Was it Zeus?"

"I don't know," he said with a slight head shake.

"You said it was no accident," she said. "Someone did it to her. She was murdered." With one arm still hooked around her calves, his other rose to curl their pinkies together on her lap. It was easier to watch their fingers twine than to look him in the eye. "I've let her down, in so many ways. If someone hurt me, if I'd been killed, nothing would take priority over finding the person responsible."

"You haven't been sunning yourself on the beach," he said. "You've been running for your life."

"Wouldn't have stopped her," she said, sealing her breath in her lungs for a moment before exhaling her words, "will our answers die with JARR?"

"It's possible. People will die. They'll have to… and sometimes that means losing intel."

Which was what she feared. "How soon? How long before… Should we stick to our plan of locking ourselves away in Beta?"

"Maybe," he said. "But there are few places as secure as this one. We can see anyone approaching and can take them down before they land, air or sea. I'm not sorry you're here. H and Styx, Zara, Raven, Swift, these are people who know how to take care of themselves, who can take care of you."

She hazarded a smile. "I thought that was your job."

His fingertips slid up her forearm. "I'd die for you, Little Red, I don't have to tell you that."

On a blink, her eyes ascended to his. "If someone hurt me, would you let anything get in the way of finding that someone? Of hurting them back?"

Rising, he cupped her face and drew her mouth to his. His kiss made her forget their troubles. It never lasted, and never would, not until they got to the end of their journey and JARR was gone for good.

His hands tucked themselves beneath her and he carried her to their bed. Her father was in one of the rooms nearby, but she couldn't ask Daire to stop. The tenderness in his kiss was a promise. The physical show of uniting their bodies reminded her how they'd always be linked, in this life and the next.

In person and in their letters, both of them had indicated they'd sacrifice themselves for this mission. The more she learned, the more likely it seemed the future they'd dreamed of sharing was impossible.

It took just a second to pull the tee-shirt she wore over her head. As Daire stood to shed his own clothes, she found her smile. His body was incredible, honed, trained, ripped, he was made to protect humanity from itself. All he wanted to do was his job and she'd got in the way of that. Got in between him and his destiny.

Olympus wanted to wring every ounce of spirit from his extraordinary heart. He'd trusted her with that and still she couldn't save it. Wanting wasn't enough. Aching to give him freedom didn't offer an escape.

He sank into her slow, bringing her focus to those intense eyes above her. He couldn't hide it; how could she ever have thought this man didn't love her? As he moved in her, she felt the completion of his soul with hers.

Her hand rose toward his face, he caught it and kissed her palm, pressing it hard against his mouth, closing his eyes like he was savoring the contact. She knew it. A lump formed in her throat as heat rushed her senses. They were finite. This could be finite. One day, one minute, they could be torn from each other forever. How could she go on without him? She wouldn't be able to. Would he? She didn't want to be the cause of his demise but couldn't save him either.

"I'm sorry," she whispered when he laid her hand against his chest. "My Heart."

"I love you," he said, almost as though he was offering his own apology. "Nothing changes that."

Swallowing hard, she closed her eyes to the sorrow that may lie ahead and gave herself to the pleasure only he could provide.

TWENTY-FIVE

THE NEXT MORNING, she woke alone. With so much going on, it wasn't a surprise Daire wanted to train and prepare, to reconnect with his men and hopefully undo any damage done by his feigned betrayal. Knowing she'd likely get in the way, she took her time in the shower and getting ready.

Navigating her way down to the family room they'd been in the previous night, it was a relief to see Zara there with Styx.

"Wow, I really thought I'd get lost," she joked. Her warmth chilled when they both stood up, solemn in their countenance. "What?" Her eyes flicked back and forth between them. "What is it?"

"He's gone," Styx said.

"Who? What are you—"

"Ares," Zara said. "Daire… He left in the dark."

"No, he didn't," she said on a snicker, but they didn't look unsure. Her smile faded. "What do you mean he left?"

"The cameras picked him up leaving the house around three," Zara said. "The chopper's gone. He's gone."

She couldn't think. Gone? Why would he go? Why would he abandon her? To go to Beta? Back to Zeus? Why would he do that? He'd gone to Zeus for intelligence, and they didn't need…

"That's not all," Styx said and glanced to Zara before focusing on her again. "There's something else. You should sit down to hear it."

"I don't want to sit down," she said, fear churning around her heart. "Was he hurt? Was there an accident?"

"No, this isn't… You'll want to be sitting down when you hear this."

Drawing it out only increased her apprehension. "Would you just say it," she snapped.

"That blood we took… Your blood… It showed… You're pregnant."

Daire couldn't be gone. Why wouldn't he have woken her or told her the plan? "If you knew he was leaving, why didn't you stop him?" she asked. "Why didn't someone come and get me? I could've talked to him. Convinced him to stay or that he needed back up. He shouldn't be out there alone."

Zara and Styx frowned at each other. "Did you hear me, Lady? You're pregnant."

"You've tried that one before," she said, sneering at him. "I'm not falling for it."

"This is for real," he said, coming around the couch to approach her. "You are pregnant."

On a blink, she sought any hint he was lying. He'd never looked so somber, so intent.

She didn't understand, couldn't figure it out. "I'm pregnant?" she asked, and he nodded slowly. But she shook her head. "No, I can't be. I can't. It's impossible."

"You and Daire haven't been having sex?" Zara asked. She winced, trying to breathe as everything wilted to slow motion. Pregnant. "It is just him, right? We know it's his."

"Yeah," Styx said, though he remained intent on her.

"Sorry, we just don't know each other that well."

Taking a step back, she wanted to disappear. Wanted everything to stop for just a minute. "I can't believe this."

"We have it here," Zara said.

She wasn't even aware of the woman coming over until a piece of paper was put in her hand.

"Who knows about this?" she asked without reading the sheet.

"Us," Styx said.

"Falcon."

Because he'd been the one to run the test.

Squeezing her eyes closed, she shook her head fast. "Why was he even testing my blood for—"

"It's part of his standard testing," Zara said. "He wanted to measure what was in your blood… What unique factors JARR may look for. In the process of that your HCG… the man's had enough kids to know at a glance."

"Oh, God," she breathed out. "Shit."

"You weren't trying?"

"The opposite," she said to Zara and showed the scar on her arm. "We're supposed to be protected." Her eyes found Styx's. "Does he know?"

"No, he was gone before Falcon told Zara," Styx said. "If you want me to—"

"No," she said quickly, grabbing for Zara's hand. "He can't know. You can't tell him."

"Why wouldn't—"

"He won't be able to do what he's got to do if he's worrying about my uterus," she recited Styx's words back to him. "I don't want you to tell Harry either."

"If you want…" Zara cleared her throat. "We have mifepristone and misoprostol here, if you want them."

"The abortion pill?" Styx asked.

"It's two pills actually, but yeah."

"Why would you have—"

"Sometimes in the course of Falcon's work, it's required." She wasn't sure she wanted to ask any more about that. "No one has to know about it either."

"We can't crowd her," Styx said, doing a shitty job of masking his offense. "Don't rush her into anything."

"I wasn't rushing her. I was telling her it was a possibility, if that was what she wanted."

"What about what he wants?"

"It's her body," Zara said. "This is her decision. Besides…" When that lingered unfinished, her head rose.

"Whatever JARR needs from you might end the pregnancy anyway."

"Shit," she said again and inhaled. "I need to…" Fumbling for the door handle, she got the door open again. "I need a minute."

She'd left her bedroom certain Daire would be around. That it would be like when they all occupied Three's house. Passing the time, training, planning, practicing. Only this time, her father would know about their relationship. It didn't even occur to her that her Heart would run out on her. But to be hit with this… She went upstairs into her bathroom and locked the door.

Pregnant.

Of their own accord, her eyes drifted down to the paper in her hand and there it was, in plain English. Pregnant. Positive.

Closing her eyes as her chin dropped to her chest, she stopped thinking. It was impossible. How could she…? How would Daire…?

Her pulse was racing. Adrenaline fueled her anxiety. How long had this child been growing inside her? Ignorance was bliss. She'd never known just how much until that second.

Having a child changed everything and yet… Anxiety ebbed. Raising her head, she tried to focus on what was going on inside her. Yes, she was confused and concerned, but there was no fear. None.

The life inside her, knowing that there was life inside her, it changed everything.

"Goddamn," she whispered to herself.

She was with child, literally. Not just any child either, Daire's child. The child of the man she loved. Her life had been easy to sideline, she could take risks when it was only her heart beating inside her. But this… it changed everything.

Calm cooled her alarm. Determination took the place of panic. They were on a clock, one no one else could know about. They weren't only fighting for their own freedom anymore; their lives were worth less than the real soul of value.

She was going to be a mother.

A quake of anticipation shook in her throat. Being a

mother was something to fear. She was wholly responsible for another life. It was a lot to process. So much about the future was unknown. No matter what, it would be her responsibility to protect her child in the face of any evil who might use him or her to punish their father… or their grandfather. How could she build a secure bond with her offspring while possibly dragging them from one anonymous town to the next just as her mother had done with her?

Whatever lay before them, she rested a hand on her stomach certain of one thing: she would never get rid of her child. She'd told Daire that in the dark once and again in the woods. Maybe it would be safer, but she would never forgive herself.

When she'd heard Daire was gone, she was bereft. Now she was grateful. He couldn't know until this was over. She couldn't put another responsibility on him.

Wherever she went, she'd have a piece of Daire with her. A piece that it was her responsibility to protect. And the best way to ensure their child's safety was to take Zeus down.

Nothing was different. That was the image she had to project. No one could know. It would be her secret. Daire told her in the woods that he trusted her to know when it would be the right time to share information. Splitting his focus, distracting his mind when he needed to have it on the job, was too dangerous.

She wouldn't tell him. Not straight away. Not that it was within her control while he was God knew where. What was he thinking? Maybe he'd be back. But it didn't matter. Worrying about her was already his primary focus and one that might lessen his attention on what was straight ahead. Throwing a child into that mix, a helpless baby, it was too much of a burden to put onto his shoulders.

So many possibilities sprang up that it was difficult to keep track. One positive stood out, one that actually made a smile bloom on her lips. She was going to have her Heart's baby.

It wasn't planned. Nowhere close. They hadn't talked about exactly what they wanted for the future. Not while it was so uncertain. This had happened at the worst possible time. The reasons against seeing the pregnancy through overwhelmingly outweighed those for, but she couldn't deny being happy. Whatever lay ahead, she'd have Daire with her so long as she protected his child. At its foundation, the news was good. They'd created life and it was a life she'd shield with every cell of her being.

Styx opened the door. Hadn't she locked it? Did that matter for a super-agent?

"Did he tell you he was leaving?" he asked.

"No," she said, running her fingers through her hair and starting toward him, forcing him to move to let her into the bedroom. "He might come back."

"I don't know," Styx said. "I don't know what's in his head." Was that his way of telling her this wasn't part of another op? "You two are so fucking stupid."

She stopped by the table to spin around. "We didn't plan this. You think this is what he wants? Now? Do you think I want it? Zara's right, they're about to bleed me dry and… I can't abort, Styx. I can't. I know there's danger ahead, that JARR could kill me or…" Her hands flattened on her stomach. "I always told him if we got into this situation, I would have to see it through. He knows how I feel about it."

"The smart course would be to take the pills," he said, walking to her. "To get rid of it before he ever has a chance to find out. If you want to do that, I won't stop you." He touched her cheek. "But this kid is a part of our fucked-up family too. Doesn't seem right to offload him just because he's too small to fight for himself."

When he managed a small smile, she reciprocated. Although it would be smart, he didn't want her to end the pregnancy any more than she did.

"We can't tell him. Or anyone. Not yet."

"I agree," he said. "I talked to Zara, she'll speak to Falcon… Though he doesn't speak to anyone anyway, makes it hard to spread gossip and rumors."

"That includes Harry. He can't know. You know he'll lecture me and blame Daire. Whenever it happened, we were both active participants."

"I don't need to know that," he said, one corner of

his mouth rising for a second before becoming serious again. "It's got to be early. You didn't show as pregnant when we were at Beta." Together as prisoners. "Unless it was just too early."

With the implant, her periods were erratic and sometimes non-existent. Except… "I had my period when we were in Vegas."

Which was after the big goodbye when the men left in their detachments, right before Zeus walked into their suite with Ares.

"So it's got to be after that… You were doing it while you were at Beta alone? That's risky, Lady."

"It wasn't all the time, just…" Once actually, in the Beast. "Once before he broke me out."

"Once is all it takes," he said. "How did you finagle that one? Wait, forget it, I don't want to know."

She turned to the bed. "And I don't want to tell you."

"There's something else…" Like being pregnant wasn't enough. She just looked at him and raised her brows, suppressing a sigh. "There's something in your blood. Antibodies that Falcon doesn't recognize."

"Is he a scientist?"

"He's a genius," Styx said. "And his cousin is a doctor. He's analyzing it and will run it by professionals at CI, but…"

"What?" She didn't like his pondering or how intense he got. "You think it's something to do with JARR? Could it be why my blood works?"

"Maybe. It's faint and has an almost anti-venom signature… but that doesn't make sense, anti-venom shouldn't linger. You haven't been shot full of anti-venom any time recently, have you?"

She shook her head. "Not that I know of."

"More likely you've…"

"I've…?"

"Been vaccinated."

"Against?"

He shrugged. "I don't know, but it's there ready to neutralize… something."

More mysteries to unpick. Asclepius should be happy he was dead. Having some unknown something in her blood should freak her out. At this point, she was barely surprised. She'd let Falcon do his job. Something would come of it, or it wouldn't.

"It won't hurt the baby, will it?"

"We'll make sure it won't. We'll get to the bottom of this, Lady. We will."

She went to the nightstand to retrieve her pendant but was brought to a screeching halt. The pendant was gone and something else occupied its place.

Sliding out the blank folded paper, she could sense his words. Why did it feel like another goodbye?

TWENTY-SIX

We're always saying goodbye.

I hope you understand this, why I had to do this. You told me you want to know the x factor, the unknown, and I'm the only one who can find it for you. My mission is to serve you and, as always, you're right. We do have to know. The next stage of this is too critical. I cannot have you hooked up to the system and then find out too late.

Don't worry about Z, he won't know we're apart for a while. Not until I go back to him. There's something I have to do first. Someone I have to talk to. I don't know how long it will take. I don't know how long we'll be apart. Just know I love you. I always love you. Every minute of every day and still it doesn't feel like enough. There are no words, LR. No words capable of conveying how I live for you.

Stay with S. The men need time to train. H needs time to bring cohesion back. They will be fired up, ready for a fight, and H has to dial back the adrenaline with a good dose of sense. It could take a couple of weeks or a couple of months, we have to be patient. It isn't easy to be apart, but we have to do this right. The longer we can wait, the more impatient Z will be and that could mean mistakes. We want him to make mistakes we can exploit.

I know you'll wonder. You'll miss me, though it won't be half as much as I'll miss you. We will see each other again. You promised me we'd find our way back to each other once and you were right. Now I make that promise to you. What I can't promise you is forever. You know why. We both know why.

Maybe there's just too much water under the bridge. I don't like hurting you, disappointing you, but I can't promise I won't prioritize you over everything else. In your letter, the one you left in the glitter for me, you told me to save humanity from Z's insanity. That you were Insignificant. You can't honestly expect me to agree with that. I told you I wouldn't be able to follow through on the same promise S made. If I can't do that for the greater good, I can't stand by and watch them destroy you.

Talking of sacrifice upsets you. I know it does. But lying with you while you slept, absorbing your beauty, and my gratitude to you for letting us be together again, I admitted to myself the truth I've been desperate to avoid. I would give my life for yours. But the truth is that may not be enough. If Z needs all of you, if I can't prevent him getting to that point, even my death may not be enough to save you. I like to think I've covered all contingencies, but it's just not possible to guarantee your safety. The process requires a part of you. If I can't prevent that, I can't prevent him from hurting you. It takes a lot for me to admit that. A lot to admit that even my complete dedication may not be enough.

I can't promise you your life, so I'm going to answer the unknowns for you. Maybe that's the last promise I can give. The least I can do. Before this ends, you'll know everything you want to know. I can't satisfy your happiness, but I can satisfy your curiosity.

I left something in the bottom of your bag. Keep it safe. When it's time, it's how I'll let you know to come to me. Don't let H see it. Keep it hidden. Temptation could jumpstart us before we're ready. I'm doing this for you, baby. Please

understand. We will find each other again.
You are my truth. My something. Your
Heart.

Her Heart was gone. Carrying guilt as usual. That was becoming habit for them both. In every way, he satisfied her. Now he had disappeared to fulfill her curiosity. Was it their conversation before bed? Something had triggered this. Something she'd done. He'd said she was safe there and had left her behind. How long would she have to live without him?

TWENTY-SEVEN

I've lost count of the days. Of the weeks we've been apart.

On Thanksgiving, Falcon went to his family in Raven and Swallow's house, while they stayed here. To watch us. They didn't say that, but I'm sure that's why. At the time, I remember writing how sure I was we'd be together before Christmas. Sitting here on Christmas Eve, in what was our room for only one night, I just watched the plane carrying Falcon's family approaching to land. How can it be that we're still apart, my Heart? Keeping Falcon and his family apart was unfair, but at least they were still in contact. And now they're here.

I don't even know if you're still alive. You don't know that I'm still alive. Maybe you're monitoring us somehow. I'd like to think that's true, but if it is, I pray you can't hear our words. Hiding the prenatal vitamins is easy. No one but Styx comes into my bathroom. Falcon's wife's pregnancies give us some cover too. No, she hasn't been around, but there are stocks here of everything we could ever need. It's almost like the guy expects he'll be cut off from the world for indefinite periods. Though, I guess he does. We've been living in his house for almost two months, and I still haven't met him. I've seen pictures but never laid eyes on him in the flesh.

Styx says that will change when his wife returns with the kids, so we'll wait and see. It still doesn't seem right that we could be endangering his family, anyone's family. I suppose him allowing them to come home suggests he recognizes we're not a threat.

H's men stay mostly in the basement still. Maybe it feels like another prison, but I can tell H enjoys putting them through their paces. Sometimes he forgets, I think, where we are, what's happening, and he'll talk to Styx about the men's progress with such beaming pride. Then somehow, he's reminded you're not here and the mood drops again.

I know what they're thinking. What they're whispering about when I enter a room and they all shut up. They think you're dead. Or you've gone back to Z for real this time. I'll admit, every day I still wake up hoping you'll be next to me, that you'll slip back into our sheets the same way you left them in the dead of night. Then it will be like nothing happened. The time we've been apart will be erased and everything will be right again, everything will be good.

Only that time can't be completely erased. Our little one has grown each day we've been apart. While the guys were out on an exercise today, Zara snuck me into some room that looked like a medical lab and did an ultrasound. She recorded it and took it back to Falcon. Apparently, this guy has everything his wife could ever need. Being so remote while pregnant, it makes sense they'd want to cover all bases. According to Zara, Falcon said we're around twelve weeks. It's a relief we're over the most dangerous time, though I can't help thinking of all you've missed.

It has to have been that day in the Beast. When we left Beta together and you took me there for the first time. Or maybe in the RV park the time you took my blood. But that was almost a week later, so... It doesn't matter. It's happened, this is the situation we're in.

You always said history wouldn't repeat itself and now I wonder when you'll find out. With no way to get in touch with you, I couldn't tell you even if I wanted to. Is this how my mother felt? She and H may have been exchanging letters, but those were months, sometimes years apart. She couldn't have told H in real time even if she'd wanted to and communication wasn't so easy back then.

Maybe if I could—

"You okay?" Styx held the bedroom door as he swung his head around it. "We haven't seen you all day."

"I'm done."

"Done?" he asked, letting go of the door to step around it. "Done what?"

"Sitting here with my thumb up my ass," she said, closing her notebook to put it on the table. "We need to leave."

"Whoa, okay," he said, reaching back to push the door into its frame. "Where do you think we're going?"

"He could be dead; you ever think of that?"

"Every damned day. You think any of us like sitting here doing nothing?"

"Then let's go," she said, standing up to head for the closet. "I'm packed, let's do it."

"You're packed because you never unpacked," he said, storming over to grab her upper arms, halting her. "You still think he'll show and whisk you away from here."

"I do," she said without shame. "I think that every day. I hope that every day. Whatever we're doing here isn't working."

"You said there would be a sign. Has he sent a sign?"

She raised her chin. "Yes."

He flattened his affect. "Okay, you suck at lying."

"You think this is me looking for a booty call? It's not, okay? Be logical."

His hands fell away. "Me? Be logical?"

"We don't know what's going on out there. We don't know if he's with Zeus, against Zeus, in trouble, hurt, dead. And all the time, Beta is sitting empty."

"We don't know that either."

"There's intel in there. What harm is it to go in and get what we need?"

"And see if your guy is hanging around waiting for you to show?"

"Maybe there has been a sign and I'm too dumb to notice. We all know what I'm like with subtle. Exile said months ago that he wanted to be at the panel. If we can get him into the JARR control room—"

"Okay, that's more than intel gathering. H will never go for it."

"We don't need Harry," she said, taking his hand, appealing to the rebel in him. "He's a pig in shit having his guys around again. If it was up to him, we'd stay here forever."

"Pissed at daddy again?"

As he sauntered toward the door, she turned that way. "You're forgetting one thing. Maybe the most major factor…" He paused to look back and she tightened her sweater over her belly. "We have to get this done before I start to show." She'd already taken to wearing oversized tops and sweaters because soon she'd have to hide in them. It helped that it was winter. Though the house was warm, the air outside was biting cold. "We're talking a matter of weeks, maybe a month, before the cat is out of the bag."

"And you want Daire to know first?"

"He didn't know first. You knew, Zara knew, hell this Falcon guy I've never met knew before Daire did. Before I did! I want to protect my child from Zeus. If we're at Beta and he gets the upper hand… I don't want to think about it. When you said it before, in the lab, he wasn't outraged, he wanted to know who the father was."

"Yeah, 'cause he was thinking Ares two point oh."

"Exactly. I will not hand my child over to him. I won't do it. If we cover as many bases as we can before I start to show, maybe we can get away with him never knowing."

"It changes things," he muttered like he might be considering it. She could only hope… and beg. "We don't want D on the back foot. If he walks in somewhere, into Beta, and you're sporting a baby bump…"

"He'll be caught off guard. We don't want him distracted. We don't want him surprised. Whatever his plan is, he'd have to adjust for the development."

"He'd hesitate."

"Right," she said. "And hesitation gets you killed. We need to do this."

"We can't get into Beta," he said. "It's not physically possible, it's shutdown."

She nodded, creeping toward him. "We can get in.

You have the Scepter, don't you?"

"H does, but I know where it is."

"So we take the key and go. No debate. No back and forth. We just do it."

"Disobey orders again?"

She smiled. "You're the rule breaker, remember? Besides, has H actually told you not to leave the island?"

"Some orders are implied," he said, as Daire had once. "But the key alone doesn't help us. We need a code to get into the building and I don't have it."

"I do," she said, startling him. "That code started my journey to Beta. It's not something I'll forget in a hurry. Do you know the route in?"

"I know the route out," he said. "The final line of escape. And they're the same."

"Good," she said, hope buzzing in her belly. "Then we have everything we need."

"You're thinking he'll be notified. You know when that code's used, it sends a signal to every base unit."

"Would you be sorry if Zeus showed up? You've been looking for an excuse to kill him for months."

"H would say it's not smart. D would point out we could get intel from him."

"If Daire is with him, he's got all the intel he's going to get. If not, Z's just walking the earth on borrowed time anyway, he won't surrender to us, to anyone, you know that."

"You wouldn't stop me?" he asked, and she shook her head. He exhaled. "Going to Beta gets us nothing."

"You got in touch with Exile once, you can do it again. We get him to the panel, he checks out whatever he needs to check out and we go to Garrick's vault."

He frowned. "His vault, why?"

"To see if there's anything useful in there, and because we need to know the order of the keys. Daire knows which one goes first because the doctor did. Garrick is the only one who holds the order of another key."

"And the third goes wherever's left," he said on an exhale, his head bobbing in understanding. "We can't get into Garrick's vault without his code. You telling me you have that too?"

"No, but you do."

"I do?"

"Garrick hasn't changed his master code in ten years," she said.

The words hit him with surprise. "How do you know that?"

"Because Daire knows that," she said. "We can do this. We're not helping anyone sitting here."

He'd had the same thoughts himself. She'd watched him grow more impatient, edgier, with each day that passed. Training distracted him, for a while, but it didn't last. Like Daire, he needed to be doing something, being useful. Since the Exodus they'd had autonomy, made choices, set their own path. Sitting by idly while his brother could be in trouble wasn't Styx's style before the Exodus, why should it be after?

"We can't tell H," he said and she nodded fast. "We have to just disappear. No looking back."

"No looking back. Agreed."

"Wait here. Get whatever you need. I'll come get you when I have the Scepter."

A man on a mission, he stalked to the door.

"Styx," she said as he opened it an inch. "Thank you."

With a single nod, he left, closing the door behind him.

This was it. They were going. Their mission had started again. She hoped whatever lay out there, she'd see her Heart. Soon. And that he'd be in one piece. Breathing was all she needed. Everything else they would figure out. She needed him alive. Her hand rose to her stomach. They both did.

TWENTY-EIGHT

"THIS IS WHERE YOU MET?" Styx asked, taking in the Buckhorn office as they entered.

As adults. "In this very room," she said, hurrying over to press the button for attention.

She held her breath. It was crazy but some part of her expected Danny to walk through the door behind the counter. He wouldn't, of course he wouldn't. Daire hadn't left her safe on Falcon's island just to come work shifts at a junkyard.

When the door opened, her smidgen of hope was dashed. Tall, blond, she recognized this guy, but didn't know him. The patch on his chest read 'Jesse.' Once upon a time, she'd have taken that as gospel. Now, with what she'd been through, whether it was true was anyone's guess.

"What do you need?" Jesse asked, then noticed Styx and became wary. "He gonna cause trouble?"

"No—"

"Maybe," Styx cut her off as he sauntered over. "I've been bored for a while."

"Ignore him," she said, brightening her smile and nudging Styx away when he came up close. "I used to live out the back with—"

"Danny," Jesse said. Pointing at her, his lips curved.

"Yeah. Yeah. I know you. You're the screamer."

Embarrassment may have warmed her cheeks as she cast a look back to Styx.

He shrugged. "You do make a lot of noise."

"This your new guy?" Jesse asked.

"No, this is Danny's brother," she said, reaching out for Styx's hand. He didn't give it, so she had to go over and get it to bring him close to the counter again. "We're looking for him."

"Oh, man," Jesse said, scratching his head. "Haven't seen him for a while, not since he came to pick up his ride a few weeks back. Don't think he left a number, but I can call Earl, see what he knows."

"No, it's okay," she said. "We just wanted to make sure he didn't leave anything behind."

Jesse shook his head. "No, but you could leave a number, I can let him know you passed through if he shows up again."

"Thanks," she said. "I hope we'll catch up with him soon."

Styx put an arm around her as they left the office and crossed the lot. "Did you really expect he'd be there?"

"No," she said on a sigh. "But it's somewhere only he and I know about. If he wanted to leave me a message…"

He'd done it before, left her a message in her mom's car. She stopped. They'd already checked around the back of the office, even though it was clear the Beast wasn't there. She'd cast an eye around for her mom's car but hadn't seen it.

"What?" Styx asked. "What are you thinking?" She stayed quiet as her thoughts lined up. "Why'd you tell that guy I was his brother?"

"Daire doesn't cut ties with an asset unless he has to," she muttered, her mind elsewhere. "He says it can pay to have allies in different areas. Maybe one day you'll need an ally here."

Taking his hand, her speed increased when they got to the street.

"I'm kind of impressed you took anything in," he said. "You don't listen when the rest of us talk."

"I do, he just has a way of… focusing me."

"Yeah," he scoffed. "You gonna tell me more about this signal he's supposed to send?"

"You think Harry will be going crazy?" she asked. "If he looks for the Scepter and it's not where he left it…"

"Trust me, he's already looked," he said. "As soon as they knew we were gone, he looked. Don't imagine he's fun to be around right now. Are we picking up the other two keys while we're here? It's Christmas Eve. The mailbox place could be closed."

She turned a smile up to him. "Like that would stop you."

It was better to let him think the keys were where he'd sent them than admit she hadn't seen them since she and Daire last had them.

"That where we're going?"

"No," she said. "Taking me and all three keys to Beta would be irresponsible. We don't have our team for backup. We don't have Daire's intel."

And she didn't want the last few weeks away from him to mean nothing. He was working to improve their hand, to assess their opponents. There was no point rushing to claim the pot when all they had was the flop.

"We need somewhere to put our heads down tonight."

"You don't care about sleep."

He stopped and dropped her hand. "Quit telling me what's in my own damn head." Stalled, she stood a couple of steps from him. "Might work with your boyfriend, doesn't work with me."

"Okay," she said, holding up an apologetic hand. "I'm sorry."

"You are not running this op."

"So you are?" she asked. "This is operation back Daire up. When we go to Beta, we'll be on limited time."

"We'll have as much time as I want."

Inhaling, she closed in on him. "You can start Minotaur and give us access to everywhere, but you can't lock the building down."

"I might—"

"You need three codes," she said. "Three codes from three principals. Do you have all three codes?"

"Ares does."

"Yeah, but we don't," she said. "We have one code. The code to unlock echo entrance. As soon as we enter that code, we're on a clock. We want to get what we can from Garrick's vault, to learn more about JARR. We don't want to run into Zeus when we're alone."

"He wouldn't assume we were alone."

"No, he wouldn't."

"So he'll bring his merc army," he said. "How do you know Zeus isn't there already? That he and Ares aren't cozied up in Beta."

"Because I would've gotten a signal."

"The only signal sent is the one from that code to the three base units." As he breathed out, his shoulders dropped. "You have H's base unit." She nodded, just a tiny confirmation. "He left it with you." Again, she nodded. "He might think he was protecting you, but you do realize if you have it, we have no way to notify Ares that Beta is up and running."

"I have faith he'll know."

"How?"

She shrugged. "I don't know. But I know if we need him, he'll show up."

"You said you need him now, I don't see him anywhere around."

"This is different, we're not in danger. Can we…" She leaned to the side, nodding that way. "Get going?"

"Where are we going?" he asked. "You don't seem in a rush to get to Beta. But you were sure in a hurry to leave Falc's, you didn't want the happy family Christmas?"

"Christmas was always just me and mom. I don't exactly have a lot of family traditions to hand down. I don't do kids and Santa and stupid sweaters around the fireplace. I got a present from my mom. She got one from me. Christmas Day is actually a great day to travel. So long as there's fuel in the car, we can put a lot of miles on the clock while everyone else is playing charades and board games. And what would you even do with kids anyway? You've got even less experience than me, so I don't see why you'd want—"

"It was the kids," he said. "You didn't want to meet the kids."

Rolling her shoulders, she tried to shrug off her discomfort. "I don't know what to do with kids. How do I know what to say to them?"

"You're gonna have your own kid in like six months. You better figure it out fast."

"Bonding will be Daire's duty," she said. "He's good with people, I'm betting that extends to little people."

He laughed, which pissed her off. "That's why you need him alive? None of this soulmates, epic love stuff, you need him to handle the child rearing."

"Look, I'll figure it out, okay? I'm just not ready to see it like that, everyone hugging and wishing each other a merry Christmas."

"A little too prophetic? A glimpse into your own future?"

"It wouldn't be my future without Daire," she said. "I don't want to see everyone else so happy and having fun when the man I love could be lying somewhere dying."

"He's not dying."

"How do you know?"

"I don't," he said. "Except so long as you're around, keeping you alive is his primary mission. He never fails a mission."

"And what if he doesn't make it," she said and stopped, so Styx did too. "When we talked about this, about what it might take to stop Zeus and JARR, we talked about sacrifice. I always said if he went, I would too. It made him mad, but it really was the truth. I couldn't imagine carrying on without him, but now…"

Her hand rose just a little, but she dropped it before making contact. It wasn't a good idea to be in the habit of highlighting the baby when others might be watching.

"Now you have the kid to worry about."

"What would I do?" she asked. "Maybe we should

hole ourselves up somewhere until the baby is born. Then Daire can stay with him, and I'll go bleed for JARR."

"Tempting as that is," he said, laying a hand on her shoulder. "I don't think it's best for the kid to know his mom died on him without a fight."

"Didn't Daire's mom die on him? He turned out okay."

"And if you're not around, what do you think happens to junior? With role models like me and H? Daire wouldn't live out there on his own, he'd be with us. Which means your kid will be running marathons by three, proficient in firearms by age six, and a covert operative by nine."

"He wouldn't want that. He wouldn't raise our child as Olympus."

"If you've gone bleeding into JARR, it's released whatever horror's inside, what kind of world is that to raise a child in?"

"I have to bleed into it for Exile and Swift to do their work. Just because I'm dead doesn't mean we lost."

"So we won. We rule the world. Even if we killed Zeus, who is Ares's family? We're what he's got and all we know is killing shit."

"Are you trying to scare me?"

"I'm trying to tell you that H raised a kid once, Ares is that kid. It's the only way he knows. Your kid is gonna be able to defend itself no matter what. That's a given if you plan to have Ares, H, or me in its life. This kid needs something else. Something Ares didn't get."

"The only way I know is running and hiding."

"Your mom loved you, she gave you tools to get through, you were a unit. Did she give you missions and punish you if you failed? Beast you if you didn't give enough?"

"No."

"Then you do have something to give this kid. He, or she, needs a balance none of the rest of us got. It needs a mom and a dad. It needs family."

Something else neither she nor Daire had. Not in a traditional sense. "That means we both need to make it out alive."

"Right," he said and smiled. "And I have to live too, 'cause I wanna hear this kid call H 'Grandpa.'"

A short laugh shook her, but her smile quickly faded. "I didn't know what it was to have stakes this high. I thought it was bad, I was scared for us, but now… If Z learns about the baby…"

"As long as he doesn't learn about it before Ares, we're fine."

"We can't put it on him. We can't burden him with another life to protect."

"One step at a time, okay?" he said. That was some solace, she nodded and tried to focus. "You want to get a vehicle and drive down there? Will only take a few hours."

"We can't go yet. Daire always gives me direction," she said, licking her lips. "I have one more idea. If that doesn't work out, we'll break into the mailbox place."

One side of his mouth rose. "Even if it's open?"

"You said you've been bored, right? I might have a better one to start with." She took his hand again. "Want to do scary and intimidating for me?"

"Thought you'd never ask, Lady," he said, hooking their joined hands around her as they started walking again.

TWENTY-NINE

DARKNESS WAS ALREADY CLOSING IN. Artificial fairy lights flashed up and down the length of the busy street. Everyone was dashing around, desperate to get their last-minute shopping done. She hadn't bought presents, hadn't even thought to. On the island, there wasn't much of a selection. If she'd been thinking, maybe she'd have considered online shopping. Her mom didn't allow that. They bought their presents early and in person. Never knowing when they might have to move fast meant preparing as far in advance as possible. For everything.

Russell Figgs, PI. She tried the door before even coming to a complete stop. It didn't budge.

"Damnit," she said under her breath.

"Don't be so easily defeated," Styx said. "Is it the guy you need or something in there?"

"I hope something in there," she said. "Figgs is not the most together guy. I don't think Daire would trust him to relay a message."

Not accurately anyway.

Styx surveyed the street, then took her shoulder to hustle her past the storefront and into an alley. They kept on going toward a handleless door in the concrete.

"When in doubt…" he didn't stop, just moved a couple of steps back and lifted his foot to slam his heel into it.

It didn't open, but he had blasted a big hole in the wood.

"You never learned finesse, did you?"

"Always more my brother's style," he said, reaching in the hole to turn the lock. It popped open and he stepped back. "Voila." Although he said that like he was presenting her entry, he went inside first. "Hey, would you look at that!"

Peeking around him, she had to smile at the man seated at the desk, glass in hand. The wide eyes, the shaking liquid. Yep, this was definitely the right guy.

"Take… take whatever you want," Figgs sputtered.

"Thanks," Styx said. "I will."

He would anyway. As he went in to check the place out, she stayed just inside the door. Less interested in her, Figgs was watching Styx. Made sense, Styx was the threat. But they couldn't hang around all day.

She cleared her throat. It took a second, but the PI's attention did eventually swing around to her. She smiled, going for unthreatening, but shock impacted him again and he leaped from his seat, dropping his glass in the process.

"It's… it's you!"

"You remember me?" she asked.

"That's a bonus," Styx said, reading the book spines on the shelves.

"So you remember the guy that left me a box before?" she asked. Figgs glanced at Styx. "Ignore him. Do you remember the guy who left me the package?"

"Ye… yes."

"Has he been here? Did he leave something for me?"

The PI's jaw moved. Was he afraid or trying to remember what to say? "I… I…"

"We're kind of on a clock here, dude," Styx said and thumped the side of his fist on the shelf as he spun. "Answer the lady's question."

"The… there's a box."

Her heart soared as her head fell back. "Oh, thank

you, baby," she said on a rush of breath.

Daire always gave her direction. Somehow, he always just knew.

"Well, come on, guy," Styx said, clapping his hands a couple of times. "Move it! Where is it?"

"In… in the…"

Going to the desk, she didn't react as Figgs stumbled away. The key in the top drawer opened the closet in the corner, she remembered and didn't need his help. No, she needed Styx's after the door was open.

"I can't reach the top shelf," she said, and he came over to get the box.

She pointed but wasn't sure he looked. Maybe he recognized the tape sealing the lid.

He put it on the circular table and produced a switchblade from his pocket to slit open the tape. When it was done, he stepped back, allowing her to do the honors. Before lifting the lid, she took a breath. Whatever was inside could be her last link, her last message from her Heart.

Money. Bundles of cash. Pushing it aside, she wasn't surprised there was a gun there too.

"Cool," Styx said, taking the weapon out to check the clip.

An envelope. There on the bottom. She swallowed. Whatever his words said, she didn't want to read them in front of an audience. She grabbed it to stuff it into her carpet bag. It was heavy. There was something in there. Something she may not want the others to see. Thank God she hadn't opened it.

She put the money in her bag too, uncovering a spare clip that Styx put in his own pocket.

Slipping a few bills from the top stack, she put them on the table and took Styx's hand. No need to hang around.

"Thanks," she said as they headed for the door. "That should cover the… door." Styx went out first. "Merry Christmas."

As they hurried out of the alley, Styx dipped closer. "Merry Christmas?"

"Spreading holiday cheer. We need a car."

"Least we can afford it now," Styx said.

"If anywhere is open to selling on Christmas Eve."

"You have an ally in town… right?"

They shared a smile. And Daire had saved their asses again. Sure, it meant going back the way they'd come, but at least they could trust Buckhorn would sell them something reliable. Reliable enough to get to Beta anyway. If they needed to pick something else up on the way, Styx would handle that. Right now, they had to get out of the cold. A heater. Some food. And then she'd read her Heart's letter. She dreaded that almost as much as she craved it. Would he say goodbye to her again?

***

JESSE WAS QUICK and efficient and didn't ask questions. He didn't ask her questions anyway, Styx dealt with the actual purchasing. Not because it was a guy thing, because he'd be the one driving it and knew what worked best for the terrain. Buckhorn wasn't a car dealership. Jesse didn't try the hard sell. Though maybe that was because Styx wasn't the type of guy most people would risk provoking. And it was Christmas Eve, he'd want to get back to the party going on inside.

The jalopy had seen better days, but it had four new tires and a dependable engine. Apparently. They'd only been driving an hour, but it had held out so far.

"You gonna open it?" Styx asked, glancing her way from the driving seat. "You've been staring at it since we got on the road."

Her carpet bag was perched on the edge of her knees, leaning against the dash. "I don't know if I want to," she said, clutching the envelope in two hands.

"You two have a real thing for the letter writing."

"We don't carry phones. Don't have email. We were both raised to be wary of digitizing anything. Then I find out people like Exile and Swift exist and I know why."

"Staring at it won't change what's inside," he said. "What's in there is in there."

"It feels wrong," she said, her fingertips sliding up the

edge of the paper. "It's stupid, but it just feels wrong."

"Wrong?"

"To get news from him while I'm withholding…"

"Are you kidding me? You can't get in touch with him. The base unit was our only hope, and he gave that to you. You're not withholding, there's been no opportunity to tell him."

"I know," she said, tightening her hold a little. "But I… I'm not sure I want to tell him." That was the source of her guilt. "Even if he was here, I don't think I would."

"'Cause you don't want to put more on his shoulders," Styx said, making excuses for her. "And that sort of suggests you'd have a choice." She didn't understand and frowned his way. "You two tend to get horizontal pretty fast when you get together. I'm guessing horizontal means naked. Loose sweatshirts won't cut it if he's down to the flesh."

"I'm not showing," she said. "I started with the baggy clothes so it wouldn't be such an abrupt change when I do."

"My point is, Lady, you can only hide it for so long. Whenever you see him again, maybe you won't be able to hide it."

He was right. Of course he was. And it wasn't so much about hiding it from her Heart. "I feel guilty," she said, her focus on the envelope again. "Like I got knocked up on purpose. Whenever we talked about it, we both agreed it would never happen for us. That it was too dangerous to have a child together. But when I took that test before, I was disappointed when it came up negative. Some part of me wanted this."

And it was a not-so-secret part. Too often she got swept into imagining them as a family. A real family. Something she and Daire never had. But the picture was a fantasy, it could never be like that. With Zeus on the warpath and JARR creeping closer every day, there literally couldn't be a worse time to be pregnant.

"You wanted to have his kid, we talked about it in Vegas."

"And now it's like I got my wish… at his expense."

"You've got the implant in your arm," he said. "It's

not a fresh scar, you didn't take it out and not tell him. You didn't stop taking the pill just to trap him. These things happen."

"Like it happened to my mom. When she got pregnant, she had no way to tell Harry either. He didn't find out until I was basically due. He got no say and told me if he had, he'd have wanted to abort."

"D doesn't want that."

"That's what he says, but the reality is so different. No amount of speculation is the same as finding out there's another life inside you. He put this life inside me and now it's my responsibility to care for it. What if I fuck up?"

"We're going to get rid of Z. This JARR thing will go away. When it does, you'll both be free to do whatever the hell you want."

South America. A life on the road being carefree… Could they take a baby with them? Had she screwed up that dream too?

"He's not here, so I can tell myself anything. His being absent gives me that excuse…" She inhaled and held the breath before sighing. "But I'm desperate for him too. I focus so much better when he's around."

"Let me worry about the focusing," he said. "And open the damn letter… What if it says he's still back there and we're driving the wrong way?"

Excellent point.

She couldn't put it off forever. The envelope was thicker than usual and heavier too. Guessing what was inside, she needed cover for concealing what she suspected was one of Minotaur's keys. If Styx saw it, he'd know she and Daire picked up the keys he'd sent to her mailbox in secret. More than that though, carrying two keys together was risky. The third could be with Zeus. If it was, and their paths crossed, he'd have everything he needed.

She tore open the end of the envelope without taking anything from inside.

Daire couldn't have known she'd dragoon Styx into getting her off Falcon's island. He couldn't know they'd be together or that they'd have the Scepter too. Now it seemed the only way to be safe was to have the three keys completely separate. One with her, one with Styx, and, she hoped, one with Daire. Everything was coming together, but until she had word from her Heart, there was no way to know if it was happening in their favor or not.

"No," she said, dumping the envelope into her carpet bag, tipping the key out while pushing the bag onto the floor. "I can't do it. I can't."

"Want me to do it?" he asked. "'Cause we're getting to the point I'm just gonna take it from you and do it myself."

"You would read my private letter?"

"Yeah," he said without hesitating. "I've stood on the other side of the drywall while he fucks you, we have no secrets, sister."

Bending over, she retrieved the envelope, shifting her clothes to hopefully further hide the key that she couldn't see in the shadow. But the envelope was lighter, whatever had been in there was now mixed in with her other things. Not the most secure, sure, but at least it remained a secret.

THIRTY

SLIPPING THE PAPER from the envelope, she unfolded it to find a business card inside. Just like the one she'd found in the PI's box at the start of her adventure. Numbers. Two rows of numbers.

"Oh my God," she whispered, running a fingertip across them.

He knew she'd know because it wasn't a mystery this time. The top number, if it was the same as before, was an access code. The bottom numbers…

"What is that?" Styx asked, his eyes flashing between her and the road.

"Coordinates. He's telling us where to go."

"Let me see it."

She handed it to him. They were together, she trusted him. Wherever those numbers led, she'd take Styx with her, so why not show him?

As his brow lowered, she asked, "What? What is it?"

"This is Gamma," he said, handing the card back. "The top number will get us in."

Without blowing them to pieces, she hoped. "Why does he want us at Gamma?"

"I don't know," Styx said. "We're headed south

anyway. We'll stop at Beta then go down there… They leave a chopper at Beta?"

"I don't know," she said. "I didn't even know they had a chopper until I was in it."

Having only gone in and out of one side of the building until that point, their vehicular fleet remained hidden in places she'd never gone.

"That's not a no. What else does he say?"

She'd tried not to focus on the words. Her Heart. She'd kept secrets from him in the past, but never like this. Still, like Styx said, whatever was there, was there, she just had to take it in.

Being so close to you and staying away is torture. I don't know what brought you back to the mainland, but if it wasn't me, we have a lot to talk about.

I didn't know it would take this long. I didn't mean for it to be like this. All I can do is try to explain and hope you understand.

Battling Zeus, protecting you from JARR, it's important, but it's taken over. Once you had a different question, a different priority: finding out what your mother wanted you to know. You thought that was the mission and I led you on, which I'm sorry for, though it brought us together, so I can't be too sorry.

Your mom was your world. Everything you thought you were was wrapped up in her. You realized it too late. Something I know all about. We've been distracted, diverted too many times.

But I am a resource at your disposal. You remember when I said that to you?

"Yes," she whispered to no one, recalling the conversation they never got to finish in Vegas.

In Three's house. In the Beast actually, before Harry interrupted.

"Yes, what?" Styx asked.

"Shh," she said without taking her eyes from the words.

I know what you were going to ask me that day, what had been on your mind. Everything else kept getting in the way, but I am done failing you. I need you to know that you can rely on me. That no matter what you will always be my priority. There's a chance with what's to come that some won't make it out alive. Don't stop reading. For once, I'm not talking about me or us.

You want an answer to what happened at the beginning. What happened before you and I ever met, as adults. To what happened to your mom, how she ended up in that wreck.

"Oh my God," she murmured, her hand covering her mouth as tears welled in her eyes. "Oh, my Heart."

"What?" Styx asked again, but she kept on reading.

You might think this is an odd time for

me to complete this mission to find the truth, but it's not. I need to know that I can pull the trigger on anyone and not worry that I'm depriving you of the answers you deserve.

I heard you. In our bedroom, the night I left. As soon as I heard your need, read it in your eyes, I knew this had to be done. I need to serve you, LR. I will get you answers.

There's a limited pool of suspects. We can take the principals out straight away because H would never do anything to hurt the woman he loved. P couldn't care less about you or your mom. And Z, we both know he didn't have the resources to keep himself safe in this country. He ran off to Europe because he didn't have the personnel to maintain security. Given that, it's unlikely he'd divide what resources he did have on this vendetta.

Don't get me wrong, Z would love to punish H, he would, we both know that. But doing it from afar got him nothing, not even the twisted gratification he'd get from causing pain. Z didn't kill H at Beta when he had all three of you because he wanted to leverage you against each other. So why would he sacrifice you or your mom when you had value. He'd already used you against H once and got his way.

I haven't completely discounted his

involvement, but I was around you before your mom died. I was watching and I saw no hint of Z near your lives.

But here's the thing… and this is why I wish I was with you right now, I did have a suspect. Back then and in my investigation so far, everything I'm finding proves I was right.

Going to Miami, sticking with you, I didn't follow up as thoroughly as I should have. Back then, I really thought we'd all die in the control room, so what did it matter?

I know who's responsible for sabotaging your mom's car—

Scrunching the paper in one hand, she closed her eyes tight, pushing the tears from her lashes down to her lap.

"What?" Styx asked. "Shit, Lady, what does it say?"

"He knows who killed my mom," she murmured, fresh moisture leaving her eyes. "Goddamnit."

"Your mom?" Styx asked. "He's looking for your mom's killer? Where the fuck did that come from?"

Breathing slow, she tried to calm down. "I told him I wanted to know." Though she hadn't known he'd take that as a signal to investigate immediately. "Someone sabotaged her car and we never found out who or why."

"That's what he's doing? Did you know—"

"No," she said, raising the paper to her chest. "He says he wants to be able to pull the trigger on anyone and know he's not depriving me of finding out the truth."

His head bobbed in assent. "That's a good point. Fuck knows how this will go down, but chances are it ends with a body count. What else does he say?"

...but the physical act is not enough. He was working on someone else's orders. Who does that leave us with?

One is too self-involved to devote resources to it, especially given that at that point, he was pouring everything into keeping Zeus from going under. Killing your mom could be a sweet gift, from his point of view, except with Z on the retreat, he already had all the favor he needed. Two and five were dead, or busy running for their lives. Three, we both know doesn't have that kind of savvy. So who's left? Four or Six. Six might be dead, but he told Z about the assassination plot for a reason. The guy was a sniveller, not a planner, not a leader. How do you think he ended up Six all these years?

Four.

Four can disappear. I told you that. It's not unheard of. But to be off the radar for so long, something's up. Even if it's not, I need to eliminate the possibility.

I'm tracking our perpetrator, closing in, I'll get my confirmation from him. If I'm right, he goes to the Laird and then I bring Four in. This is not a mercy, baby, they don't deserve mercy, but I will await my Heart's orders. Once I have all the pieces together, I'll let you decide their fates.

I haven't forgotten about Z and we do need to know what else he may have in store. I heard you. Like I said in the letter I left in our room, I will find out everything before I come back to you.

Use the card. Follow the numbers. Wait for me. I'll come home to you, LR. Being away from you is torture and the fire that drives me. I love you. Always.

You are my truth. My something. Your Heart.

"He wants me to go to Gamma and wait."

"We'll go to Gamma after Beta."

"Maybe we shouldn't go to Beta."

Although it had been her pushing for it. Helping him gain intel had felt noble at the time, now she was hyperaware her Heart could have a plan. One she didn't want to mess up.

"We're going to Beta," Styx said. "You said you have the code. That we could get in."

"We can," she said. "I mean I could get in, but maybe we should wait for Daire."

"No can do," Styx said. "There's a plan, we have to stick to it."

"What plan? I thought we were making this up as we went along."

"We were. Until I told Exile to meet us there."

"He's waiting for us?"

His eyes narrowed on the road. "I don't think he waits for anyone," he said. "But he'll be at Beta tomorrow. We eat. We sleep. Then we make the rendezvous."

Exile. Rendezvous. Their itinerary had taken shape. She'd set them on this course and couldn't argue against it now. Daire might want her sitting somewhere safe and waiting. Unfortunately, things didn't always go to plan.

THIRTY-ONE

"ARE YOU READY FOR THIS?"

Sitting in the car by the Beta keypad that would open the gate, she wasn't sure what to do but nod.

The last time they'd been there together, they'd been running for their lives. Or, more accurately, Styx had been running and she'd been hanging over his shoulder.

Accepting her nod, he reached out of his window to input a code. Maybe a guest code. Maybe his. Maybe someone else's. It didn't matter. The real test would come after he stopped the car and they went to the door. She was the only one with the entry code. Could she rely on her memory? It had been six months since she'd used it.

"Leave everything," Styx said, parking the truck facing the gate.

He killed the engine and jumped out. She couldn't afford to second guess herself. She'd told him they'd get in and had to believe they would. Her doubt could cost them time and progress.

She got out, closing the door a second before he locked the vehicle.

The darkness seemed to exist in its happiest state around Beta. Why did they have to meet Exile at night? The place was spooky and unsettling at night, especially in its dormant state.

"Pandora."

The voice in the shadows startled her to a stop.

Styx didn't lose a step. "Echo entrance to control room. One route in, one route out," he said as a figure appeared from the black cloak over the corner.

Exile.

The woman at his side was taller than her, but not by much. The pair weren't touching, but they didn't need to, they carried the same air, almost like they shared an aura. She didn't quite get it, something just bled from them, like their proximity was necessary above all else. Something she could understand.

"Kero," Styx said as he stopped by the keypad and looked back at her. "Get us in, Pandora."

Did they need her? Maybe not. Exile and Kero bypassed the gate somehow. Though Daire told her that was an isolated system, maybe security was different and easier to penetrate.

Inhaling to fill her lungs, it was the worst kind of déjà vu to be standing there looking down at the thin glowing outline of each key on the pad.

"What's the hold up?" Exile asked. "You fuck me around on this—"

"Give her a second," Kero said.

Having another woman around offset the testosterone, at least a little.

Her pulse raced. Going inside again, there. It seemed counterproductive. But this was on their terms, it wasn't like before. No one was there to imprison them. To beat and torture them.

Imagining Daire was there behind her, like he had been the first time, she began to input the number. As her thumb moved toward the last digit, she paused. "Two, not a three," she whispered to herself.

"If you're not sure, why—"

The light around the keypad flashed green twice.

"Fuck, you did it," Styx said, grabbing her neck to pull her head to his lips.

After a quick kiss in her hair, he went to open the door.

"Should we check it out first?" Kero asked.

"Anyone left inside is dead," Styx said, opening his hand to her. "We're on a clock now."

They went inside and up the stairs. Just like Danny had, he paused before opening the door at the top. When it gave without requiring security, he actually exhaled a laugh. Their pace increased as they traversed corridors and stairs. Maybe a minute later, they were outside the control room.

She wouldn't have known that if it wasn't for the look Exile and Styx exchanged. The first time she'd entered that room, Harry was there with a gun. This time, they hadn't given anyone time to get there before them.

And instead of Danny, Styx was the one turning the handle and popping the door from the frame. He rushed inside and went to the control desk. The massive screens were blank, just like before. Everything was sleeping. Dormant. Waiting for life.

Styx went to the central section and opened the cover. He produced the Scepter from his pocket, showing it to Exile as he pulled out one of the seats and set his laptop down in front of the buttons and keys of the control desk.

"Ready when you are," the hacker said, opening his computer.

It wasn't like any other laptop she'd seen, but that was actually reassuring. They needed something superior to get through whatever Minotaur might throw at them.

Styx put the key into its custom slot, pushing hard at the last moment. A thud sounded. Then nothing and… A light above the screens, right there in the middle, began to flash.

"Is that a good sign?" she asked.

"There's life," Styx said, sitting at the opposite end of the control desk. "We should be able to…"

He typed in a few commands, the small screen in front of him flashed and then blanked.

"Leave it," Exile said, typing on his own computer. "I got it… I got it…"

"But I haven't—"

"Doesn't matter," Exile said. "This is my playground."

His focus didn't waver, his eyes stayed on the screen as a stream of letters, numbers, and symbols crossed it.

"You interfaced?"

"Oh, I'm more than interfaced," Exile said, his lips thinning. "It's art."

"Want me to drop to my knees?" Kero asked.

"Leave me with my girl."

Kero smiled as she turned, which seemed odd. Kero must've read her confusion because she paused. "The computer. I'm the other woman."

Okay, so the guy loved his computer, which made sense. What didn't make sense was why the woman was so calm.

"Putting the number into the keypad downstairs…" she said, compelled to ensure Kero knew they were in trouble. "It sent a signal to three devices. We have one. The other two are with—"

"Zeus and Poseidon, I know," Kero said, wandering around, taking in the space. "You want to show me around this heap of bricks?"

"Zip it and stay put," Exile said.

"I don't like to make it too easy for him," Kero said to her, ignoring her lover. "I get bored when he's playing with his toys."

"We could go to Garrick's vault," she said, seeking Styx. "Get in there and see what we can find."

Styx left his seat. "You good, Exile?"

"Just fine."

Kero came to her side as she and Styx went to the door. "He'll be busy for hours… Anything to eat in this place?"

"Bring me a cupcake," Exile called, putting another smile on Kero's face.

Styx took them into the corridor, leading the way. With Minotaur online, security panels worked, doors opened, the building was alive again.

"You're not what I expected," Tess said to Kero.

"Because Exile's such an asshole? Yeah, he takes some getting used to."

"How did you meet?"

"I stalked him," Kero said and shrugged. "Sort of. I was in a jam and he was my last resort."

"He forced you to be with him?"

"No! God, no. If anything, it was the other way around. It took time to worm my way in and even then, he pushed me away in some pretty… cruel ways."

"But you stuck around?"

"We can't let them get their way when we know what's best for them," Kero said. "You don't find that with Ares?"

"He's harder on himself than anyone else could ever be. The truth is, with everything we've been through, if we both didn't want to be together as much as we do, we'd have ended things months ago. We always find our way back to each other and when we do…"

"You can't help yourselves? Exile's entirely the opposite. Or he used to be. He has no problem refusing sex… He's turned on by more than the female form… it's complicated. And if he thinks he knows best, he won't hear anything else."

"I think they're all like that," she said.

When they laughed, Styx spun around. "You think this is your book club? Stay on fucking alert."

"What's going to happen?" Kero said, as nonplussed there as she had been upstairs in the control room. "We're alone in a building that was locked down until a few minutes ago."

"We don't know if—"

"We know Exile's in the system," Kero said. "I know you've been running for your lives for quite a while, but trust me, nothing happens in this building that my guy doesn't make happen. That means, you're safe so long as you're with me. If he wanted to kill me… No, wait, he always wants to kill me, but he's a pro at resisting that urge these days. If he kills me, the sex stops, so…" Kero widened her smile. "We're safe."

"Did you leave anything here?" Styx asked her, deadpan.

"I… don't think so. Nothing important."

"We can check Ares quarters," Styx said. "Stop at the armory, get some weaponry. Stock up."

"Your plan isn't to stop here?" Kero said.

"Z has his merc army, and whoever One is paying for security. He could be on his way here already; he could've mobilized the second he got the notification Minotaur was active again."

"If Z gets here, we're fucked," Styx said. "He outnumbers us. Your guy needs to do his digital recce fast."

"And I thought Exile was paranoid."

"Paranoid keeps us alive," Styx said. "Let's just move fast."

Weapons. Cash. Beta kept hoards of provisions in its bowels. Styx might not pay much attention, but he knew his way around. When they got to the main vault, he wasted no time in grabbing a cart to load it with supplies.

"It's amazing," Kero said. "All this shit just lying around in the middle of nowhere."

The shelves towered higher than anyone could reach and seemed to extend for miles. File cabinets stood around the perimeter of the room.

"Help yourself," Styx said, dumping a metal crate at the front of his load.

If Olympus was no more, they'd have no use for all the equipment.

"We're on the bike," Kero said. "But we will definitely come back."

"You won't get back in without the code," she said. "And I'd give you it, but without a key, Minotaur won't—"

"By now, Minotaur is my flame's bitch," Kero said. "Don't worry about that."

Styx told Kero to help herself. That had to extend to her too. And there was something in there she wanted. Something important.

"Where is the DNA?"

Styx pointed to the corner. "Results and comparisons are in the red one. The physical samples are in the fridge on the other side."

Samples.

Good.

"Why do you need DNA?" Kero asked.

"Because one of Zeus's big plans is to blackmail Ares's father. Without the evidence, that would be difficult to do."

As she went to the red filer, Kero crossed to the refrigeration unit. "These would be best in an incinerator," she said after opening the doors.

"Takes too long to fire it up," Styx said.

In the filer, everyone was listed in alphabetical order. Ares was right there where he should be. She pulled out the file at the same time the fridge door closed at the other end of the space.

"Ares," Kero said, holding up the vial.

"You ladies ready?" Styx asked, pushing his cart toward the door. "We'll stop at Poseidon's vault, then load up the truck."

They went into the corridor and Styx paused to code the door lock before continuing between them to lead the way again.

"What are we looking for in Poseidon's vault?" Kero asked.

"Anything on JARR," she said. "Specifically, if there's anything about the order of the keys. We need to know that before we can open the operator's panel."

"Exile wants a look at it."

"I don't know if we can get in without the code."

"Who knows the code?" Kero asked.

"Poseidon," Styx said and glanced at her. "Maybe Ares."

"Maybe?"

"Ares chose the code," she said. "When he was a kid. I don't know if he remembered it or not."

"He'll remember," Styx said. "If it's your life or the code, he'll remember."

Unfortunately, memory didn't work that way.

Styx pushed his cart to the end of the corridor and abandoned it to open a door to their left.

"You're leaving that stuff there?"

"We have to go up a floor for Poseidon's vault," he said, holding the door for them to go into the stairwell first. "You better be right about his master code."

"I'm right," she said.

Daire was right. She trusted him through to her bones. They ascended the stairs. Oddly, her Heart's apparent betrayal had strengthened her certainty in him. He'd had every opportunity to turn his back on her and cast her aside. He hadn't. He wouldn't.

She had to stop her hand moving to her stomach again. No matter what happened to her, so long as their child was allowed to be born, her Heart would give that same dedication to their offspring.

THIRTY-TWO

POSEIDON'S VAULT looked more like Asclepius's lab than it did the room they'd just been in on the lower level. Though it was five times the size as the doctor's evil lair.

The three of them stood just inside the thick steel door looking at the cabinets and drawers, the glass shelves with their vials and technology existed side by side.

"Okay, you guys know his system, don't you?" Kero asked.

They looked at each other. No. They didn't. How were they supposed to find the needle in this haystack?

Exile might be busy for a while, or he could be done in seconds, they didn't know. What she did know was Styx didn't want to hang around any longer than was absolutely necessary. And they couldn't adopt the "take everything" approach they'd used at the doctor's. For one thing, they didn't have time to pack everything, for another, they didn't have the space to carry it. Styx wouldn't want to do numerous trips. Even if he did, where the hell would they put it all?

"Take the hard drives," Kero said, stepping closer to the central workstations.

"The what?"

All she saw were screens and keyboards.

Kero went over to crouch at the solid unit accommodating the equipment and touched a seam. Shit, maybe they weren't solid. She twisted to look up at Styx. "Get me in here."

Styx was actually smiling when he went around to the other side of the central unit and crouched to do something over there.

"You know what to do?" she asked.

"Exile will. All I have to do is get the drives. If there's anything useful on there, he'll find it."

"Here," Styx called and Kero went around to join him.

Without Kero's help, she and Styx could've been there for days. Time was against them. The sooner they could get out of there, the more miles they could put between them and any principals who could potentially be on their way.

By the door was a stack of metal crates, she pulled an empty one from the top and went around to join them. With that many terminals, there would be more than one hard drive. She put the crate on the floor by Styx.

Kero seemed formidable in her own right. Had she always been so fearless or did Exile bring it out in her? Daire gave her strength, she understood that confidence, knowing the man she loved would go to any lengths for her.

She couldn't do much to help so wandered around, absorbing whatever she could. It was by accident that she saw the box marked "*Whist*." That had been used on her. It was potent. Opening the cabinet, she took out the box to slip one of the bottles out. So small and so dangerous. So useful. Putting the bottle in her pocket, she closed the box and started to hunt for the darts and the gun that went with them. Maybe they'd need it, maybe they wouldn't. But so long as it wasn't in Beta, it couldn't be used against her.

Yes, Beta would have more stores, but at least this meant they could possibly fight fire with fire.

It took at least half an hour for Kero and Styx to go around and remove every hard drive and hunt for hidden systems. In that time, she found what she sought.

A laptop sat on top of the full crate when she turned,

dart gun in hand.

"What's that for?" Kero asked, nodding at the weapon.

"Insurance."

"Come on, ladies. Work isn't done yet."

No, it wasn't, and they'd have to stay alert.

The way Kero had spoken of Exile made it obvious she trusted her guy completely. Tess wasn't sure what to make of the hacker. He made no secret of prioritizing his self-interest. His motto seemed to be, "what's in it for me." He needed a reason not to do something criminal versus the opposite.

Still, when the three of them went outside to load up the truck, she felt uneasy. Outside, in the darkness, they didn't have the protection of the building or the man at the helm.

"We'll stop by Ares quarters and—" The blast of sound came in the same moment Styx jerked back. "Shit." He grabbed both women and pulled them down to a crouch behind the truck. "Shit!"

"What was that?" she asked. Kero had blood on her hand. Where did that…? When Kero touched Styx's chest again, Tess put the pieces together. "Oh my God." She pounced closer. "You're shot."

"We need to move," Styx said.

"Guess we're not alone anymore," Kero said. Another bang, and another. The ground around them splintered and popped. "They're using hollow points." Their ally rose just enough to snatch a med bag from the top of their pile and curved around Styx to check his back. "No exit."

The two locked eyes; she didn't like what their silent exchange implied. They were too serious. Too solemn.

"Count of three…" Styx said, shoving the tailgate closed as he got the keys from his pocket. "Everyone in the truck. We need to get the fuck out of here. Fast."

"No," Kero said, stealing the keys to thrust them at her. "You're driving—"

"I don't know my—"

"You want to dig the bullet out?" No, she really didn't and shook her head. "You're driving. Styx in the back."

Another shot, rounds came faster, blasting the ground around them. "One… Two…"

"Fucking move," Styx said, huddling over her to force her around to the driver's side.

He opened her door to force her inside before opening the back door to get in himself. She turned the key and nothing. Shit. This better not be the moment that… The back doors closed, and she glanced back to see Kero helping Styx take his jacket off.

The side window shattered.

She jumped, thrust back into the peril of the moment. "Shit," she said, turning the key again.

This time there was life. She threw the truck into gear and sped toward the gate. No time to pause for gates to grant exit.

"Floor it," Styx said. "Don't hesitate."

"Shit," she said again, slamming the gas pedal to the floor.

They smashed through the barrier and in almost the same second an explosion lit the air. That was no Christmas display. They bumped across the concrete onto the dirt track with a trail of explosions bursting the ground in their wake.

"That's a security weakness Ares will want to fix," Styx said and hissed in a breath. "Shit."

"Lie the fuck down," Kero said, crouched between the two front seats, facing into the back.

"Is he okay?" she asked, the ting of bullets hitting metal echoed as the explosions silenced.

"I don't know yet," Kero said.

Fabric tore and there was more cursing.

"What was that?" she asked. "Who was shooting at us?"

"I don't know," Styx said. "Best guess, Zeus had sentries. Guys he sent to watch the building in case anyone was dumb enough to come ba—fuck!"

"Okay, you're tacky," Kero said, her voice calm yet rough around the edges. "You need to calm down. You're running on adrenaline and going into shock."

"Who's shocked?" he asked. "I've been shot a bunch

of times."

"Lie there and shut up," Kero said. It sounded like the woman was hunting for something. "I don't have anything for a local. I have needles and no drugs."

"Just do it."

"Fuck the macho bullshit. You keep losing blood and your body goes into shock, you'll shut down. Who keeps your Pandora alive then? You don't want to be awake for this."

"Do we have a choice?"

"Fuck," Kero whispered.

Suddenly, she had a thought and grabbed the bottle from her pocket. "Give him this."

"What is it?"

"The Whist."

"Shit," Styx said, his voice weaker. "Just fucking do it."

"How much?" Kero asked, ignoring him.

"Give it," Styx said. She tried to glance back, to see what was happening. Styx was drawing the Whist into the needle. "Lady, you have orders."

"Orders?" she asked, her head snapping front to back, checking him and the road. "What orders?"

"The card," he said. "Dump the rest of us and get there. Whatever it takes."

"Styx," she said, her eyes blurring. "I can't, I—"

"He's out," Kero said. "Thank fuck."

She hadn't slowed the vehicle. They raced along the dark road cutting through the forest. She'd driven that route with Danny. With Daire. Conscious and unconscious.

"Will he be okay?"

"I get the bullet out, clean the wound… I can sew him up. It doesn't look like it punctured his lung, but I'll find out… He's still bleeding bad."

Too much blood loss would be detrimental. She couldn't lose Styx, he was her friend, her brother, and he'd put so much on the line for her and Daire. They couldn't just—

"Oh my God," she gasped, trying to look into the back again. "Exile! We just left him—"

"Don't worry about him."

"Why didn't we go back into Beta? Why did we—"

"Because the building corners us," Kero said, distracted by what she was doing. "If we holed up there, they'd keep us under siege. Even if Ex could lock the building down, where would we go? We don't trap ourselves with no route of escape."

"But he's back there alone. They'll kill him."

Kero snickered. "No, they won't. You haven't noticed how useful my guy is? To use him, they'd have to get their hands on him. And that won't happen. My flame always has an exit strategy."

"I can't believe this," she panted, checking the rearview. "It doesn't look like anyone's following us."

"They'll be awaiting orders or think they can get to whoever's left inside. From how I understand it, no one can kill you until they've used you for JARR."

"Yes, but—wait, they could be tracking us. They might be—"

"Let's see…" When she glanced back, Kero had a device in her hand. "Pull over."

"What?"

"Pull over." Slamming on the brake, she brought them to a stop at the tree line. Kero grabbed her arm, pulling it into the backseat to fill her hand with fabric. "Keep pressure on that."

She shoved her hand toward Styx, forcing her to lean between the seats to hold pressure on his chest wound. Kero jumped out in a crouch. She couldn't see where the woman went. All she could see was Styx's pale, expressionless face. Even in the shadow of the truck, it was easy to see he'd been hit hard. A chest wound. He was lucky to be alive. They could've lost him. Just like that. Life could be taken in a blink.

Kero got back in and closed the door. "Done. Get moving."

"Done?" she asked, driving again.

"Tracker destroyed."

"Is that why they let us inside? To tag our vehicle? To find out where we were going?"

"Maybe. More likely, they weren't on site. God knows

how long they've been out here with nothing going on."

Zeus wouldn't care about leaving people in isolation or how long they were left there. It couldn't be easy to be ordered to watch an inaccessible building while you were sitting in freezing conditions outside in the middle of winter.

"I'm sorry about Exile."

"Seriously," Kero said. "He's fine."

"How can you be sure?"

"Because if his heart stops, I'd get a buzz."

"A buzz…?"

Kero held up her arm for a second. "Our chips are connected."

"Your chips? He chipped you?"

"He's been chipped much longer than I have," Kero said. "But yeah, I'm chipped. It's how he'll find me."

So they were being tracked, just by someone on their team. "Will he be mad you left?"

"He'd be madder if I stayed put or went back for him. We've been in situations like this before. We've talked it out a bunch of times."

Daire would probably tell her to get herself safe too. She'd be one less thing he'd have to worry about if he was running for his life.

"How's he doing?"

"We'll have to get antibiotics," Kero said. "Ex will have supplies if he catches up with us first. We should find a motel, let Styx sleep this off. He'll be sore when he wakes up, unless we can get him some of the good stuff."

"Medication," she said. "Painkillers. If Exile doesn't—"

"Don't worry so much," Kero said. "If we have to break in somewhere to steal pharmaceuticals, we'll break in and steal them. You've got to be willing to do whatever it takes in this life… Helps that Ex will hack any system to erase the evidence."

"He's got you out of jams before, hasn't he?"

"You have to trust your guy. Think Ares would abandon you?"

"No," she said. "He always gives me direction…"

The Scepter. If Exile didn't shut Minotaur down and take the key out, Beta would be ripe for the taking. Even if he did, who was to say he'd hand it back to them. They might have just given a criminal the key to the store, literally.

She'd been right. It was too dangerous to have keys together. They shouldn't have them together at all. Switching track, the best way to ensure safety was to protect their advantages. She didn't need a key for Gamma, Minotaur wasn't on. As far as she knew, the failsafes hadn't been activated down there.

Rather than head for the highway, she went a different way. Kero was still in the back dealing with Styx and didn't seem to be paying attention to where they were. She kept up as much speed as she could, getting there as fast as possible.

She stopped the truck in the trees, with nothing else in sight.

"Where are we?" Kero asked, glancing around.

"I have to do something," she said, lunging across to scramble in her carpet bag. When she found the key, she wrapped it in a shirt and grabbed a bottle of water as she got out. "Wait here."

Maybe it was madness, but it just seemed to be good sense. Moving as fast as she could through the trees, she turned to ensure the truck was out of view before hurrying to the clearing. The lake. No Beast. No surprise. It was comforting just to be there, in the spot she and Danny once enjoyed each other. But nostalgia wasn't her motivation.

"Behind the rock at the tree line where you left your clothes safe and dry when we went skinny-dipping.," she whispered her Heart's words as she went to exactly that spot.

Checking around, she ensured no one was watching when she dropped to her knees to scrape at the dirt. It was hard, compacted, but she grabbed a rock and pounded at the ground until she had a hole around a foot deep.

Pushing the shirt wrapped key down, she covered it over, patting the dirt back into place. She opened the water and took a sip before pouring the rest over the displaced area. The water would help settle it again and if it froze, all the better.

Her hands were dirty, so she went to the lake to clean them fast. If she got back into the truck with muddy hands, it would be obvious what she'd done.

She wanted to protect them. All of them. And sometimes that meant a little misdirection. It was done. Now Styx was her focus. He had to get better, and she'd do whatever was necessary to care for him. Whatever was necessary.

THIRTY-THREE

It's so quiet.

Kero's been gone less than an hour and I'm climbing the walls. Getting Styx into the motel room was difficult enough, now sitting here, watching over him, I feel the strain again.

I'm sorry. I should be saying that to Styx, I will say it to him, but I feel like I've let you down too. He's your brother. We talk about him protecting me, you tell him I'm the primary mission, and then he's the one injured.

As bad as I feel about that, as scared as I am for his wellbeing, I can't stop thinking about you. Out there. Alone.

I didn't do much to help Styx, Kero was the one who jumped to action. She's formidable. So formidable it's enviable. She doesn't panic, doesn't feel fear, she just acts. Why can't I be like that? I find myself surrounded by all of these capable people and it just makes me feel more inadequate.

I should've pushed H harder, demanded that he train me to look after myself. I don't want to be the reason anyone gets hurt. I don't want to be the reason we lose someone important to us. Anyone.

And you're out there. Alone. Kero and Exile have a connection, a physical connection that assures them both the other is okay. Why can't we have that? I know you're strong, you're the most skillful man I've ever met, but I still fear for your safety. I worry about you. Every minute I worry. I thought it was bad before, that the not knowing was hard when it was just us. But now...

If we don't make it through this, if I don't make it through, know that I love you, so much. Know that however it happens, you brought me comfort in my final seconds. I love you and if I never see you again, if we never find each other, understand I'm grateful, for so much. Grateful for you. Above everything else.

Like you said, how we met brought us together. I'm happy it happened, that we got to know each other as we did, without the darkness.

Your letter... what you're doing out there... I can't even find words capable of describing my awe. It feels like you're always holding me up, always going to incredible lengths to provide for me. What do I give you? Nothing. I'm not able to provide for you in the same way. It seems unfair that you *have to be our strength all the time. You are our rock. Our touchstone. Our guiding light. All I do is hold you back and make you vulnerable. Why do you put up with it? Why would you want to be with me? It doesn't se—*

The motel room door flew open, and she surged to her feet as Exile came striding in. He didn't say anything, just slammed the door and stalked to the chair in the corner to sit and open his laptop.

"Are you… okay?" she asked.

"I'm pissed."

Okay, yeah, she could see that. "Kero's—"

"She's on her way back."

Had they spoken already or was he just going by her chip?

"I'm sorry that… Did they hurt you?"

"They pissed me off," he said, typing. "'Cause I had to go out my way to murder the fuckers. That was Z?" He stopped typing to land his narrow, intense glare on her. "We're done fucking around."

"What does that mean?"

"It means if your guy wants a piece of the action, he better get his ass here."

She stepped closer. "I have no way to get in touch with Ares, I'm waiting for his signal. And Styx needs time to recover. The more time the better."

"Yeah, well, I don't have time or give a shit."

The door opened again, but Exile kept on scowling at her.

"I leave you alone for two minutes," Kero said, closing the door and coming to hand over a bag of drugs and medical supplies. "What's going on?"

"I'm pissed," Exile said, typing again.

"That's no newsflash." Kero looked at her. "How's our patient?"

"Still sleeping. The Whist can last a few hours."

"Do you know how to set up an IV?"

"No."

Kero took the bag back to head over to Styx's side. "Come here and I'll show you."

"Don't get attached," Exile muttered.

"You sit over there and seethe."

"I don't want another one of your damn pets," he said. "You never fucking learn."

"Walk out the door, Flame."

"I'm sorry everything went this way," she said. "If we'd known there were people there—"

"Did you scout it?" Exile asked.

She turned to him. "What?"

"Did you scout the site?"

"Did we?" Kero asked. "Shut up, we're not taking their shit out on each other. I gather they're dead." Exile went back to his typing. "How many were there?"

"Four," he said and paused in his typing to look at her again. "What signal's your guy sending?"

"Excuse me?"

"You said you were waiting for Ares's signal. What is the signal?"

Should she tell him? Without Styx or an ally of her own around, she had to decide who to trust. It was the intent work of Kero that helped her decision.

"Each of the three principals has a base unit," she said, talking more to Kero than Exile. "Zeus and Poseidon have theirs. Ares had Hades unit… he gave it to me. When it's time to meet, he'll send a signal to the base unit."

"Give it to me," Exile said.

Horror flared her eyes. "No."

"You want your guy back? Give me the damn unit."

"I shouldn't—"

She stopped when Exile stood up to dump the laptop on his chair.

"Okay, everybody stop," Kero said, standing up to put herself between them. "We're all pissed off, we got shot at. One of our team took a hit. Adrenaline's high, we are not going to turn on each other."

"Finish whatever shit you're doing, we're leaving."

"No."

"Cupcake," he warned.

"You want to leave, leave," she said. "Have I ever stopped you? You want to stomp out your bullshit, go stomp it out. Did you forget why we joined this madness in the first place? This JARR, whatever it is, it's a cousin to the Point. Benjamin's funding came from somewhere… I didn't ask enough questions. You know how dangerous the Point could be."

"I stopped that, didn't I?"

"But to stop this one, you need to be at the operator's station. We're in this because it's a global threat. We can't sit back and hope it will pass us by. If we want to fix this, we have to be in it. You are the only one who can fix this. It's your fault for being so damn good at what you do."

"I don't trust them."

"You don't trust anyone."

"I trust you."

"And I'm the one telling you we have to be here."

"They shot at you."

"And you killed them," she said. "I kept myself alive, didn't I? You know you don't get rid of me that easy. How many times have we been here? Arguing about what's the best course? You know why we're here, Flame." Kero crept closer to her guy. "You know we need to do this… Don't you?" Sliding her hands up his chest, she coiled her arms around his neck. "How will we be bad together if we're dead, my love?"

"What happened to fuck the world?"

"I still say fuck it, but it's hard for us to live in it if it doesn't exist."

He groaned in frustration. "I don't play well with others."

"Something I've always known about you," Kero said, a smile in her words. "I love you."

Though it was said in a whisper, it didn't feel like Kero cared who heard her. As she drew her guy down for a kiss, Tess turned her back to give them privacy. Love. Witnessing it made it seem so simple. It was anything but.

Maybe it was the life they lived, the danger they were always running from, but nothing seemed simple.

Daire, her Heart, was out there, and she wanted to know he was okay. Styx, lying out on the bed, seemed peaceful, more at ease than he could ever be while they were fighting the threat. Z had so much to answer for, Olympus did. Even if they triumphed, the damage Olympus caused wouldn't be erased. It was in them. All of them. Her, Daire, Styx, even Harry and Garrick. It took something from them and crafted the people they were. Without it, maybe they'd all fall apart.

Her carpet bag was on the bed by Styx. She opened it up to rummage inside. The base unit. She hadn't spent much time examining it. Though there were times she'd stared at the blank screen, wishing it would spring to life and link her to her Heart again.

Purpose sped her stride toward the kissing couple. "Do what you need to," she said, interrupting their moment by thrusting the device their way. "Don't contact Zeus or Poseidon, not until we've brought Ares up to date."

"We're in control," Kero said as Exile took the base unit. "We're stronger. We have everything they want."

"And more," Exile said on his way to pull the chair over to the dresser so he could work on a solid surface. "If Ares is out there, if he has so much as a watch on his wrist, I'll find him."

"He will," Kero said, setting her hand on her shoulder. "We'll concentrate on Styx. Get him back to full strength."

The guy had taken a lot of hits. Before meeting in London, he'd endured captivity and torture. After their capture and imprisonment in Beta, his own brother beat on him. Now he'd been shot. Why did it seem one guy was bearing the brunt of the pain? It wasn't fair, but there wasn't a damn thing any of them could do about it.

THIRTY-FOUR

WHEN SHE OPENED HER EYES to the empty bed, they drifted shut again without any alarm. No, it took a second for that to hit her full force. She sat up, looking left and right. Exile was still at his computer. Kero slept on the other bed. Their patient had been in the bed when she lay down. Where did he go?

"Styx," she said.

"Bathroom," Exile said without missing a beat.

She leaped up and ran, but stopped at the end of the bed to ask, "Did you sleep?"

"He doesn't need to," Kero mumbled from behind her.

Apparently, she wasn't as asleep as it appeared.

Styx.

Hurrying to the bathroom, she opened the door and went straight in. "What are you doing?" she asked.

In only his underwear, the dressing on his chest was a stark contrast to the dingy room around them.

"I'm going to take a shower," he said.

"You can't do that. Go lie down in bed. You need to rest… I can't believe you're up."

"It was a gunshot," he said. "I'm not dying, Kero got

it out, we're fine."

"We are not fine," she said, marching closer. "What would I have done if you died? Huh? What would I tell Daire? What would I tell Harry?"

"That I went out a fighter," he said, hooking a hand around the back of her neck to tug her closer and kiss her head. "I told you to go to Gamma."

"I wasn't going to leave you, especially not with the Whist in your system."

"Yeah, that shit's a kick in the sack," he said. "Now I know why you were so pissed at being shot full of it." He touched her stomach. "Everybody okay?"

"I was scared," she said. "You cannot be chill about this. You were shot."

"I've been shot before," he said, going to turn on the shower. "It's not that big a deal."

"It's a big deal to me."

"You were scared, I heard you," he said. "Ex took care of the threat, we're good."

"Those were sentries. That's what you said. Just because the shooters are dead doesn't mean the threat is gone."

"No, which is why I'm going to take a shower and we're getting back on the road."

Her shoulders moved as she tried to hold onto her confidence. "I gave the base unit to Exile. He says he can contact Daire."

"And you want him to come running back from what he's doing?"

"Did Exile tell you what he found last night? Was getting him in there worth it?"

"We haven't talked about it yet, but it was worth it. Ex can't be near tech without absorbing new information. He's a sponge."

"I miss him."

"D," he said, resting a hip on the vanity. "You've been missing him for months."

"Kero was so together last night. If we'd been alone... I'm not sure either of us would've made it."

"We don't think like that. We got the job done and everyone on our side is alive."

"Daire said you used to break missions down, go back over what happened, talk about potential weaknesses and alternate ways to do things."

"Yeah, but that was Olympus and we're not Olympus anymore. We run things our own way now. You gonna help me in the shower?"

"If you need help, yes, I will."

He smiled. "Yeah, 'cause that's what I want to tell my brother."

"He trusts us."

"He trusts me to keep you alive. That's what I don't think you realize. If we hadn't made it out last night, that would've been on me. Not you."

"It shouldn't be that way."

"Maybe, maybe not, but I can't let us be vulnerable like that again."

"What does that mean?"

"Our friends are on their way," he said. "I'll shower and rest until they get here. After that, we're moving out."

"You mean H? His people."

"No," Styx said. "If there's a showdown, we'll call them, but we need to be able to move fast, be quick and discreet."

"Wreck?" He nodded. "I don't want other people to die for us either. If Exile's spoken to Daire—"

"If they'd talked, I would know," Styx said. "We need to eat something, get our strength back."

It wouldn't be a bad thing to get something into the patient, so she nodded along. "Okay, food and backup."

Then they'd talk more about what came next. Had she jumped on Exile contacting Daire because she was so desperate to see him? Her motivation was difficult to unpick. What was best for the mission? For the people involved? Was she just being selfish and weak?

***

"SHE'S BEEN GONE A WHILE," Tess said, leaning back on the headboard. "Should we worry?"

"About Kero?" Styx asked, his lips curling as he went back to checking the weapons he'd retrieved from the truck. "Not while Exile is still alive."

"He can't protect her all the time."

Though it may not be the smartest thing to question the man's ability while he was still in the room. They'd been sitting there for more than half an hour and the guy hadn't said a word. The crate of hard drives was still beside him, so he was busy. Still, it was unnerving somehow.

"He doesn't have to be with her to protect her," Styx said. "Whatever jam she gets herself in, he can get her out."

"He can't get her out a hospital bed if someone shoots her."

"Maybe not, but he can assemble the world's best doctors at her bedside and has every cutting-edge tool at his disposal, experimental and proven. Biological and technological."

"How?"

"Everything is digital," Styx said. "He can access email, book flights, pay people, and hack any private or government facility. If he needs it, if she needs it, they can get to it."

Her mother raised her to suspect technology. To be aware of being tracked or pursued. If Exile wanted to find someone, anyone, he'd be able to.

The insight skewed her view on something she'd written to Daire. "What if he needs something?" she asked. "What if he's the one shot? Can Kero do the same for him?"

"Opal takes care of her if I'm down," Exile muttered.

"Opal?"

Kero came in carrying a box of food that smelled incredible. She hadn't been hungry until the scent assaulted her.

"What did you get?" A buzz silenced them. "What was that?"

"It sounded like—"

Styx stopped when Exile picked up the base unit.

"Oh my God," she said, rushing over with Styx and Kero not far behind. "Was that—"

"LR?"

Tears flooded her eyes. "Oh my God." She crouched closer. "I'm here, baby."

"What's going on?" he asked, his voice a tenuous but welcome glimmer of their connection. "How did you—"

"Ex," Styx said behind her, laying a hand on her shoulder. "Got a report?"

"Not over this line," Daire said, his voice heavy with concern. "You get my package, LR?"

"Yes," she said, wishing they could be alone.

"You follow my instructions?"

"We took a detour," Styx said, answering for her.

"Beta. That was you?" How did he know they'd been at Beta? "You need to get out of there. Pieces are moving."

"We left Beta," she said. "In a hail of bullets. Styx got shot."

"Thanks," he said, squeezing her.

"Bad?"

"No, I'm good."

Like it was no big deal. "Kero saved his life."

"You need to follow the package. Both of you. I need more time. Hole yourselves up and wait." Not such a bad suggestion when Styx could do with the recuperation time. "H?"

"Where you left him."

"Good. At least one person can follow instructions. I have your answers, LR. But I'm tracking the source, I do not want to walk away from this now. Can you wait a little longer?" Every minute without him got harder. "If you say the word—"

"I can wait," she said, thinking of the child in her belly. With witnesses and on a line he didn't trust, she couldn't give him the news. "Are you safe? Hurt?"

"I'm fine," he said, some of his worry easing. "Working for you, baby. Ex there?"

Exile's gaze moved to Kero's. "Yeah."

"This'll go faster if you give me everything you can

on Four."

"I'm not your fucking friendly neighborhood hacker. I don't give a shit about Four."

"Two, Three, and Five have been neutralized," he said. "One has to be last and Six is complicated, but it's Four I really want. We really want."

"Why?" No response. "You want my help, you give me the script."

"I don't know how secure this line is."

Exile tapped a key on his keyboard twice. "Completely."

"If you want his help, you show trust," Kero said. "Didn't I bail your brother and your girl out last night?"

Was this calling in a favor? Evening the chit. Kero could be cutting when she needed to be.

"Four instigated the hit on Helen." Her mother. "I can't get to the why unless I can get to Four. Something doesn't add up and I don't want to be blindsided. If Four initiated that, I'd guess Four was more involved in the plan to assassinate Zeus than we previously thought."

"Four set up Two," Styx said. "Prompted Two to make the play, so it would land on him if Zeus found out."

"Which is exactly what happened," Daire said. "Zeus murdered Two and Five for introducing the operation."

"That doesn't explain why Helen was killed."

"No, it doesn't," Daire said. "Somehow, it has to be linked. The plot to kill Zeus fell apart. The Exodus happened. Do we believe the Six just went back to their lives and forgot about it? No. The assassination failed and somehow Helen's death was the backup plan."

"If they couldn't kill Zeus, they wanted to kill Hades? Or have them kill each other?"

"That's what I'm thinking. Whether they killed Helen or Pandora, it didn't matter. If H found that out on his own, if he learned about the death, he'd be on the warpath."

"And take Zeus down himself?" Styx asked. "So either way we have Zeus dead."

"And potentially Hades. We know Zeus has a backup plan with JARR, I'm willing to bet he has a backup plan for his death too."

"Four has been on the run since the Exodus," Styx said.

"We need to know why. Is Four running for their life or laying low until the plan runs its course?"

"Maybe they want to remake Olympus," Kero said. "Without the current principals involved."

"Maybe."

"You benefit most from that," Exile said. "Wasn't the great Ares cultivated for the top spot?"

"Yeah, well I don't want it. They brought me the mission to assassinate Zeus first, before they took it to H. I said I didn't want it."

"So they kept you out of whatever came next," Kero said. "Shame."

"Yeah. I didn't know I'd need to be on the inside of anything back then," Daire said.

"Four whispers to Two and Five to instigate the plot to assassinate Zeus," she said. "Which put them in the firing line, saving Four from being to blame when things went wrong. After the Exodus, we think Four still had designs on rebuilding and went to plan B. That meant killing me or my mom to fire up H, potentially leading to Zeus and Hades killing each other." She paused for a moment. "What did Four want Olympus to be? What did they want to rebuild?"

"I don't know," Daire said. "Which is why I need to get my hands on Four. Ex, you were in Minotaur?"

"Yeah."

"That was why you went to Beta?"

"Yes," Styx said. "And we swiped a bunch of hard drives from Poseidon's lab. Ex is trawling through them, if there's something on the order of the keys, he'll find it."

"You have to keep the keys far away from each other," Daire said. "We can't risk Z getting them. If he gets the keys, Pandora's next. Did you shut Beta down again?"

Everyone looked at Exile. "Yeah. And I got your precious Scepter."

"The Scepter?" Daire said, confused. "You woke Minotaur with the Scepter?"

She could almost feel his intrigue burrowing into her. "That's the only one of the keys we have," she said, hoping to sound normal and not provoke others interest.

"The only one?"

"Mm hmm," she said, trying not to flinch. Exile had the Scepter, or, at least, she hadn't seen him hand it to anyone else. The Bolt was with Daire, and she'd buried the Trident next to their skinny-dipping rock. "That's good though. Like you said, we have to keep them far from each other. Safe and dry." Like her clothes. "We have to be careful, I don't want to be next."

"The keys don't matter as much as the intel right now," Styx said. "One way or another, we have to find out what else Z knows that we don't. What's the ace?"

"Power," Exile said, attracting all of their attention. "The ace is power. It's a backup plan. If either of the financial or biochemical attacks fail, the system will take control of the grid."

"The power grid?"

"For the continent," he said. "At least."

"Shit. How do you know that?"

"Because I was in Minotaur," Exile said. "Tracking the connection between Minotaur and JARR wasn't that hard. If I'd had more time…"

"We can get you more time," Styx said. "If you think you can shut it down—"

"I can't," he said. "Not without triggering the attacks."

"We're going to stop the financial and biochemical attacks," Kero said. "Does that mean the attack on the power grid is inevitable?"

"If the continent loses power, everything stops working," Exile said. "Zeus can hold governments to ransom for as long as he wants. And if JARR is in the system anyway, there's no telling what else he might be able to access."

"Zeus is no tech whiz," Styx said. "How would he—"

"Poseidon," Daire said. "That's why he's keeping Poseidon close."

"Even Swift could neutralize Poseidon."

"Which makes you and Swift two of the most important people in what's to come."

"Others could do it."

"Do you know anything more about the order of the keys?" Styx asked.

"No, but once I'm done with Four, I'll join Zeus. We've been in touch, I'm keeping him close."

"Where is he?"

"Europe," Daire said, which got snickers from Styx and Exile. "One is still with him, best I can tell."

"And Six?"

"Reluctant. He wants to see the proof. The DNA evidence. Zeus can't get at that right now, but Six is not taking any chances about calling his bluff."

She looked at Kero, who was looking right back. "We got the DNA. We pulled it from the vault, it doesn't exist in Beta anymore."

"That's good," Daire said. "Destroy it. Don't wait."

If Zeus wanted proof to dangle over Six, he'd need a sample from Daire. When he was a kid, he wouldn't have resisted, now there wasn't the slightest chance of anyone getting hold of the great Ares without his consent.

"Meet you in Texas?" Exile asked.

"Works for me," Daire replied. "Styx, hole up with her."

"Roger," he said, though he didn't sound that wild about it.

"We're almost there, LR."

"I miss you."

The words just tumbled out, but she wasn't sorry they'd escaped.

"I love you," he said, without caring there were others listening apparently. "Remember what I trust?" Their love. And Exile's too. "Be safe, baby."

And the base unit went dark.

For a few seconds, no one said anything.

"Okay," Styx was the one to break the tension. "Guess we all have our orders. Let's move out."

THIRTY-FIVE

Why does time go so slowly? Every day I wake up and I still think of you. I want to touch you, to tell you about my dreams, to plan our lives. It's not meant to be, is it? It's been seven weeks since I last heard your voice on the base unit and I try to keep faith in our future, but it's so difficult. We feel so far apart in so many ways. What happened to our easy days when loving each other was enough? Or maybe I'm kidding myself, was it ever like that?

Gamma doesn't feel like home. I know I've said that before. That I keep thanking you for what you did to make my suite special. What really makes it special is knowing you were here, that you once existed in this space. If I could imagine us together again, maybe I could settle here. But the truth is, all I want is you, the Beast, and the open road.

When Styx and I got here, there was gratitude for the time. He didn't say it, but I felt it. I wanted him to have the time to recuperate, to get better, and back to full strength. He's been training harder every day. Every single day I see his determination grow. He's tired of being here. Tired of sitting still and doing nothing. I am too, but what choice do I have?

It's getting harder and harder to hide. With H and his men here now, I worry every minute that we'll be found out. I try to hide the evidence. Why? I don't know. I don't want to go ten rounds. Maybe it's because I feel guilty you don't know. It doesn't seem right that the world should know before you. I'm so aware of it and soon I won't be able to hide Bump.

Having your child inside me brings a fortitude I never knew I could have. Styx trains me, as best he can, in how to fight, how to protect myself. Only when H isn't watching or we can get away with it of course. I like that Styx wants to empower me and to give me the tools to protect what's ours, but it's terrifying too. Could I really be expected to use these skills against someone? While I'm carrying Bump? I don't know if what I know will be enough. If I will be enough. If our child has to live with just one parent, it seems right it should be you. You're so much more capable, so much more loving than I could ever be. Bump needs you, my Heart. I need you.

Z is still out there. He wants JARR. H and Styx talk about training, about what's to come. They talk when I'm not around, H knows you guided us here, but I don't know what else he knows. H and I have gone back a step, a few, I guess. It's like our early days and we don't have you around to steady us this time. Sometimes I think H is avoiding me, then I wonder if maybe I'm avoiding him. His men offer a distraction, they keep him busy. So long as he's busy, he's not discovering my secret.

Since H and his men arrived a couple of weeks ago without the Kindred, there's been talk of joining forces, of the Kindred coming here to Gamma to train. But there's hesitation. I don't fully understand it. Maybe they're sick of their family being disrupted for a showdown that it seems will never come.

Why do I do this? Write to you like you'll ever get these messages. I fill pages and pages with words you'll probably never read. Will we see each other again? I almost can't believe it. Why is it so difficult to be apart? I love you, I know that, and I miss being in your arms, but it's more than that.

What I'm going through now, with Bump, it feels like the future. Yet every time I try to make plans, everything ends in a question mark.

Should I be setting up home here? I need a nursery, a crib, all the things I don't have. When you left me on Falcon's island, I was scared I wouldn't get to see the pregnancy through. That Zeus would bleed me so dry that Bump wouldn't make it.

The terror I feel now is so much

more devastating, so much more potent. What if I have this baby before Z catches up with us? A baby, our baby, would be so vulnerable. How can I protect something so small? So young and helpless?

H's suggestion he'd have asked my mother to abort makes so much more sense now. Is that what I should've done? Have I damned us all by seeing this through? I'm sorry, my Heart. I never wanted to weaken you, and now I've made you weaker than ever before.

"How are you doing?"

Looking up from her notebook, she appreciated the steam rising from the cup Tulsi brought across the room. Didn't matter that they were in the desert, creature comforts were more valuable than they'd ever been.

"Thank you," she said when Tulsi put the cup down on the table next to her and sat in the middle of the couch.

"I think Wreck's getting broody," Tulsi said.

She closed the notebook to put it aside and picked up the cup in both hands, cradling it tight while turning to her friend.

"Brooding?" she said. "Your guy does that better than anyone else."

"He keeps bringing up Bump," Tulsi said, eyeing her stomach.

She opened her arms to present her stomach, knowing how Tulsi liked to touch it. Her friend was her saving grace. Having someone to talk to, a woman to talk to, was more valuable than she could've imagined. Her bump wasn't obvious beneath her baggy clothes, though it soon would be.

Tulsi came closer to lay a hand on the baby. "Is he moving yet?"

"Sometimes I think so. I'm only nineteen weeks," she said, sipping her milk. Actually, eighteen weeks six days if her and Falcon's calculations were right. "In another few weeks, there will be no mistaking him wriggling around."

She sighed.

Tulsi's hand rose to her cheek. "You're doing everything you can."

"He's going to miss everything," she said, lowering her cup. "I could lose him any minute and he'd never know he was a father."

"He'll know," Tulsi said, showing a wide smile that was intended to encourage hers. "He will. And he'll be ecstatic."

"It's been seven weeks since I heard his voice. Even if we do get through this, the man deserves a break, not a child foisted on him."

"The baby, you and the baby, will be his reward. I know it."

"You've never even met him."

But Tulsi wasn't dissuaded. "No, but it feels like I know him. You and Styx talk so highly of him… I'm eager to meet him, I'd love to."

"And I'd love to make it happen," she said. "If I knew where on the planet he was, I might."

"We'll meet, I know we will. Soon. And we'll give this baby the welcome it deserves."

At that point, all she wanted was her child to be born healthy, without constant threats looming over them.

"We always said history wouldn't repeat itself," she said, stroking Bump. "But here I am pregnant, while the child's father is off out there saving the world somehow. Saving us from the threat that wants to take us down… Am I going to end up like my mom? Terrified. Paranoid. Teaching my child all these rules to keep them safe? What kind of life is that?" She scoffed. "I know what kind of life it is because it's my life."

"No. You won't be the same. Daire said he'd never walk away from his family, didn't he?"

"It's different," she said. "The reality is different. He might not have a choice." She swallowed. "And then I think of his mom, she died and left him with Harry…"

"You are not going to leave your child," Tulsi said, taking her cup away to put it back on the end table. "You're going to get through this. We're going to get you through." She linked their fingers. "Let's go downstairs… see if there's any dessert left."

With a smile, she rose from the couch to venture into the Gamma corridors. Given there was no threat in the building and Daire was responsible for setting up security, she didn't have to fear the walls around her. In Beta, it paid to be wary, but in Gamma she could explore, get lost and find herself again. If only that worked in life too.

The kitchen was usually tended by Harry's men. An adjoining mess was where they ate. If they weren't training, the men could be found there, or in the giant recreation room beyond.

Tulsi slowed as she did when no noise carried from any of the rooms.

They looked at each other. "That's weird, right?"

"Yeah," she said. "Where is everyone?"

It wasn't just silent. It was empty. And when she went to the window at the end of the rec room, the row of vehicles inside the gate was new too.

"Did they leave us behind?" Tulsi joked.

She shook her head. "They didn't leave. Someone arrived." As she crossed the room, she grabbed Tulsi's hand to pull her along. They went down a floor, but in the stairwell, she stopped.

"Wait here, Tuls, be absolutely silent."

The hope was allies had arrived. But if whoever was there warranted all the men being on alert, it could be an enemy in their midst.

Tulsi nodded, showing she understood. It might have made more sense to leave Tulsi upstairs, but if something happened, if they had to move fast, she didn't want to risk her friend being abandoned.

The moment she opened the door, she heard ruckus. With laughter and jeering, it seemed to be good natured. No gunshots or explosions. As she went down the corridor, intending to see what was going on, the calmer voice of her father carried from the room she was about to pass, so she paused.

"It's dangerous," Harry said. "You sure you can keep your head?"

"I did before." Her lips parted. Her Heart. Right there. He'd come back. Why didn't she run in there and throw herself at him? "This is it. No fuck ups. Once it starts, it happens fast."

"We take out Z and the problem goes away," Styx said. Was it just the three of them in there? "I can do that quick and easy."

"We're not rushing in there blind," Daire said. "I've been away for months; I don't know how much his forces have grown. We don't know how secure his stronghold is. The only way to get the intel is to join his side."

"It's risky."

"We have control. Minotaur will protect us."

"Is Ex ready to take JARR apart?"

"Kero's on him," Daire said. "Swallow's got a lead on our biological element."

"Everything's coming together," Harry said. "Are you sure you don't want to stay a while?"

"I can't switch off right now. My head has to stay in the mission," Daire said. "The sooner I get out there, the sooner we can finish this shit."

"You look tired," Styx said.

"I'm not the one who got shot," Daire said in a more familiar tone. "Thank God they missed that beautiful face, huh?"

Styx laughed. "And Ex got to have all the fun."

"While you were being cared for by two beautiful women," Harry got in on the teasing. "Are you complaining?"

"About the earache Tess gave me after, yeah," Styx said. "That woman's relentless."

Silence descended.

It didn't linger long.

"She's upstairs," Harry said.

"She'll bust something seeing you."

"No." Daire's response was abrupt. "I can't see her

now."

For a second, it was like her heart stopped beating.

"What the hell shit you talking?" Harry asked, his anger apparent.

"Yeah, there's no guarantee when you'll get out," Styx said. "You might not get this chance again."

"No," Daire said again. "I know it's a risk, but now isn't the right time."

"The right time?" The roar from Harry was unexpected. Her father was offended, but why? "Think you're some player—"

"Whoa, Harry," Styx said, sliding into the role of mediator.

"I raised that boy better than to play with women's hearts for kicks! He doesn't deserve it! Doesn't deserve her! If I had the chance to be with Carrie one last—"

"I'll drop to my knees for her!" Daire's anger eclipsed his mentor's. "You don't fucking get it! You didn't love Carrie at all if you could watch her heart break and still turn your back. I'll walk in there, take one look in her eyes and fall to my knees. You think I would go back? You think I could walk away... again? After all this fucking time... The things I've done! The things she's seen me do... I know there's a chance she'll never forgive me, that I'll never have her again. I know what I'm doing could cost me her love. I didn't think I'd ever pay that price, that anything would make me sacrifice her, but it's for her! I'm doing this for her! To keep her safe."

"She won't understand," Styx said, somber. "This is taking a lot out of her."

"Yeah," Daire said at a lower, forlorn volume. "She deserves better. Maybe after me, after I take care of all this shit, she'll find someone to make her happy. Someone without the baggage."

"It's been months," Styx said, his voice thick with sympathy.

"Believe me, I know, I feel every day. Every minute."

"She misses you."

"You can't guilt me more than I already feel," Daire said. "Everything I've done is for her."

"Yet you're running away from her," Harry said. "You sure this is about keeping your focus?"

"I love her, more than anyone can ever know."

"And you're worried you might lose her," her father said. "In Beta, when she's hooked up to JARR—"

"I can control it."

"What if you can't?" Harry asked. "What if it takes all of her?"

"So I should just give up? Let Z do whatever he wants and cast her aside? You're her father. How can you think that way?"

"I don't," he said. "And I know all about using the mission as cover. It's easier to focus on the mission. We're trained for that. Trained to complete objectives. Relationships aren't always so straightforward. Love isn't straightforward."

"Mine is," Daire said, full of determination. "Loving her is the only absolute in any of this."

"But you want to walk away from her when she needs you."

Her father was pushing hard, though his words were sort of gentle. Styx was quiet and that didn't bode well. Closing her eyes, she leaned on the wall, flattening her hands at her sides. He better keep his mouth shut. He had to keep his mouth shut. Knowing about Bump wouldn't make Daire's job any easier.

"I have to walk away. I'm the only one Z will let get close."

"You going overseas?" Styx asked. "Want someone on your six?"

"Too dangerous."

"Fuck dangerous," Styx said.

"He's back in the country anyway."

"How long until we hear something?"

"No longer than ninety-six hours. By then, I'll know the plan."

"And we'll converge on Beta," Harry said. "You need a key."

"I need the Scepter."

Maybe that was his reason for being there. Except he

should have the Bolt. If he'd read her hint right, he'd know where the Trident was too. In their last conversation, over the base unit, he'd said the keys shouldn't be together.

Given they were racing toward the confrontation, they shouldn't put the keys together now. Her Heart was right it would happen fast once it started.

"Don't look at him like that, H," Styx said. "This is for Tess."

"I'll tell him I traded Tess for the Scepter," Daire said.

"Good. That will explain why you don't have her with you. What about the last few months? What are you going to tell him about what you've been doing?"

"The truth," Daire said. "He'll be just as interested to know that Four started this whole thing."

"Could be torture and murder in your future," Styx said. "You up for that?"

"Knowing Four caused Tess so much pain? Will be a walk in the park."

"You'll impress Z," Harry said. "Laying the instigator at his feet."

"If it gets me in deeper, I'm all for it," Daire said. "You got blood stores? Everyone should donate as soon as possible."

"We're on it," Styx said. "Don't worry. We've got her."

"Thanks. Deal with the prisoner, get the truth for her. She should hear it from his lips."

"You want us to give her a message?" Harry asked. "She'll find out you were here and didn't see her."

"We know the truth, old man," Daire said. "That's all that matters to me."

When she smiled, a tear trickled from her eye. Her hand jumped to her lips, holding in the gasp that threatened. He wanted to stay in his mission mind and not be distracted. Her Heart said he'd drop to his knees for her, and she wasn't sure she was strong enough to send him away again.

Pushing off the wall, she returned to Tulsi in the stairwell.

"What's going on?" her friend asked.

"It's coming together," she said, taking her friend's arm as they ascended the stairs. "Cherish your guy tonight. Cherish him while you have him."

Because he could be taken from her at any second. When they amassed at Beta and the two sides faced off, there was no guarantee everyone was making it out alive.

THIRTY-SIX

SITTING ON HER BED, she watched the door. Just watched. Anticipating… nothing. In a daze it was difficult to expect anything. Yet when someone knocked on the door, somehow, she knew her father would be on the other side.

He opened the door to look around it. "You doing okay?" he asked. She raised her brows though her head move was kind of a nod and a shake. "Can I come in?"

"You're in charge around here," she said on an inhale. "Yes, Harry, come in." He entered and closed the door. She spoke before he was halfway across the room. "You sent Styx with him, didn't you?"

He stopped. "How did you…?"

"I heard your conversation," she said. "I know he was here."

"You didn't come in?"

"I need his head to be wherever he needs it to be, Dad. Like he said, the sooner he gets out there, the sooner we can finish this shit. But you sent Styx to tail him." Was it experience or hope that told her that? "Tell me you did."

"Yes," Harry said. "He said he didn't need anyone but—"

"He'll know Styx is there."

"Styx knows how to hang back," Harry said. "This isn't intel gathering. We're not monitoring him because we don't trust him. It's backup. I want Styx close if his brother needs him. Doesn't matter if he knows."

"You don't have to convince me," she said, sliding to the edge of the bed. "I feel better when they have each other's backs too. You gave him the Scepter?"

"Yes."

"Good," she said. "We're making progress."

"I didn't expect you to be so... calm."

"Guess experience really does make a difference. I want Daire here. I want them both here. Happy and safe. But that won't happen until we deal with Zeus. Until we purge JARR. Believe me, I want it done more than anyone."

"Styx, he... he said it's time. To tell you it's time."

She smiled. "I bet he did."

"Time for what? What don't I know, Light-Sprite?"

Styx could've told Harry about Bump any time. Either he didn't want to be the person with Harry when he found out or he was respecting her ability to choose the right moment.

"Do you remember..." she asked, her mind in a more intimate place. "The last time you saw her... mom?"

His flash of surprise wasn't drawn in shame. "Yes."

"What did you say to her?" she asked, contrasts of heat and ice ricocheting around inside her. "Did you tell her you loved her?"

"Yes."

"Promise her that you'd find a way..." Her nose began to tingle, by now, she recognized grief welling within her. "That you'd find your way back to her?" He said nothing, just grew more rigid. "You meant it, didn't you?" Except they hadn't found their way back to each other. Her mother died without ever seeing her soulmate again. "Daire meant it too."

"We're going to protect you," Harry said, as certain as he'd probably been telling her mom they'd be together again. "But I need all of the information. You can't hold back. If there's something I need to know, you have to tell me."

Great theory, the practice wasn't so simple. "Will we

know when Zeus gets to Beta?" she asked, choosing not to spill the secret at such an emotional moment. She might appear calm, but inside she was terrified for her Heart. "If Daire's already woken Minotaur, we won't get a signal from Zeus, will we?"

"No," Harry said, coming over to sit on the bed with her. "Daire will send a message or Styx will. Though if he's right that Exile has control over Minotaur, Zeus will be looking for a way to track him down."

"Do we know where Exile is?"

"Downstairs. With the Kindred and our men."

"So this is it," she said. "The calm before the storm. The final countdown."

"Swallow has secured what she believes to be the biochemical agent."

"Here?"

"It's being stored in state-of-the-art facilities owned by CI, their family's company."

"That's one less thing we have to worry about."

"Swift should be able to focus on the power grid, but we have to be ready for anything."

"Has he contacted Zeus already? Daire, I mean."

"I don't think so," Harry said. "If he has any sense, he'll wait until he's closer or just appear without warning. But he's carrying a prisoner, that can complicate things."

"A prisoner?"

"Four."

"Because he wants Four to admit their role in the assassination plot?"

He nodded once. "Which works in our favor. When Zeus is mad, he's distracted. We may be able to use that to our advantage."

She frowned. "I thought Daire left a prisoner here."

"He did. Left one, took the other," Harry said, standing up to offer her a hand. "It's someone Daire says you know… The man responsible for sabotaging your mom's car."

She wanted to know. Wanted to take her father's hand and face the villain who'd stolen her mom's life. But, at the same time, returning to her grief could weaken her. Without Daire around, she wasn't sure she'd hold it together.

But what choice did she have?

Putting her hand in Harry's, she stood up. "Take me to him."

They returned to the floor where Daire had been, where she'd heard the conversation. Bypassing that room, they went into the next. Harry's men were there. Exile and Swift were typing away on separate laptops in the corner. The Kindred, or more specifically Swallow, noticed when she and Harry entered.

Zara, also known as Swallow, shot to her feet. "Pandora," she said and rushed over, winding around the men and furniture in her path. "How are you doing?"

"Good," Tess said, holding onto her smile as their eyes locked.

If Zara had been with Daire, she knew he was still in the dark about Bump.

"We want to see this guy," Harry said. "Boze, Lowe, you're with us."

"Will two men be enough?" she asked.

"We'll come with you," Zara said. Before she'd even turned around, Raven and Caine were on their way over. "Just in case. This guy's a piece of work."

Yet when Zara took her hand and offered a warm smile, Tess felt her company was more about support than physical backup.

"You good?" Swift called without taking his eyes from his screen.

"We're good," Raven responded.

They left together, following Harry through the building, though she probably knew it just as good as he did.

"Did you meet Wreck and Tulsi?" she asked, still holding Zara's hand.

"Briefly," Zara said. "They're going to meet the Fox Den guys who'll offer logistical support. We have a team arriving soon too."

So many people. Good. They needed numbers. Yet she felt the weight of responsibility. These people were standing up against evil, would everyone make it home?

"I don't know how to…" For all the times she'd written to Daire and said the words, it wasn't as easy with people she wasn't so familiar with. "I really appreciate all of you… coming here. Doing this."

"You don't have to thank us," Zara said, letting go of her hand to put an arm around her. "This is what we do. And Rave needs to brush up his skills… Sometimes he gets lazy."

"Lazy?" came the gruff question behind her.

Zara was smiling as she glanced back. "You have to admit I've been on top a lot recently."

"What guy would refuse that?" Caine asked. "You need a real man to take control, you just mosey on along to my room."

"Go for it, baby," Raven said. "Just the reason I need to put a bullet between his eyes."

"You don't need a reason. Just an opportunity," Zara said. "Why do you think I never leave the two of you alone?"

"Do you think they'd really hurt each other?"

"They have, plenty of times," Zara said. "Where do you think Caine got his scar? That was over a different woman though…" Zara tipped her head back but didn't turn. "You've never scarred a man for me, have you, Beau?"

"What happened when you kissed another guy?"

The smile that twisted Zara's lips was all pleasure. "We weren't together then."

"I was right there with you, baby."

"They do like to get macho sometimes," Zara said, pulling her closer. "Ares is the most levelheaded of all of them. You're lucky you have him."

"Doesn't feel like I do these days," she said on a sigh. "But I know he's doing what's necessary."

"He misses you," Zara said. "There's a different kind of strain on him than usual."

Which didn't reassure her at all. If Daire was distracted, if his head wasn't in the game, he could get hurt. Maybe walking away hadn't been the right thing to do after all.

They exited the stairwell into a gray corridor. The rest of the building didn't feel so cold, but they'd descended enough that she knew they were underground already.

Harry took them to a door and input a code before placing his fingerprint on the top panel. "I don't have to tell everyone to keep their cool in here," he said, meeting her eye. "You want to walk away any time, you walk."

Her mouth was suddenly dry, so she nodded.

Harry opened the door and went inside with Boze and Lowe on his flanks. It felt like she stood there for an age, steeling herself to what might happen inside. Zara gave her a squeeze and that was enough to get her feet moving. One step followed another until she was in the concrete room, staring through bars at a man she hadn't thought about in months.

"Patrick."

"Pandora."

Well, if that wasn't proof he wasn't who he'd said he was, she didn't know what was. In a tee-shirt and jeans, his appearance was grubbier than she'd expect from him. His hair was a little longer, his eyes sharper. From the faded bruises and scabs on his face, it was obvious he hadn't come willingly. She didn't care. How could she have trusted this man?

Her mom was right. People who insinuated themselves into her life couldn't be trusted. She'd shared her grief with this man. The letters. The confusion. And he'd just lapped it all up without uttering a word of truth.

"You sonofabitch," she said, and strode just a step before Zara held her back.

Her friend leaned in to whisper. "Don't give him the satisfaction."

But it was hard to be calm, hard to play it cool. She was no super-agent; everyone seemed to forget that a lot. Still, Zara was right, if they wanted answers, she had to restrain her anger.

"You murdered her," Harry said, his voice darker than she'd ever heard it.

In this open concrete space, there were bars on three sides of them. A cage for a criminal, for their enemy, and it was exactly where he deserved to be.

"I did a job," Patrick snapped. "I did my goddamn job and you people hunted me down for it. Who the fuck gave you the right—"

"You murdered her!"

"Yes!" Patrick hollered back. "I was paid to do a job. Isn't that what you do here?" He made a deliberate show of scanning the room. "This is a professional set up. That guy who came after me, he was a professional. You're all professionals... just like me."

"We don't murder innocent women," Harry said.

Was that true? She wasn't sure.

"We have rules. Morals."

"When it suits you, I bet," Patrick said. "Where were your morals when I was being beaten and kidnapped? This is false imprisonment. Where are your morals now?"

"She deserves justice."

"And you think taking me down will give her that?" Patrick said and laughed. "You're fucking kidding. I was a pawn. A playing piece, I wasn't the instigator. I told that other guy, you should have some professional fucking courtesy."

"We don't give courtesy to scum," Harry said. "Did you even think about what you were doing? About what your actions would cause? Did you care at all about my daughter?"

Patrick's eyes narrowed as they slid to her. "Oh," he said, getting the setup. "You're her father..."

"And you murdered my mother," Tess said, venturing closer, passing Boze to stand by Harry. "Why?"

"Money, sweetheart."

"No," she said, shaking her head. "Why did you approach me? Why come to the club and talk to me? What was that? Were you paid to do that too?"

"Yeah," he said without shame. "My client wanted your mom dead. It had to be her. I knew exactly when she'd be the one in the car. You were a valuable source of information. Every detail I reported, the pot got a little sweeter."

"What did it matter? What was the motivation?"

"Destruction," Patrick said. "I don't know the details."

"Tell us what you do know."

But as he considered the people in the room, he

retreated to sit on the bed behind him. "Why should I?"

"You want us to pay you?" she asked. "Fine, you get ten million dollars."

His mouth curled. "I'm not that dumb, sweetheart."

"Maybe we'll let you keep your life."

"If you kill me, you'll never know the why. You'll never find out the truth."

"We know who paid you."

"Yeah. Do you know why?"

"As you said, destruction," she said. "I guess your client wanted to end the organization."

"No," he said with a head tilt. "Wasn't as simple as that."

"We know everything you told the guy who brought you here," she said. Though that wasn't entirely true, there was no reason to give Patrick scope to manipulate them when Daire wouldn't withhold. Not from her. Just because she didn't know then didn't mean she never would. "I don't think we need you at all."

"Didn't tell him everything," Patrick said, brushing a hand down his thigh. "I didn't tell him the end goal."

"The end goal?" Harry asked. "You said that was destruction."

"Of life. Certain lives. To create chaos so there could be a victor."

"Your client wanted to be the victor?" Harry sneered and scoffed. "Your client is bound and gagged, trussed up and on the way to their own execution. Guess we know who wasn't triumphant."

"You think?" Patrick said, his smile sinister in its certainty. "How do you know this isn't playing out exactly as we want?"

"We? You just called yourself a pawn. This isn't your master plan."

"Maybe not, but I did my job. I'm good at my job and once this is through, my fee's gonna skyrocket."

"You think you'll be around to collect? To work?" Harry asked. "You're exactly where we want you."

"And you're exactly where we want you," Patrick

said. "All of you. It's like you have the script or something."

"You expect us to believe you?"

"Believe what you want," Patrick said. "I don't care. Just don't think you're in control here. You're nothing. None of you."

"You're the one behind bars."

"That won't last," Patrick said, resting his back on the wall. "You have your moment. Believe you're winning. Whatever. That confidence is exactly what we're relying on."

"Is it?"

"Yes."

"You think you can taunt us like that and get away with it?" Harry asked, creeping closer. "You can't begin to imagine what we're capable of. Of what we can do to make you talk."

"Try it," Patrick said, pouncing to the edge of the bed. "What does it matter? What does it change? Your slut's still dead."

Oh, shit.

"Don't you fucking—"

"No more pussy for you, old timer. Fuck you and your whore, she deserved it! You all fucking deserve to go down like dogs. That bitch thought she could run, thought she could get away? I fucking showed her what a dumb, stupid, little cunt of a—"

The blast of a gunshot came before she saw her dad's hand move. Shock froze on Patrick's face. Blood trickled from his forehead as his body slumped to the floor.

"Wonder if that was in his script," Caine said, almost snickering.

Still stunned, she turned enough to see Zara wrinkle her nose. "Okay, maybe we should've talked about not killing our only source of information."

"He did exactly what I would've done," Raven muttered and turned to exit.

Patrick was dead. That wasn't the plan. Was it?

"We'll take care of it," Boze said, patting his Stratego on the back.

Everyone else filtered out before Harry turned. In his

own shock, she wasn't sure he'd fully processed when his eyes rose to hers.

She went over to take his hand. "We don't need him," she said, offering a tight smile. "Let's go find some dessert."

Murder wasn't an everyday thing, but her father was no stranger to it. Bawling him out wouldn't change a thing and she couldn't say she was sorry. Patrick killed her mother and had to pay for that crime. All Harry did was claim some justice. Nothing would make them whole but losing Patrick didn't make the world a poorer place that was for sure.

THIRTY-SEVEN

This is my goodbye.

It's been three days since you left here. Three days since I heard your voice. Everyone is preparing. Provisions are being packed. Weapons loaded. Munitions checked. It feels like the eve of war. I suppose it is. After all the posturing and jockeying, the time for confrontation can't be put off any longer. Tension hums in the air. There's anticipation. Expectation. It's setting me on edge.

I heard you say ninety-six hours. With bated breath, everyone waits. I wait.

What lies on the other side of this?

For so long, I was scared. Then I just wanted the end to come so this would be over. I don't know what I feel now. Hope, that maybe we'll both make it through. Fear for Bump. What will happen when they hook me up to JARR? I still hope that perhaps we're afraid for no reason. If JARR only needs a few drops of blood, it could all be over fast.

I have to hope. I have to. If I don't, or I consider waiting until Bump is born, we'd be more vulnerable. Right? Making these choices on my own is so difficult. I wish I had your advice, that we could make these decisions together.

Something is coming, something is about to change. Styx told me a lot of what you do is waiting for something to change. We're on the cusp of that. Will it be something good or is this going to be the end for all of us?

Sitting in the corner of the rec room, people had been coming and going all day. Serious expressions of concern had taken the place of their ease. Everyone was switched on. Alert. Ready. It seemed she was the only one struggling.

Tulsi came in with Zara. She put her notebook aside when it was clear the women were aiming for her.

"How are you doing?" Tulsi asked.

"I get asked that a lot," she said, trying her best to smile. "I'm not sure I deserve the concern."

"You deserve it," Zara said as she and Tulsi sat on either side of her. "If you want to sit this one out—"

"I'm the only one who can't sit it out," she said, her hand moving a little higher on her thigh. "One of two anyway."

Unfortunately, her child was in it because she was in it.

"Have you told Harry yet?" Tulsi asked.

Her friends had asked this more than once over the last few days. She suspected they already knew the answer to their own question.

"It's not about hiding it from him," she said. "It's not

even about avoiding the lecture and the I told you so."

"He needs to know."

She shook her head. "He doesn't. I can't put it on him, I can't. What will it change? Telling him just adds another variable. One that could make him hesitate. Hesitation gets you killed."

"I don't know that I'd feel any different," Zara said to Tulsi. "In an ideal world, he'd know, but his knowledge doesn't change anything. We still have to go there. Tess still has to be hooked up to the machine."

"It could hurt her baby."

"We know that," Zara said. "But what's the alternative? We run and hide until the baby's born? Its father doesn't even know it exists. Zeus won't cut her any slack. The baby being out and alive in the world will only give him another avenue of manipulation."

"He kidnapped me when I was an infant," Tess said. "Used me against my parents to get his way. At least this way I have a chance of protecting my child, while they can't be taken away from me."

"I'm going to stick with you," Zara said. "You and the little one are my primary concern."

"No, I don't want you walking into danger."

Zara smiled and reached for her hand. "I'm Kindred. Danger is what I do."

"Raven's okay with that?"

"Unfortunately for him, I don't believe in double standards. If he's allowed to do it, so am I. It wasn't always easy, but he's pretty much resigned to it now."

"I don't want you getting hurt because of me."

Zara leaned closer. "It won't be because of you. Zeus is pulling the strings."

"Or so he likes to think," a new female voice said, attracting their attention. Kero. Just inside the doorway. "Ex got a message. It's time."

She didn't know how else it could've happened. Of course it was low key. Ants started dancing in her belly. Zara gave her hand a squeeze and the three women stood up to hug.

"Will you be okay here on your own?" she asked Tulsi.

"She won't be on her own," Kero said.

That was worrying. A new discomfort crept in, more like dread than plain old anxiety. "You're not coming?"

"The Titan chip is installed here," Kero said. "If Ex needs into the system, it's easier if someone's here to let him in."

"If he needs to send JARR here? I thought the point was to delete it."

"We don't know how it's going to go down."

And maybe Exile didn't want his woman lost in among so much of the enemy while he was focused on something else.

"Let's hope no one gets shot," she murmured.

"Swallow's got skills," Kero said, nodding her way. "Stick with her."

A glowing recommendation. Not that she really doubted Zara or anyone on their team.

"I need my bag."

Before she could take a step, Zara caught her arm. "Leave anything important here."

"Leave it here?"

"It'll take about a day to drive down there. Carry only what you need to survive. Everything else stays here or with the team's supplies."

"Because…?"

"You're going in there as Ex's prisoner," Kero said. "Zeus knows Exile was in Beta's system. That he runs Minotaur."

"How does he know that?"

"Just trust me," Kero said. "Ex traded the Scepter—"

"Which he got when he shut down Minotaur," Zara added.

"For me," Tess said. "Why would he do that?"

Kero's smile was smug and proud. "Because he knew something no one else did."

"What?"

"That Minotaur needs more than just a key now," Kero said. "That pussy is purring to my flame's tune. Zeus thought he could rock up and get in there, Ares thought it too, according to the line he's feeding Zeus."

"They thought the keys would get them in," she said. "The keys and the code, like before."

"Right."

"But it won't?"

"No," Kero said. "They need Exile's help, his permission."

She frowned. "But wait, I thought… Aren't Zeus and Ares and their people at Beta?"

"Mm hmm," Kero said. "They strolled on up to the door like nothing had changed."

"Oh my God," she said impressed and maybe a little smug too. "Zeus can't even get in the building."

"Not until he gives my flame what he wants."

"JARR," she, Zara, and Tulsi said at the same time.

Kero shrugged and sighed. "What can I say? The game turns my guy on… almost as much as the tech."

Though it was amusing to imagine Zeus coming up against a literal brick wall trying to get into Beta, she had to be wary too.

"Exile is… Can we trust him?"

"We're a little too deep into this to second guess him now," Kero said without any offense.

"And Kero isn't necessarily the most impartial party," Zara said.

"If I'm going to hand myself over to this guy, to play his kowtowed prisoner, I have to know we're not setting ourselves up for a fall. If Exile wants the same as Zeus—"

"If he did, he'd have it already," Kero said. "He was there, at Beta, with you. We could've locked you and Styx up and just waited for the keys to be brought to us." She inhaled. "That said, sometimes my guy gets a little… dazzled."

"Dazzled?" Zara asked with concern. "What does that mean?"

"Sometimes the code it… transfixes him, I guess you could say. He's intoxicated by it."

"You think Exile will get drunk on power?"

"Oh no, not that. If he wanted power, he'd have it. He doesn't care about power. Just if you think he's being sucked too deep into the intellectual argument…"

"We should…?"

"Just ask him what's the point," Kero said.

That made little sense. "What's the point?"

"He'll know it came from me," Kero said and stepped aside. "Can we get going?"

As Zara and Tulsi headed for the door, she retrieved her notebook. Before she'd even straightened up, Harry came into the room. The other women paused, but not for long, then they exited without her father saying a word.

He closed the door. Ominous? Maybe. But expected.

"You know Exile got word?" he said. She nodded. "We'll load up to drive down there, set up base away from Beta. You and Exile will go in alone." She nodded again. "If you feel unsafe—"

"We're all unsafe," she said. "Yeah, I'm scared, that's what comes with not calling the shots. But Daire's in there. I don't think of it as leaving my team or being alone, I'm going towards the man I love. So long as he's alive, I don't have to worry about a thing."

"You have so much faith in him," Harry said almost in wonder. "Sometimes it's difficult to face…"

"That I have faith in him?"

"That your mother likely had the same faith in me."

Oh, she hadn't appreciated the weight of guilt her father carried around.

"It wasn't your fault," she said. "It could just as easily have been me in that car."

"And you think she would've forgiven me that?"

"I don't think you need to be forgiven," she said.

"I got complacent. It had been so many years. You and your mother…"

"Were old enough to look out for ourselves. I didn't suspect anything was wrong."

"Your mother did," he said. "You told me as much."

Not that she wanted to speak ill of the dead, but…

"Mom wasn't always… together. She got paranoid sometimes."

"What you call paranoia, I call good sense. She kept you alive all your life. You underestimate what a task that was, how incredible it was that she achieved it for so long."

She'd underestimated the gravity of the task until being faced with it herself. Even if she and Bump made it out, they may still be faced with a life on the run. Especially if Bump's father, uncle, and grandfather were left behind… or worse.

"Did you miss us?"

"Every day," he said without hesitation.

"And mom, if she'd… if she hadn't gone through with the pregnancy or given me up… would you have wanted to know after the fact?"

His brow creased. "You weren't unwanted, Tess. There was nothing we wanted more than to be a family. Zeus and Olympus… those threats were real. By staying in ranks, I kept him from pursuing you… at least, I thought I did."

"If you'd stayed with us, it would've been worse," she said. "If you'd gone back on your word and left Olympus again after Zeus let us go…"

"He'd have dedicated his life to tracking us down… and wouldn't have let you live."

"While he had us, we could be used against you. If he killed us, he'd have lost that control."

"He could kill one of you," he said. "And for the remainder of our lives, we'd know that death was on my head. That I could've prevented it."

Though it was infuriating, she exhaled a laugh. "Don't need to look far to know where Daire got his sense of responsibility from. Not everything is under your control. Not everything is your burden to bear."

"You tell him that?"

"All the time," she said and smiled just a moment before him. "He wants to make you proud."

"He wants to make you proud," he said, his smile fading. "He tells himself that he does what's necessary to keep you alive, to keep you free. Even in his darkest moments, when he wants to give it up or walk away, when he's tired and beaten, at the edge of his sanity, he reminds himself of your love, that you still need him even when you're apart."

Because that was what Harry told himself too. She didn't have to ask, it was written all over his face.

She crossed the room to take his hand. "It's just a little longer," she murmured. "We get rid of JARR. We get rid of Zeus. All of that will go away and we'll all be free."

"Zeus has an army."

"So do we."

He shook his head. "Not like this. He's used these last few months for recruitment."

"He can't have been training them."

"He doesn't need to. The men Ares trained would've passed along his teachings." Harry's teachings. "And Zeus doesn't care about these men, he needs warm bodies who can point and shoot. When Ulysses Sherwood is in a corner, his strategy always begins with outnumbering the enemy. If he's built his ranks the way I think he has, the way intelligence tells me, we could be overwhelmed just by sheer numbers."

"We're smarter," she said. "We're stronger. There's no one else I'd rather have at the head of our ranks."

Startled, he blinked. "You mean if Daire wasn't an option."

"He does better with your approval, when you steady him. He lives to be your soldier."

"No," Harry said. Shaking his head, he cupped her cheek. "He lives to be your partner." His thumb moved across her face. "Let's go get him back, huh?"

Worried tears may escape, she nodded and let him take her hand to lead her out. The end was coming, it was right there on the horizon, would any of them live to see beyond it?

THIRTY-EIGHT

ONLY THREE VEHICLES pulled off the road to stop in an abandoned parking lot. The rest of their convoy kept on going.

"What's happening?" she asked as her father and Zara got out of the two other vehicles.

"Time for the switch," Wreck said from the driving seat.

What she'd been dreading. Time to close the final distance between her and Beta.

Popping the door, she slithered out of the truck and forced her legs to take her to her father.

Before she could say a word, a motorbike roared into the parking lot from the direction of Beta. It circled them once and stopped in front of her father's truck. The rider took off his helmet: Exile.

"If you're done with the theatrics," Zara said, but Exile didn't care.

If she hadn't seen him and Kero together, she'd think he didn't care about anything at all.

"We're less than an hour out," Harry said, bringing everyone's focus back.

"Even less on the bike," Exile said.

"I don't want to go on the bike," she said, restraining instant panic.

Riding bitch, holding on to Exile, meant holding her body close to his. No way he'd miss Bump if she was squashed up against him.

"Doesn't matter how we get there," Exile said.

"Then it doesn't matter if we use a truck."

"You can use ours," Zara said. "Hades can take Swift."

"I need to talk to that asshole," Exile said.

"You don't make many friends, do you?" Zara asked as she and the hacker went toward the Kindred truck.

"We'll be an hour behind you," Harry said, coming in close, stealing her focus. "Exile will get you inside and should be in the system. Me and my people will do what we can about their numbers."

"It's dangerous," she said. "Are you sure it's smart to go straight in for a confrontation like that?"

"Zeus's knowledge on troop formations is limited. He'll expect us to descend at some point after Beta is accessed. Don't forget we have Raven."

"He can't take out an army."

"As long as they remain outside, the only barrier is reloading," Harry said, resting his hands on her shoulders. "Have heart, Light-Sprite. This will all be over soon."

"Raven knows not to shoot Daire, right? That he's on our side."

"This is what we do. We've trained our whole adult lives for showdowns like this. Something unexpected will happen, it almost always does. But we'll adapt." He got serious. "If anything goes wrong, if we have to abort—"

"Follow Daire, I know," she said. "I don't have to be told that. He'd get me out before I realized anything was wrong anyway."

"You won't be alone in there. We'll do everything we can to get you out as fast as possible."

Only if they got rid of JARR as quickly as possible. If not, she'd have to wait in Beta. It was impossible to neutralize the threat until she opened it to the world.

"That's not the only objective though, is it?" she asked. "Getting me out has to be secondary."

"I would never say that to Daire," he muttered. She offered a brief smile. "Approaching after Exile has insinuated himself into the system will divide resources and attention."

"Which should buy Exile and Swift more time. Will Swift come in?"

"He'll work off site. Separating them increases our chance of success."

Because if they were both within range of Zeus and a weapon, they could both be taken out in seconds, screwing their objective.

"What do we think about Garrick?" she asked. "Can he be trusted? If it goes to shit, should we—"

"Daire has been close to them for a few days and in regular contact before then. He won't bare himself to Garrick. Revealing his duplicity could be dangerous."

"If Garrick feels like he's in a corner, he could drop the dime on Daire to save himself."

He stroked her hair. "You don't have to worry about Daire."

"Focusing on him gives me a break from focusing on me." And the child in her belly. "Thank you for this, Dad." His frown deepened. "You don't have to be here, doing this, helping me or Daire, but you are."

"This was my mess before it was yours," he said. "And I love you. Both of you." Her and Daire… Was that what he meant? "We'll get it cleaned up, then we can all start living."

He faltered. His thoughts probably went back to her mom.

"You know what we never did," she said, taking his hand. "We never had that talk about your relationship with mom. I bet there's a lot of stories you could share."

"You lived with her all your life, I bet there's a lot you could too."

So maybe she wasn't as far from them as it seemed.

"Time to move, Pandora," Exile called.

The men in Harry's truck rearranged themselves after

everything from the Kindred truck was moved into her father's. Raven was already astride the motorcycle holding the helmet out to Zara as she tucked her hair into her shirt.

"We're right behind you," Zara shouted over, taking the helmet.

She nodded and smiled, trying to show the confidence she felt inside. Still, it was difficult to cross the asphalt to join Exile. He was nice enough to open the door for her, though he didn't hang around to close it. Climbing in, she fastened her seatbelt and waited for him to get them underway.

Twenty, maybe thirty, minutes of the journey went by and neither of them spoke. The dark road ahead and behind felt desolate without the visible support of their allies. Knowing they were nearby, that they intended to fight with them, was as abstract as knowing Daire was up ahead. She should be optimistic about seeing him again. Somehow, Zeus erased all hope. He was at Beta. Waiting. For her and her child.

"You've got some chutzpah," Exile said, resting his wrist on top of the wheel.

"Because I spoke out against riding your motorcycle?"

"Going into this place…" he said. "Believing you'll get you and your kid out of it." Her attention flew to him, but he kept on looking straight ahead. "You've got a lot of faith in Ares. I thought my girl had a lot in me, but shit… you're expecting miracles."

"How do you know…?"

He may be a digital God, but there was no electronic record of her pregnancy anywhere. Even if there was, why would he look?

He glanced at her stomach. "Sweater only hides so much. Bigger question is how does Hades not know? He doesn't, does he?"

The side window was a better option than his judgment. "He has a blind spot."

"Sees only what he wants to," Exile said. "Ares know?" She shook her head the tiniest fraction. "It's his, right?"

"Are we girlfriends now?" she snapped. "You figured it out, clever you."

"I didn't do shit," he said. "And I don't give a crap."

Her chin descended. "Kero noticed?"

"I don't spend a lot of time checking other women out. Kero's enough of a handful on her own." The slight rise at the corner of his mouth suggested something private, maybe intimate, was on his mind. "You know I don't give a shit about you."

"Hadn't spent a lot of time thinking about it."

"I'm doing this to keep my girl alive, to keep her happy."

"I understand."

"Don't expect heroics, not from me."

"You do your thing and I'll do mine."

"Right. Which is why I'm not slowing this train down. If it costs you, your baby, your whole damn family, I don't care. I'm cutting this shit off. Doing whatever's necessary."

"That's all we need you to do."

He glanced her way then back to the road. "Guess no one told you."

"Told me what?"

"It was meant to kill you," he said. "JARR, it was designed to kill its gatekeeper."

"It needs all of my blood?"

"I don't know how much it needs, but the minute your blood hits the system JARR releases a toxin."

Tension spread through her muscles. "A toxin? Like poison? Why?"

"To paralyze its pray. It's slow acting. You don't even realize it's creeping up on you, it takes just a little piece of you at a time. You get foggy, reflexes slow, it takes your fight and eventually suppresses your ability to breathe. It's smart. The system keeps you exactly where it needs you. As you give it life, it takes yours," he said. "The gatekeeper is one use only. Once JARR is up and running, it doesn't need you anymore."

"Zeus always wanted it to be me." Her child. If it was just her and it was necessary, she'd give her life. But she wouldn't give the life of her baby. "We can't go. We can't do this."

"Oh, we're going."

"No," she said, wrapping her arms around her stomach. "This baby deserves a chance."

"Re-lax," he droned, loose and indifferent. "I said 'meant to kill you' not 'going to kill you.'"

"What's the difference?" she asked. "If they wanted it to kill me—"

"You were vaccinated."

"Vaccinated?"

"That unknown signature in your blood is the vaccine, you're immune to the toxin."

"Why? Why design it to kill me only to vaccinate me?"

"The designed to kill you part was Zeus." No surprise there. "The doc and Poseidon didn't know until after JARR was locked by your blood."

"How did they find out?"

"Paperwork always screws you," Exile said. "Or Zeus, in this case. He was the only one who knew about the toxin until the invoice showed up in the doc's lab. Asclepius started digging, got the formula, and went to work developing a vaccine."

"That doesn't tell me why."

"Maybe he liked you or he had a thing against killing kids, I don't know."

"Or maybe I was the test case," she murmured.

"Whatever. You're immune. You're fine."

"How do you know all this?"

"The hard drives," Exile said. "Poseidon kept notes. His journal said a lot about you and your folks… and Zeus. It's a surprise Olympus lasted as long as it did. Poseidon always thought Zeus and Hades would kill each other… He made it a point to be useful, to temper his allegiance to both sides and know as much as he could."

In the hope of saving his life. So far, it was working for him.

"Who else is vaccinated? Was the formula in his notes?"

"Some of the components were mentioned, but the doc kept the formula to himself. You were the only recipient."

Maybe the formula was in Asclepius's journal. "Why didn't you tell us this sooner?"

"Us?" he asked. "Everyone knew… except you."

And she'd been too caught up in hiding her pregnancy to apparently notice others were withholding.

"Ares didn't want me to know?"

"Ares is an asshole."

"I heard you didn't get along," she said. "He doesn't expect heroics and has his brother. He doesn't need you."

"Does he?" Exile asked. "Have his brother?"

She'd just assumed Styx would be nearby. But he'd been sent to back Daire up. If her Heart didn't need back up, where did that leave Styx? Hiding somewhere on the perimeter? Waiting for his team to show up?

"Did the message mention him?" she asked. "Someone sent you a message."

"Came through Poseidon, but yeah, I got a message."

"And Styx?" she asked, trying to maintain her calm while he infuriated her.

He shook his head once. "Not on the inside."

So Daire had no one.

"Is anyone?" she asked, organizing her thoughts. "No one can get into Beta, can they? Because you put some hex on the system?"

"A hex on the system, I like that," he said, slouching a little more. "Yeah, I did. No one gets in there until I let them."

"Are they there? Waiting?"

"Should be," he said. "Doesn't matter. They need both of us, so no one will be angling to hurt us."

In theory. "That was why we came first. Alone." Or so others might think. "Doesn't that make it easier to aim and fire at the rest of our team?" She shifted her body some more toward him. "Is that why Kero stayed behind? You didn't want her to get hurt?"

"Kero knows the contingencies," he said. "Don't be worrying about her."

"But you don't give a shit," she said. "About the rest of us. Oh my God, you're leading them into a trap."

His frown appeared in an almost huff. "You don't know shit," he said. "You know what I'm going in here to do? Shut this shit down, remember? How you think Z will feel about that?" He wouldn't be happy. "Do I give a shit about your team? No. Do we need them to get out of there in one piece? Possibly. I hedge my bets, lady. If one route doesn't work, I might need another. No one goes down just for kicks. Your team is useful."

"You're using them," she murmured.

He glanced at her. "And what the fuck are you doing with me? I'm here 'cause I'm such a swell guy?" No, he wasn't. He was putting himself on the line. Yes, he wanted to complete his work to keep Kero safe, but he was also just one man. He could've told them to fuck themselves, to stick with Swift and forget about him. He was helping, for his own reasons, but it suited theirs too. Everyone in their team was using the others one way or another. "It's a job. We don't get dead, we live to do another one… We die? The world keeps on turning. No one's mourning us."

"I don't want to die alone," she whispered.

God, how ridiculous had she been back then?

"Lucky for you, it's unlikely, at least if you're dying today. Once you're hooked up to that machine, if it wants all of you, Zeus will keep on feeding it. The room will be full of people… Not that they'll be swooping in to save you."

Daire would. Even if it damned the world, he might not be able to stop himself. She wanted his love. Needed it. But she didn't want the world to pay the price for it.

"If it happens," she said, tightness growing in her chest. "If JARR needs all of me, you know how to destroy Beta, don't you?"

"It's in the system."

"Do it," she said, all determination. "Do it and make sure I go down with it. Get out. Get Ares out. And let it burn. Let JARR and Beta burn."

"Why would you—"

"He doesn't need to know," she said. "Tell Styx he

doesn't need to know."

"About his own kid?"

"How will it change the situation?" she asked. "Ares, Hades, neither of them needs to know. Styx will take care of the others. I know you don't give a shit about me but consider it a dead woman's final wish. Kero would understand."

"You think you know her?"

"I think any woman in my position… Any woman losing her life and the life of her child… She's hurt enough, she doesn't need to take the people she loves down with her. Please, Exile, he doesn't need to know."

His eyes met hers for a second before returning to the road. "He doesn't need to know."

Even though it wouldn't be his fault, Daire would struggle enough with the guilt of her death. He didn't need to know they'd lost their child too. It may be a small mercy, but if she was dead, it would be the last one she could give.

THIRTY-NINE

ONCE AGAIN IN THE DARKNESS, they approached Beta. Light came from beyond the trees, brighter than ever before. White in its luminescence, it wasn't welcoming. Usually, the building reveled in its shadowy cloak. Anything new implied unknown, and unknown definitely wasn't good.

"What's with the light?" she asked. "It's not for our benefit."

It couldn't be. They knew where they were, where they were going. They didn't need a beacon to follow. And Zeus wasn't that hospitable.

Being that it was night, and Zeus feared exposure, she couldn't figure out why he'd do something so overt. Shouldn't he and his people be hiding, in the trees, in some camp somewhere ready to pounce? Why would they be announcing their presence to the world?

Unfortunately, they rounded the final curve and her eyes adjusted to the new angle, providing a horrifying answer.

"Oh my God," she whispered, her hand rising to her open mouth.

The building was in the background. Massive spotlights illuminated the foreground as men worked to remove concrete and restore earth displaced by the explosions from their frantic escape last time.

Rebuilding might seem odd, but the why wasn't her first concern. The sheer number of men working on machinery and with hand tools to do what had to be their master's bidding was astounding.

Her hand fell to her lap. "There are so many of them."

"And that's the night crew," Exile said. "Imagine how many might work in the day."

She didn't even notice his hand until it curved around the back of her neck. "What are you doing?"

"Making this easier on both of us."

He squeezed hard and her head began to swim. He was… Her vision darkened to nothing.

She awoke with a start.

"Take it easy."

Who was…? Exile.

"What the fuck did you do?" she meant to snap, but her words came out foggy.

"Got us inside," he said.

That was her first hint to check out where they were. Familiar utilitarian paint adorned the walls of the long room. At the head of it, up just a few stairs, was a control desk set into the middle of a large metal structure with a matching fixed chair to the side. The wrist restraints didn't bode well.

"This is the JARR control room," she said, seeking confirmation, which she got in a nod. Checking out the bare walls and opaque glass doors at the other end, she couldn't work out what was going on. "Why are we alone?"

"We're alone in the building."

That she didn't expect. "Why? How did you swing that?"

"Z didn't have much choice. I want in first and he has the keys, I can't do anything until the startup process is complete."

"So why would you…?"

"Because maybe we can work out how much of you this thing needs before we put Zeus in the driving seat."

For her benefit? From the man who'd been so

adamant he didn't give a shit?

"That kind of sounds like you care," she said, sliding her hands down the arms of the leather chair she was sitting in. "Was Ares out there?"

"On some errand," he said, crouching in front of the control desk. "Lucky for you."

"You mean lucky for you," she said. "You think if he saw me unconscious, he'd just let it slide? This could've been over before it started." Her hand rested on her stomach. "Did you—"

"I was careful," he said, rising to go to the end of the structure to crouch by the wrist-restraint chair.

She couldn't see exactly, but it looked like he was doing something with his hands down there. "What are you—"

A clang heralded a large metal panel coming loose in his hands. "JARR was put together piecemeal," he said, setting the panel against the wall and returning his focus to whatever he'd uncovered.

"It was built largely by outside contractors," she said, rubbing her temple. "No one person knew what they were creating."

"The bonds are the weakness. Where one part is connected to the other."

"Like a jigsaw," she said, forcing herself to stand and go over.

"Right… It also makes everything take twice as long because the steps are protracted. He twisted to look up over his shoulder, revealing what was in front of him. Another metal panel. This time with a square embossed in the middle. "Blood first."

"That's it?" she asked. "I put my blood on that square and we're in?"

"It's the first step, not the last one," he said, standing up. "We don't have much time."

"We can't take as long as we want?"

"Zeus would only give us ten minutes."

"Fuck him."

"Great plan," he said, deadpan. "Except we want to

be into the JARR process before the others show up to create anarchy."

"Right."

"We want Zeus fighting a battle and his focus split. Not one then the other."

"Okay, so I have to bleed."

"You have to bleed," he said, producing a knife from his pocket.

"Wait," she said, yanking her hand behind her back before he could reach it.

"Time's a ticking."

"Yeah, I… My blood has to be living, we know this system can break it down and measure what's in it."

"So?"

"If it reads something that's not supposed to be there, something new, or it thinks I'm the wrong person, this could end fast."

"Right, but why would it…" His gaze dropped to her stomach. "The kid."

"I don't know if it makes a difference, and we can give this a try, but—"

"Be ready to haul ass," he said, reaching around to snag her wrist. "I hear you."

Their eyes met as he put the blade to her fingertip. Holding her breath, she closed her eyes and hissed at the sting of pain that came with him piercing her skin.

Exile pulled her down to smear her beaded blood across the dark square.

Time dragged as they watched and waited. What did they expect? What would happen?

With a quiet whoosh, the panel slid aside to reveal a large keypad bearing symbols, not numbers.

"What are they?" she asked, recognizing some. "They look like…"

"Greek letters," he said. "We need a password."

"Shit," she murmured. "We're so screwed."

"Not if you know it."

She stood up and he wasn't far behind. "I don't."

"Who does?"

"Ares is the only one."

That she was sure of anyway.

Exile's head tilted. "And he didn't tell you?"

"No."

"You're sure?"

Though he was annoyed, she smiled. "Trust me, Ares knows better than to give me hints. If we're waiting for me to figure this out, we'll be here for weeks. He knows I'm terrible with…"

"Terrible with… what?"

"Oh my… Maybe you can be good with subtle," she whispered his words. A surge of adrenaline hit her. "My Pandora. The password is my Pandora, but I don't know how to spell that, how—"

"I've got it."

He went to the other end of the desk and picked up a backpack that he dumped on top to produce a tablet.

A beep distracted her. And another. When she looked down, a tiny red dot was flashing in the corner of the panel they'd revealed.

"Uh… I think it's getting impatient."

"I hear it," he said, poking at the screen as he returned to her and crouched again.

Her heart pounded as he pressed buttons on the keypad. Nothing indicated whether each input was right or wrong. He stopped typing. Was that it? Was he done? How many shots did they get? One and done or would they get a do-over?

Nothing happened for so long that she actually took a step back. "Will it warn us before it kills us?"

"Probably not."

And all around the top of the room were vents. JARR could be filling the room with poison gas, and they'd never even know it. How smart would it be for the system to kill its gatekeeper?

The beeping started again. Faster. More frantic. Almost panicked.

Exile stood up. "Maybe we should—"

The panel slid aside just like the previous one, only it

went the opposite way. And they were in.

"Oh my God," she said as he returned to his crouch.

"The keys," he said, his fingertip grazing the metal by three oblong holes at the top.

And beneath, a metal tube, narrower at the tip, jutted up at an angle toward the chair at their side.

"That's it," he said, pinching the solid tube between his thumb and forefinger.

"What does that tell us?"

"It tells us…" Nothing good if his tone meant anything. "It doesn't want you to bleed fast. It's only capable of taking a small amount of blood at a time."

"Which means?"

He stood. "Either it wants a little of you to get started… or it wants you hooked up the whole time it's active."

"Shit," she said.

"Yeah. And I can't do anything without the keys." He pointed to the desk holding his backpack. "There's a panel there. Two. I guess when we get started, they'll open."

"That's where you'll work?"

He nodded. "I patched Swift into Minotaur, so they can monitor what's going on. I don't know how much time I'll have to link him into JARR."

"So this could all be on you."

"On us," he said and inhaled. "It's time to let the other side in."

She and Exile may not be the best of friends, but she'd rather stay there, alone with him, than have to see Zeus again, especially if her minutes and hours were numbered. But what choice did they have? Exile was right, it was time.

She nodded her acceptance and he started typing on his tablet again. Daire. She had to think about him. Seeing him again would be difficult because they couldn't be them, they couldn't greet each other like they wanted to. Once it was over, they'd have time to cherish each other. She had to believe that.

This was it. No going back now.

FORTY

EXILE MOVED THE CHAIR she'd started on up to the desk, so he'd have somewhere to work when the fun began. He did whatever he did on his tablet and then they waited.

"How long will this take?" she asked, wrapping her arms around herself as she paced.

"For them to get here or to shut JARR down?"

Even she didn't know which she meant. Exile was concentrating on his tablet, typing something on the keyboard he'd attached a moment ago. His backpack was now beneath him, tucked between his shins and the desk.

"What are you doing?" she asked. "JARR isn't even on."

"Minotaur is," he said, a picture of calm. "And my girls are together." Whatever that meant. "Swift's out there too."

"Does that mean they're in position?"

She'd feel better knowing their people were close by and not in danger. Before Exile could answer, the door opened. The hacker didn't flinch, but she stopped, braced for whoever may join them.

When Daire marched in and stopped, the door swung shut behind him. She didn't know what to do. What to say.

Why was he alone? Were they being monitored?

"Little Red?"

"Oh, my Heart," she said and rushed forward as he strode her way.

She stopped dead a few yards later, tensing as she realized what would happen if they embraced. After being apart for so long, it was only right he'd expect her to want to be in his arms, and she did. She did want to be there. She wanted to race to him, to leap up, coil herself around him and never let go.

"Babe?"

"No," she said as he frowned. "Oh, God."

"He's gonna find out sometime," Exile muttered, still he hadn't even turned around.

She swallowed. "We opened the coded panel," she said, ignoring her Heart's concern to turn on a professional air that would no doubt confuse him. "It accepted my blood." And his password. "We need the keys."

Going over there, she hoped distance might get them through this. Instead, when she peeked, her Heart's scrutiny was acute. When he'd betrayed her in the plan with Styx to return to Zeus, she'd forgiven him. It hadn't even been a question in her mind that she would.

Now he might think she blamed him, that she was mad he left the way he did and for so long. She wasn't thrilled about it, but that didn't change her love for him.

"Lift up your sweater."

Oh, God.

"Told you," Exile muttered again.

The guy really wasn't helping.

"Do you have the keys?"

"Tess," Daire said, warning thick in his tone as he stepped closer. "Lift up your sweater."

She should've known. The guy knew her body better than she did. He'd seen more of it, been intimate with more of it, than she'd ever got to grips with.

Sorrow welled within her. "I'm sorry," she whispered.

"Oh my God," Daire breathed as the door opened again.

Mercs she recognized from her last stay came in first. There was a pause and then Havers appeared, holding the door for Zeus to swan in, Garrick at his back.

"Pandora," Zeus said, glee almost glowing from behind his arrogant shell. Who was she kidding? It wasn't a shell, no, that was him through and through. Disgusting. Smug. Selfish. "Can you believe we find ourselves here?"

"Weren't we always destined for it?" she asked.

He stopped. "Interesting you should talk about destiny."

Daire stepped into Zeus's eyeline. "We don't need a crowd."

"No, we don't," Zeus said and raised a hand. A bunch of the soldiers moved to the perimeter of the room, facing the wall rather than into it. "But it's nice to have them around."

"You want witnesses?" Daire asked. "You want intel to reach their ears?"

Zeus considered that a second, then inhaled. "Get them out of here."

"Havers, you stay," Daire barked. "The rest of you outside, reinforce our lines."

Like they had all the time in the world, Zeus sauntered to the middle of the room. She was in no rush, but to see him so casual pissed her off. She could die there. Her child could die and… Daire knew. He knew the truth. She'd tried to protect him from it, now that was impossible. And she may never have the chance to explain.

"It's time to produce the keys," Garrick said.

Unlike Poseidon to be so forward. Maybe he, like the rest of them, just wanted to get this over with. Daire knew which key came first; he'd told her as much. That information likely came from something he read in Asclepius's journal. Her journal. Garrick knew where another of the keys came in the lineup. Had he told Zeus or was he withholding that information until the crucial moment?

"We should savor this," Zeus said, raising his arms like he was hosting a party. "All of us together again."

It had been months since she and Daire left him and Garrick in that LA hotel suite. "We're not all together," she said, happy to contradict him, even if it wasn't smart. "You're missing your third."

"We don't need him," Zeus said, not discouraged. "If nothing else, the time that's passed since the Exodus has taught me that. We don't need Hades."

"Funny," she said, showing him a smile just because it would piss him off. "It's taught him the opposite. You're superfluous."

"I am here. I am in charge."

Maybe it was sick, but she always felt a curl of pleasure in her gut when her words frayed his control. All the soldiers probably bowed and obeyed to every word he uttered. It would never be her. She would never be his subject.

"The people you need are here of their own free will," she said. "I am here because I choose to be. Exile is here because he chooses to be. We don't need you." They needed the keys, and she wasn't sure who held them. "If you want to do this, we do this now, or we walk away."

"You don't speak for Exile," Zeus spat.

"No," Exile drawled, turning his chair, "but your oratory is bullshit and I'm getting bored. Produce the goods… if you've got them."

"We need time to get our people situated inside."

"That's what you're doing? Buying time? Show us the keys."

"You got Minotaur online without one," Daire said to the hacker. "Want to tell me how you did that?"

"No."

"Might affect how this goes down," Daire said. "The process as far as we know it is the first key must be in Minotaur before being retrieved and used in JARR. Right now, you're not using a key. Do we have to start all over?"

If Exile had to shut Minotaur down, would the failsafes be triggered?

"Minotaur will take the key," Exile said. "Shut it down and bring it online the traditional way."

"The timing will have to be right," Daire said. "You shut it down, I put the key in and bring it online a second later." Exile nodded once and her Heart's focus shifted.

"Havers go to W3 supply room and get us walkies."

Havers went rushing out the room without asking a question.

"Just like the old days," Exile said, pushing back in his chair. "You miss them?"

"Not even a little bit," Daire murmured and turned his back to her again.

He couldn't even look at her. This time wasn't like when he was ashamed or feared he'd disappointed her. His head stayed high, he just wouldn't let his gaze touch her.

"We should bring them here," Garrick said.

"Who?" she asked. "Bring who here?"

The principal stayed focused on his counterpart.

Zeus was dismissive. "Later. I'm not sure they deserve to witness this. Our inner workings are not under their purview."

Someone sure did sound haughty. Kind of explained why the Six had come up with the plot to assassinate him in the first place. The Six, that's who Garrick had to be talking about. But they couldn't be there, could they? Didn't Daire say Two, Three, and Five had been neutralized? What did that even mean?

Havers came back and rushed over to present Daire with the walkie-talkies.

Her Heart tossed one to Exile. "Channel Two."

"You need the keys?"

"I know which one we start with," Daire said, on a mission as he marched out of the room.

A few moments of silence passed.

"You may as well sit down," Zeus said, though it took a moment for her to glance his way. "The chair was made for you, Pandora."

"You knew it was bullshit, didn't you?" she asked. "Asclepius said there was an accident, that I wasn't meant to be the gatekeeper. He said somehow, mysteriously, the drill instructions were mixed with the live ones, and I ended up in the hotseat. That was you, wasn't it?"

"To have that leash on H's neck…" he said and drew in a satisfied breath, "was intoxicating. He'd do just anything,

anything at all, so long as I had you. I wasn't going to give that up."

"But he didn't know, not at the time. You didn't taunt him with it, so what use was it?"

He leaned her way. "I always had it. That weapon. The bomb to drop on him whenever I chose. He had no idea the axe swung above him. Any good strategy begins with a contingency. Never box yourself in. Always have a backup plan."

"Your whole life," she said. "It's all been about manipulation. Nothing in your life is genuine. You have only what you've been able to connive and steal. Olympus could've been something incredible. If it had been handled in the spirit that was intended... If it was given to anyone but you..."

"This is the life I chose," Zeus said. "And now I get to watch you wither and disappear... Imagine how Hades will feel about that."

"I don't have to," she said. "If I lose my life today, I can take comfort knowing yours won't last much longer."

They stared each other out until an abrupt alarm blared through the air. This wasn't a subtle beep, it was a sharp blast. Once. Twice. Then silence.

"He's bringing it back online," Exile muttered. "Work fast, Ares."

Maybe the hacker hadn't been listening to her and Zeus or he just didn't care. Likely the second. But he was facing the desk, poised to react to whatever may appear on his tablet screen.

She didn't know how long it would take to bring Minotaur online the legitimate way. At least they hadn't been gassed... yet.

"When he turns it off again," Garrick said slow, "he'll have ninety seconds..."

"He knows," she murmured, fixated on the door.

Until Minotaur was off, they could breathe easy. After that... They were waiting. For something to change.

FORTY-ONE

HER BREATHING SEEMED HEAVY. Each exhale was a puff of anxiety, each inhale desperate in its hope. This was it. No matter how many times she'd imagined that moment, it was nothing to the experience of being in it. Noise faded until a whine vibrated in her ears. It wasn't real. Was her mind tuning in, or maybe out, of reality?

She could be dead in just a few minutes. Keeping her hands at her side was so difficult. They wanted to cradle her stomach, to reassure the child inside that they would be okay. Her fingers curled into fists, she had to be strong. If Daire would only come back, if he could be with her, touch her, hold her—

The door opened and Daire raced in, focused as he ran toward her. But she wasn't his aim. Still, he didn't even look at her. He swept around the end of the desk and plunged a key into the first slot. He surged to his feet and they watched, waiting for acceptance or rejection.

The slot went green; the one next to it turned amber. The final key slot and the light above the blood tube glowed red.

"We're good," Daire said and turned at the same time she looked toward Zeus.

She gasped. Zeus, still in his chair, gripped the arms tight. Garrick, standing just at his shoulder, held a gun to his head.

"Get them here," Garrick said.

"This isn't the time for this," Daire said, trying to alleviate the tension.

"You disgusting snake," Zeus snarled. "You think I fear you?"

"Don't think I won't do it," Garrick said, creeping a little further around, his weapon still trained on his target. "Get her here now." Zeus said nothing, just sat there seething. "The countdown's started, Sherwood. We don't get the next key into the system within eight minutes, the whole thing shuts down."

"Then we'll do it again and again," Zeus said. "You think we need you? My men could destroy you in seconds."

"You know nothing," Garrick spat. "If system access fails now, we don't get back in for thirty days. You want to stand here a month? JARR is my creation. I know more about it than any of you could imagine!"

"Ares!" Zeus snapped the command. "Finish this!"

Garrick strengthened his arm. "If he moves or anyone touches me, you will never know the traps set into the system. JARR is complex, its ability to recognize a fraud would astound you. You can't trick my masterpiece. It will destroy itself if an imposter tries to access its data. I won't lose it now. No one will jeopardize my life's work. No one."

Daire and Exile seemed to make eye contact for just a second.

Zeus was distracted. "Put the damn key in! Do it now!"

"Which is next?" Daire asked. Either he didn't know or wanted them to think he didn't. "Garrick?"

"Not until she's here."

"Her? Her? You pathetic fool," Zeus said, his knuckles whitening. Was that fear or fury? "Why is everyone around me so goddamn weak? You're weak! All of you! You do this to me? Betray me? For a woman? You're no better than Hades."

"Spoken like a man who's never been in love," she whispered, her gaze on the floor by Daire's boots. "I'm not surprised. It's not possible for you to love anything more than you love yourself, Ulysses."

"You, your father, this idiot, it's not love, it's sex. Your conscience demands you make it into something it's not. My love…" Zeus roared and raised his hands to smack his palms on the arms of the chair, "is for Olympus!"

"Olympus is dead," she said through gritted teeth, her eyes cutting to his. "You're the pathetic fool!"

"Anyone want to put the key in?" Exile asked, turning his chair. "Anyone at all?"

"Get her here!" Garrick shouted.

"Havers," Daire barked, "bring our guests."

"Ares!" Zeus scolded.

Havers was already out the door.

Light on the exposed panel caught the corner of her eye. The amber slot was flashing. "Time's running out," she murmured.

"You want the key…" Garrick said, hatred curling his lip as he pushed the barrel harder against Zeus's head. "None of you deserve JARR's bounty."

"They're on their way. She's on her way," Daire said, his voice even and calm. "Let's put the next key in. Buy ourselves more time. You don't want to risk her life, do you?"

"You don't want to buy time," Garrick said. "Not if you ever felt anything for Pandora. We use the keys and it will expect blood. Her blood. And it won't wait eight minutes."

"She's here," Zeus said. "We have Pandora. Start bleeding her now for all I care."

"We can't waste her blood," Garrick spat like Zeus was an idiot. "It can't be replaced, substituted, or diluted in any way. If JARR detects a false supply, it will erase every iota of data we need. Everything it's spent its life collecting. No one's life is at risk if we follow the steps. If we do everything right."

"And if your precious love doesn't get here and JARR shuts down for thirty days, what do you think will happen to you in that time?" Zeus asked. "What do you think I'll order my men to do to you?"

Always getting someone else to do his dirty work, Zeus hadn't changed at all.

"You better hope she gets here, or you won't see the next thirty days."

"Maybe I should grab a coffee," Exile muttered, turning back to the desk. "Anyone got Sudoku?"

The hacker's attention went to Daire as her Heart's head moved. The men's eyes met, she couldn't see Daire's face, but was absolutely sure they did. Exile gave the slightest nod. What was that? Could they have a plan?

The door opened again. One came in, former President Byron. Not a her. The new Six was next, Daire's father, Richard Merrill. The woman who came in before Havers was new to her, they'd never met.

The woman passed everyone else to get to Garrick who held an arm out toward her. "My love," she said, wrapping both arms around him.

"Everything's on schedule," Garrick said, holding her close.

Zeus surged up and lunged, knocking Garrick's gun arm aside. A shot razed the air, someone wailed, JARR beeped, and movement echoed. It was madness. Mayhem. Daire backed up, pinning her between him and the machine, the chair also blocked her way. She couldn't see anything. Couldn't see what was going on, what had changed.

"I should kill you now!" Garrick called out.

His new confidence, his aggressive attitude, it was out of character, at least the character he'd portrayed. He'd been conning them the whole time. The hapless, harmless gofer routine was a ruse, it had to be.

"We need the key," the woman said. "He must have it on him."

"Yes," Garrick agreed. "Ulysses, give us your key."

They were waiting on Zeus to hand over a key? The beeping grew louder, the flashing sped. Laying her hands on Daire, she tried to ease him aside, but he stayed put, pushing back against her insistence so much that Bump was squashed between them.

"I will not!" Zeus said. "You will never—"

"Do it!" the woman called. "Do it! He must have the key—"

"You stay silent—"

"Kill him! Do it, James! Kill him!"

"You take orders from me! Don't you—"

A shot. One single shot. For a moment, everything was still. Daire's shoulder descended and she leaned to the side to peer around him. Blood. She noticed blood pooling on the floor beneath Zeus's head before reality sank in.

"He's dead," she said.

Styx would be disappointed not to do it himself. Maybe Harry too.

"Search him," the woman's voice was strong, in control, and it was a shock to see the weapon in her hand.

Garrick went to do as she said, searching the deceased Zeus's pockets until he came up with a key. He stood and only took a couple of steps before tossing it to Daire. Immediately, her Heart crouched to slot it in. The beeping stopped, that keyhole turned green and the final one went amber.

"Where's the last?" Daire asked, standing to full height.

"Are you with us, Ares?" the woman asked. "If you're not, we don't need you."

"We need him," One said. "That's Ares."

The woman's expression turned to disgust as she stepped aside to look back at One. The former president was on the ground, blood beneath him too, except it was his thigh he cradled.

"You're nothing to do with this, Byron," she snapped. "The only reason you're still alive is because we don't need the attention of an investigation into your death." Her eyes narrowed on the pale Six. "You could be of use, if we choose to give you the White House."

She was no slouch. Confidence came easy to the stranger who perhaps wasn't so unknown.

"Four is a woman," she said, putting pieces together. "That's who she is. She's Four."

"Let me see her," Four said. "I've been eager to meet

you, Tess." Daire edged aside enough to let the women see each other. "I'm sorry about your mother, but she would never have let you come here. We needed you separate from her. For this moment."

"And to piss off my father."

The woman shrugged. "It never hurts to have your enemy's focus divided. While they squabbled among themselves, we got into position… With Ares, we knew you were safe, and your father would never hurt you."

"That's what you plan to do."

"We need your blood," Four said. "Your warm blood." She gestured with the gun. "Sit down."

Daire turned around. She blinked up at him, but he wouldn't look at her. Avoiding her gaze, he manhandled her into the chair.

"Don't do this," she said when he grabbed her wrist to force it into the restraint. "Not like this. We can't do this."

"Ares is Olympus," Garrick said. "Once you're gone, it will be all he has left."

"No," she said. Fighting against her Heart clamping the other metal restraint on her wrist was fruitless. "He knows better. You don't want to work for them. You're better than this."

She was appealing to him like he was hurting her, and he was, but not in the way her words portrayed. They'd killed Zeus and shot a president; God only knew what else they were capable of. And now, in that position, her Heart was vulnerable. They held the weapon, and Ares was a threat if he wasn't on their side. She couldn't watch him go down, not like this, not at all.

Her Heart stood and twisted to extend an arm toward Garrick. "Gimme the key."

Garrick looked at Four who gave him the nod and he retrieved a key from his pocket. Again, Daire caught it and he went to the panel.

"Baby," she breathed as he closed his eyes and pushed the final key into its slot.

One beat. Two. She couldn't feel anything but the pound of anticipation pulsing from every form in the room.

A metal drawer whooshed open at the base of the panel. The slots were green, the light above the metal tube flashed amber.

"You have to get the blood in," Garrick said with an almost frantic urgency. "You have to start the line immediately."

Daire had already taken the packet from the drawer and ripped open the lid. Without hesitation, he attached plastic tubing to the metal inlet. Everything was fast, deliberate, no mistakes. He was the efficient warrior.

The beeping started again, louder, more insistent. Yet it was slower, like the trudge of a funeral procession. With caution, he attached the needle to the tube.

What were they going to do? They were cornered. Four had a gun trained on them. If they tried to run, to fight… The room was wide open, cover didn't exist. And their baby… Daire would put himself between her and danger, she didn't want him hurt. There had to be a better way than rushing and hoping, but… what?

Her arms barely moved in her fight against the restraints. "My Heart," she begged in a whisper, tears skittering down her face. "Baby…"

His head turned and their eyes locked. "I told you I wouldn't be capable," he murmured and actually flashed her a dimple before taking the needle to his own arm.

"No," she screamed as her love pushed the line into his own vein.

FORTY-TWO

DAIRE'S JAW CLENCHED as blood drained from his arm, routing through the transparent tube into JARR.

No one else could see what he'd done. No one but her. His blood… JARR didn't want his blood, and the toxin—the blare of an alarm heralded instant darkness.

The curse in the air was only too aware.

One gun flashed, and another from the control panel. Was that Exile? Who was shooting? She couldn't move! Couldn't get up to shield her child. A third shot. In the pitch black, disoriented by the alarm, everyone was in a panic. Everyone except the hand that touched the back of hers to lift it away from the chair. Her wrists were free. She was free. Slithering out of the chair, she crouched with Daire just as red light scorched the air.

Grabbing for the tube, she yanked the needle out of his skin. "Why did you do that?"

"Stay behind me."

"No—"

But he was already rising, creeping along the front of the control desk.

"Good, you did good," Daire said to someone, Havers, he was with them.

Her Heart smacked Exile's shoulder and swiped the backpack now on the desk.

"Get the fuck out of here," the hacker said, his fingers working fast on his keyboard. "This will lock the building down the second the data's gone."

"You can't stay here," she said, but he probably didn't hear her over the alarm. "Exile! You have to get out of here!"

Daire grabbed her hand and pulled her away from the man fighting to save the world from JARR. Her Heart took her out into the corridor and stopped, letting her go to sink his hand into the bag.

"Get him out of here," Daire said to Havers who was paying close attention. Get who—Merrill stood close. "You get out of here alive 'cause I say so, Merrill. Take him to Hades."

"Not Styx?"

"Stay the fuck away from Styx," Daire said and shoved the young soldier. "Keep your head down, shoot to kill." Daire slapped a couple of clips into the boy's hand, his other held a weapon. "Do not hesitate."

"Hesitation gets you killed," Havers said.

Daire smacked the boy's upper arm and he immediately started to move, Merrill close behind him.

"Where's Styx?" she asked as Daire took two guns from the backpack. One went on his belt. The other stayed in his hand and he tossed the backpack onto his back. "Baby?"

"He's in the control room."

"But Beta's shutting down."

"It's gonna do a lot more than that," he said and grabbed her hand.

"There's a toxin. JARR releases a—"

"I know," he said, "we don't have much time."

"I don't want to—why did you do that? I'm immune to the toxin, I could've—"

"You think I would take the chance with your life?" he asked, anger creasing his expression. "With our child's life?"

She snatched her hand from his. "What are either of us without you? This baby needs a father."

Pushing her back against the wall, he bent his knees to get in close. "Right now, it needs its mother thinking straight. I'll get you out of here. You do the rest."

"We can't leave Exile—"

"JARR will self-destruct."

"That's what Garrick said," she murmured. "That's why you and Ex looked at each other…"

"As for its failsafes, they will trigger if Ex and Swift can't control them."

"He could die."

"We all could," he said, grabbing the side of her head. "Your priority is our child."

Blood streaked his arm. "You're bleeding!"

"Look at me," he said. The web of blood was terrifying, thick, staining his skin. "Tess!" Her eyes jumped to his. "I've gotta get you out of here and we don't have a lot of time. I need you to move fast and trust me. Can you do that?" She nodded once. "Are you sick? Hurt?" She shook her head. "When we get outside, it will be loud, and it will be frightening. Focus on me. Only on me."

"I love you."

"Good. Come on."

He took them down the corridor, the red light flashing everywhere as the alarm echoed in every hall. It wasn't like before. When she and Styx ran from Beta before. Pressure squeezed her from every side. It almost felt like the air was getting thinner, that it was getting harder to take a breath.

They went downstairs, just one floor. He swung her around, flattening her back to the wall as he crowded in against her, but he wasn't getting friendly.

He took the walkie from his belt to his lips. "Extraction sierra foxtrot," Daire barked into it and hooked the device onto his belt. "I need both hands. You have to hold onto me so I know you're close."

"I can only get so close," she said, hooking a finger into his beltloop. His gaze dropped to her stomach. "I'm sorry."

"Don't apologize," he murmured under his breath. After a second, his expression shuttered and he tensed. "The fighting is concentrated around the front. If we move fast and quiet, we'll get you out of here."

He turned around to redirect her hand to his waistband. "Stay alert."

The moment he opened the door, she was blasted with noise. Gunfire. Explosions. Lights directed at the sky and along the ground lit the night with menacing color and precision.

Her feet didn't want to move, but when he did, she just went, sticking nearby as he surveyed the yard. Low, he turned this way and that, keeping her at his back. He shot once. And twice. She flinched but kept moving. They went through a gate, over a ridge...

The sound of fighting faded. No, it wasn't quieter, something else was drowning it out. Seeking the sound, a second later she identified it coming from the air. A chopper, descending just a few hundred feet in front of them.

Daire stuck one of the guns in his waistband and snatched her hand to pull her around in front of him, pushing her toward the landing helicopter. It was dark, she couldn't see much of the black beast. The door was open, it was only when Daire boosted her up into the front seat that she recognized Falcon.

"I thought you didn't come into the field," she said, but he'd never hear her.

Falcon put the headset around her neck.

Daire fastened her safety belt. "Keep her safe!"

And that was when it hit her.

He wasn't coming with her.

She grabbed his arm, shaking her head. "You go, I go!"

"Not this time, Little Red."

His pupils were dilated, his eyes almost fogged. The toxin was doing its work.

"Don't do this!" she screamed.

He boosted up to kiss her fast. "I'll be waiting for you on the other side!"

"Please don't! Please! Stay with me!"

He cupped her head to direct her ear to his lips.

"Those are my men back there. On both sides. I need to have my brother's six." A lump dammed her throat. She couldn't see through the tears, but he kissed her temple. "I love you. Both of you." His eyes snapped onto the man behind. "Do whatever it takes!"

Falcon reached over her to slap something into Daire's hand. "We didn't have time to test it!"

"I only need an hour!" Daire called back, then switched his focus to smile at her. "It was always gonna end this way."

He dropped back, planting his feet on the ground. A weapon much bigger than his handguns was tossed past her from behind. Daire caught it and saluted, pulling the door to trap her inside.

"No," she whispered, but he was already backing away.

Instinct begged her to throw herself out after him, but her baby, their baby. As the chopper rose, numbness crept in. Their eyes were locked right up until he jolted to the side, startling her. People. There were people approaching his position. Shooting. He dived for cover, but went to his knees, his hands dropped too. The weapon was on the ground, he wasn't shooting back. The toxin! It was doing its work, slowing him down, paralyzing him. He had no defense, no way to fight back while the toxin slowed his reflexes, incapacitating his breathing.

The flash of weapons broke through the mire, coming from all directions. Every direction.

He was alone there. She'd left him alone. Run from the danger while he stayed to face it. How would she ever forgive herself? How would she explain abandoning her Heart to their child?

From around a side mound another figure appeared, running, flat out, the flash of his weapon's muzzle going almost constantly even as he dropped to a full-pace body slide coming to a halt by Daire.

Friend or foe?

Styx! He pushed Daire aside and picked something up. Many fighters closed in on their position. They needed to defend themselves. Brother fought with brother, or they would, after taking care of each other. Could he help? Styx was there, if Daire was… at least he wouldn't die alone.

Their people were there, that's what Daire said. Harry. Styx. Exile. Zara. All of them were down there somewhere. As they got higher, the blasts quieted, but the scene was astounding. Beta burned. Vehicles crashed. Lives were being lost. The lives of her family. And she may never know what became of any of them.

FORTY-THREE

NOTHING PROCESSED. She couldn't process any single piece of information. The journey was quiet and they landed without her moving a single muscle.

Falcon turned everything off and got out, but she stayed there, exactly where Daire put her.

The door opened.

"How is she?" a female asked.

"She hasn't said a word."

Daylight broke over the nearby building. Gamma.

Tulsi came into her eyeline, but she still didn't move. "How are you doing, honey?" How was she supposed to answer that? She couldn't feel anything. She felt nothing. "We packed some supplies for you. Falcon's going to take you home."

Home? She didn't have a home.

"You hear anything?" she managed to whisper. Tulsi shook her head. "Kero?"

"Left. About an hour ago."

"We left Exile inside."

Tulsi came closer, sliding a hand over hers. "This was never going to be easy."

No. Not when it felt like everyone knew this was

predestined. Was she the only one on the outside looking in?

"Wreck was with them."

"I know," Tulsi said and moved aside when Falcon came over to take her headset and safety belt off.

"We have to move," he said, though maybe not to her.

"Kero shut Gamma down," Tulsi said, linking their fingers again.

"Why?"

"It was the plan," Tulsi said. "We can't risk it falling into enemy hands. Everyone has to lay low. The order is to limit contact until the Olympus threat is fully neutralized."

Maybe it was because she wasn't supposed to live, but she hadn't thought much about what would come after the showdown.

"Go into hiding," she said, her body heavy. "To live on the run."

"It'll be over soon."

A weak laugh seeped from her tired lips. "I've been telling myself that a long time. It's a lie. It's all a lie."

Who did she have if her Heart was gone? Her father? Styx? Her family was gone or running for their lives. How could she raise a child in safety with so many unknowns? In the JARR control room, she'd been disoriented, shocked, scared, she couldn't even remember seeing One or Four after Daire's blood touched the machine. Were they dead? Was Garrick? Had Exile perished chasing JARR in the midst of its self-destruction?

"Have faith in them," Tulsi said, squeezing her digits. "Give them a chance to make this right."

"Wreck might never come back. Rowdy. The people involved because of us. Because of…" Anger at least gave her the energy to throw the belts aside and jump onto the asphalt. "Fuck it."

"Fuck what?" Tulsi asked, hurrying after her as she marched around the chopper.

"I'm alone, right? Shit, it all seems so pointless." She stopped to drive her fingers into her hair, holding her head, digging her nails into her scalp. "None of it meant anything.

None of it!"

"What do you mean?"

Her hands dropped to Tulsi's shoulders. "My mom died. This all started because my mom died and I didn't want to be alone. I grabbed onto Danny, I clung with such desperation because I didn't want to live the rest of my life alone."

The grief was all-consuming. Every part of her grew heavy. As her hands slid away, she dropped to the ground, her body quaking in a pain so deep it crushed her bones.

"You're not alone," Tulsi said, snatching her chin, forcing her to look up. "You are not alone, Tess." Her friend's hand slid onto her stomach. "You have a support system. And you have this child. No matter what happens. No matter whether your guy makes it or not, you have this piece of him to care for. You're right, maybe Wreck won't come back…" Fear bobbed in Tulsi's throat. "And if he doesn't, if him and Rowdy don't make it, I'm alone too. And I don't have any part of him to cherish."

There was no need to hide it anymore. Touching her stomach, she got strength from what her Heart had given her. Life, such as it was, wouldn't ever be the same again. She had to give this child life. To raise it aware of exactly how valued and loved it was.

"I don't know what to do," she whispered.

When Tulsi smiled, a tear dripped from her lashes. "Falcon's going to take you back to his island. Devon is there and they have a doctor. You can give birth there safely. They will look after you."

"Why should they?"

"Why shouldn't they?" Tulsi asked. "They help people. It's what they do."

Maybe they'd hear word from Raven and Zara. Whoever made the plan had to know about the baby. That meant not Harry or Daire.

"Styx," she murmured. "He put this together."

Tulsi nodded. "He wants you to be safe." And he was the only one who'd known about the baby before they left. "Him and Zara talked about it, I think. It's a good plan…

Please don't push all of us away. We want to help."

"I can't ask them to care for me and a baby."

"According to Zara, Devon loves babies. And they're expecting their own soon. You're due around the same time. You can help each other."

It wasn't like she had a list of better options. Even if she felt awkward, she had to think of her baby. Without insurance or even a fixed abode, how could she give birth in the world? On the street? How would that be best for her baby?

"This way!" Falcon called, attracting there attention.

There was something in his hand. Her carpet bag. She'd given it to Zara before they left and assumed it went in their truck. Obviously, it hadn't.

"The things we do for love," she said on a sigh and took Tulsi's hand.

The baby had to be her focus. The life inside her. The next generation. And it would be different this time around. No more secrets. No more lies. She'd make sure her child knew exactly where it came from and how much it was loved.

EXTENDED EPILOGUE

ONE

Six months later.

"AND THIS…" Tess said, stroking the back of the baby tied to her body in a sling, "is the glitter."

His little head was tucked under the fabric, his eyes closed. She ran the back of her index finger down his cheek. Being only five weeks and one day old, the kid had an excuse for not gawping at the ceiling. "Oh, what am I doing here, honey? Why did I drag us here?"

She sighed, her focus drifting toward the lockers. Either he'd been there and she was about to have a glimmer of contact with the man who may or may not be living anymore or…

"We came all the way here, didn't we?" she asked the sleeping baby, resting a hand on his warm back. "We'll do this, then get a strawberry and vanilla milkshake. Won't be as good as the ones Aunt Bess makes for Aunt Devon, but we'll make do." Taking her time, she was in no rush to reach the locker. "You know Grandma and Grandpa used to come here too. It wasn't always a roller-rink, which is why Daddy had to teach me to skate the first time we came here together." She curled a little closer. "Prince had more to do with my success, but we won't tell him that." The heat of her baby was motivating. "One day Daddy can teach you too…"

Had she just lied to her little one?

Passing the desk, it was impossible not to relive their first time there together. How Danny crossed the room with such easy purpose. How he'd gone to the desk and grabbed what he needed without anyone else seeing him. His ability. His lithe movement. His stealth. His strength.

Funny, she'd reminded herself of these things so often. It wasn't about admiration, though she did miss having his body on hers, it was about faith. The man was capable. He knew how to take care of himself. And he was out there with his brother, and her father too. At least, that was her hope.

Stopping in front of the lockers, she licked her dry lips. "Seven across, three down."

Steadying her breathing, she approached. As her fingers rose to the cool metal, her heart jumped. Please. She needed this. Needed to know he was still alive. Every second of doubt crashed together in a crescendo so abrupt, it winded her. Her sinuses stung; her eyes already watered. Easing aside the door, her fingertips skimmed along the ceiling of the locker to the seam she'd missed first time she'd been there.

If it hadn't been for her Heart…

Her lips parted, air dried her tongue, and her eyes closed in a silent plea. With gentle pressure, she released the flap and… nothing. Blinking, there was nothing, there… How was she supposed to…? It couldn't be. After all these months? They'd exchanged letters there when they'd only been in Miami a day. Yet, somehow, in the six months since they parted, he hadn't got there, not for a second.

That meant only one thing.

Pain in her chest opened her mouth wider.

Like life was mocking her, *Slow Hand* rose in the air. That song. Danny's song. It ridiculed her hope. Forcing the flap back up, she planted a hand on the door to slam it.

The little one shifted his head. Cradling it through the material, she rested her forehead on her knuckles, her palm still on the metal before her.

She'd thought she could give him his father. Some

part of him. A small… something.

"Don't fucking test me," she whispered like the magic words could grant her a reprieve.

Nothing could.

Nothing would.

He was dead.

That was the only explanation.

Daire knew of this place. Harry. Styx. They all knew and any one of them could've left her a message. Yet there was… nothing.

Could all of them be gone? Had they died together? Was her son the only morsel of him left?

How could it be? How could she…? She'd promised her child love. That he'd be cherished and adored. She'd promised him they wouldn't be alone.

"Make out time." Her head moved a millimeter at the echo of those masculine words. Was she delusional? Had to be. They couldn't be real. She couldn't have just heard… Those words were… Warmth slid onto her shoulder; the weight of a hand settled by the curve of her neck. "Babe, come on." She couldn't believe it. Couldn't hope it might be true. Maybe she was dead too. The heat of his mouth rested on her hair. "My Something."

Spinning around, a desperate yelp left her lips when their eyes collided. His intensity softened as his dimple deepened.

"My Heart."

"Always," he said, ducking to marry their mouths.

TWO

SINKING INTO THE GIFT OF HIS KISS, she descended into bliss. He was alive. With her. There in front of her. His fingers in her hair, tipping her chin up, angling their mouths to deepen the plunge of his welcome tongue. Her Heart. Her whole world. No… Not exactly.

Laying a hand on his shoulder, she pushed. He didn't want to give in, to part their mouths and she couldn't claim to want it either, but he had to know. He had to understand the truth.

Increasing her pressure, she got him to put just an inch of space between their lips.

"Little Red," he breathed the words like they were vital to his life.

"There's…" she said, unable to open her eyes. Her mind was in disarray, sense wasn't easy to come by. "There's someone else…" The proximity of his mouth swayed back. She opened her eyes, eager to check he really was her Heart. "I have to tell you there's someone else…" resting a hand over his at the side of her head, she guided it down to the curve of the head beneath the sling, "who wants to meet you."

His lips rose as she cradled his hand around their little one.

His smile slowly faded. "I wanted to be with you," he murmured.

"I know."

"I was overseas and when I heard—"

"It's okay," she said, smiling in hope he could reciprocate. "We were okay. We're okay."

His smile came when his eyes descended. "He was early."

"Impatient," she said, her muscles loosening. "No idea who he gets that from."

His whisper of a laugh was heartening. "You called him Oscar."

"You like it?"

"Yeah," he said, stroking the baby tucked inside the fabric that kept him covered. "He's perfect."

"You can't see him."

His gaze found hers. "I don't need to see him to know he's perfect. He came out of you."

"Out of us," she said, her pinkie curled around his at their sides. Truth was often heavy. "I'm not sorry I had him. We didn't talk about it, but even if we had—"

"Hey," he said, touching her cheek. "I'm not sorry either. We did talk about it."

"Before it was a reality, and you were always against—"

"The woman I love carrying my child?" he asked. "I was never against that. I just needed to know I'd be able to keep you safe. Both of you."

And that was the twist of the blade. "I promised him a milkshake," she said. "We should sit. Talk."

Excitement bubbled beneath the weight of the possible outcome of their conversation. She could throw herself into him. Demand without answers. But their son deserved better than his parents being so caught up in each other that they couldn't plan for his security.

With their fingers linked, Daire led them across the building and chose their table, seating himself facing the door. Did that mean danger was close or that old habits died hard?

"I'll be back," he said, touching their son as he bowed

to kiss the top of her head.

Watching him at the counter, she wasn't sure taking her eyes off him was an option. Maybe he'd vanish again. Disappear like he had in the past. She didn't blame him for going, it was necessary. Safety was important. Maybe if Oscar wasn't in their lives, if he wasn't a factor, she'd be less understanding. Though…

When he turned to come back, her smile ascended slowly. Curiosity joined his.

"Is this real?" she asked.

He sat, pulling his chair closer to hers. "It's real, baby." Scooping up her hand, he brought it to his lips. "Not that it's easy to believe."

"You didn't think we'd be here again? That we'd ever be together again?"

"Sometimes I didn't want to let myself believe," he said against her knuckles. "But you were the something that kept me going every day."

Trepidation crept in. "Did Harry and Styx—"

"They're okay," he said, his other hand curling around her palm as he straightened her fingers to kiss each tip. "Harry about blew something when he found out he was a grandfather."

"He didn't know I was pregnant," she said. "Styx was the only one…"

"He supported you better than I did."

"That's not true," she said, bouncing to the edge of her seat, laying her free hand on his face. "You were our something too. Mine and Oscar's. I made him all these promises and I… I was scared I'd never deliver. That we'd be alone… like me and my mom."

"I told you that would never be us," he said, tucking her hair away from her face. "Being apart, it was difficult, I know. I wanted to come back to you every second. But I had to know… I had to finish it."

"I understand that," she said, her knees moving deeper into the vee of his thighs as she got even closer. "What happened? With Garrick and…"

"He and Four had a bunch of contingencies.

Different sites all over the damn world. And Zeus's army were more than happy to follow Four's money. The guys I trained, and some of the others, were with us… And I spent more time with Exile than I ever want to again."

A server came over with their milkshakes. The way Daire's eyes cut to the woman, it was clear part of him was still in soldier mode… or maybe he was concerned with protecting his family.

When the woman left, she took his attention back. "Garrick? Four?"

"We caught up with them," he said, offering his cherry to her lips. The hints of them meant everything, so she didn't hesitate to pull the fruit from its stalk with her teeth. "Garrick first. We rounded him up and sent him off with one of the Laird's lieutenants. Garrick was the brains in the operation, so she wasn't far behind. Not sure how much love was there, Four let him go pretty easy."

Guilt joined her pushing the stone to her lips, he took it, but concern was written all over his face. "I let you go pretty easy," she said on an exhale of shame. "I shouldn't have let you go back there alone… with the toxin in your system. It was a battlefield. I let you go into danger."

"That's exactly what you should've done. I could focus because I knew you were safe. And with Oscar now… You did exactly what I needed you to do. Exactly what any mother should."

Leaning back, she checked her son. "Are we safe here?" she asked, stroking his cheek. "Is there danger?"

"No, baby," he said, caressing her outer thighs. "I wouldn't be sitting here if there was danger around. I'd be out there eliminating it."

Like Harry had during her childhood. If their life was going to be the same, this moment could be fleeting.

She ignored her anxiety to loosen the sling. "Whenever we're out, he's always in the sling. It keeps him close to me in case we have to move fast." As the fabric freed the little one, she scooped him out to present him. "So you better be right." She smiled at the tease, and the way his eyes widened. His lips moved too, like he was moistening them, could he be nervous? "Meet your son, my Heart."

"Shit."

"Not a good start," she said, easing the infant into his father's arms. "No swearing in front of the baby."

"Right," he said, his large hand dwarfing the little one's head as he raised him to admire his tiny face. "Babe…"

His wonder was humbling. Some of that excitement bubbled through. "He's gorgeous, isn't he?"

"I can't believe how…"

Oscar wriggled, his lips parting in a grumble. She urged him closer. "Don't let him get cold."

He'd been tucked against her heat and comforting heartbeat. Quickly taking off the sling, she didn't ask before guiding Daire into it, giving him the opportunity to hold their son close.

"I don't know if this is—"

"It's okay," she said, tightening it and sitting back again. "Just keep him close. He's safer with you than anywhere else in the world." Picking up her milkshake, she enjoyed it and the sight of son settling against father without a care in the world. "I told him you'd teach him to roller-skate."

"Give the kid a chance, LR," he said. "We've got more important things to cover before we get to skating."

Sliding closer, she leaned in to whisper. "It's okay, he's definitely yours." Startled, his gaze leaped to hers. Restraining her smile, she said, "he likes disco music."

"Oh, thank God," he said in a rush like he'd been worried. "You know I'd have to disown him otherwise."

She laughed and put the milkshake down. "Whenever I played it, he'd kick harder, like he was dancing in there."

"I'm sorry I missed it."

"You didn't. Devon insisted on recording everything… I may have sworn at you a few times in delivery."

"I deserved it."

"No," she said, her fingers finding their way into his hair. "You gave me the most incredible gift. I thought my love for you was the biggest thing I could ever feel, then our son was born and…" He turned his head to guide her palm to his mouth. "I don't want to keep you a secret." His brow creased.

"I didn't know Harry and I blamed him for so much. I know now he didn't have much of a choice, but I want my—our child to know who you are... maybe have a sibling somewhere down the line." She swallowed. "It's a lot, I know, I don't expect everything to be... I want you to visit him."

"Visit him?"

"I'll explain it to him. You don't have to worry. He'll never blame you for—"

"No, I won't visit," he said. Grief stunned her once again. "I won't visit him; I won't visit you. It's over now, it's finished. This is it."

That didn't sound like the Daire she knew. "Because I had our baby? How can you turn your love off like that? What? It just evaporated?"

His scowl grew fierce. "What? No..." He took a breath. "Olympus is over." He glanced at Oscar. "I didn't want that word ever breathed around him." But his certainty was absolute. "What was is no more. Whatever happens from here is our life. Us. Together. South America's next, as soon as you're ready." He threaded their fingers together. "We're giving this little guy what we never had. He'll know his parents. His family."

"Harry will see him?"

"Yeah," he said. "What did you think? He'd reject Oscar? Shit, if he tried that, I'd put a bullet in him myself... or is it that you... You don't want Harry in his life? I swear to you, he won't mention—"

"No, I want Harry to know him. I want Styx to know him too. I want him to have a family. I promised him he'd be loved. Our friends, our allies... he's important to them. Devon and Bess cried when we left... We went to Tulsi's, I doubt her and Wreck will wait much longer to start their family."

His brows rose. "Wreck wants a kid?"

Her grin burst. "He was amazing with Oscar. He's not a typical uncle, but Oscar will have a lot of over-protective uncles. Will you teach him to protect himself?"

"You want me to?"

"Yes," she said. "I don't want you to be his CO, I

don't want you drilling him every minute. I want you to be his father, but we never know what he might face in the future. And if we don't let him train at least a little, Harry won't have a way to bond with him."

That was meant to be a joke, but he wasn't laughing.

"Would you feel the same if we had a daughter?"

She couldn't believe the accusation in that question. "You think I want to birth soldiers for your war?" She scoffed. "Sure! We better get to the doctor and figure out how soon you can put another one in me. We're wasting precious time." Rising, anger burned in her. "I'm going to the restroom. Should I take Oscar? Do you plan to split, or will you be here when I get back?"

"I told you, I'm not going anywhere."

Walking away from him was the smartest thing to do. In public, she didn't want them arguing, that would divide his focus. Whatever his faults may be, whatever hers were, Oscar would always be the priority.

THREE

TESS WANTED TO BE with her Heart. Wanted them to always be together. She'd been so desperate to see him, to have him in her life again. Now he was there, she was almost afraid to trust it. Maybe that was why she lingered in the restroom washing her hands.

Having her Heart back was a privilege. They had to value their union instead of making assumptions. What happened to their trust? Their intimacy? She'd told him once he had to fall in love with her again. Maybe that was it. They'd spent so long on guard, apart, scared for each other, that it wasn't easy to relax and just accept nothing was tearing them apart.

Time to put ego aside and figure out what they wanted, what was best for their boy.

A new determination joined her on her exit from the restroom except… the table was vacant. Terror grabbed her. What could've happened? Danger. It could only be…

A group by the skate desk shifted and there they were, father and son surrounded by at least ten adoring women.

Oscar was a babe magnet apparently. Styx would love that. Her lips quirked and she covered them with her curled fingers, hiding her laugh. She gave them another few seconds before going over there. Stopping about ten feet away, she listened to the cooing and swooning.

Daire's eyes met hers, his smile glowing in them. Pride. His awe had become a satisfaction. The honor of fatherhood outweighed any gratification she'd seen in him before.

"My wife," he said, extending an arm her way, forcing the women to back off a little.

Not yet, but she didn't mind the title.

"Oh, you're so lucky," one of the women said as she got closer. "He's gorgeous."

"Which one?" she asked, happy to tuck against her Heart when he put an arm around her.

"We're gonna skate now, ladies, but it was a pleasure to meet you all." The women dispersed, smiling, blowing Oscar kisses. "I'm sorry." He kissed the top of her head. "I don't want to fight."

"Well, we're going to," she said, tipping her head back to look up at him without separating their bodies. In fact, she twisted closer, resting her hands on her Heart's torso beneath Oscar. "We're parents now. Sometimes we might disagree on what's best for him. So long as we both keep what's best for him at the center of everything, we'll find ways to compromise. I don't want him growing up desperate for your approval, but the truth is, he probably will. Don't most kids crave their parents' approval?"

"Yeah, but he'll never doubt it," he said. "We'll tell him we're proud. We'll make sure he knows he's good enough. That he can never disappoint us. We'll be honest with him. Work things out as a family. And you're right, I should make sure he can take care of himself because I want him to be safe, and being the oldest, he'll feel responsible for his siblings."

"Plural?"

One corner of his mouth curled. "We'll need a bigger trailer."

She laughed and relaxed. "I often wondered what happened to the Beast. I'd love to show him one day."

"One day," he said, wrapping his arms around her. "Want to take the little guy skating?"

Though she put pressure on her hands, he didn't budge. "I'll watch from the sidelines."

"Oh no," he said, keeping an arm around her while turning. "We're taking Momma with us, aren't we?"

"Momma hasn't been on wheels since the last time we were here," she said. "She doesn't want to end up on her ass."

They moved to the desk where two pairs of skates waited. "Clearly, she's forgotten what a good teacher I am."

"No, we talked about that," she said. Daire picked up both pairs and led her around the desk to the seating by the lockers. "That's why I said you'd teach him too."

Whirling her around, he planted her on one of the benches and held her skates toward her. "Now he can just get a feel for it."

"You sure you want to try it with the sling," she said, slipping her feet from her shoes.

"Are you kidding?" he asked, straightening his back. "I love this thing. He's secure and I still have both hands. I can run drills and the kid can sleep through the whole thing."

She pulled on her skates. "Harry will be pleased to hear that. But no standing on your head, okay? That's where I draw the line."

"Guess Grandpa just got bumped down the pecking order."

Their oddball family might be unusual, but Oscar would get used to it… or the rest of them would get used to him. Already it seemed the baby was making the rules and that was just fine by her.

FOUR

BACK ON SOLID GROUND, or rather in solid footwear, Oscar was done with roller-skating and rooting against his father.

"I have to feed him," she said, rising to her feet.

But when she tried to reach for Oscar, Daire turned to the side. "I want to show you something."

"You can show me after," she said, opening her hands. "He needs to eat."

"He can eat."

"I don't like to be unprotected when I—"

"Babe," he said and just crooked a brow. "We've met before, right? You want your own phalanx, consider it done."

"Okay, but he eats every couple of hours." She'd fed him before they came into the roller rink, but they'd probably been skating for two hours. "He sleeps and eats and poops, that's pretty much it... Unless you want a demonstration of his lung power?"

"Trust me," he said, slipping an arm around her to guide her away from the desk where they'd returned their skates.

Oscar's head moved as he sought sustenance. Their son might be the most precious thing alive, but he was not patient. Not even a little bit.

At least it seemed like Daire was moving for the door. She could feed their boy in the parking lot. It wouldn't surprise her if her Heart had figured out exactly which vehicle was hers. And he'd have his own…

They walked out the Rotunda doors and she stopped. Yes, her rickety RV was where she'd left it, almost in the middle of the lot. And he had figured out it was hers because he'd parked right next to it.

"Oh my God," she whispered. Eyes wide, she rushed forward a few steps, passing father and son. When she turned back to him, tears weighed heavy on her lashes. "The Beast."

"At your service," he said, pulling her back to kiss her head. "It's our home, right?"

The moment couldn't be more perfect. She'd be able to feed her son in the same place he'd been conceived. When they got over there, she was about to ask for the key when the door burst open. Harry appeared.

"Dad," she said, though he was scowling at the man beside her.

"What took you so long?"

"We were skating."

"You took my five-week-old grandson roller-skating?" Harry asked, still unhappy. "Let me see him."

"Hey, no," came the voice from within. "I knew first, I get first go."

Her head snapped around. "Styx?"

Daire was already smiling. "Inside," he said.

Harry stepped back and gave her a hand to leap up into the Beast. Her father hugged her. Styx was sitting in the corner of the dinette like he had all the time in the world.

"So you popped?"

"Come give me a hug," she said when her father stepped aside.

Styx exhaled a grump, but pushed himself up and met her midway, coiling both arms around her so tight, it was impossible to disguise that he'd been worried. Maybe he just missed her, but it felt like a little more than that.

Once they parted, he fixed on his brother. "You

didn't teach the kid not to corner himself in a new potentially hostile environment yet?"

"We're friendlies," Daire said. "He's got good instincts."

"And none of you have experienced a diaper yet," she said, resting on the kitchen counter. "Our boy can clear a room in seconds."

"Our boy?" Harry asked.

She looked from him to Daire. He passed Harry to run his fingers into her hair. "I told him everything Oscar was your choice. I'll stand by the mother of my child no matter what. Whether she wants all of us involved or none of us. No matter what, our forces are dedicated to your protection. Oscar's protection."

Sometimes it was impossible to believe her love for him could grow anymore, then he went and said something like that.

Distracting herself, she loosened the sling as Daire held their child.

"Can I feed him here?"

"Do you want me to feed him?"

Smiling, she took Oscar into her arms. "We travel light," she said, resting her lips against him. She'd missed her boy and the faintest hint of his father in his hair reminded her how she'd missed being near his father too. "Devon offered us a pump and bottles, but…"

"You travel light," Styx said, folding his arms. "Smart."

"Can I use the bedroom?"

"Stop asking permission, Little Red." Daire's hand slid down the back of her head to guide it to his lips. "It's your room."

In the bedroom, everything was the same, just as she remembered. The comfort. The security. Still, it felt a little peculiar to slip off her shoes and prop the pillows up to sit down and raise the hem of her top.

Oscar was an amazing eater. She put all her breast-feeding success down to him… well, him and Devon.

"You talk?" Harry's voice carried up the trailer.

"Don't need to," Daire said.

"We should eat and get on the road," Styx said. "I've spent too long on my ass."

"You should hibernate," Daire said. "You keep going too long, you burn out."

"Says the guy who's never been off his whole life."

Her boy's eyes were closed, but his mouth worked overtime. Already it seemed like she took their closeness for granted when it was something to be cherished.

"Daire," she called out, raising her voice enough to get his attention without distracting their little one.

"Baby?"

"Come here," she said and only had to wait a second for him to appear.

"You okay? What do you need?"

Subduing her smile took effort. "Don't panic," she said and raised an arm. "Come over here."

"Is he okay?"

She gave up the fight with her smile when his fingers slid into hers and she pulled him down to sit on the edge of the bed. "Yes. You shouldn't miss anymore of him. See how smart he is?"

Daire watched him for a few beats. "He's strong." His little mouth moved fast as he gulped down his food. "Is he getting enough?"

When he showed her a frown, her fingertips moved to the crease between his brows, trying to assuage his concern. "Yes. He's hungry, he'll slow down in a minute. He likes his food."

"Good. That's good, right?"

"More than good," she said, nodding at his side of the bed. "Sit with us."

He was on the edge of the bed, but that wasn't the same as him relaxing with them. She wanted him close, wanted him to appreciate all their son's nuance. No one would know him better. Her Heart was a sponge with everything, their son would be no different.

Oscar ate until his little stomach was full and was already drifting back to sleep when his mouth broke suction.

"Here," she said, easing Oscar into his father's arms. "Will you burp him?"

She didn't even have to ask, Daire was already rising, propping Oscar on his shoulder to rub his back. "There's something of yours in the drawer, Momma," he said, bobbing his chin toward her nightstand. "It kept me going in my weakest moments."

"It?" she asked.

Her Heart was already turning away. "You want to come say hello to your minions, son," Daire asked, wandering down the hallway.

She smiled again. Already she could tell he was proud of their little one. His approval meant a lot to her. Until that moment, she hadn't given it much weight. Not only did she want Daire to accept their son, she needed him to dote on him. Thankfully, she wouldn't have to wonder whether he did, he oozed esteem.

She didn't think much of opening the drawer until she laid eyes on what he meant. Her pendant. Their pendant. He'd kept it. Cared for it. Her fingertips met the cool metal. It kept them together, even when they were apart.

Harry's authoritative voice boomed from the kitchen. "You need to move him—"

Oscar's little belch cut his grandfather off and all three men exclaimed their praise.

Tucking herself away, she was in no rush to interrupt the bonding moment.

"Now the two of you need to learn how to change a diaper."

"We got his bag from next door," Styx said.

Next door would be her RV parked next to the Beast. She wasn't even surprised her father and Styx had already rifled through, and apparently stolen, some of their things.

"You stole from Tess?"

"In case we had to move fast," Styx said like that justified it.

She stifled a laugh. Some things would never change.

FIVE

SHE LISTENED AS HARRY TALKED his protégés through changing a diaper. Each seemed to be taking in the steps, as proven when Harry quizzed them on the process after.

"Good," Harry said. "Everything he needs is in the diaper bag. We'll top off supplies."

"How does the sling work?" Styx asked.

"We'll take the RV; his car seat is in it."

Wait. She leaped to her feet. That sounded like they were discussing taking Oscar out. She hurried to the hall. At the other end, Daire was showing Styx how to secure Oscar in the sling.

"What's happening?" she asked, walking down the trailer. "Where are you going?"

"You don't have to do all the feeds yourself anymore," Harry said. "We'll get supplies. Bottles. Sterilizing equipment."

"When can he have real food?" Styx asked, pulling the fabric of the sling tight. "That's gotta be soon, right? We want him strong."

"No," she said, shaking her head, but as she tried to pass, Daire put an arm around her to hold her at his side. She looked up at him. "Are you going with him?"

"He'll be safe with his grandpa and uncle," he said. The smile was probably meant to reassure her. "You trust them."

"I…" Stys was stroking Oscar's back, his hand looked huge against the tiny infant. "I've never been apart from him."

"He's just eaten," Harry said. "Burped. Diaper change. He'll sleep for a couple of hours."

Her father knew babies. He'd raised Daire alone and been part of her life at a young age. It wasn't a lack of trust, she just… "We've never been apart."

"We won't let anything happen to him," Styx said, almost offended. "I've been keeping this kid alive since before any of you knew he existed."

That was true, he had known first.

"Okay," she said, slipping away from Daire's side to go over and kiss Oscar's head. "Be good, little one." His eyes were already closed. "Have him back in an hour. And don't go too far."

"Yes, Mom," Styx droned.

Harry opened the door to depart, and Styx was quick to follow with Oscar.

Wincing, she spun to face Daire, but he was already smiling. "I'll go check they secure the car seat right."

"Thank you," she said, tilting her cheek to welcome his kiss as he passed.

When the door closed and she was left in silence, she wasn't sure what to do with herself. For all those times she'd worried about being alone, it was only then she appreciated how Oscar had been her crutch. Since learning of her pregnancy, they'd been together. He gave her something to live for, to focus on, a reason for being.

She could take a shower. Lie down. Relax knowing her son was safe. She didn't doubt Styx or Harry's ability to keep him safe, she just wasn't sure what to do with herself without him.

Daire came back inside. "Cargo's secure."

"Our son is not cargo," she said, but smiled when he

did.

They were alone. She swallowed. It hadn't occurred to her until… he came over, sliding his hands onto her hips, easing her back against the dinette.

"Want me to rev your engine?"

Memories. Happy memories. From a lifetime ago.

"I do," she said. He boosted her onto the dinette table, but her hands were quick to land on his, stalling them from going any higher. "But I…" Why were her lips suddenly so dry? Damn, he was hot, incredible, the perfect guy, and the only one she wanted. "I haven't done this… since… the last time we did this."

"Good," he said, running his fingers into her hair, tipping her head back to kiss her slow.

She eased back. "Have you?"

"You're the only one for me, Little Red. You know that. There will never be anyone else."

He kissed her again, his hands drifted down her back, pulling her pelvis closer. "I had a baby. Things are different—"

"My baby," he said, cupping her head and meeting her eye. "You had my baby."

"Yes."

"I love you, Temptress. And I won't leave you ever again."

"We get our forever?"

"Yes, we do."

His lips sank onto hers again. She let herself enjoy it. The tender press of his kiss was so precious. So many times she'd feared never experiencing it again.

They were together.

It was only as he picked her up and her arms twined around his neck that she accepted the truth. They'd found each other. Somehow, they'd come together again, and he was giving himself to her. To their son. To their life together.

"Daire," she whispered as he took off his tee-shirt and freed her from her top.

The maternity bra wasn't sexy, but she wasn't sure he even noticed. He kissed each of her breasts and her lips again before trailing his lips through her cleavage and down her belly. Without losing his mouth's connection to her body, he shed their pants.

A self-conscious part of herself wanted to stop his mouth's expedition, to draw him back up to kiss her again. Instead, she loosened, trusting him with her heart and her body as she always had.

They'd come so far, overcome so much. She didn't have to worry about him rejecting her, not when their souls were entwined and their destinies meshed.

He kissed her clit, circled and flicked it, teasing her pleasure, warming her hormones. Sex. The only time it came to mind was when she thought of him. He'd visited her dreams and teased as he did then, slipping his tongue into her, parting her folds, arousing her desire. She needed him and didn't ever want that dependence to change.

They were alive, they'd made it through alive. If nothing else, they had to celebrate the life that had been gifted to them. There was talent involved. Skill. But luck had been on their side, no doubt about it.

"Baby," she breathed, her hips rising to his mouth. "Oh, baby, I need you… please."

Her fingers fisted in his hair, but he was already kissing his way back up her body. While she begged, he spoiled her with his kiss, his caress. Every second they'd been apart rushed together in the deep need of pleasure hidden within her. She'd pushed it down. Kept it restrained. Held it back for him, knowing he'd give it to her again one day.

Hoped.

Anticipated.

Dreamed.

Their lives had followed different paths for months. Neither could've been sure that they'd be together again. Moments of pessimism had slipped in. She'd wondered if maybe they'd shared their final moments by that chopper at Beta.

But they hadn't. They were there. In their bed. Where they'd said goodbye and he'd promised to do whatever it took to get back to her. He had. He'd kept his promise.

Tears of joy and relief slipped from her eyes as he pushed into her. Their eyes met and overwhelming gratitude burst within her.

"Daire," she whispered, reaching for his face.

"I love you."

"My Heart," she said, her hips rising to meet his as their bodies sank into instinct.

They knew how to be together, how to link themselves in the most intimate way and cherish every second. She'd never take it for granted again. Whether this was their last moment together or just one of a million that would follow, they'd always appreciate each other.

SIX

"BEER?"

The question made her smile. "No… thanks." She raised her head to look down the trailer at her confused lover by the fridge. "I'm breastfeeding."

His joy eclipsed confusion fast. "Right. You're on Omega."

She laughed. "Not quite," she said, shifting when he came over to lay on his side next to her. "We should talk about this." Laying a palm on his shoulder, she stroked a scar that hadn't been there before. "You got shot."

"And cut," he said. "I got plenty of bruises and wanted you there to kiss every single one better."

Pushing him onto his back, she straddled him, but stayed close, tucking her head under his chin. Seconds became minutes, they just lay together, savoring the moment. He had to have doubted like her. Doubted that they'd ever find each other again.

But now that they had, now that they were together in their bed again, the time apart faded to nothing.

"I missed you," she whispered.

"I missed you too," he said. "I missed Oscar. I'd never met him but—"

"He missed you." She raised her head to meet his eye. "And he needs you. We've been through so much, you and me... and him... When you put the JARR needle in your arm—"

"I knew there was a toxin," he said, stroking her hair from her face. "Exile told us, Falcon was working on an antidote, had been since he found the markers in your blood."

"But you didn't know it would work," she said, recalling what Falcon said about testing. "And you went down, I saw you..."

His hand kept moving, soothing her. "Styx was there. Yeah, I got knocked on my ass, but he covered me, that's what we do."

"You said he was in the control room."

"And he was... until he heard the needle went in my arm."

"You should've given it to me, putting it in me wouldn't have poisoned me."

"Would it have poisoned Oscar?" he asked, though neither of them could know. "When Garrick said JARR would self-destruct... It was a gift we couldn't pass up. We spent so much time talking about counteracting the failsafes... Ex and Swift could stop the attacks, yes, but the data would still have existed. We couldn't let it get into the world. Destroying the data was always a priority, as to how we could go about it... We needed the data destroyed."

"And Garrick told you how to do it."

"It will destroy itself if an imposter tries to access its data."

"You were that imposter."

"Ex and Swift were always going to mop up the mess."

"But doing it the way you did... Beta shut down."

"Did more than that," he said. "By the time the sun rose, most of it was ash and rubble."

"Oh my God."

"Yeah," he said. "The site's clear now."

"Clear?"

"We took it apart, removed everything down to, and

including, the foundations… Can't even tell it was ever there."

As astounding as that was, she believed him. Her Heart and her father were both that thorough.

"How do you feel about that?"

"That the place I met the woman I love has been wiped out? Happy, actually… We don't need that place anymore. Nature can have it. Nature and the dead."

"The dead?"

"Those that fell there are still there… Including One."

She sat up, her fingertips trailing down his torso. "The investigation is ongoing. It's been on the news."

"Yeah, and it will be for a while… Ex will drip in what needs to be dripped. They'll never find him."

"He bled out or Beta took him?"

"Beta probably got him first," he said. "He was injured and had no support… We didn't do an autopsy."

"Zeus there?" she asked. He nodded. "You buried him?"

"The incinerator survived," he said. "It was the last thing we took apart."

"Their ashes are scattered at the site." Somehow, that was fitting. "Think we'll ever take Oscar there?"

"I think we'll take him to our spot. As to how much we'll tell him about Olympus… that's up to you."

And it was something she went back and forth on. "I don't want to lie to him… secrets only hurt in the long run. But…"

"You don't want to scare him either."

"He'll know you're capable… that you and Harry and Styx… that you have skills."

"Especially if you want us to pass those on."

She sighed. "It depends on what comes next. What comes after South America?"

"Whatever you want. Suburbia. Little League. Parent-teacher conferences."

"How do we earn a living?"

"Beta left a bounty."

"For Gamma," she said, then her head tilted. "What's

happening with Gamma?"

"It's there," he said.

Expecting more, she leaned in, but he said nothing. "Didn't you stock it with what was in Beta? What about your people? About your men? Harry won't just retire, there has to be a plan to keep going."

"In a different form, yeah."

"Elysium," she murmured.

"Yeah, because you told Styx about that."

"It wasn't a secret... What's wrong with Elysium?"

"Nothing."

"It will be a better operation. More moral, less murky... Harry's a know-it-all, but he's not pathological like Zeus. You and Styx will keep him steady."

"Me?" he asked, his brows rising. "No, not me."

Her shoulders went back as his hands explored her body. "You're abandoning them?"

His hands dropped to her hips. "You want me to be a part of it?"

"Harry needs you. Styx needs you. And what else are you going to do? Flip burgers in a fast-food joint?"

"I have other skills."

"And you will be successful no matter what you choose to do. Oscar and I are yours. That's a given. We want you to do what will make you happy."

"I want you safe."

"And you're a control freak." She smiled, pressing her palms to his pecs. "You'll be happier to be in the know than on the outside. What if you hear Styx is in trouble? What if he gets hurt and you weren't there? How mad will you be if Harry keeps you out of the loop? Harry can't be in the field forever. He needs eyes out there."

"I don't want to be apart from you. I want us to be a family."

As her smile grew, her fingers drifted into his hair. "We will be. We are. I've lived at Gamma before. It's the safest place for Oscar."

"He won't have a normal life."

"Because we live where his father works?" she asked.

"Of course he will. It's no different to living on a military base. Millions of families across the world do that. Gamma is not that far from civilization. We could send him to school. He can have friends. Go to birthday parties… And you can coach Little League."

"His friends won't think it's weird he lives in a military compound?"

"He'll tell them we're in private security," she said. "It's the family business. Kids in Vegas will be used to all sorts. And I'll bet people won't ask too many questions… But if you want to get a house, we can do suburbia and you can commute to Gamma."

"And if I have to go into the field?"

"You wouldn't be the first person to travel for business." Whatever was in his head, he was processing something, maybe making plans. She touched his jaw. "This is our life together. Ours. I want both of us to be happy. It doesn't have to be one or the other. You don't have to pick between your family and your men. Oscar and I shouldn't take anything away from your life, we should enhance it."

"You do," he said, his fingers threading between hers. "You've been carrying the weight of this family alone. It's not my job to get you pregnant and split. What the hell kind of father does that make me?"

Although his jaw tightened, and angry tension racked his body, her lips curled again. "Stop doing that."

"What?"

"Beating yourself up. Blaming yourself for everything. Taking responsibility for everything… You did get me pregnant, but I was there too. And I wanted this. I didn't want to admit just how much, but I told you I was disappointed when the test was negative. I wanted to have your child."

"You want to have another?"

She laughed. "Give a girl a minute."

Wrapping his arms around her, he flipped her onto her back. "The life you're suggesting… Our family has to be the priority. That means when we're ready, we have another, and another, and as many as we want. We make decisions about what's best for our family before everything else."

"Do you want to walk away?" she asked. "If that's what will make you happy, we'll do it. Do you want to walk away from your people? From Harry and Styx and the men you went to war with?" Her sincerity didn't crack his façade. Something in him held back, something wasn't right. "My Heart?"

"No," he said in a snap response. He stared into her for a few seconds then leaped up off the bed. "Goddamnit."

"What?" she asked, sitting up.

He stalked down the hall and spun around. "How the fuck can I say that to you? After everything you've been through? How could I be thinking about dragging you back?"

"You're not dragging me anywhere," she said, scooting to the end of the bed. "What do you think I want? You think I want you home by five every night so I can put your dinner on the table? You think I want us staring at the walls day after day? You're a soldier, Daire. Whether you go into the field or manage your men from the base, that's up to you. I told you that I wanted Oscar to have a family. Look at the people he has in his life. The Kindred, Wreck and Tulsi, Harry, Styx, our people find strength in standing up for what's right. Elysium won't be about grabbing power, it will be about standing up against the bullies, about fighting for the vulnerable."

"How do you know that?"

"Because I know you, and because I've seen it. It's what you and your people have been doing these last six months. Even Exile, in his own fucked up way, was doing the right thing. You didn't let it go because it would be easier, you fought on until the threat was contained. It's okay that you don't want to walk away from it. I would never ask you to."

"I love you," he said, striding back up the trailer to crouch in front of her. "I don't want to make you unhappy." He scooped up her hand, holding her knuckles at his lips. "I don't want to drive you away."

"You found me once, you'd do it again," she said, though he didn't respond to the joke. "Okay, then we decide today, nothing between us is classified. Maybe I won't always know everything. You don't have to go into every detail every day, but if something is going to take you away from us, if you are in the field, I know everything." He nodded once. "And you write me as often as you can when you're out there… You have to say goodbye to us too, me and Oscar. No just disappearing. You kiss us goodbye every time."

"I promise."

"And you marry me." That he hadn't expected. "Before South America. We do it as soon as we can get ID."

His smirk became a kiss on the back of her fingers. "Your passport's in a closet panel."

"My London passport? You kept that?"

"I've been waiting to marry you since Miami."

"We're in Miami."

"Then it's perfect."

His chin rose. By the way his eyes moved to their top corners, she could tell he was hearing something she wasn't.

"Get dressed?" she asked.

"Get dressed."

They just got done putting their clothes on when someone pounded on the door. "Jump to!"

That was Harry. Panic hit her as Daire went storming down the trailer. What was wrong? Why did her dad sound angry? Had something happened with—

Just as Daire got there, Styx came inside, without Oscar.

"Oh my God, where is—" Harry came in, carrying the baby, and her heart slammed against her chest. "Don't do that to me!"

Styx was amused, Daire didn't see the funny side either. "You'll pay for that."

"Oh yeah?" Styx asked. "What are you gonna do? Report us to the school board?"

Her Heart looked back at her and she nodded. "Never pays to be on your CO's bad side."

Styx became serious.

Harry's ease ebbed too. "What does that mean?"

"It means you're getting him back," she said, going over to take Oscar from his grandfather. "Was our boy good?"

"No, hey, you don't change the subject," Styx said. "My CO?"

"I guess it's different now you're the three principals," she said, retrieving a blanket from the closet. "Lay that out on the floor for me, Heart."

Daire took it from her to put it on the floor by the couch. She sat there, laying Oscar on his back next to her.

"Thought you were leaving this life behind."

"We are for a while," she answered for Daire, smiling at her baby. "South America waits… You two aren't exempt from that either. We need a family vacation. All five of us are going away together."

"You want to take them on our honeymoon?"

She smiled up at Daire. "Babysitters on hand twenty-four seven? Yes, I do."

"Honeymoon?"

"We're getting married too," Daire said. "Today."

"There's a three-day waiting period in Miami," Styx said.

"Not if you take a four-hour premarital course," Daire said and winked at her. "I checked."

"There's no waiting period for non-residents," she said. "I checked better."

Daire laughed as he dropped onto the floor next to her.

"What are we doing in South America?" Styx asked. "What's the play?"

"No play," she said. "A vacation…" She laid a hand on her son's stomach as she turned her smile up to Styx. "You could invite Kingsley… if you want…"

"Kingsley," Harry said, frowning. "Why would…" But a quick scan of their faces told him why. "Jesus, was anyone following my goddamn orders?"

"Thank God Daire wasn't," she said, looping her arm through his. "Otherwise, you wouldn't have your beautiful grandson."

Harry looked down at the wriggly Oscar. "Your mother would've adored him. I'm sorry she isn't with us to see this."

"She's with us," Tess said. "She's in all of us. Oscar will know her. We'll make sure he does."

Her father crouched to stroke the little one's head as he muttered, "The things we do for love."

Daire wrapped his arm around her, pulling her in against him. "I'd die for it."

"Live for it," she said, smiling as he ducked to align their mouths. "Live for love, My Heart."

"Live for love," he said, bringing his lips to hers.

Thank you for reading this tale!
If you can, please take the time to review.

~

Ask your local library for more Scarlett Finn novels!

~

For all things Scarlett Finn
check out:

www.scarlettfinn.com